P9-CEB-217

THE MAN WHO FOUGHT ALONE

By Stephen R. Donaldson

The Chronicles of
Thomas Covenant, the Unbeliever

Lord Foul's Bane
The Illearth War
The Power That Preserves

The Second Chronicles of
Thomas Covenant, the Unbeliever

The Wounded Land
The One Tree
White Gold Wielder

Mordant's Need

The Mirror of Her Dreams
A Man Rides Through

The Gap

The Gap Into Conflict: The Real Story
The Gap Into Vision: Forbidden Knowledge
The Gap Into Power: A Dark and Hungry God Arises
The Gap Into Madness: Chaos and Order
The Gap Into Ruin: This Day All Gods Die

Short fiction

Daughter of Regals and Other Tales
Reave the Just and Other Tales

THE MAN WHO FOUGHT ALONE

Stephen R. Donaldson

A Tom Doherty Associates Book  New York

This is a work of fiction. All the characters and events portrayed in this novel are either fictitious or are used fictitiously.

THE MAN WHO FOUGHT ALONE

This book is printed on acid-free paper.

Edited by Patrick Nielsen Hayden

Design by Jane Adele Regina

A Forge Book
Published by Tom Doherty Associates, LLC
175 Fifth Avenue
New York, NY 10010

www.tor.com

ISBN 0-765-30202-0

First Edition: November 2001

Printed in the United States of America

0 9 8 7 6 5 4 3 2 1

To “the boys”—

Don Westervelt

Rich Jacobs.

You’re irreplaceable.

Acknowledgments

My particular thanks to Howard Morhaim and Evelin Yourstone-Wheeler, both of whom went out of their way to help me with this book.

Carliss Swilley's remarks about Chinese antiques have been extrapolated from Fang Jing Pei's exhaustive *Treasures of the Chinese Scholar* (Weatherhill, 1997). Details about the history of Wing Chun have been condensed from "The Truth about Wing Chun's Past," by Benny Meng and Richard Loewenhagen, *Inside Kung-Fu*, May 2000, Vol. 27, No. 5.

Author's Note

I wish to emphasize that this is a work of fiction. I have done everything I can think of to ensure that the general information it contains is accurate. But I have not based any of the characters here on anyone I have ever known, read about, or heard about. Nor do the schools have any "objective correlative" in the real world. A student of Shotokan myself, I have nothing but respect for all martial arts and admiration for all true martial artists. The opinions and attitudes expressed by my characters belong exclusively to them.

In addition, I can state categorically that Fumio Demura *sensei,* Bill "Superfoot" Wallace, and Benny "the Jet" Urquidez have never attended a martial arts tournament in Carner.

THE MAN WHO FOUGHT ALONE

1

For two weeks Ginny concentrated on taking care of me. Ordinarily she didn't have much tolerance for inactivity, but she stood it with as much grace as she could muster. She force-fed me pills, changed my bandages, stocked the pantry and fridge, picked up tapes and books to keep me from driving her crazy, and generally made herself responsible for my recuperation.

A week or so after being shot, I could walk upright most of the time, and her regimen of vitamins and antibiotics had just about knocked out the infection. But I still couldn't move fast, or think very quickly, or tie my shoes without groaning.

She even kept the apartment clean, which was usually my job, since even her best friends never accused her of being tidy. Compensation, I think. If you've got a mind like a ledger, you surround yourself with the most ungodly mess. But if your head could stand in for a witches' cauldron, you're inclined to clean everything in sight. Whenever she mopped or dusted, I had to bite my tongue so that I wouldn't nag her about missing the corners.

I kept my mouth shut because I didn't want to punish her for taking care of me. It wasn't her fault I had a hole in my stomach.

We were private investigators—by which I mean, she was. Ginny Fistoulari, owner and sole proprietor of Fistoulari Investigations. Tall and good-looking. So good-looking, in fact, that you would've considered her beautiful if you liked broken noses. Mid-thirties. Lean and poised, ready for anything. And keen as a hatchet.

Or she used to be, until she lost her left hand during the case that first got me in trouble with el Señor, Puerta del Sol's only real crime lord. For a while afterward, she felt so maimed and maybe unloved—or unworthy—that she could hardly figure out how to go on living. But now, after a period of what you might call disarray, she'd started to regain her edge. She wore a stainless steel prosthesis—her "claw"—with two hooks that worked like pincers off the muscles of her forearm. She could pick up all kinds of things with it. Also punch holes in double-glazed windows. And because the edges of the hooks down near the base were sharp, she could cut things with it—tape, string, cloth, even rope if it wasn't too thick.

Years ago I was her partner, but I'd lost my license. Negligent manslaughter, the commission called it. I'd killed a man whose only crime was being nearby while I was drunk. Other than that, he was just a cop trying to chase down a purse snatcher.

Unfortunately he also happened to be my younger brother.

Since the purse snatcher had a gun, I wasn't indicted. In one sense or another, I'd tried to stop him with "necessary force." But Puerta del Sol's licensing commission would never re-certify me, so now I was just the hired help at Fistoulari Investigations.

I wanted to be Ginny's partner again. I wanted to earn it. But I wasn't there yet.

I'm Mick Axbrewder. I always liked to say that no one calls me Mick, but the truth was that people by the busload did it practically all the time. Everyone who elicited even a smidgen of restraint from me did it with impunity. I probably hadn't actively punched out someone who used my first name since my last binge.

I was what you might politely call a recovering alcoholic. Back in my drinking days, I had "the courage of my convictions," if nothing else. Put your hand on me, and I broke it. Call me Mick, and I rearranged your face. But now? *Some*thing had replaced that kind of courage, but I wasn't exactly sure what it was.

That's probably all anyone actually needs to know about me. Everything else is just more of the same.

I'm too tall. And I used to weigh too much, but recently a thug named Muy Estobal put me on a .38 caliber diet, and I slimmed down nicely. On those days when my vanity poked its battered head out of the closet, I was proud that I had to tighten my belt an extra notch to keep my pants up.

Indirectly, Estobal was the reason Ginny and I came to Carner. His version of a diet involved shooting me in the gut—which didn't do much to improve my already sour temper. In a fit of pique, you might say, I thanked him by breaking his neck. Unfortunately he worked for el Señor, and his boss took exception to his demise. After a week or so, the crime lord succeeded in running Ginny and me out of town.

Or maybe I should say she got me out to keep me alive. But any way you looked at it, we were pretty far from home. After our last job, we drove here in Ginny's worn-out Olds, with me sprawled along the back seat hugging my guts most of the way. She found us a cheap apartment in a building that looked like a poster child for Genteel Poverty, and we moved in for the duration.

She'd chosen Carner for the simple and sufficient reason that she had a contact here who might help her get a job while we waited for el Señor to get tired of craving my blood.

When I was feeling optimistic, I thought Ginny and I were back on the road to being partners. Maybe even to being lovers. The rest of the time I knew better.

Most of the time, her bedside manner stank. She detested being my nurse. But I was used to that. What I couldn't adjust to was the way I felt with our caretaking roles reversed.

For six months after she'd lost her hand, I'd been the nanny. And she'd hated it—hated it so bad that it charred her heart. But she hadn't believed that she had any choice, so she'd turned as much of her anger against herself as she could. In the process, I'd damn near lost her.

You'd have thought that might make me more sympathetic now. For some reason, it didn't. I disliked my pain, hated my general uselessness, and positively loathed being dependent on her. Occasionally I was so charming about it that I said things like, "I guess when this is over we'll be even."

She gave me one of her special glares—the kind that made complete strangers duck for cover—but she didn't pretend to misunderstand. Instead she muttered, "I'm not keeping score."

"Maybe not. But you were. The one who feels like a cripple always keeps score. This time it's my turn."

"That's right." She turned her glare on one of the chairs and watched it cower. "And the way I count, if you don't shut up about it we're never going to be even."

She was using her take-no-prisoners voice. If I hadn't been such an asshole, I probably would've winced. The chair sure did.

Sometimes—mostly late at night after she went to bed, and I

couldn't distract myself with inane remarks—I got the distinct impression that I was living on borrowed time. She'd made a point of renting an apartment with separate bedrooms. In the dark hours I was sure that her reasons for wanting her own room had nothing to do with letting the wounded man sleep soundly.

When irritation and waiting got the better of her during those two weeks, she made phone calls. Business, most of them. We'd left Puerta del Sol in a hurry, and she still had details to take care of—banking, mail, credit cards, the leases on her apartment and office, insurance, that sort of thing. And she harassed the commission regularly.

They'd suspended her license after I killed Estobal. Not because of him, but because she'd killed our client. Which didn't exactly make the commission feel all warm and fuzzy about her. She'd done it in self-defense, but the ethics committee still took joy in delaying her reinstatement.

Naturally she wanted her license back.

Since she needed a job, she also got in touch with her contact—the reason we'd driven to Carner instead of some other, more familiar city.

In college, she told me, she'd been friends with a man named Marshal Viviter. Just friends, she told me. After college, he'd been a cop in Puerta del Sol for a few years, so they'd stayed friends. But he was ambitious, and when he quit the force to become a private investigator, he'd left Puerta del Sol because—she told me—he wanted to work somewhere with more money and a bigger client base. Apparently Carner fit his requirements.

As it turned out, the city supported an entire gaggle of rent-a-cops and snoops. Which made sense in a town where so much cash changed hands all the time. But he'd made a success of it, despite the competition. His ad in the yellow pages—"Professional Investigations: proven, prompt, discreet"—was ostentatious enough to sell cosmetics.

Her first call to this Viviter left her smiling, something that I hadn't seen in more than a week. Until her face lifted, I hadn't realized how much strain she carried around. Marshal, she reported, had more clients than he could handle. He wanted her to come in for an interview, discuss the situation, but off the top of his head he didn't see why he wouldn't be able to put her to work right away.

For some reason, I didn't ask the obvious question. Put *you* to work? Not *us*? Maybe all those antibiotics had killed off my intuition as well as my common sense. Instead I challenged her.

"Does he know about your license?"

If I'd been listening to myself, I would've known I was in trouble. Whenever I started to act like a professional nag, something went wrong. But I wasn't paying any attention.

Her smile disappeared like closing a shutter. "Of course he knows," she snapped. "What do you think? I can't get a job unless I lie to prospective employers?"

I waved a hand airily. Axbrewder the effete invalid. "You know that's not what I meant. I'm just surprised that he's allowed to hire you with your license suspended."

She studied me for a minute, then sighed. Got a grip on herself. But her smile didn't open again.

"The laws are different in this state. His whole office rides on *his* license. He can hire the homeless if he wants to. As long as he accepts responsibility for everything they do. If they screw up, it's his problem."

She shrugged. "That's why he needs an interview. He's known me for a long time, but he still has to be sure what he's hiring." Her attention trailed away. "We haven't seen each other for years."

I let it go. What lay behind it was too scary to contemplate.

But the second time she called her old friend, they talked for a long time. On the phone in her bedroom, with the door closed. And when she emerged she wore an expression that I'd never seen on her face before.

She looked wistful.

Ginny go-for-broke Fistoulari, the eager racehorse champing at the bit. She looked wistful?

I was splayed out on the couch at the time. I sat up, acting like my stomach hurt worse than it actually did. "So what did he say?"

Ignoring my performance, she shook her head absently, her mind still on the phone. "Nothing, really." Hell, she even sounded wistful. "We talked about old times. People we used to know." A faint smile softened her mouth. "There was this guy in college. We figured out he was cheating on his exams. Of course, we didn't want to snitch on him. But we also didn't want him messing up the curve for the rest of us. So we worked out this elaborate con to trick him into betraying himself."

She drifted farther away. "I can't remember the last time I had that much fun. Now everything matters too much."

For some reason, my heart had started to jump and spatter like beads of water on a hot griddle. I was only convalescent, not stupid. The Ginny I'd known for years hadn't cared much about fun. Or she hadn't let it show—

Mostly because I wanted to be able to recognize her again, I asked, "Did you tell him about your hand?"

Then I flinched to myself. That question was a low blow, and I expected her to lash back.

But she didn't. Instead she simply turned away, picked up her purse, and walked to the front door. Without a word, she left the apartment.

All of a sudden I felt more completely alone than any time since we'd left Puerta del Sol. Actually, I hadn't felt that alone since I'd caught her in bed with another man.

Because she hadn't said it, I told myself for her, Axbrewder, you are *such* a nice man. You didn't feel bad enough about it when she was maimed and dependent, and hated herself even more than she hated you? You want her to go back there?

Unfortunately that didn't relieve my alarm. Sweat oozed inside my bandages, and my heart rattled around in my chest like it'd broken loose.

I couldn't pretend there was nothing wrong.

Making a production out of it, I got to my feet. But I didn't fool anyone. I wasn't well yet, but I was a hell of a lot closer to it than I'd been for a while. No matter what I felt like at the moment.

Exercise was supposed to be good for me, so I started pacing. At first I couldn't be bothered to stand up straight. But then I managed to stiffen my spine and do better.

One of my more ambiguous gifts was an ability to recall conversations pretty much word-for-word. Now I couldn't help remembering the last time Ginny and I'd really talked to each other.

First she'd said, *I thought I'd have to carry your self-pity and your stupid drinking around on my back for the rest of my life. I wanted to believe I was strong enough, but I knew I wasn't.*

When I'd asked her what she wanted to do about it, she'd answered, *The truth is, I don't know what I want. I don't know how I feel about you. I don't like* cripples. *I don't like being one, and I don't like you when you're one.* But then she'd corrected herself. *I want you to go away with me. Somewhere we can* think. *If we have reasons to go on, I don't know it right now. And if we're finished, I'm not going to admit it until I've had a chance to* think.

Before that conversation, I'd believed she was going to say goodbye. When she'd insisted instead on taking me out of el Señor's way, I'd nearly collapsed in relief. But now I wondered how I'd contrived to confuse myself so completely.

She'd had a week and a half to think. Judging by appearances, she'd reached conclusions I suddenly didn't want to hear.

I don't like cripples.

Since she wasn't there to argue with me, I decided to exercise with a bit more fervor. Proving how tough I was, I took a bandsaw to my guts by attempting a push-up—and almost survived the experience. Which did wonders for what I liked to call my clarity of mind. *If we have reasons to go on, I don't know it right now.* Obviously I wasn't ready for *that*. Muttering curses, I levered my body upright on the arm of the couch and went back to ordinary pacing.

I promised myself that I'd apologize when she came back. But when she did, the words stuck in my chest.

She looked at me just once, straight and hard. "No, I didn't tell him." Her tone reminded me of push-ups. Like me, she'd almost survived. "I can't exactly hide it, but I'd rather deal with it in person."

Then she concentrated on ignoring me for the rest of the day.

From then on I drove my exercises harder. I probably would've been well by now if I hadn't given myself peritonitis by neglecting my pills. One thing for sure, I knew how to be crippled.

That had to change. This time, I promised myself—this time I'd be stronger.

Naturally pacing got old. Also it made Ginny twitch. So as soon as she bought me a pair of sunglasses I started walking outside. I did laps around the blocks in our neighborhood until I had them memorized. Since push-ups were too much for me, and I didn't even want to think about sit-ups, I started on squats. The first day I worked my way up to one.

That night I was so sore I thought I'd torn something inside. But I kept at it.

Against no detectable resistance, I began to pick up some of the cleaning chores. And from there I planned to move on to cooking. I thought I'd be able to handle that. In a week or so, I told myself, I'd be ready to go back to work. Then she could stop waiting for me.

The next Monday, she went for her interview with Professional Investigations. She didn't ask me if I felt well enough to go along—she just went by herself. Which made my bowels squirm in ways that resembled entry wounds. But I still tried not to understand. Apparently I'd forgotten how to trust my intuition.

So I decided to cook a special meal to welcome her back. Also, presumably, to congratulate her. First I cleaned the apartment the way it should've been cleaned all along. I even took my life in my hands and cleaned her room, just to show that I never did actually learn anything from experience. Then I took over the kitchen.

But she didn't come back. She didn't call.

Eventually the first meal was ruined, so I made another one. I defrosted the fridge, which didn't need it, and scrubbed out the pantry, which did. After a couple of years, the sun gave up and let electricity take over, but I didn't turn on any lights. Or the TV. Or my optimism. Instead I stripped down my .45, took a fine brush and gun oil to all the parts, then put it back together so that the mechanism clacked with the surgical precision of a guillotine. Next I greased fresh rounds and nestled them in the magazine. Finally I oiled and polished my shoulder holster until the leather flexed like skin.

After that I sat alone in the dark. Outside, Carner shone like a nuclear blast, but I kept the blinds closed and contemplated my sins.

She didn't show up until after midnight. I heard her heels outside the door before she got her key into the lock, which gave me plenty of warning.

She came in without turning on any lights. Apparently she thought that she could avoid disturbing me. She may have been humming under her breath, but I couldn't be sure. My heart laid down a barrage so heavy that I didn't trust my ears.

We talked about it in the dark.

I kept it simple. "Where were you?"

"I had my interview," she answered softly. I couldn't tell whether she was glaring at me or not. But every word had the force of a bullet in flight. They were so accurate that she might've been using tracers. "Marshal showed me around. We had dinner. We talked.

"I didn't try to keep track of the time."

No, of course not. Why should she?

My next question sounded thick, labored—congested by bandages and self-neglect.

"Did we get the job?"

Her voice might've come from anywhere in the room. "Not *we.* *I. I* got the job. You're on your own."

A gulf opened at my feet. I sat still and hugged my chest so that I wouldn't fall into it.

She pushed it wider. "We'll stay here until you're well enough to find work. Then I'll move somewhere else." No ground remained between us. "Or you can move, if this rent's too high."

When I couldn't say anything, she went into her room and closed the door.

That was a good thing. I didn't really want her to hear me whimper like a beaten hound.

2

That night I didn't go to bed. For an hour or two, I paced. After that I sat up in one of the living room chairs, holding my .45 like an offering in the palms of both hands, and trying to think. Or I told myself I was trying to think. What I meant was that I didn't want to feel.

Sometime around 4 A.M. I pulled off my bandages and took a shower. That was probably safe enough—a good three weeks had passed since I was shot—but it felt like baring my soul.

By the time Ginny got up to start her first day working for Marshal I-can't-remember-the-last-time-I-had-that-much-fun Viviter, I had myself dressed. As ready as I was likely to get. I'd shaved so hard that the follicles on my face still cringed. I'd eaten as much breakfast as I could stomach. And I'd put on my best—which was also my only—suit.

As soon as she took a look at me, her face turned belligerent. If I tried to foist myself off on her now, she'd probably give me a new gut wound to match Estobal's. I had other plans, however.

Wanting to prove I could do it, I faced her head-on.

"I still have about five hundred dollars in the bank." I sounded like I was chopping wood. "But I don't have any cash, and I need wheels. I can't hunt for a job if I can't get around."

Hell, in a city like Carner I might not be able to reach an ATM without a car.

While she studied me the hostility drained out of her eyes. I'm sure she heard self-pity in my voice, but apparently she'd picked up determination as well. Frowning, she chewed on the inside of her cheek for a couple of heartbeats. Then she said carefully, "You aren't ready."

She sounded just a touch unsure of herself.

I liked that. Somewhere deep inside, I was angry enough to

catch bullets in my teeth. The more I managed to keep her off balance, the better.

"That's my problem, not yours," I told her. "Leave me some money. I'll pay you back."

She wanted to argue with me—I knew the signs—so she tried to get mad. "Goddamn it, Mick—"

I stopped her there. I was fast when I needed to be, and I already had my hand in her face, with my index finger pointing rigid as a gun barrel between her eyes. "Don't call me that. You fucking know better."

She took a deep breath. A struggle I couldn't identify conflicted her reactions. Now that she'd decided to walk out of my life, she may've felt guilty about it. Her grey eyes held a hint of violet, like a threat of bruises or thunder.

As she let that breath go, she said, "You're right, Brew. I know better."

Like flipping a switch, she turned businesslike and started fishing in her purse. "I can only spare twenty bucks right now. But I'll leave you the company credit card." She'd kept Fistoulari Investigations alive on the assumption that we'd manage to get home someday. "You can use it until you start getting paid. And I'll have more cash at the end of the day."

With her claw, she pointed two tens and a piece of familiar plastic in my direction.

I took them. What the hell else was I going to do?

She also gave me my antibiotics. I took them, too.

By the time I'd put the money and credit card in my wallet, and dropped my pills into a pocket, she'd left the apartment, closed the door behind her. I was alone again, lumped in the middle of the living room floor like a pile of unsorted laundry.

Which meant that I had to face the consequences. I'd staked out my ground. Now I had to stand on it somehow.

Unfortunately I didn't know a soul in Carner. And my résumé wasn't likely to inspire confidence. I'd spent too many years being drunk. Not to mention dependent.

But I'd decided during the night that I didn't mind making a fool of myself, if I had to. In reality, of course, I *did* mind, but since I couldn't imagine any obvious alternatives, I might as well swallow it. Add it to the list of pains in my gut.

On the theory that what's good for one pain is good for another—pharmacology as sympathetic magic—I took my pills. Then I picked up the phone book and located the nearest rent-a-relic agency.

The address wasn't much help at first. The yellow pages included a rudimentary map, however, and eventually I deduced I was only fifteen or twenty blocks away. Presumably I could walk that far. I'd been practicing.

Carner's climate didn't exactly encourage pedestrians, but it was still winter, so the heat didn't kill me. By the time I reached Acme Cars Cheap, I was wearing just a shower, not an entire hot tub.

Once the credit card cleared, Mr. Acme put me in a perky Subaru that would've been small for someone half my size. And he deigned to sell me a real map. After that, I was ready to embark on my new career, Indignation-For-Hire.

The map, and the complexity of the route I had to take, confirmed the impression that reading the paper and watching TV had given me. Carner was only two states away from Puerta del Sol, but it might as well have been in a completely different world. It made the city I called home look like a hick town.

For one thing, it was huge. A crooked valley between low rumpled hills confined its downtown to some extent, but its suburbs and malls, convention centers and car dealerships, parks and stadiums—there were a lot of stadiums—lapped away from the valley in every conceivable direction, sending out ripples of fresh concrete, glass, grass, and stucco to cover every viable patch of ground and dirt for a thousand square miles. And with all that room, Carner was still crowded. It had enough inhabitants for a Third World country. The airport was so vast you could've staged an invasion of Europe from it. Two beltways four lanes wide spread out the traffic jams while three freeways pumped in more cars. Hundreds of buses crawled the streets as if no one ever needed or wanted them to get anywhere. Some of the malls could've hosted Alpine skiing events without any significant remodeling. Hell, even the city Animal Shelter occupied a building the size of a cathedral.

But Carner wasn't just huge, it was new. In fact, practically everything you could see anywhere looked new. Towering offices, banks, and hotels by the dozens clotted the horizons downtown, breaking the sky into pieces like construction blocks. Some of them had so much glass on their sides that sunlight came off them whetted keen as knives. If the skyscrapers hadn't spent so much time shadowing each other, the reflections would've driven every sane human being in the vicinity blind. As it was, even on cloudy days Carner's denizens wore sunglasses welded to their faces. Otherwise they wouldn't have been able to walk downtown, never mind drive.

That section of Carner was so comfortless and artificial, so full of buildings pretending they weren't identical to each other, that it should've ceased to exist as soon as the sun went down and you couldn't see it anymore. Darkness doesn't ordinarily tolerate pretension on that scale. So, I learned, the city fathers had ordained that the sun didn't set. When the actual sun ignored their designs, they replaced it with so much glaring incandescent neon, sodium, and halogen illumination that you wouldn't know night ever happened if the city didn't cool off occasionally.

The suburbs weren't that bad, but they weren't much better, either. There the zoning board allowed trees and grass, which took some of the glare off the cement, but still didn't prevent the houses, apartment buildings, mini-malls, and convenience stores from looking like they'd arrived prefabricated from some happily rich Developers' Heaven.

And all of them were *lit*. Carner spent electricity like a city that owned its own public utilities. Streetlamps as harsh as spotlights guarded the roads. At night every right-of-way looked like a landing-strip. Lights watched over the mansions, malls, dealerships, privacy walls, and stores. Even in the ghettos, you couldn't go to a park at night without getting a tan. And as the sun set the stadiums seemed to go off like nuclear blasts—except your average thermonuclear device probably wasn't that bright.

One way or another, Carner did its utter damnedest to look like a place where no one had any secrets. Every furtive human desire or deed must surely have withered away decades ago, shamed to death by all that illumination.

As far as I could tell just watching the news and reading the paper, most of the cash that kept the place going came from sports. Professional, university, college, high school, *middle* school, for God's sake, minor league, semi-pro, amateur, tour, back-room—you name it, Carner had it. Most of the high schools sprouted gymnasiums on the scale of Olympic venues, plus separate amphitheaters for football, track, and tennis. Even the churches worshipped with basketball courts and swimming pools in their basements. Every citizen who wasn't an athlete either owned, supported, worked for, or watched spectator sports, and well-toned bodies insulted their own mortality at every imaginable opportunity.

All that dedication to sweat and injuries, as well as franchises, concessions, merchandising, nutritional supplements, and TV contracts—never mind good old-fashioned gambling, the foundation and tombstone of the American Way—gave me hives. That, and the incessant pitiless glare of the lights.

I was completely and entirely out of my element. The kind of people I could really understand and talk to didn't even come out of hiding until after dark. And they sure as hell weren't *athletes*.

Nevertheless Ginny's contact flourished here. I didn't see how.

By the time I found my way to "Professional Investigations: proven, prompt, discreet," I felt more than a little shaky. So far, being on my own was the shits.

But that changed nothing. I still didn't know a soul in Carner.

I had two different plans, depending on how much Ginny had told Marshal Viviter about me. If he knew enough to recognize me, I intended to ask for advice, contacts, a reference, whatever. Hell, I had to ask *some*body. But if my name didn't mean anything to him, I wanted him to give me a job.

For a while during the night, my famous intuition had gone into overdrive. Now I felt sure that despite all the time she'd spent talking to her old friend recently, Ginny hadn't said much about me.

For one thing, I guessed, she was ashamed of what had happened to our relationship. She wanted a clean start with Viviter, no baggage or self-justification. And no limits. Because she was already half in love with him—or so my sore stomach proclaimed vehemently. All that fun and all those happy memories made my contribution to her life look pretty abject. The last thing she wanted to do with him was discuss a former lover. Especially a former lover who made her feel ashamed.

I could've been wrong, of course. Intuition is like that. Sometimes it functions like effective prescience. And sometimes it leaves you facedown in your own muck.

But even if I was right, I still had to ask myself why I wanted to risk undermining her by trying to get a job with Professional Investigations. At the moment, the only answer I had was that I didn't know where else to turn. To pacify my conscience, I promised it that I'd be straight with Viviter—and that I wouldn't give away anything Ginny might've kept to herself.

What I hadn't figured out, of course, was why Viviter would even bother to talk to me. My inspiration didn't stretch that far. But I didn't let that stop me.

With my obligatory sunglasses clamped to my face, I squeezed like a circus trick out of the Subaru and went to meet Marshal Viviter as if he were the Oracle at Delphi.

Nevertheless I distrusted Professional Investigations before I even left the sidewalk. Its offices—they took up the whole eighth floor, I discovered—were in a massive glass-and-concrete skyscraper that also featured title companies, lawyers, accounting firms, and sports agencies. It was, I told myself acidly, no place for a private investigator. People like Ginny and I were in the pain business—uncovering it, containing it, avenging it, occasionally relieving it. We needed seamy offices in run-down buildings that made no pretense of tidiness, never mind sterility. We didn't belong in an edifice where people got rich riding on the backs of their clients.

And inside the place was worse. It had scarlet carpets so thick that if you dropped a coin you'd never see it again, and potted trees ten feet high positively gleaming with health, and wall after wall of mirrors clean enough to focus surgical lasers. The expensive air was so balmy it must've been imported from a beach somewhere. Polite functionaries hovered everywhere to assist the bewildered. Where I came from, the elevators could've been rented out as apartments.

Bordellos should look so good.

Professional Investigations wasn't just successful, it was bloody triumphant. Ginny's college boyfriend had raised pain-for-profit to a level I couldn't even imagine. Of course, this was Carner, not Puerta del Sol. But still— It seemed to me that Marshal Viviter must be a proven, prompt, discreet scumbag, as dirty as death almost by definition. The only reason I didn't turn my back and leave was that Ginny obviously had a good opinion of him. And I still didn't have any choice that I could see.

Girding up my loins, as they say, I braved the foyer, got directions, and rode the elevator up to the eighth floor.

For once there wasn't any glass. The agency probably didn't want its clients to feel like they were being watched. A tasteful brass nameplate on the rosewood door announced:

Marshal Viviter
PROFESSIONAL INVESTIGATIONS
proven, prompt, discreet.

The door opened without a sound when I turned the knob.

On the other side, I found myself in a lobby that might've been small by the standards of the rest of the building, but that was still bigger than Ginny's entire office in Puerta del Sol. Cushioned armchairs and deep loveseats which matched the carpet—here a reassuring taupe instead of scarlet—arranged themselves decorously among the potted plants, end tables, and ashtrays. Deliberately meaningless paintings in muted colors softened the walls. As soon as I closed the door, I felt like I was in the waiting room of a funeral home.

Three other people had taken up residence ahead of me, a youngish couple with anxiety as thick as stage makeup on their faces, and an older businessman digging his heels into the carpet like he wanted to hurt it. They glanced at me when I entered, but didn't pay any real attention.

The far end of the room sported several doors, but still no glass. In front of them, a receptionist at a sleek rosewood desk presided over an intercom/phone console and a computer monitor. By then I felt so intimidated that at first I didn't notice she wasn't blond, or pretty, or even especially polished. And I didn't realize until I got closer that she was sitting in a wheelchair.

Like the outer door, the desk had a brass nameplate. This one introduced her as "Beatrix Amity."

"May I help you, sir?" Her tone, like her mild smile and her remote gaze, was perfect for the job—impersonally welcoming and relaxed, without a hint of intrusion. Her capable hands rested on the desk as if they were at my service.

I coughed at a sudden dryness in my throat. Now that I'd spotted the wheelchair, I also saw plastic runners over the carpet behind the desk, presumably so that she could move around easily. And at least two of the doors had electric eyes to open them automatically for her.

"My name's Axbrewder," I informed her with an uncomfortable rasp. "I'm here to see Mr. Viviter."

"Do you have an appointment, Mr. Axbrewder?" She managed my name smoothly, like she practiced it every day.

Warming up to feel foolish, I shook my head. "Afraid not. But I want you to tell him I'm here anyway. I think he'll see me."

That was pure bullshit—and she probably knew it, too—but she kept her opinion to herself without any visible strain.

"Certainly, Mr. Axbrewder." She turned to her console. "May I say what this concerns?"

I tried to smile, but only managed a spasm. "I'd rather you didn't."

"As you wish," she replied immaculately. The merest hint of a frown warned me that I was out of line. "I'm sure you understand that Mr. Viviter is quite busy. We usually insist on appointments. Otherwise his schedule becomes impossible.

"If you'd like to take a seat—?" She nodded toward the chairs, promising me nothing.

I didn't move. Whether or not what I wanted made sense, I wasn't any good at backing down. And I've never been gracious about it when I feel intimidated.

"And I'm sure you understand, Ms. Amity, I wouldn't do this if I didn't consider it important. I'm not rude by nature." Then I shrugged. "Well, maybe I am. But I'm also housebroken. I would've made an appointment if I could afford to do things that way."

Unpersuaded, she faced me steadily and waited for me to say something reasonable.

Floundering inside—and determined not to show it—I said, "If Mr. Viviter wants to know why I'm here, ask him why he spent the money to make it easy for you to do this job. That isn't something you see every day," despite the Americans with Disabilities Act. "Not in places like this, where the décor is sacred enough to worship."

Apparently this episode of "Adventures in Charm, with Mick Axbrewder," was just like all the others. Sometimes even I wondered why I didn't change the channel.

"Mr. Axbrewder." For all the mark I made on her, Beatrix

Amity might as well have been cast in teflon. "I don't need to ask him. I already know the answer. Now if you'll please be seated?"

I got the message. She wasn't going to touch her intercom until I parked my ass somewhere else.

Suddenly, however, I didn't mind. For no particularly obvious reason, I found that I believed she played fair. Another intuitive leap. Despite my manners, she'd make an honest effort to get Marshal Viviter's attention for me.

Maybe Professional Investigations took the pain business seriously after all. Why else would Beatrix Amity work here, when she could've spent her time complaining about an employer who treated her wheelchair like a hindrance?

Since I'd claimed to be housebroken, I retreated to one of the loveseats and lowered my aches into its embrace. From there, I watched her work her intercom. But some trick of the soundproofing prevented me from hearing what she said.

I couldn't relax anyway, so the absence of magazines didn't bother me. I guess they weren't necessary. Viviter's clients weren't people who waited around much. Within five minutes after I sat down, the other people in the lobby had been escorted to privacy through doors behind Ms. Amity. Their guides looked more like stockbrokers than rented snoops. But one of them walked with the kind of jerk you get when you're wearing an artificial leg.

Apparently hiring the handicapped was fashionable this year. Maybe I'd get lucky.

While I waited, I tried to believe that Viviter would actually see me. But I couldn't carry it off.

Nevertheless I knew who he was as soon as one of the inner doors let him into the lobby. He had to be Ginny's Marshal Viviter for the plain and simple reason that I hated him on sight. He was everything I wasn't—fit, affable, good-looking as sin, and so sure of himself that you could've used his radiance to toast bread.

He stood maybe three inches shorter than me, a couple taller than Ginny, but he obviously kept himself in a whole lot better shape. Every ounce he carried must've been muscle of one kind or another. And he knew how to dress. His tailored suit was businesslike without being formal, and expensive enough to suggest that he was good at his job without implying that he got paid more than he deserved. He wore his hair tousled, which gave his charm a boyish tinge. His eyes were so clear you'd think he polished them on the hour, and he smiled easily without seeming soft or diffident. When I thought back, I realized that I'd seen a picture of his chin in the dictionary under "rectitude."

Where I came from, no one looked that good unless they were too dirty to live. Ordinary innocence—not to mention honesty—had more flaws.

He grinned at Beatrix Amity, then looked straight at me. "Mr. Axbrewder?" A couple of steps brought him close enough to stick out his hand. "I'm Marshal Viviter. You wanted to see me?"

Graceful as a wounded bull, I heaved myself upright. Hoping to score a couple of points, I took his hand and squeezed. But his grip was strong and dry, and I suddenly had so much sweat on my palm that I might as well have shaken his hand with a used dishrag.

No question about it, my whole life would've been simpler if I'd ever learned how to turn and run.

Gritting my teeth, I managed to croak out, "Thanks for making time."

"No problem. I had a cancellation." He said that so smoothly it must've been a lie. "Come on back to my office. We can talk there."

I'd expected him to say, I'm glad to meet any friend of Ginny's. Maybe he planned to mention it later.

A touch on my arm steered me in the right direction, just in case I was having second thoughts. I wanted to hack his hand off, maybe break his wrist on general principles, but he removed it almost immediately. Among his other virtues, he was too professional to touch his clients unnecessarily.

Beyond the door, halls seemed to run here and there for no particular reason. Presumably they accommodated offices, file storage, rooms for conferences or interrogations, maybe even a law library. But none of the walls or doors had any windows. Professional Investigations kept everything it did private—at least as far as the paying customers were concerned. If Ginny was in the building, I could work there for a week without laying eyes on her.

I couldn't tell the difference when we reached Viviter's office.

If I'd been here on my own, I wouldn't have found it without divination. He seemed to pick a door at random and open it for me. But as soon as I walked in, I knew this was *his* office, the real thing, not some convenient impersonal substitute.

For one thing, it had enough space for volleyball practice—so much space, in fact, that a sculpted rosewood desk which could've slept three fit in perfectly. And for another, it featured one entire glass wall, giving anyone who wanted it an expansive view of the canyons between the skyscrapers. Venetian blinds managed the sunlight without defusing the impression that if you got too close you'd fall out. Dark wooden bookcases with glass fronts softened the other walls. Heavy frames held the full spectrum of diplomas, certificates, and licenses. But that window dominated the room.

Viviter must've chosen his office to remind his clients that they stood on the edge of an abyss. *Ergo* they needed him.

"Have a seat." He gestured at a selection of armchairs while he crossed behind his desk and sat down in one of those executive chairs that looked like it floated on air and gave massages while taking dictation. When I didn't join him, he added, "Please?"

I needed the reminder because the window kept tugging at my attention. With an effort, I picked a chair facing away from the glass and eased myself into it.

I assumed that he'd noticed the pain I carried around, but if he did his clear gaze didn't give off any hints. "Now, Mr. Axbrewder," he began, "what can I—?"

I interrupted him. "Call me Brew." I needed to do *some*thing to disrupt the effect he and his window had on me.

He raised a manly eyebrow. "That's your first name?"

I shook my head. "It's Michael. But I haven't used it since I was born." Actually since my brother was born. We were the Axbrewder boys, Mick and Rick. I hated the reminder—but it helped. Memories like that put calcium back in my spine. Sounding a bit stronger, I finished, "Brew suits me."

He was comfortable with that. "Fine. I'm Marshal." He may've been comfortable with anything. Shifting gears smoothly, he remarked, "Beatrix tells me you're interested in our employment policies."

Apparently nothing slipped past him. He even knew that I needed help getting started.

"Indirectly," I admitted. "What I want is a job."

He didn't react. "And what does that have to do with why I put in a few carpet-covers and electric eyes for Beatrix?"

"Nothing, really," I said, hoping that the hole in my guts didn't show. "I was just trying to get her attention."

This was what I'd come for, so I forged ahead.

"I'm a private investigator," I told him, taking the go-for-broke approach, "but I lost my license a few years ago on a negligent manslaughter charge. Since then I've been working for another investigator. I'm in Carner mostly because I don't know where else to be. But I'm new here. I don't have any contacts, and you might not recognize my references." Before he could ask me why I'd picked him, I added, "I got your address out of the yellow pages. Your ad's bigger than anyone else's."

I did *not* want to reveal anything that Ginny hadn't already told him.

He grinned cheerfully. "Do you always leave that many gaps on your job applications?"

No doubt women fell down dead when he looked at them like that. Since I hated him, I didn't smile back.

"Some days are worse than others. What do you want to know?"

He still hadn't mentioned Ginny.

He spread his hands like a man who wanted everything. "If you don't have a license, what are your credentials?"

He made my position easier by reminding me to be mad at him.

"This, mainly." Glaring indiscriminately across the desk, I took out my .45 and thunked it down in front of him. "*That* I have a license for."

This time he raised both eyebrows. "That's *it*? Your credentials are an old .45 heavy enough to break your foot if you dropped it?"

"No." I faced him head-on. "I'm also a really lousy shot."

For a second or two, I thought he might laugh out loud. But his laugh was probably as affable and self-confident as the rest of him, and I didn't want to hear it, so I tried to distract him with a real answer.

"I've been doing this for a long time, and I can watch out for myself." While I talked, I retrieved the .45 and put it away. "When I'm on a case, I don't take no for an answer. I'm not particularly smart, but I'm stubborn as hell. I'm good with secrets. I can follow orders. I don't cheat—and I don't sit on my hands while other people cheat. And I've told enough lies in my life"—mostly to myself—"that I'm starting to hate them.

"Oh," I finished grimly, "and I'm a recovering alcoholic." Just in case he wondered how I felt about negligent manslaughter.

He studied me hard enough to leave holes in my head, but he still sounded cheerful. "And you're rude to receptionists. You should add that to your list."

This wasn't an interview, it was a damn game. He didn't like what he'd heard from Ginny about me, and now he was just entertaining himself while he waited for an excuse to throw me out.

Or else I'd pissed him off by leaning on Beatrix Amity.

Ignoring my stomach, I sat up straighter. "I forgot that one. But it's trivial. I'm also rude to employers."

This time he did laugh. "And I guess you have a gift for it, too."

Then he leaned back in his chair, folded his arms behind his head, and lost his sense of humor.

"I'm sure everything you say is true." I couldn't help noticing that he didn't seem to sweat. "But from my point of view it isn't much. Unless you want to fill in some of those gaps—?"

Since he hadn't asked a specific question, I didn't volunteer anything. Without specific questions, I didn't know how much I could tell him.

"In fact," he went on after a couple of moments, "from my point of view it's worrisome. Experience tells me that lousy shots who commit negligent manslaughter have a tendency to repeat themselves. And recovering alcoholics don't have a very good track record in this business." By which he meant that sooner or later the pain got to them, and they started drinking again.

"This is a clean, professional organization, Brew," he explained patiently, like he wanted to be sure that I understood the problem from his perspective. "Around here we dot our i's and cross our t's. We play by the rules, and our clients get honest work for an honest buck. We guarantee discretion—we're serious about it." Just for a second he gave me a glimpse of steel. "But the last time an investigator who was 'good with secrets' worked here, he ended up homeless.

"I'm willing to talk about this," he finished, "but you haven't given me much to talk about."

That sounded pretty final. Just because I was desperate didn't mean that he had to help me. In any case, I didn't think that I could stand working for a man who made me look like a pile of uncollected garbage.

"Never mind." I almost managed to stand up without wincing. "I get the message. Sorry I wasted your time."

Putting on a show of dignity, I headed for the door.

He waited until I had my hand on the knob. Then he suggested casually, "Leave me a phone number, Brew. In case something changes."

I was primed to say, Fuck that. But before I got my mouth open, I remembered that I didn't know my way out of here. If he didn't escort me, I might never find the lobby again.

I might stumble around until I ran into Ginny.

That went *way* beyond acting like a fool. I still had enough sense to know that coming here put me on what you might politely call shaky moral ground.

Awkward as a marionette, I walked back to the desk, picked up a pencil, and scrawled my number on a scrap of paper. Then I stood there stiffly with nothing to do while I waited for him to get up and guide me out.

Glancing at the number, he started to his feet.

And stopped abruptly. Still only half upright, he took another look at what I'd written.

When he finished standing, I could tell by the look on his face that I'd made a mistake. He wasn't angry, but he was scrambling inside. I could almost see him chasing implications behind his mask of mild surprise.

"You didn't tell me," he remarked quietly, "you know Ginny Fistoulari."

I shrugged, mostly so that I wouldn't compound this foul-up by swearing at myself out loud. That damn woman hadn't told him *any*thing about me. Anything he could use, anyway.

Swallowing at the anger in my throat, I gave him as little as I could. "She's the investigator I worked for after I lost my license."

With a sigh, he dropped back into his chair. "Sit." The steel was back in his voice. "Start over again. How long have you known her?"

I ignored him. Steel didn't scare me.

"I told you," I said carefully, "I already got the message. You didn't take me seriously when I walked in, and you still wouldn't if you hadn't made the connection. I do need a job. But if you change your attitude now, you're doing it for the wrong reasons.

"Get me back to the lobby, and you can forget we ever met."

Ginny hadn't told him *anything* about me. She hadn't so much as mentioned my name.

His stare didn't waver. "Wait a minute." With one hand, he waved my indignation away. "You said you wanted a job. You asked for help." His tone took on a flensing edge I hadn't heard him use before. "You didn't tell me that my *attitude* mattered. You didn't tell me you're qualified to evaluate my state of mind.

"Put your damn crystal ball away, or your degree in psychoanalysis, or whatever the hell it is you think you're using, and sit down."

For a heartbeat or two, I couldn't move. I wanted to take a swing at him, but unfortunately the damn sonofabitch was right. I'd made about ten assumptions that I couldn't justify, and most of them involved thinking that I knew what went in his head. Which was what usually went wrong when I tried to talk to Ginny.

Hell, I didn't even *know* this guy.

I crumpled back into my chair and braced myself on its arms to ease the pain in my guts.

"Listen, Marshal." For a while I let the way I hurt do the talking. "She's an old friend of yours. You've already given her a job. I may look like trouble, but I'm not trying to cause any." Not anymore. "I came to you for help because I'm lost here. But I don't want to tell you anything she hasn't already mentioned." Stiffly I concluded, "She has her own reasons for doing what she does."

I didn't see him move a muscle, but somehow I could see his attitude shift again. He put his flensing knife away.

"OK," he said slowly, "fair enough. That explains some of the gaps." He touched his hair quickly, checking the tousle, then went on, "But there's at least one I need filled in. If you don't do it, I'll have to get an answer out of her. That"—he paused to look at me hard—"might make your problems worse."

At least he was willing to be specific. That helped.

"Which gap?"

He didn't hesitate. "Why did the two of you leave Puerta del

Sol? She doesn't want to talk about that." He glanced briefly out the window. "I thought she was settled there."

No shit she didn't want to talk about it. She couldn't explain without telling her old boyfriend about me. And she'd made her desire to keep me out of the discussion obvious.

I suppose I should've kept my mouth shut. But I figured I had a right to answer that particular question. *I* was the one who got shot and couldn't go home.

Trying not to think about bullets, I asked, "You remember el Señor?"

Unexpectedly Marshal grinned. "Re*mem*ber him? I still have nightmares about him—and I never actually had any trouble with him. He used to make some of the cops I knew sweat shit."

That, as they say, was gratifying. Without meaning to, I relaxed a bit.

"He sent one of his goons to cap a client of mine." I caught myself. "I mean a client of *ours*.

"I got in the way."

"So he shot you," Marshal put in. "That's why you have trouble moving. The wound hasn't healed yet."

I shrugged. "I couldn't think of anything else to do about it, so I broke his neck."

"Which 'he'? Who did el Señor send after you?"

I hesitated, then answered the question. "Muy Estobal."

Marshal laughed out loud. "Muy Estobal?" Amazement filled his face. "Christ on a crutch. You broke Muy Estobal's *neck*? I didn't know he *had* a neck. My God, Brew, you ought to proclaim yourself a hero. You should have *placards* printed up."

Then he gradually turned sober. After a moment, he drawled, "Makes you wonder why Ginny didn't tell me, doesn't it?"

Not me. I already knew. "Marshal," I warned him, "this is what I was afraid of. I don't want to confuse things for Ginny here."

He dismissed my scruples. "Don't worry about it. She's a big girl. And I'm not that easy to confuse. I just like explanations. They're cleaner than guesswork."

But he didn't give me a chance to respond. Apparently he wasn't interested in my version of Ginny's mental state. Instead he stood up all at once, like he was immune to gravity and scar tissue.

"This makes a difference, Brew," he announced. "I remember

Puerta del Sol well enough to be impressed. But I still need to think about it. I've already given Ginny a job. And, as you say, we've been friends for a long time. I don't want trouble. Or conflicts of interest.

"Tell you what," he went on briskly. "I'll call you. Before the end of the week. If I decide I'm not comfortable putting you to work myself, I'll give you some names and a reference. That should help you get started."

I hated him. I didn't want to feel grateful. But I had trouble controlling it. Trying to fend it off, I said the most graceless thing I could come up with.

"You're going to rely on what Ginny says about me?"

He stared at me humorously. "What do you think I am, crazy? Of *course* I'm going to rely on what she says. So far you've avoided mentioning any other names I can use."

Damn. Damndamn*damn*. He was still right—which I disliked so much that I actually blushed. In particular, I hated having people be nice to me when I needed to stay angry.

Muttering, "You didn't ask," which was only marginally true. I appropriated his pencil again and wrote down the names of a couple of honest cops back home. Then I added two or three of Ginny's clients who wouldn't have forgotten me. None of them knew where I was anyway.

When I finished, he grinned as if I'd pleased him somehow. "All right. This almost looks like a real job application."

Charming me out of my underwear the whole time, he helped me locate the lobby. Then he shook my hand again and sent me off on a surge of clear-eyed bonhomie. Apparently he expected me to have as much confidence in his promises as he did.

Eventually I found my way down to my car. It seemed to fit me better than it did before. I must've shrunk in the past half hour.

The Subaru's AC worked, but it didn't help. By the time I got back to the apartment, I'd sweated right through my suit.

3

Two days later he called me.

By then the apartment was so clean that you could eat off the floor under the fridge. I'd tightened the covers on my bed until your eyes bounced when you saw them. The windows had the clarity of Marshal Viviter's gaze, and I'd beaten the rugs practically threadbare.

Under other circumstances, I would've called that plenty of exercise. But not this time. In addition, I'd flagellated my body until I'd achieved an actual sit-up, and the first five push-ups were almost easy. If this part of Carner had offered any shade, I probably could've walked five miles. Just to keep in practice, I took two showers a day.

Meanwhile Ginny and I didn't talk to each other much. Because of her work schedule—or her social life—she came back to the apartment at irregular hours. When we were both there, and awake, we attempted a couple of aimless conversations, but they didn't accomplish much. I asked how her job was going. She said fine. She asked about my search for work. I said I was waiting for an answer on one prospect. At some point, she remarked on the state of the apartment. She may've been trying to suggest that I should beat the pavement instead of the rugs, but I didn't react, and she didn't push. In every way that mattered, she'd already moved out.

Mostly to stave off the sensation that I'd been abandoned, I spent a fair amount of my time fuming. But being mad at her just made me feel even more alone, and being mad at myself was so normal that I did it on auto-pilot anyway, so I concentrated on manufacturing disgust for Marshal Viviter.

Anyone who looked that good, I told myself, and made that much money in that line of work had to be crooked. A moral pretzel. With plenty of salt so it tasted almost like food. He'd been toying with me the whole time I was in his office. No doubt he and Ginny had already milked my squirming for hours of innocent hilarity. If he called, it wouldn't be to offer me anything I needed. He'd be looking for some way to keep me on his hook.

I told myself.

Which gave me a charming motivational lift, like one of those leadership seminars where they teach you to achieve comparative excellence by tearing other people down. But it didn't do much for my morale. Soon I'd start to dissolve in my own acid.

When the phone finally rang I was sitting practically on top of it. You'd have thought that I wanted to hatch the damn thing. Since I was in Stoic Mode anyway, impeccably resigned to the vagaries of my fate, I snatched up the receiver before the end of the first ring.

"God, Brew," Marshal chuckled, "what *kept* you? I've been waiting here for nanoseconds."

Obviously he knew it was me—as Ginny's boss, he could be sure that she wasn't here—so I didn't bother to introduce myself. Swallowing my lungs, I croaked, "Sorry about that. I didn't expect the head of Professional Investigations to make his own phone calls. I was just trying to be rude to your receptionist again."

"Well, at least you're consistent," he conceded. "That's a virtue. I guess."

Before I could muster another of my elephantine ripostes, he went on, "Considering the mood you're in, you probably won't ask why I called, so I'll just tell you.

"I've got a job for you." Then he corrected himself. "I mean a job possibility. But if you can keep that sunny disposition under control, I think your chances are good."

Luckily I was sitting down anyway. Otherwise I would've been forced to collapse somewhere. My heart had attempted a triple toe-loop in my chest, missed the landing, and gone into a skid. For a moment or two, I couldn't remember how to breathe. Somehow I managed to say, "Tell me about it." I may've been panting.

"When you were here," he began promptly, "I mentioned conflicts of interest." Apparently one of his professional gifts was the ability to sound casual and serious at the same time. "I was talking in generalities then, but now I have a more specific complication on my hands.

"Professional Investigations"—proven, prompt, discreet—"has been hired by a woman named Mai Sternway. She's separated from her husband, and now she thinks he's stalking her. She says he wants to intimidate her so that she'll be afraid to go after the kind of divorce settlement she deserves."

Right away I wanted to know why he'd violated her confidence by telling me her name, but I didn't get a chance to ask.

"That's not a problem, as far as it goes," he explained. "Some research and a few hours of protection a day. We do that type of work all the time.

"The problem is that now her husband, Anson, also wants to hire us."

When he said that, my stomach twisted around the memory of Estobal's bullet. I thought I knew what was coming.

"Ordinarily I wouldn't even listen to him," Marshal remarked like he expected me to believe him. "But what he wants doesn't have anything to do with his wife. And he isn't the kind of client I enjoy turning down. There are too many other things he might want to hire us for down the road. I hate to burn a bridge like that. So I let him go into detail.

"It's still a conflict of interest." Marshal's disembodied voice conveyed a shrug. "Or close enough that it's too messy for me. But then I thought of you—"

Damn him anyway, I was right.

I cut him off. "You thought of me," I retorted with massive sarcasm, "because *I* don't care about conflicts of interest."

"No." Without much effort, he matched my good humor. "I thought of you because you need a job. And if you get this one you won't be working for me."

I bit down on my tongue and waited for him to go on. Sudden relief made me light-headed. At the moment I didn't care whether I trusted him or not. I could decide that later. Right then I wanted a job as much as I'd ever wanted a drink.

"It's only for three days," he said, "but I think it could turn into something steady. If you'll tone down your hostility long enough to pay attention."

"Go on," I told him noncommittally. The receiver had started to make a dent in the side of my head, and I could feel the pressure building on my brain, but my arm refused to relax.

He sighed, then got down to business.

"Anson Sternway runs a karate organization called the International Association of Martial Artists. It's what I think of as an umbrella organization. Individual karate schools and martial artists sign up as members, and in return the IAMA provides inexpensive insurance and promotion, publishes newsletters, runs seminars on subjects like 'effective business practices' and 'advanced *kama*'—whatever that is. In addition, it sponsors tournaments.

"Apparently karate tournaments are big business. People from around the country—or around the world, for all I know—get together and pound on each other to win trophies. According to Sternway, these tournaments are already a cash cow, and their popularity is growing every year."

I did my best not to sound impatient. "And—?"

"And," Marshal told me, "this weekend, starting tomorrow, the IAMA is holding its 'world championships' right here in Carner. At one of the convention hotels." Of which Carner had a few dozen. He paused for effect, then added, "They need extra security."

I wanted to ask, For *what*? I couldn't imagine a room full of Bruce Lee wannabees needing *any* security. But I kept my mouth shut. Even if the job was just an insurance boondoggle, I needed it.

I needed *work*.

"Under normal circumstances," Marshal was saying, "they don't have this problem. Their contract with the hotel relies on hotel security. There's always trouble with petty theft and crowd control. It seems these tournaments are like zoos where they lock in the spectators and let the animals run free. And I gather a few of those martial arts suffer from testosterone poisoning. Sometimes they try to settle their differences outside the ring. But hotel security is usually adequate to the situation. The hotel's insurance covers the losses.

"But this tournament isn't normal. This time one of the member schools wants to display some kind of 'antique martial arts artifacts,' for the edification of the assembled." Marshal paused to swallow his lack of conviction. "According to Sternway, these 'artifacts' are valuable, and the insurance company has balked at the added risk. The hotel has been asked to hire extra security—which is an expense they didn't take into account when they negotiated the contract. Naturally the hotel wants the

IAMA to pick up the tab. On their side, the IAMA wants to insist on the terms of the contract. Eventually they agreed to split the cost of hiring Professional Investigations."

"But you have a conflict-of-interest problem," I put in so that Marshal wouldn't try to explain it to me.

He completed the thought for me. "But *you* don't. That makes you ideal for the job.

"I suggested that Sternway hire you instead. I told him you cost less than we do." I could hear Marshal grinning. "He's agreeable. But he wants the hotel to make the final decision. On the grounds that they're legally responsible anyway.

"I've set up an interview for you with their Chief of Security this afternoon. If you get the job, you'll be working for them. You'll answer to them, and they'll pay you."

Someone had to say it, so I did. "I don't have a license."

He dismissed that. "Don't worry, these people won't ask." I pictured him rolling his eyes at the ceiling. "I've already vouched for you." Then he seemed to shift gears. "Of course," he admitted, "you'll be out on a limb. If it breaks, I won't be there to catch you. The rules around here give private investigators a lot of slack, but not *that* much."

For some reason, he didn't mention that if I screwed up he'd look pretty bad for recommending me.

I had a question about that, but he didn't give me a chance to ask it. Still sounding casual, he said, "There's just one detail I haven't mentioned. I want you to keep me informed. Tell me how it goes, what happens, give me your impressions, that sort of thing."

Well, shit. And there I was, all set to believe that he was actually offering me help. My anger came back in a rush.

"Just a second," I snarled. "How do you *spell* 'conflict of interest'? Are we talking about the same thing? I'm supposed to work for *them* and report to *you*?"

If I gripped it any harder, the receiver was going to crumple.

"No, you idiot," he retorted. I'd finally succeeded at pissing him off. "Damn it, Brew, what would it cost you to jump to a *harmless* conclusion every once in a while? I'm not asking you to violate professional ethics. Or confidentiality."

With both hands, he shoved exasperation through the phone at me.

"You'll be working for the IAMA and the hotel. You won't be working for Anson Sternway. And his wife is my client. I'm supposed to protect her. If he goes ballistic and does something crazy, I don't want to be taken by surprise. All I'm asking you to do is warn me if you pick up any hints of trouble.

"You want the truth? I don't trust either of the Sternways. They both have perfectly reasonable explanations for wanting to hire me. And I haven't heard any disturbing rumors about them. If either of them is nuts, I don't know about it. But coincidences like being approached by both of them make me nervous."

In his place, I probably would've flayed my skin off. But he was too fucking professional for that. He'd already recovered his equanimity. Which gave me one more reason to hate his guts.

"I'm doing you a favor here," he finished patiently. "But I'm also covering my ass."

Somehow he'd outmaneuvered me again. I didn't want to admit it, but the bastard had a good point. I was starting to wonder if he was *ever* in the wrong.

"All right," I muttered, trying to slow my heart down. "Maybe I was out of line. You're doing me a favor." Then I objected, "But I don't understand why."

"You said you wanted a job." He sounded puzzled by my attitude.

I shook my head, even though he couldn't see me. "That's not an answer." Hyperventilating discreetly, I took a more dangerous tack. "Ginny must've said something to convince you I'm worth the risk."

That made him chuckle again. "It wasn't her. I talked to one of your buddies in Puerta del Sol. Detective-Lieutenant Acton."

He was making fun of me. I didn't have any cop "buddies" in Puerta del Sol. They all hated me. I'd killed one of them once—and the fact that he was my brother only made it worse. Acton was just honest.

Still, it seemed to imply that Marshal hadn't talked to Ginny.

"By coincidence," he went on, enjoying himself, "I knew Acton years ago. When I asked him for a reference, he fell on the floor laughing. Then he gave me his version of your adventures with el Señor. That convinced me you aren't really as stupid as you try to look."

I felt a surge of irrational gratitude, an almost transcendental relief that whether or not I got this job didn't depend on Ginny. But I tried to ignore it. Marshal still hadn't answered my real question.

"You say you want me to warn you if I think this Sternway might be dangerous to your client. That's pretty slim. What do you really get out of helping me like this?"

"Think of me as your agent," he suggested. He was having too much fun to take me seriously. "They get ten or fifteen percent. I want you to be polite to me at least that much of the time."

Damn, he was slick. For a man who talked as glibly as he did about professional ethics and conflicts of interest, he sure knew how to avoid questions.

But I didn't have the energy to keep pushing. I needed most of my resources just to manage the way I felt about a chance to work, so I conceded the field. Politely.

"I'll try. You aren't an easy man to be courteous to. But I want the job. I'll do whatever it takes."

Then I added, "Just tell me one more thing." Mostly because I didn't want to get my hopes up. "Why do you think this might turn into something more?"

"Pure speculation at this point." Marshal talked faster now—a man who wanted to get off the phone. "While Sternway was trying to talk me into his security job, he implied it might lead to more work, maybe with the IAMA, maybe with a developer named Alex Lacone. It seems Sternway works with Lacone as a consultant of some kind.

"Let's take it one step at a time, shall we? First things first. Are you in?"

Oh, I was *in*, all right. I hadn't left myself a lot of choice. So he told me names, addresses, and times. Also how much I'd get paid. Then he wished me luck and hung up.

After listening to the dial tone for a while, I put the receiver down carefully and spent a few minutes just letting my squeezed head throb. The job paid less than Ginny made in Puerta del Sol, but it was still more than I'd expected. Carner was beginning to sound like the Promised Land, flowing with milk and money.

I didn't trust it. Promised Lands have a way of turning into war zones when you aren't looking.

But I needed the work.

Torn between gratitude and distrust, confusion and hope, I

checked my watch. Fortunately my interview was still three hours away. I could use the time. Once my skull moderated its complaining, I heaved myself into motion.

I wasn't hungry, but I ate something anyway. Practicing self-discipline. Then I left the apartment and coaxed ignition from the Subaru's timid engine. While the belts squealed to wind up the air-conditioning, I unfolded my map to figure out where the hell I was going.

4

The Luxury Hotel and Convention Center wasn't what you could call centrally located. In fact, it was more convenient to the airport than to the rest of Carner—which made some sense, considering that The Luxury's more expensive competitors already occupied most of the prime real estate near the stadiums. At least it was easy to find.

I was still a couple of hours early when I spotted the hotel. By Carner's standards it wasn't particularly huge. Nevertheless it could've swallowed the population of a sizable town. At first glance, it looked like The Rubik's Cube that Ate New York, partly because it *was* a cube, as wide and deep as it was tall, but mostly because some stoned hotel designer in a moment of perfect hallucination had decided to paint the damn thing with uncoordinated colors in random blocks maybe forty feet square.

In front of the entry-portico—a required feature for modern hotels—a fountain sprayed sheets of water that never seemed to reach the ground. Since I didn't like the building, I hoped this wasn't really where the IAMA meant to hold its tournament. Unfortunately a tall stream of running lights around the rim of the hotel identified it as The Luxury Hotel and Convention Center, and a blazing marquee between the fountain and the street announced:

WELCOME
IAMA
World Championships.

Oh, well. Abandoning the Subaru in a parking lot that could've landed jumbo jets, I crouched behind my sunglasses until I reached the hotel lobby. Then I started to familiarize myself with the place.

For Carner, The Luxury was pretty generic. I didn't have any trouble locating the convention facilities, which took up at least the first four floors. They may not have been the best facilities in town, but they offered enough space to hold Billy Graham's latest "crusade" plus the entire Mormon Tabernacle Choir. A reduced version of the hotel marquee told me I was in the right place. It said:

IAMA World Championships
9 A.M. to 9 P.M.
Friday, Saturday, Sunday.

Smaller print mentioned guests I'd never heard of—Bill "Superfoot" Wallace, Benny "the Jet" Urquidez, Fumio Demura.

I had less than two hours left, so I got serious.

For a start, I studied the hall itself, which turned out to be a rectangular cavern the size of a tennis stadium, with a high sound-baffled ceiling and the moral equivalent of Astroturf for carpet. Lines of tape on the floor marked out twelve squares in two long rows—presumably the competition rings. At one corner of each square, a tall pole raised the ring's number so everyone could see it. Exactly five folding chairs had been placed along one side of each square, with two more on the left. More tape indicated aisles between the rings. Outside the rows, chairs on adjustable tiers rose like bleachers toward the distant walls.

At one end of the hall, a dais with a clear view of the rings held a row of trestle-tables draped with green cloth. The tables sported a couple of microphones. On both sides of the dais, large sections of the floor had been roped off like staging areas. Maybe Sternway's "antique martial arts artifacts" would be displayed in one of them. What the other was for I couldn't imagine.

Already I had to adjust my preconceptions. Until I looked around the hall, I hadn't realized that I'd expected something less elaborate. I'd known vaguely that karate was a growing sport. But if I'd risked a guess at the size of the IAMA's championships, I would've said forty competitors, max, with maybe twice that many spectators. Obviously this tournament had other ideas.

When I was confident that I knew the layout well enough to cope with hundreds of people blocking my view, I located all the fire-alarm boxes, phone jacks, and security cameras in the vicinity. Then I turned my attention to the hall's access points.

There were six, three sets of double doors spaced out along each of the longer walls roughly opposite each other. On one side, of course, they opened toward the hotel's lobby, restaurant, and bar. On the other, service corridors led to the kitchens, offices, storerooms, and laundries which handled conventions. This was the part of the hotel I worried about. If trouble wanted to sneak in or out, it would probably go through here.

So I spent the rest of my available time wandering those corridors, paying particular attention to the ones that ended in exits. They were all windowless and blind—apart from the occasional security camera. Once I got used to them, however, the pattern seemed simple enough. Several times I encountered people who worked there. But they left me alone after I told them that I had a 1:00 P.M. appointment with their Chief of Security, and I was getting acquainted with the hotel so I'd be ready to talk to him.

With fifteen minutes to spare, I went back to the lobby and asked the bell captain for directions to my appointment. Five minutes after that, I found myself in an office midway down a long hall which left the lobby from one end of the Reception desk.

Like the rest of The Luxury, the Chief of Security's office was essentially generic, decorated in Mid-Level Functionary, with a painfully artificial fern potted in one corner, a couple of modest desks, and a large marker-board calendar scrawled black with employee schedules and convention dates. The man who held my future in his hands was named Bernie Appelwait, and he wasn't glad to see me.

He was a short unshaded cartoon-sketch of a man, with the kind of pallor that made you want to slap some color back into his cheeks. A swirl of white hair, watery eyes, swollen knuckles, and a larynx like a goiter made it obvious that he was getting on in years, and age hadn't been kind to him. In fact, it'd made him downright bitter—or so my instincts told me. Whenever he opened or closed his mouth, he did it vehemently, like trying to snap flies out of the air. The rest of the time, he moved and talked like a worn-out wasp, whining with threats he didn't have the energy to carry out.

When I offered him my hand, he ignored it. His glare conveyed the impression that I'd just proposed to rape his mother's cadaver.

Oh, well. Viviter had asked me to be more polite. Taking a crack at good manners, I dropped my hand and remarked mildly, "My name's Axbrewder. We have an appointment."

I didn't need to ask who he was. A silver badge on his navy blazer and a plaque on his desk both identified him.

His mouth snapped. "I wondered when you'd bother to get here."

I made a production out of checking my watch and looking innocent. "Am I late?"

He snorted. "You've been here so long we could've wrapped this up an hour ago. I would've come to get you, but I wanted to see how much snooping you'd do on your own."

On the inside, where he couldn't see it, I gave him a bow. Maybe he wasn't nice about it, but he knew his job. Security cameras and employee reports had enabled him to keep track of me.

"Mr. Appelwait," I explained more sharply, "I want the job. The way I figure it, I won't be much use to you if I can't find my way around the hotel. So I came early to look at the layout."

If he appreciated my diligence, he didn't show it. "So you can get out fast."

I blinked. "Why do I want to get out fast?"

"After you snatch those 'artifacts' everyone's so fastidious about, you'll try to leave before we can catch you."

"After I—?" For a prospective employer, he had a hell of an attitude. Just for a second, I considered turning my back on the whole thing. Forgetting all about Marshal and his help. Before I said something I might regret. But I swallowed the impulse. Instead I stared at him. "You aren't serious."

He went on glaring. "Doesn't matter whether I am or not. Watchdog Insurance is." He snorted again. "They're afraid I'll hire some crook who just wants to rip them off. Like I wouldn't know a hard luck rent-a-cop when I see one. Besides, I bet you can't tell the difference between antique Chinese ivory and plastic flatware. You're lucky they condescended to let me make this decision. If they were here, they'd tell you to stand on your head so they could interview your crotch."

Finally I got the message. He didn't have a problem with me. His grievances faced in other directions. He thought he deserved more respect than Watchdog gave him.

I could live with that. "This is just my opinion," I ventured, "but I think you've been insulted."

"It wasn't an insult," he retorted. "It was a fucking affront." His teeth tore off chunks of air and chewed them out again. "Little insurance twerp who still eats Pablum for breakfast thinks he can tell me how to do my job.

"Call me Bernie. 'Mr. Appelwait' takes too long."

I relaxed a bit. "That suits me, Bernie. Call me Brew."

Buzzing harmlessly, he dismissed the idea. "I'll call you Axbrewder." Something that might've been a smile sneaked across the background of his glare. "Remind myself not to like you."

"You're in no danger," I assured him. "Even my friends think I'm an acquired taste."

He treated me to a show of disbelief. "You have friends? Now I'm impressed."

I wanted to make a snappy comeback, but I couldn't think of one, so I dropped it.

Slowly he moved around one of the desks and lowered himself into a chair with a circular cushion on the seat—a piles-pillow. When he was comfortable, he gestured me to a seat across from him.

Folding his arms behind his head, he leaned back and got down to business.

"I won't bullshit you, Axbrewder. At my age, I don't have the patience. This situation caught us by surprise. And Watchdog dithered too long. I don't have time to make a project out of hiring extra security. If I turn you away, I'll have to accept whatever I can sublease from Professional Investigations, or one of the other agencies.

"Viviter referred you. Him I don't like, but his rep's clean." Bernie rolled his eyes. "In fact, if he weren't so full of snot he'd squeak when he walks.

"Besides, it's only for three days. What're you going to do? Crack the hotel safe when I turn my back? Burgle the rooms? Even guys like you aren't that stupid." He sounded like he meant, Guys like us. "As far as I'm concerned, the job is yours to lose."

I started to say, "I'll take it," but he cut me off.

"Don't be too eager. This kind of work is boring, but that doesn't make it easy. By nine tomorrow, that hall will be a zoo. I'm told we have 'martial artists' from all over the world staying here. They may even be famous, I wouldn't know. As far as I'm concerned, they're just a bunch of gooks in pajamas. But they all have their cliques and flacks and fans and teams, and their 'revered masters.' And then they bring their equipment, which they leave everywhere.

"On top of that, they're all so tanked on competition hormones they think they don't need hotel security to keep an eye on them, and they as sure as shit don't need ordinary safety precautions like keeping the aisles clear and obeying the fire regulations. And on top of *that*"—he was starting to enjoy himself—"they'll have an audience of several hundred devoted 'experts' who can't tell the difference between kung fu and cunnilingus."

I tried to look austere so I wouldn't laugh. "Rather like me in that regard," I remarked.

He chuckled, then snapped his mouth shut. "Don't do that. I already told you I don't want to like you. I'm trying to convince you this job isn't easy."

Raising my hands to placate him, I murmured, "Sorry."

"I can see that," he drawled.

When he'd recovered his glare, he resumed.

"The hours are long. From eight in the morning until past midnight, you'll be up to your navel in gooks who don't have any use for you, and the only real reason you'll be there is to watch for petty theft. Wallets, watches, jewelry. And equipment." Shaking his head in disbelief, he explained, "According to claims from past tournaments, some of that gear is worth stealing. Even here, where they sell Nikes and crotch-cups on every block.

"But," he informed me, "we'll have guards on those artifacts all the time. That's our only major concern, and you won't have to worry about it." He didn't need to say why. I was an outsider. No matter how he felt about guys like me, he trusted his own people more. "Your job will be to circulate, control disturbances, clear the way for the paramedics when someone gets hurt, and try to catch petty crooks.

"It won't be enough to keep you awake. In a normal year, the claims from this tournament hardly amount to a thousand bucks.

But I don't care about that. If you *don't* stay awake, I'll fire your ass so fast you won't be able to find it for weeks."

I waved my hands again. "Enough, Bernie. You already said it. I'm 'a hard luck rent-a-cop,' and I need the paycheck." Looking straight at him, I added, "I don't expect you to cut me any slack. If I can't do a job like this, I should be in some other line of work anyway."

He nodded once, sharply. "You got that right." Then he changed gears. "You're stiff when you move." He didn't ask why. "Can you stay on your feet all day?"

I shrugged. "Try me. I'm stubborn."

"I'm sure you are." His glare had a charm all its own. "But now that we've talked about it, you won't be able to file for disability when you decide we crippled you."

He was just doing his job, so I didn't get mad.

"I'll expect you here," he announced, "at eight tomorrow. After that, I'll comp you a room for the rest of the weekend, spare you driving back and forth. You don't get a uniform. I don't want you identified as hotel security. You'll see more if people don't know you work here. I'll supply everything else."

While he talked, he tilted back to his desk so that he could toss me a couple of forms to sign. I glanced at them to make sure I knew what they were, but I didn't bother reading them.

The main advantage of a complimentary room was that I could avoid Ginny for a couple of days.

While I scrawled my signature, Bernie added, "You've already done your snooping, so we'll skip the tour.

"Any questions?"

Ginny would've had questions—the kind he meant—and if I'd strained my brain I might've been able to think of an example. But my interests, or my instincts, ran in different directions. Which made us pretty effective when we were together—and made me feel like I only had half my senses when we weren't. As far as I was concerned, this job wasn't about petty theft, and "gooks in pajamas," and security. It was about Marshal Viviter and Bernie Appelwait. And, presumably, Anson Sternway.

I didn't ask the questions Bernie expected. Instead I asked him what I wanted to know. But I did it obliquely, just in case he felt inclined to take offense.

"I guess you're prone to liking people too much, but I have to say, you hide it well."

He glared harder to cover up a wince. "Women, mostly. Since my wife died." He paused, and I thought he was done. A moment later, however, he admitted, "But recently I'm having the same trouble with men. I see a guy with an honest face, and suddenly I want us to be friends for life.

"Take my advice, Axbrewder. Don't get old. They say it beats being dead, but I say, don't talk to me until you've tried both."

Sounding more than ever like a wasp, he rasped, "Now shut up and get out of here. I have work to do."

On command, I climbed to my feet—stiffly—and headed for the door. Bernie Appelwait wasn't going to die of old age. If someone didn't feed him a little respect soon, he'd die of emotional starvation.

As I opened the door, he stopped me. When I turned around, I saw him leaning toward me with his elbows propped on the desk top, pointing at me with a finger that couldn't straighten all the way.

"One more thing, Axbrewder. Leave your iron at home."

Just for a second. I didn't understand him. Sounding particularly intelligent, I said, "Huh?"

"This is a hotel," he explained acidly, "not a bordello. We don't want anyone shot. We don't even want guns going off. It's bad for business. And Watchdog won't cover it. We'd rather get robbed."

"No problem." I attempted a smile to cover my confusion. He must've noticed the bulge of the .45 under my jacket. "It's just bluster anyway. I can't hit anything."

Before he started buzzing around the room again, I closed the door and left.

Outside The Luxury, heat shimmered on the parking lot, distorting everything, and the pavement felt vague under my heels. Without sunglasses I would've been too blind to find the Subaru. The way it slumped between its wheels made me think its tires were melting. When I got in, the vinyl of the seat scorched me through my suit. I didn't realize how hard I was sweating until drops of water smeared my glasses.

If this was winter in Carner, I sure as hell didn't want to see summer.

With the AC straining, I drove back to the apartment.

Along the way, I asked myself what to tell Ginny. I liked the idea of just keeping my mouth shut. After all, she'd pretty much stopped talking to me. But I didn't trust that reaction. Most of our problems came from not talking to each other.

Manfully I decided to explain everything. Which included my conversations with Marshal. It would do me good to clear the air. If I ever managed to grow as old as The Luxury's Chief of Security, I didn't want to be bitter about it.

But that night there wasn't any air left to clear. Ginny didn't come home.

5

If I slept that night, I didn't notice it. My heart suffered while my brain fumed. Marshal, I thought, she's with Marshal. In his bed. Tasting all that handsomeness— She'd had an affair less than a month ago, hadn't she? Why not another one now?

Meanwhile my heart insisted that she was in trouble. Marshal had given her a dangerous assignment, and I was her partner, but I wasn't there to back her up.

I didn't know how to endure it. How had we come to this, when all I'd ever wanted was to stand beside her?

Sometime after midnight, I called Sam Drayton in Puerta del Sol.

I considered him a friend, even though we'd spent less than a week together. He and his wife, Queenie, had been involved in the case that eventually convinced Ginny to get me out of town. And Queenie had nearly died, accidental victim of a cocaine overdose aimed at someone else.

I had no business calling him. Of course. He had his wife to take care of. An overdose that massive might've burned out her brain, leaving a husk where an open and lovely, heart-wrenching woman had once been. The last thing he needed was frantic phone calls in the middle of the night from men who were big enough to fend for themselves.

But he knew things I didn't, and he'd helped me before.

As soon as I heard his voice, I knew I'd gotten him out of bed.

"Sam," I said. "It's Brew."

Then I seized up. I had no *business* doing this to him. No business—and no right. Even his silence over the phone seemed to ache for rest.

But he didn't try to get rid of me. "Brew." Recognition sharpened his tone. "Where are you? Are you all right?"

He knew I was on the run from el Señor. He knew why.

I couldn't tell him where I was. Safer for both of us. And the sound of his weariness closed my throat on everything else. Awkward as a cripple, I replied, "It doesn't matter." Desperate inside, and afraid to show it, I asked, "How's Queenie?"

"Brew." From somewhere Sam mustered the strength for severity. "Did you call me at 1:37 A.M. to ask that?"

He was my friend. "No," I admitted. "But I want to know."

The memory of the way she'd been hurt felt like Estobal's bullet in my gut, leaden and cold.

His voice sagged. "It damaged her. She's lost seven or eight years of her life. They're just gone. She has no idea how we met, or how long we've been married, or what she did before—" His throat closed, too. He had to force out words. "But at least she remembers me. And she's recovering well in other ways. Balance, mood, reflexes. She may remember more as she gets stronger."

Maybe I shouldn't have bothered him in the middle of the night. Nevertheless he was definitely the right man to call. The right friend for me. He understood—

My eyes burned, for Queenie as well as for myself. "Thanks for telling me," I said, my voice hoarse. "She's a terrific woman." I would've prayed for her if I'd thought my prayers ever did any good. "She deserves better."

"So—?" he prompted.

So why *did* I call?

"Ginny and I are safe," I told him. Fighting obstructions that crowded my chest. "Don't worry about that."

"So—?" he repeated. It was still the middle of the night.

Despite his exhaustion, I made him wait while I took a couple of deep breaths and fought to clear the bullshit out of my way. Then I said simply, "She doesn't want me for a partner anymore."

Sam didn't hesitate. "She *said* that? You've been known to do some mind reading when you think no one will notice."

I was in no condition to recite her exact words. "She got a job without me. She told me I'm on my own. She didn't say much about what she wants."

Although I could guess—

He paused to think. Not long, but long enough to scare me. I was afraid he'd ask me why I cared.

Then he said, "Brew, I know this is difficult for you. But you're stronger than you realize. You work hard not to realize it. If you admitted the truth, you'd have to take responsibility for yourself.

"I'm not talking about drinking. I'm talking about *not* drinking. You pin that on Ginny. You tell yourself you don't drink because you couldn't survive if you lost her. But it's *your* decision, Brew. You're the one who chooses. Every day." He sighed. "Then you lie to yourself about it.

"I can't make you face the truth. I wish I could—but I'd probably be dangerous if I had that much influence on people."

Now his tone suggested a smile that I remembered vividly, full of friendship I hadn't earned. "Queenie remembers you and Ginny. We talk about you from time to time. In the morning I'll tell her you called.

"I'm going back to bed."

When he hung up, he left me with the sensation that I'd come *this close* to knowing what he meant. But the obstacles in my chest had become storms, and I couldn't go the rest of the way.

I should at least have told him that I still wasn't drinking.

The next morning before I left the apartment, I wrote Ginny half a dozen notes. They said things like, "Pack your stuff and get out. You can stay with Marshal." Or, "I'm working at The Luxury this weekend. Give me a call when you get a chance." Or just, "Are you all right?" But I tore them all up.

I probably could've called her. Or called Professional Investigations and left voice mail for her. But I didn't do that either. Instead of clutching after her, I went to work.

By 7:45 I was back at the hotel with my suit clean and my sunglasses polished. The .45 I left in the Subaru under the driver's seat. Armed with nothing except concern and sleep deprivation, I headed across the parking lot to tackle my new job.

The first job I'd found for myself—sort of—in more than a decade. Certainly the first job I'd faced alone.

Ginny was fucking Marshal right now.

She was in trouble—she needed me.

Sam's advice seemed impossibly far away, like a voice you hear in dreams.

The lobby was already busy. Men, women, and kids dressed in warmup suits or martial uniforms clustered around each other, obviously waiting for the convention hall to open. Various parents and instructors kept tabs on the kids as best they could. A number of the competitors carried what I assumed were weapons in cloth or canvas cases like ski totes, and everyone seemed to have a gear bag. But I wasn't on duty yet, so I ignored the details. Instead I trudged across the lobby to Bernie's office.

I found him there, apparently handing out duty assignments to half a dozen men in hotel Security blazers with badges pinned to their breast pockets. Practicing my manners, I withdrew and started to close the door, but he gestured me into the office with a vehement flap of his hand.

As soon as I'd complied and shut the door, he announced, "Men, this is Axbrewder. Watchdog insisted on extra security, so he'll be working the tournament with us."

By way of introduction, he listed a handful of names I didn't try to remember. His guards nodded at me like I was none of their business. Or maybe they were just bored. Hotel security wasn't usually what I would've called stimulating work.

"I want you to know him by sight," Bernie went on, "because he won't have ID. He's undercover"—he snorted the words—"so the rest of us can concentrate on staring at antique artifacts.

"Just for variety, we'll use channel seven." Dutifully the guards unclipped walkie-talkies from their belts and clicked the dials. "Max will be on the monitors as usual, since he seems to be the only one who can sit there and stay awake. Coordinate with him. I want two of you on that display at all times, and two more nearby."

His men nodded again. They'd all done work like this before.

"And remember," Bernie added, "nobody goes off duty until the night shift is in place. Watchdog won't cover us unless we have a full crew. Plus Axbrewder.

"Let's go." He slapped his hands together. "Sternway wants to open the doors as soon as those gooks deliver their display."

Murmuring to each other, his crew left the office.

While they filtered out, he handed me up a cell phone. "You don't get a radio. If anyone sees it your cover is blown, but every hotshot here already has cellular. Just hit 'send' if you need something. It's set to dial straight in to Max. He can patch you to me." He indicated a small receiver in his left ear. "Or get the paramedics. Or the cops.

"Just be discreet about it."

"No problem." Hiding the way my hand shook, I slipped the phone into a pocket. "But if I have to call from the men's room, you can't hold me responsible for the background noise."

Glaring, Bernie stifled a grin. "Just don't puke on the air. Max has a sensitive stomach.

"Come on." He pointed me at the door. "Sternway wants to meet you. Since he's paying half your wages, he'd like to know what he's getting."

I didn't waste any more time on jokes. They were for my benefit anyway, not Bernie's—an attempt to defuse my anxieties. I'd lost something a hell of a lot more critical than a hand. I hardly knew who I was anymore.

If Ginny were here, I could've done this job in my sleep.

Nevertheless I wanted to do it right. As soon as Bernie joined me in the hall, I asked, "Who's delivering these 'artifacts'?"

"They belong to a local karate school, *Essential Shotokan*," he explained as we walked. "Or to their *'sensei,'* a gook named Nakahatchi. That's something I don't even try to understand. Nakahatchi's a Jap, but the display is supposed to be Chinese. Has something to do with martial arts history." He grunted under his breath. "*Essential Shotokan* is responsible for it until it gets here. They'll probably have a damn parade when they deliver it."

We strode briskly across the crowded lobby. "The problems you've had at past tournaments," I asked while I had the chance, "were they random, or did they look organized?"

He stung me with another glare. That may've been his way of smiling. "Stop trying to impress me. If I knew the answer, I would've mentioned it already. Hell, if I knew somebody was running a team through here, I would've pulled in the cops.

"But I've always suspected—" Abruptly he paused, turned a frown on the ceiling. "If you want to know my personal reason for letting Watchdog pressure me into hiring you, that's it." Then he jerked into motion again. "Maybe I'm getting paranoid. The punks we've caught in the past act like kids looking for thrills."

Which meant nothing. A decent team wouldn't have much trouble avoiding guards as obvious as hotel security.

In the direction of the tournament, the crowd thickened. Competitors and spectators wanted into the hall. Bernie had to slow down, pick his way. I followed as unobtrusively as I could, and after a bit of squirming I reached the nearest doors a couple of steps behind him. He held a door open for me, then let it close when I was inside.

"Don't worry," he muttered, although I hadn't said anything. "Your cover's safe. The gooks'll think you're one of the dignitaries."

Nodding, I took a quick moment to look around. Since my previous visit, someone had hung a huge satin banner above the long table at the head of the hall. Orange letters on a black background said simply:

International Association of Martial Artists.

By the door, a large poster listed the day's events and starting times. Some of the terms were obvious—"masters," "junior division," "black belt." Others—*kata, kumite, katame, kobudo*—didn't convey a thing.

Arrayed in front of the head table were maybe a hundred trophies, ranked by size. A *hundred*, for God's sake. That was way too much self-congratulation to suit me. They all sported a black wooden frame like a formal oriental arch on a pedestal, with a gold figure under the arch doing an impossible kick. The small ones looked to be about two feet tall. The big ones, eight or ten of them, were practically my height.

At the back of the hall a registration table had been set up, but at the moment no one attended it.

The air felt almost frigid. The Luxury had cranked up the air-conditioning so that the hall wouldn't get too warm later.

At least twenty people had gathered ahead of us, clustered in front of the head table—two guards, ten or so men and women in business suits, plus nearly that many more, all men, wearing formal versions of the martial uniforms I'd seen in the lobby. Now I understood why Bernie called them "gooks in pajamas." Less than half of them were Asian, but they all could've been dressed for bed. Some of the outfits were bright silk pants and shirts with wooden buttons. The rest were wrap-around white canvas. However, the wrap-arounds wore black belts that had been knotted and re-knotted until they'd started to fray white. The silk suits had bright sashes in contrasting colors.

Privately I inclined toward sneering at them. These people had dedicated themselves to something that didn't seem real. What the hell was a "martial art" anyway? If they considered violence an art, they were all crazy. And if they'd turned it into a sport, it was just a game. Sports followed rules. Violence didn't.

Roughly half the business suits sported lightweight audio headsets. Presumably they'd supervise the tournament. As Bernie led me closer, I saw that most of the suits and a majority of the canvas wrap-arounds wore identifying patches, either over their hearts or on their left shoulders. The patches had the yin-yang symbol picked out in orange on black, with the letters IAMA below it. I guess the silk pajamas didn't want needle holes in the fabric.

One of the suits appeared to be holding court for his assembled vassals. He was Marshal's height, but leaner, and maybe ten years older, judging by the lines of authority on his face and the distinguished mix of grey in his black hair. He seemed perfectly relaxed—he didn't even use his hands while he talked. But something about his carriage reminded me of C-4, passive and malleable until you stuck in a detonator. His pale eyes moved constantly, but without urgency, as if he searched for something that he didn't need to find in a hurry.

Once I'd noticed his resemblance to an explosive, I caught hints of the same thing around him. A fair number of the suits and pajamas stood with a kind of concussive ease, as if behind their calm they were already in motion. Apparently my preconceptions needed adjustment. Joke or not, these men and women took the martial arts seriously enough to spend years training.

Outside this hall, in the world I understood, no one except a predator stood like that.

Despite the arctic conditions, a trickle of sweat slid down the small of my back. Explosives made me nervous. Filling my lungs, I took another crack at relaxation.

The man holding court acknowledged Bernie with a nod as we approached. "Mr. Appelwait. Glad you could join us. We're ready. As soon as Nakahatchi *sensei* arrives, we can get started."

His voice was flat, studiously devoid of inflection, implying nothing. But the angle of his gaze suggested scorn.

Bernie cleared his throat. "We're ready, too, Mr. Sternway." Making an effort to be polite—in his own way. Then he added, "You wanted to meet the private investigator I hired."

"Yes, certainly," Sternway responded. "We should all meet him. We want to avoid confusion if any problems develop."

He'd hardly said six sentences, but already his lack of expression bothered me. I wanted to poke him in the ribs, just to get a reaction. I didn't like the sensation that he sneered at me simply because I couldn't stand the way he did.

"Good idea." Brusquely, Bernie introduced me.

Sternway and I shook hands. His grip was firm and dry—and oddly threatening, like a fist full of blasting caps. The easy balanced way he reached out and then withdrew made me feel like I'd been put together out of Tinker Toys.

Bernie's voice sharpened sardonically as he went on, "This is Mr. Postal. From Watchdog Insurance. And Ms. Messenger."

Two of the business suits not wearing IAMA patches stepped forward, and the man took my hand. He was short and babyfaced, with the kind of muscles you get when you overcompensate in the gym for the fact that you have to look up at everyone.

"Sammy Posten, Mr. Axbrewder." He had a twerp's voice, no question about it, but until he pronounced his name—Post*en*—I didn't realize that Bernie had been mocking him. "Watchdog Senior Security Adviser. I hope you're as good as Marshal Viviter says you are. There's a lot at stake here."

I wanted to tell him that Viviter had a wild imagination, but I didn't get the chance.

"Or there will be," the woman at his shoulder put in, "when the chops arrive." Without apparent effort, she displaced him to commandeer my hand. "I'm Deborah Messenger, Mr. Axbrewder."

An isolated part of my brain wondered, Chops? but I ignored it. The radiance of her smile evaporated every other thought in my head.

If I'd only seen her picture, I wouldn't have called her beautiful—or even pretty. But in person none of that mattered. The lines of her sleek black suit, particularly the plunge at her neck and the brevity of her skirt, called attention to the way her body swelled and dwindled in all the right places. And above that her face seemed positively luminescent, with gleaming lips, soft cheeks, auburn hair, and lustrous brown eyes.

Suddenly I didn't feel tired anymore.

Scrambling for any excuse to keep her hand, I asked thickly, "If he's Senior Security Adviser, does that make you Junior?"

She laughed in a low voice, just for me. "No. It makes me a Security Associate."

Her smile resembled a grin of conquest.

Reluctantly I opened my fingers, let her touch trail away. "And just how much *is* at stake?"

"We aren't sure," she answered, still privately. "Mr. Nakahatchi insured the chops for two hundred thousand dollars, but that's low. The real value may be quite a bit more. This situation came up too suddenly for an adequate appraisal."

In a sports town like Carner, experts on Chinese antiques were probably rare. Still, two hundred thousand bucks sounded like real money to me. Real enough to explain Watchdog's anxiety, anyway.

Slowly normal activity wandered back into my head.

Just in time. Sternway didn't seem to be in the mood for digressions. He took charge again.

"Mr. Viviter did recommend you, however, Mr. Axbrewder. And you've satisfied Mr. Appelwait. Let's continue."

Still in no rush, he introduced me to three business suits with headsets—Parker Neill, Tournament Coordinator, Sue Rasmussen, Master of Ceremonies, Ned Gage, Director of Referees—and a handful of pajamas with impenetrable names like Hideo Komatori, *Sifu* Hong Fei-Tung, Master Song Duk Soon, and *Soke* Bob Gravel. Apparently "*sifu*" and "*soke*" were titles, like "master" and "*sensei*." Some of them bowed, others shook my hand, but none of them took any real notice of me. I guess I didn't look dangerous enough.

Where was Ginny when I needed her?

Next Sternway turned to other matters, pulling his court around him. Sammy Posten joined them, although the courtiers ignored him. Deborah Messenger lingered near Bernie and me.

Just having her close made my back teeth hurt, and my palms itched like they were starting to grow fur. But I was supposed to be working, so I tried to stifle my hormones. Instead of drooling on her jacket, I asked Bernie, "What're 'chops'?"

Before he could reply, his walkie-talkie chirped. He took it off his belt, listened, said, "We're on our way," and put it back.

"That's what they call the artifacts," he growled under his breath. "Ridiculous name." Then he headed for Sternway's court.

"Mr. Sternway, Mr. Nakahatchi is out in the parking lot."

"Good." Sternway looked at his Tournament Coordinator. "We'll open the doors as soon as the display and security are in place." A small gesture of one hand broke up his meeting.

As if on cue, all the suits except Posten and Bernie's men turned to the head table, along with most of the pajamas. Only Hideo Komatori and *Sifu* Hong Fei-Tung—one canvas, one silk—joined Sternway's entourage as he drew Bernie with him toward the lobby.

I tagged along, partly because I was pretending to be a dignitary, but mostly because Deborah Messenger did the same.

"A chop," she told me, "is like a small block print." She had a gift for talking to me as if no one else existed. "You ink one side and press it to a piece of paper to print something, usually an Oriental character—an ideogram or *kanji*. These are carved out of ivory. Instead of traditional characters, they print"—she shrugged delicately—"pictures of martial arts.

"I don't know much about Chinese antiques," she finished, "but the workmanship is exquisite."

I would've asked her more questions, just to keep her talking, but by then we'd reached the doors, and the crowds outside made conversation impossible.

With Bernie clearing the way, Sternway led us through the lobby to The Luxury's formal entrance. Under the portico, we were awaited by a shambling old Dodge station wagon surrounded by white canvas pajamas.

At first glance, I had no idea which one of them might be Nakahatchi *sensei*. They were all men, they all wore black belts, and half of them were Asian. But then Hideo Komatori cleared up the matter by approaching an older man whose belt had been worn almost to tatters and bowing deeply. At once, everyone else bowed back, and the older man murmured, "Hideo-*san*."

Next Nakahatchi and Sternway bowed to each other. After that, the rest of Nakahatchi's people started unloading a long display case from the Dodge while Bernie positioned his guards and Posten bustled around getting in everyone's way.

Deborah Messenger consulted briefly with Bernie, nodded approval at what he told her, and stepped back to rejoin me.

As the case came into sight, *Sifu* Hong Fei-Tung made a small hissing noise like a curse.

I studied him as unobtrusively as I could. Apparently he was Chinese—unlike Hideo Komatori and Nakahatchi. And Bernie had already suggested that displaying these chops publicly might have undercurrents I couldn't evaluate. Still, the intensity of the *Sifu*'s reaction surprised me.

His face and eyes and nose, even his mouth, seemed flat, like he ironed them every morning—unmarked by age or pain, although grey spattered his eyebrows and brush-cut hair. And he didn't move a muscle. Nevertheless I could see anger steaming off his whole body. Inside his silk, he remained quiet, untouched. Yet his anger radiated enough heat to fry bacon.

Sternway must've heard him, too. The IAMA director turned a look like a warning on Hong Fei-Tung, threatening as a fuse. His eerie relaxation matched the *Sifu*'s. If anyone lit a match, they were both going to go off.

Nakahatchi gazed into the distance placidly, apparently unaware of his surroundings.

The *Sifu* didn't back down. In a viscous acidic tone, he pronounced softly, "Forgeries. The true chops are lost."

At that, Nakahatchi's students clenched like they'd been stung. Their *sensei* may've been oblivious, but they weren't. Without warning, their indignation crowded the portico.

Nakahatchi wasn't oblivious, however. Still placidly, he intervened by turning to Hong Fei-Tung. With his eyes lowered humbly, he gave the *Sifu* a deep bow.

He might've been forty-five or fifty, short and compact, with sparse hair and a hint of dullness like fatigue or premature aging in his eyes. His features had more definition than Hong's, but they remained distinctly Asian. The only lines in his face were two deep seams on either side of his mouth that looked like trenches in a battlefield, cut to carry out an old war.

"Forgive my presumption, *Sifu* Hong." His voice was more guttural than Hong's. If he hadn't spoken mildly, the contrast would've made him sound crude, almost brutish. "I cannot aspire to your understanding of these matters. To us the chops are precious, and we revere the wisdom they contain. They have been entrusted to my care. It is my wish to share them as openly as I may, without dishonoring them—or my responsibility for them."

Hong Fei-Tung snorted disdainfully. "They belong to China. They are dishonored in Japanese hands."

That was an insult. It must've been—even *I* felt it. Ominously the students set their case down and gathered in a clench around their *sensei*. But Nakahatchi didn't rise to the offense.

"That," he answered quietly, "is a matter which I must respectfully defer to my masters."

"*Sifu* Hong," Sternway put in, "we've had these discussions before. They can't be resolved here. Nakahatchi *sensei* wishes to share the chops in a spirit of martial brotherhood. For the present, that's enough."

When Hong moved, I shifted toward him. If he wanted to start a fight, I meant to stop him.

For the moment, at least, I'd forgotten all about the pain in my stomach.

But *Sifu* Hong surprised me by aiming an elaborate bow into the air between Sternway and Nakahatchi—a flourish that seemed to involve a couple of steps and several complex arm movements.

"Sternway *sensei*." His tone hadn't changed. "Nakahatchi *sensei*. I mean no personal disrespect. These questions will be considered at another time."

No personal disrespect, my ass. If Hong had been any angrier, he would've spit in both their faces.

Nevertheless Sternway and Nakahatchi bowed back like completing an arcane ritual. Giving each other "face," maybe. By degrees Nakahatchi's people relaxed. Talking softly, they went back to their case.

Bernie must've seen me move. He met my gaze and nodded. Apparently he approved.

Sammy Posten looked around in confusion, palpably clueless. Smiling, Deborah Messenger moved away to exchange a few words with Nakahatchi—compliments, I assumed.

Then the case slid the rest of the way out of the Dodge, and I got my first glimpse of the chops.

I couldn't see what the fuss was about. The case was polished black mahogany with a glass lid, and shaped like a coffin for some odd reason, but larger, maybe five feet by eight. It must've held a hundred or more chops—yellowed blocks of ivory nestled in precise rows on a cushion of screaming scarlet brocade. Each one was about as thick as my two thumbs, and intricately carved, but still they conveyed nothing to me. I would've had an easier time placing a value on the elephants that supplied the ivory.

While Nakahatchi's people shouldered the case, Deborah joined me again. Before her smile could send me back into shock, I asked in a whisper, "What the hell was *that* all about?"

"I'm not entirely sure," she admitted. Then she explained, "The question of what they're worth isn't simple. Even a forgery that good could be precious, for the craftsmanship alone. But unfortunately the issue here is more than just the difference between, say, a nineteenth-century knock-off and an eighteenth-century original. The content, the information carved on the chops, also matters. I'm told that the originals reveal something important about the martial arts. Something with authority. If the chops are forgeries, the information isn't authentic.

"In theory a forgery could have been made anywhere, at any time—and belong to anyone. But if the chops are originals, they're a Chinese national treasure."

That didn't quite answer my question. I persisted. "But if they're fake, what does it matter who owns them? Why is Hong in such a snit?"

She shrugged. "Who knows?" I loved watching her shrug. "You'll have to ask Mr. Sternway. I don't understand the politics involved."

At last the case was ready to move. Solemn as a cortege, with Sternway and Nakahatchi in the lead, hotel security on both sides, and Bernie bringing up the rear, the display climbed the portico steps. As the lobby doors slid aside, a gust of colder air welcomed the procession into The Luxury Hotel and Convention Center.

Sternway put his hand on my arm and pulled me to his side for a moment. The instant he touched me, my guts remembered the path of Estobal's slug, and I wanted to break Sternway's fingers. But Marshal had advised me to be polite, so I didn't slap the hand away. Instead I matched Sternway's stride.

He didn't glance at me. "If those two decide to go at each other," he warned softly, "don't get in the way. They'll eat you alive."

Oh, really? Two short middle-aged guys in pajamas didn't exactly terrify me. But it probably would've been rude to say so. Obliquely, I remarked, "I've survived worse."

He flicked me with a look that said, No, you haven't, then let me go.

I was starting to enjoy all this respect. If the situation didn't improve soon, I might tell Marshal to go to hell. Resume my normal charming demeanor. Fuck the job.

Right, I snarled back. And then what?

For maybe the third time already, I wasted a breath ordering myself to relax.

Together, Sternway and Nakahatchi parted the crowd like Moses. Apparently everyone except me took them seriously. The waters closed behind us, cutting off my retreat, but at least we didn't have any trouble reaching the tournament hall.

Once we were inside, the cortege headed along the bleachers toward the roped-off area at the near side of the dais. I detached myself from the procession to take another look around and think. There were questions I wanted to ask everyone in sight, but they'd have to wait. I wasn't directly responsible for the security of the chops. This job I needed so badly had different requirements.

In the middle of the holding area, Nakahatchi's people stopped, unfolded legs from the display case, and set it down neatly in the exact center of the space. Sternway and Hideo Komatori exchanged a few words with Bernie while the Watchdog advisers listened. Then they all moved outside the ropes, and Bernie put his guards in position.

The other pajamas, including *Sifu* Hong, had spaced themselves out around the hall, presumably setting up stations for their various schools. At the head table, Sue Rasmussen, the Master of Ceremonies, stood deep in consultation with the Director of Referees, Ned Gage. But Parker Neill, Tournament Coordinator, seemed to be doing the same thing I was—taking a last look around before the confusion started. I wandered over to join him.

He was slightly plump, with fleshy cheeks, a nose that couldn't decide on its own shape, hangdog eyebrows, and an unnatural sheen to his dark hair that suggested dye or sweat. His shoulders sagged. If I hadn't become so sensitive on the subject, I might not have noticed the trained ease hidden behind his blazer and his IAMA patch.

He gave me an absent-minded nod, his attention elsewhere. "Axbrewder." Something that resembled boredom tarnished his gaze.

Since I couldn't look relaxed, I took a stab at affability. "Call me Brew, Mr. Neill. Axbrewder sounds like a medication. Something they give you for gas."

He smiled distantly. "OK, Brew. I'm Parker. Us functionaries don't stand on ceremony here."

The implication being, of course, that under other circumstances he would've expected more formality.

I plunged in before he could wander away. "Parker, I've never been to one of these before. I don't really know what to expect."

"Oh, it's pretty simple"—he could answer without thinking about it—"once you get used to the noise, and the crowding, and the people who block the aisles. The audience is supposed to stay on the bleachers, but we'll spend the whole weekend asking them to leave the tournament floor.

"Events are held in the rings. For *kata* and *kobudo*, the judges sit in those chairs." He gestured at the folding chairs at the edge of each ring. "There are score-keepers. Time-keepers and referees for *kumite* and *katame*. Sue announces the events and the winners from the head table. For the lesser events, we award the trophies right away. The rest we give out Sunday night.

"That area"—he pointed at the roped-off space opposite *Essential Shotokan's* display—"is like an 'on-deck circle.' Competitors go there before their events to get instructions, have their gear inspected, and do last-minute warmups."

He smiled humorlessly. "We always run late. But it all gets done eventually."

There were probably fifty questions I could've asked while I had the chance. But I wanted to understand the answers, so I kept it practical.

"Where do the competitors warm up when it isn't the last minute?"

Still on auto-pilot, Neill told me, "They're supposed to find space outside the aisles. Some go out to the lobby—which the hotel doesn't like. And a fair number use the corridor outside."

He nodded at the service doors. "Usually they don't get lost."

That would complicate security, but it wasn't my job to say so. Bernie and The Luxury presumably had an understanding with the IAMA.

Just to keep Parker talking while I thought, I commented, "You must need a hell of a lot of judges. Where do you get them?"

Maybe all his smiles were humorless. "That's the price black belts pay for their rank." Or maybe he really was bored, despite his responsibilities. "If they want to compete, or watch their students compete, we expect them to do it. But even they aren't enough. For the kids' events, we use brown belts when we have to."

At least they didn't dragoon spectators. That was a comfort.

"I guess you've done this before," I offered, hoping to touch something a bit more personal. But he just nodded. The marginal attention he'd allowed me began to drift away. It seemed that no one here could think of a reason to take me seriously.

I made one more attempt.

"Forgive my ignorance. I don't mean to sound rude. But I can't help wondering what makes Mr. Sternway so important? Where does he stand in the martial arts world?"

What did he have that made him a match for Nakahatchi and Hong?

Parker Neill turned to look at me.

"Depends on how you approach it," he explained without much interest. "The IAMA was his idea. A resource for individual schools and *karate-ka*. It provides access to insurance, advice, advertising, tournaments, seminars. He started it, and he runs it.

"But it wouldn't work if he couldn't command respect. There are hundreds of styles and thousands of schools, and they tend to be pretty self-involved. They're 'true believers,' they all think they own a truth no one else understands. If an ordinary businessman tried to launch an organization like the IAMA, he'd be laughed out of town."

Parker's attention wandered again, but he kept on talking.

"Sternway *sensei* is an eighth-*dan* in Shorin-Ryu. They don't go any higher than tenth. In fact, he's my *sensei*. And Sue's." He nodded toward the Director of Referees at the head table. "*Anson Sternway Shorin-Ryu Bushido* is one of the biggest schools in

Carner. He proved himself all around the martial arts world for a couple of decades before starting the IAMA. And he's friends with people like Bill Wallace and Fumio Demura.

"The IAMA couldn't exist if Sternway *sensei* weren't so highly regarded."

I got the picture. I couldn't help noticing, however, that Parker sounded just as bored talking about his *sensei* as he did explaining the tournament. Sternway may've been the god of Shorin-Ryu—whatever that was—but he didn't inspire enthusiasm in his Tournament Coordinator.

Maybe, I thought sourly, Parker had been worn down by Sternway's air of superiority.

Some of the IAMA blazers now moved toward the doors. Presumably they were about to let the hordes in. Neill had work to do, so I let him go.

As far as I knew, Alex Lacone wasn't here.

He was my only hope for another job after this weekend.

6

The minute the doors opened, noise poured into the hall. Men, women, and children in pajamas and warmup suits, all jabbering at once, mobbed the IAMA blazers at the registration table while the first influx of spectators tried to choose seats without knowing where the events they were interested in would be held. Before I could decide on a vantage point, the whole space had begun to rumble with tension, expectancy, hopes, stifled fears. The ceiling seemed to settle a few inches, clamping down like the lid of a pressure cooker.

As far as I could tell, no one paid any attention to the display of martial arts antiques.

For the moment, at least, I didn't have anything particular to do. The hall was too self-absorbed to need protection. Even a thief whacked out on crack or angel dust would probably know better than to start poking around until people settled into the tournament and got careless. Assuming Bernie's men would even let someone enter in that condition.

So I concentrated on trying to acclimatize myself. Tune my nerves to the pitch of the noise and the press of the crowd, the clamor of hormones and anticipation. The more familiar I became with it all, the better my chances of spotting trouble.

In my present frame of mind, I had a long way to go. Ginny's absence ached in me like the loss of a limb.

Virtuously practicing my ability to pick details out of the human in-rush, I scanned the hall until I spotted Watchdog's Security Associate, Deborah Messenger. She was talking with Sammy Posten across the rings from me, near the head table and the display—although from this distance it looked like he did all the talking, gesturing erratically while he worked himself into a lather over something or other. She listened the way you listen to your commanding officer when you know he's crazy and you plan to disregard his orders as soon as he turns his back.

I let my interest carry me casually in her direction. Along the way, I did my level best to look like a dignitary.

At the doors, the in-rush had slowed. Apparently the crowd wouldn't reach Big Bang proportions for a while yet. The bleachers were less than a third full.

Sternway, Sue Rasmussen, Ned Gage, and Parker stood together at the head table, consulting over long sheets of paper. Near them, another blazer—presumably a record-keeper of some kind—sat in front of a laptop. A couple of pajamas in black belts were already "on deck," warming up with punches that wouldn't have stopped an angry preschooler and kicks I could've done myself—if both my legs had been ripped out of their sockets first. Around the walls, less ostentatious contestants—"*karateka*"?—changed their clothes and stretched.

I thought I might cross in front of the dais toward Deborah Messenger. But before I got that far, the cluster at the table broke up, leaving Rasmussen alone with one of the microphones. She didn't look like she was about to use it, however, so I deflected myself in her direction. Presuming on my exalted status, I ascended to the head table. I still needed a lot of general information.

The Master of Ceremonies was a short blonde with flouncing hair and a scrubbed and open cheerleader's face. Her confident demeanor suggested that she could chat happily with total strangers during a nuclear holocaust. Nevertheless something about her conveyed the sense that she'd disappeared into her blazer—that Sue Rasmussen in other clothes would be a different person entirely.

She smiled like a flashbulb as I strolled toward her, but I didn't take it personally.

"Time to start, Ms. Rasmussen?" I asked. Just breaking the ice. The dais was the perfect vantage point. I could watch the events as well as the crowd. Once I adjusted to the tournament's rhythms, the particular ebb and flow of its manufactured tensions, I could spot disturbances from here better than anywhere else.

Being a dignitary had its advantages.

Sue Rasmussen shook her head. "Not yet. Registration is still hard at work. I won't go on duty for another ten or fifteen minutes."

I took that as permission to ask her questions. Gesturing out at the hall, I inquired, "This is as busy as it gets?"

Widening her eyes, she pretended to be shocked. "No way." Then she lowered her voice. "We don't usually admit it, but we schedule the less popular events on Friday. Too many people aren't free until the weekend. So we do kids and color belts, since their parents and instructors are the only ones who pay attention anyway. And all the *katame*, which—"

" '*Katame*'?" I interrupted.

"Grappling," she explained easily. "Some of the best techniques in the world are joint locks and throws, but even at their best they're hard to see from the stands.

"Of course"—she laughed politely, her hair bouncing—"if we didn't have any crowd-pleasers today, no one would come. At least not until the Bill Wallace demonstration this evening. And we need judges. So we'll do most of the team *kumite*—sorry, sparring—this afternoon, and finish the color belts before we start the brown belts tomorrow morning.

"Still," she admitted, "the real crowds won't be here until Saturday and Sunday. That's when we'll hold the black belt events. And the Masters'."

I nodded like I understood. "So team sparring is popular." Why wasn't I surprised? Carner seemed to have a bottomless appetite for watching people in pads thump each other. "What else?"

"Well, the demonstrations, naturally." As she went on, she sounded more and more like a cheerleader. Maybe she got off on wearing that blazer. "Bill Wallace is *famous*. They call him 'Superfoot'—you'll see why. Benny Urquidez could probably outpoint a tiger. And Demura *sensei* trains his students beautifully.

"Then there's individual sparring. Black belt *kata*—I mean forms. And the Masters' divisions. Don't miss them, they're really impressive. *Kata* and *kobudo*, weapons. And then the finals, the grand championships. You won't see *kata* and *kumite* like that anywhere else. Sunday night this place is going to rock."

That sounded like my cue to burst into applause, but I didn't. Instead I remarked, "I wonder why. What's it all *for*?" All this sanitized violence? "Why do you do it?"

I guess my cynicism showed. Her manner stiffened. "Don't

dismiss it until you've seen it, Mr.—" Her voice trailed off. She'd obviously forgotten my name.

"Axbrewder," I supplied.

"Mr. Axbrewder." The cheerleader was gone. Now she sounded like an indignant schoolmarm. "This is part of any martial artist's education. We'll see an extraordinary display of knowledge and expertise. And competing here brings people as close as possible to testing themselves in real life. We keep it safe, Mr. Axbrewder, but we put on as much pressure as we can. If martial artists don't know how they react to stress, they can't learn to deal with it."

She was actually better looking when she got pissed off. If she tried to deck me, she might be downright beautiful.

I kept at her. "You make it sound like altruism, Ms. Rasmussen. Surely that's not all the IAMA is interested in?"

The blazer at the laptop flicked a quick glare at me like I'd insulted his mother. Then he turned back to his LCD.

Rasmussen's tone froze. "No, of course not." Apparently she'd just written me off her Christmas list. "We're also here to promote the martial arts in general, and the IAMA in particular.

"But," she insisted, "this isn't about *money*." She said the word like it tasted bad. "Everyone who works here is a volunteer. And I assure you, we wouldn't do it if it weren't worth doing for its own sake. The martial arts are *good* for people, Mr. Axbrewder. If we want to share the benefits, we have to grow."

"Excuse me." Dismissing me, she turned back to her paperwork and the microphone. "We'll be starting soon. I need to get ready."

Some days I could take a hint. "Thanks for your time." I bowed insincerely. "You've been very helpful." Then I crossed the dais and stepped down to the main floor.

Under other circumstances, I might've asked her, *Good* for people? What the hell's *that* supposed to mean? But at the moment I was more curious about why she sounded defensive when she mentioned money.

Unfortunately I'd spent too much time talking to her. While I was on the dais, the Watchdog people had disappeared. I couldn't believe that Posten didn't plan to attend the tournament. If I was right about him, he'd want to defend the chops with his personal vigilance. But maybe a Security Associate's job didn't involve standing around for days while nothing happened. Maybe I wouldn't see Deborah Messenger again.

Well, drat. She'd caught my interest in ways that I hadn't felt for a long time.

But there was nothing I could do about it, so I decided to look for Bernie. I wanted to know what he'd say if I spent most of my time up on the dais, acting exalted. And I could always think of more questions for him.

I was near Nakahatchi's chops. Hotel Security had started letting a few people into the display area for a closer look. They all wore pajamas—apparently the competitors took the antiques more seriously than the spectators did. Before I moved away, I heard a man in a white canvas suit and brown belt sneer at the case, "Big deal. It's still just Wing Chun."

"What's wrong with Wing Chun?" a woman in silk countered sharply. I couldn't tell what the color of her sash meant.

"Kung fu," the canvas snorted. "Soft styles. They're for girls. You can't really use them."

Soft? I wondered. As opposed to what? Hard?

The woman didn't back down. "Says you."

The man gave her a nasty grin. "Says the IAMA. Why else do the soft styles have their own divisions? You wimps don't even compete with the rest of us in *kata*." The woman tried to interrupt, but he kept going. "Except in the finals. And the soft stylists always lose."

Getting mad, the woman retorted, "That's because the judges don't know shit about it. It's so unfair."

She had more to say, but I walked off anyway. Parker Neill had already warned me about true believers.

Against the wall past the edge of the stands, a small group of pajamas crouched in postures that made them look like models for a nonrepresentational sculpture. Other competitors, most of them pretty young, threw out punches and kicks. Some of them squatted or jumped while they struck.

Involuntarily I rolled my eyes. I suppose it made sense that kids and teenagers did this stuff. Hand-eye coordination, aerobics, the discipline of a specific skill. But surely grown-ups had better uses for their time?

Without warning I heard a burst of static as Sue Rasmussen turned on her microphone. When the noise in the hall subsided, she started to talk.

I expected a conventional master-of-ceremonies spiel, so when she proclaimed, "Ladies and gentlemen, welcome to the IAMA World Championships," I tuned her out to concentrate on locating Bernie.

But I shouldn't have. Suddenly the audience and everyone else stood to attention. When I looked where they faced, I saw Anson Sternway alone in the middle of the tournament floor. In a loud voice, Ms Rasmussen announced something that sounded quaintly like, "Hay sucker dock-cheat, ray," and the whole crowd—with the exception of Bernie and his guards—bowed to the IAMA director.

Holding his fists at his sides, Sternway bowed back.

The next thing I knew, the tournament was underway—and I was feeling foolish. If everyone here thought that Sternway deserved a bow, I should've joined in. Acting like a dignitary was part of my job, and I'd already fluffed it.

At least now I knew where to find Bernie. While competitors and judges scurried to answer Rasmussen's preliminary instructions, I filtered in my boss' direction.

He stood like he was asleep at one of the closed doors. Until I reached him, I wasn't sure he had his eyes open. Since no one paid any attention to us, I figured I didn't risk my cover by talking to him, but I kept my voice low anyway.

"You and Parker Neill should get together. You have something in common."

"What's that?"

"You're both bored out of your skulls."

Turning his head, Bernie gave me one of his amused glares. "And you aren't?"

"I would be," I said piously, "if I didn't want to earn my paycheck."

Briefly I described the advantages of watching for trouble from the head table. He accepted the idea without much interest.

"You dignitaries have all the luck," he muttered. "The rest of us get to stand around the walls for the next three days."

"That's why they pay you the big bucks," I told him. Then I

changed the subject. "I'm still trying to make sense out of all this. I don't understand the people who run it."

I also didn't understand why Nakahatchi wanted to show off his revered chops here. Was he serious about sharing them? Or was he just trying to rub Hong's nose in them? Was this whole world that petty? But I didn't expect Bernie to know the answer.

As if the reasons for my question were simple, I asked, "What can you tell me about Anson Sternway?"

I hadn't forgotten Marshal's instructions. And Sternway had already pissed me off.

"Nothing." Bernie's jaw snapped shut on the word.

"Really?" I let my surprise show. "I thought you've been dealing with him for years."

"I have." He was all the way mad now, not just faking it on general principles. "But I work for The Luxury. I don't discuss people who do business with my employer."

He faced me so that I could see his anger. "Get it straight, Axbrewder. I told you what I think of the tournament. That's different. But if The Luxury wants Mr. Sternway's business, so do I. Anything I might know about him is private."

Then he turned away. "On top of that, he signs half your check. I talk to him about you. I don't talk to you about him."

I nodded. I should've seen Bernie's reaction coming. When you pay for hotel security—or a private investigator—you hire loyalty as well as confidentiality. Not to mention diligence, and maybe even good judgment.

"My mistake," I told him softly.

Chewing bile, he snorted, "Damn right."

"I know better," I went on. "I'm just out of my element. Where I come from, people don't try to deck each other for entertainment." Maybe I didn't understand sports at all. "I'm looking for a handle on all this."

"That," he retorted, "is why I haven't already fired you." Then he relented a bit. "I can tell you one thing. That woman"—he indicated the head table—"Rasmussen. She's a lawyer. She handles Mr. Sternway's negotiations with the hotel. And she plays hardball. Bargain basement rates aren't enough for her. She wants two or three suites and maybe thirty more rooms comped. Discounts on food. Airport shuttles. We wouldn't put up with it, but the IAMA sells out the hotel. For the whole weekend. And let me tell you, these people *eat*."

He glanced at me. "Considering what they charge for registration and spectators, they must turn one hell of a profit."

My, my, I thought. And the tournament isn't about money? Curiouser and curiouser.

I wanted to think about that. I touched Bernie's shoulder briefly to thank him, then wandered away.

Around the hall, the tournament was heating up. Events already occupied half the rings, and more were getting ready. Competitors warming up, teachers hectoring their students, and friends helping each other stretch used just about every possible patch of floor, but that didn't stop the crowd, or even the spectators, from being in constant motion. People shifted in all directions, following Rasmussen's instructions, or improving their view of particular events, or just working off jitters.

Meanwhile tension and active bodies accumulated against the chill of the AC. If the hall got warm, the fact that I hadn't slept would start to cause problems. Vaguely I wondered whether I'd call too much attention to myself by dragging a caffeine IV around behind me.

From the rings, yells punctuated the general hubbub. They were probably supposed to sound fierce, but the kids' voices in particular gave me an impression of pain. Being stubborn about it, I ordered myself to relax, and went to take a look.

Except for the differences in size and rank, all the kids competing in the four rings at the far end of the hall might've entered the same event. At each ring, five judges sat holding clipboards while as many as fifteen or twenty kids lined up opposite them. Most of the kids looked lost, but one or two acted like they already understood bloodshed. Parents who should've been in the stands squeezed as close as they could get. From the corner, a scorekeeper called out a name, and a kid moved into the center of the ring. Alone, the kid performed a bowing ritual, shouted something Oriental, and went to work.

Presumably this was *kata*, forms. The kid moved through a series of steps, turns, kicks, punches, blocks, all obviously choreographed. At intervals one of the movements included a yell. Most of them came out sounding like questions—or pleas for help. After a minute or so, the kid stopped, repeated the bows, and withdrew. The judges held up their clipboards to the scorekeeper. Then another kid was called to compete.

Trying to understand, I watched most of one event, even though it made me queasy. At first I thought each kid had different choreography. That at least made the *katas* interesting to compare. But then I saw more and more of the patterns repeated. Apparently the forms were inherited. Traditional. All these kids had been taught to duplicate someone else's ideas about violence.

Muttering disgust under my breath, I turned away. As child abuse, this form of competition struck me as more elaborate, but less useful, than ordinary domestic brutality. A kid who got hit at home at least learned what hitting *meant*, for God's sake. As far as I could tell, these kids were being taught to act out lies.

If I wanted to survive this weekend, I'd have to concentrate on watching adults. Them I could hold responsible for their own illusions.

As promised, unfortunately, the adults—including a few teenagers—were engaged in grappling, *katame*. It looked just like wrestling to me, and I couldn't pretend I cared. Sure, the more you knew about leverage and joints, the better. But every ground-scrabble I'd ever seen or been in eventually came down to muscle and bulk. Here, however, the grapplers had the shit supervised out of them. The center judge and the four corner refs called breaks whenever a competitor drew breath. Then they awarded points arbitrarily, and after a while the scorekeeper announced a winner.

No question about it, I was having a wonderful time. For a couple of minutes, I drifted into a waking nightmare where I went out on the floor to teach some of these true believers what real pounding was all about.

Fortunately I was on duty—and this was a job, not a cause. It didn't have anything to do with me. If I earned my paycheck, I could forget the rest.

With an effort, I resumed trying to tune in to the tournament so that I could feel its rhythms and interruptions without being distracted by particular events. Let the yells and foolishness of the competitors, and the uncomfortable squirming of the crowd, sink into the background, where I could monitor them automatically instead of trying to evaluate them objectively.

What I really *wanted*, however, was someone to talk to. Someone who could explain all this.

Or Ginny. But that was a separate problem.

Halfway through the morning, I arrived back at the head table. The heat and the crowd and the yelling climbed along my nerves, and I was starting to feel stupid. Luckily someone had juiced up the AC, and the heat didn't get any worse.

Rasmussen and Parker Neill were there, along with the record-keeper and a couple of people in street clothes who looked like they might be reporters. In the staging area, Ned Gage directed an increasing press of traffic—*karate-ka*, judges, instructors. Down on the floor, younger kids received their trophies while older ones competed in other rings. A trickle of competitors and spectators visited the chops, but they weren't keen on it. Maybe Watchdog had overrated the danger.

The Master of Ceremonies left her microphone to approach me. She still looked mad. Apparently my earlier disrespect was like the German invasion of Russia—never forgotten, never forgiven. "Mr. Axbrewder," she demanded, "don't you have a job to do?"

Obviously she didn't want me on the dais.

"I'm doing it." By then I was in no mood to placate her. "I can see better from here."

"So what? If you see anything, you'll be too far away to do anything about it."

"Ms. Rasmussen," I retorted heavily, "I don't know anything about karate, and I sure as hell don't know anything about karate tournaments. But I know my job. If you want me to do it better, let me ask you some real questions. Then give me some real answers."

She didn't bother. Turning away sharply, she went back to her microphone. When she announced the latest *katame* winners, she didn't sound angry at all. She knew how to turn it on and off.

I didn't like that much. Being such a paragon of self-control myself, I naturally distrusted it in others.

Time crept along. I made another circuit of the hall. Fascinated—or horrified—in spite of myself, I watched a few rounds of kids' sparring. They flailed away at each other with such seriousness and ineffectuality that I wanted to barge into the ring, take them by their ears, and send them to their rooms. Fortunately they wore so much gear—Styrofoam on their hands and feet and heads, shin-protectors, presumably cups as well—that they were in no danger of hurting each other, even by accident. I couldn't figure out how the refs chose winners. Divination, maybe.

By the time I got back to the head table, Neill had gone elsewhere. But Sternway was there, accompanied by a man I hadn't seen before. Ignoring the IAMA director's stolid demeanor, the other man carried on an artificially animated conversation with the reporters.

The reporters were done shortly. Sternway and his companion withdrew to the back of the dais—possibly the most private spot in the hall—and Sternway beckoned me to join them.

I obeyed. I figured I knew what was coming.

For once I was right. "Mr. Axbrewder," he said flatly, "this is Mr. Lacone. Alex Lacone." Then he told Lacone, "Mr. Axbrewder is a private investigator. I've mentioned him. The Luxury hired him to provide extra security, on Marshal Viviter's recommendation."

"Mr. Axbrewder." The other man and I shook hands. His voice seemed to boom even when he spoke quietly, but no one turned to look at him, so maybe he didn't attract as much attention as I thought. "Good to meet you. I've been looking forward to it."

He was a big guy, about my size, only heavier—and a truckload heartier. An incessant grin split his square face, exposing perfect teeth that would've been blinding by sunlight. With his cosmetic tan and precise grooming, he looked like a poster boy for an expensive salon. But under the tan his skin tone was slack, and the lines around his eyes and mouth ran deep, which made me think that he'd lubricated his way through too many power lunches. I knew the signs.

In a budget like his, I was petty cash. Since I couldn't imagine why he'd been looking forward to meeting me, I asked, "What's your interest in all this, Mr. Lacone?"

He chuckled easily. "I can't help it. I'm a developer, Mr. Axbrewder, and I live in Carner. That means I like to build things, and I'm interested in sports.

"Unfortunately most of the other sports are already taken.

There isn't much room for me." He beamed so that I wouldn't think he was complaining. "But karate is still on the rise. In fact, it hasn't even begun to tap its potential markets." He swept the hall with an expansive gesture. "I want in on the ground floor."

He wasn't likely to stop there, but I encouraged him anyway. "That's quite an ambition. What does it mean in practical terms?"

Sternway regarded me with a hint of distaste, but he didn't interfere.

The developer never turned off his grin. However, it had enough channels to hold my interest. This time he tuned it to an aw-shucks station. "It's simple, really. I'm building a martial arts complex, Mr. Axbrewder. I call it 'Martial America,' and it's already pretty impressive, if I do say so myself."

Sternway offered a nod that could've meant anything.

"I'm leasing the finest *dojo* facilities in the country," Lacone went on, "to any school that wants to locate with me. In fact, I already have four fine schools, including *Essential Shotokan*—you've met Nakahatchi *sensei*, haven't you?—and Master Song Duk Soon's *Tae Kwon Do Academy*. Two more will move in at the end of the month, one of which is an authorized Gracie Brothers Jujitsu franchise." Apparently that was supposed to impress me. "I'm hoping I can persuade Sternway *sensei* to join me. I'll give *Anson Sternway Shorin-Ryu Bushido* and the IAMA the best space and the best deal in North America.

"But I'm aiming higher." Now his grin transmitted an inspirational glow, gospel music filtered by easy listening. "I'm a dreamer, Mr. Axbrewder, and I like to dream big. If I weren't a damn good developer as well"—he chuckled again—"I'd have put myself out of business years ago.

"My master plan for Martial America includes as many as twenty schools of all kinds, a tournament facility twice this size, and a hall-of-fame-style museum, a complete education center, repository, and promotional outfit for any martial art in the world. The perfect home," he pointed out in case I missed it, "for Nakahatchi *sensei's* Wing Chun antiques, for example. Including stores, of course, where you can buy anything and everything that has to do with the martial arts."

Sternway hid his reaction. He hid all his reactions. But he didn't look to me like he believed in Lacone's "dream."

"Sounds expensive," I remarked. The martial arts were supposed to be *good* for people. "Who's paying for it?"

Lacone turned up the volume on his grin. "It'll pay for itself. In fact, it'll make us all rich.

"But still," he admitted with less enthusiasm, "it takes money to make money. You know that. Down the road, I'll need to bring in some pretty heavy players.

"For now, I'm concentrating on my core schools. If enough famous martial artists locate with me"—he glanced at Sternway—"Martial America will promote itself. They'll attract attention, we'll get more and more ink, advertisers will become interested, and the whole thing will snowball."

I didn't think he'd ever seen a snowball. Not in Carner, that's for sure. But he finished confidently anyway.

"Then we'll be off and running."

I nodded noncommittally, feeling a bit baffled. I couldn't imagine why Marshal thought Lacone might be good for a job.

Apparently the subject bored Sternway. Shooting his cuff, he checked his watch like he wanted an excuse to be somewhere else. Then he surprised me by suggesting to Lacone, "Tell you what. Why don't the two of you join me for lunch? We can get to know Mr. Axbrewder a little better."

While I raised my eyebrows, the developer beamed in Sternway's direction. "Sorry, Anson. No can do. Sammy Posten is bringing one of Watchdog's underwriters out here to discuss Martial America's coverage. We're supposed to belly up to the trough in about twenty minutes."

He still hadn't mentioned anything that suggested a job. Which was natural, I told myself. He knew next to nothing about me.

Sternway shrugged, then looked a question at me.

I wanted a chance to make him squirm a bit. And I could think of plenty of questions for him. "I'll need to check it with Bernie," I answered promptly.

He didn't betray a reaction. "We can do that on our way out."

We both shook hands with Lacone again, and I followed Sternway off the dais.

If nothing else, having lunch with the IAMA director would help confirm my status as a dignitary.

We found Bernie where I'd left him, but Sternway didn't give me time to ask his permission. The director simply announced that he was taking me to the coffee shop. When Bernie acquiesced with a dyspeptic nod, Sternway drew me out of the hall.

I rolled my eyes for Bernie's benefit as I passed. Taking a swing or two at Anson Sternway was turning into one of my life's ambitions. He'd been "important" too long—he'd gotten into the habit of presuming on his own authority. The prospect of asking him a few subversive questions added a dash of adrenaline to my bloodstream.

Unfortunately I had to wait my turn. As soon as we were seated in The Luxury's coffee shop—a generic space complete with a single plastic flower, garish and cheerless, on every table—and had ordered some food, he started on his own questions.

His approach unsettled me a bit. He didn't seem to care that I was stone ignorant about him, the IAMA, or the martial arts. While he pried into my qualifications, experience, and training, he paid no particular attention to the answers. In fact, he hardly looked at me. Despite his air of impenetrable self-possession, his gaze slid away whenever I tried to make eye contact.

I might've thought that he was just killing time with me while he waited for someone more substantial to come along, but he didn't carry himself like a man who killed time. Instead he reminded me of a coyote circling a lost lamb—pretending disinterest while he made sure the lamb wasn't just bait.

When he did pounce, however, I couldn't figure out why he'd been so cautious about it.

What he really wanted to understand, apparently, was my connection to Marshal Viviter. In view of Marshal's recommendation, why didn't I work for him directly? And if he wasn't inclined to hire me himself, why did he think I was good enough for tournament security?

That, I had to admit, was a fair question—although I didn't know why it mattered. But I couldn't give it a fair answer, not without violating Marshal's confidential relationship with Sternway's wife. So instead I told him that my qualifications had nothing to do with it. The problem was a practical one. A former partner of mine already had a job with Professional Investigations, and Marshal suspected that we'd cause trouble for each other. Otherwise he wouldn't have hesitated—ha!—to hire me himself.

Sternway seemed to accept that. At any rate, he didn't push it. But I still didn't understand his concern.

When I'd flagged down the waitress for a fresh pot of coffee, I moved the plastic flower out of the middle of the table, giving myself a clear shot at him. Then I took my turn.

"You already know, Anson"—he'd been calling me Brew, and I wanted to sound polite—"I'm a complete stranger to this whole world. The martial arts. Schools. Tournaments. If you could explain a few things, it would help me do my job."

He granted me a glance. "Go ahead." Maybe he thought I'd appreciate his condescension.

I bared my teeth, metaphorically speaking. "Where I come from," I told him, "violence means blood. Guns, knives, clubs, fists—if the guy using them doesn't actively want you dead, he sure as hell intends to hurt you. He's *serious* about it.

"But you've got kids in those rings, wearing so much gear that if they fell down they wouldn't be able to stand up again. From what I've seen of the sparring, the refs stop the action as soon as anything even comes close. And in the forms—the *kata*?—your contestants attack imaginary opponents who cooperate with every move."

Somehow I caught his gaze. Leaning forward, I faced him squarely and counted the seconds until his eyes slipped away.

"If I were being gentle, Anson, I'd say it all looks like a game. But honestly, it looks like a lie. You're selling an illusion here. Isn't that true? You give out trophies the size of gazebos to convince the 'winners' that they're heavy hitters, they can whip whole platoons of thugs, no one sane is ever going to mess with them. But in fact I haven't seen anyone who'd survive for twenty seconds on the street. It's all just charades."

He didn't last long. His gaze wandered off by the time I mentioned trophies. If I'd succeeded at making him uncomfortable, however, he didn't show it. His voice had about as much inflection as a concrete floor.

"Of course it's an illusion. A tournament is sport karate, and all sports are games. They depend on rules to keep people safe, and real violence isn't safe. That's obvious."

I hadn't expected him to be so open about it. "Then why do you do it, if you know it's a lie? Other sports *use* violence. Some of them." Football, for example. "Karate is *about* violence. That makes the lie dangerous."

"Because," Sternway repeated like he thought I was stupid, "no one would participate if it weren't safe."

He scanned the room, possibly counting the plastic flowers. "Where do you suppose the money comes from?" he asked rhetorically. "People want to compete. That's human nature. They want to prove they're the best. And for every man, woman, or child who wants to prove they are the best, there are a couple hundred more who want to see them try.

"That's how it works. First *karate-ka* pay for a chance to prove themselves. Then spectators pay to watch. When they've generated enough interest, newspapers report the result. Advertisers recognize a chance to promote themselves. Winning means more. More people want to compete, even more want to watch, newspapers and sponsors increase their vested interest. The eventual outcome is the NFL, a multi-billion-dollar business dedicated to the love of competition."

He'd started to scare me. "But that's less dangerous," I insisted. "Those games aren't *about* violence."

He sighed. Just for a moment, he actually looked at me.

"That's where you're wrong, Brew. What we do here isn't a lie. It's simply not the whole truth."

Probably he could've told me how many other people were in the coffee shop.

"The skills we test," he explained without any obvious patience, "are a starting point, a foundation. A *karate-ka* who can handle competition has begun learning to handle real violence. Serious martial artists pursue additional training to improve their skills further. That's the difference between a master and a student."

He, of course, was a master. Eighth-*dan*, whatever that meant. Worshipped nationwide.

I felt sorry for his students.

I wanted to ask, So *you* understand real violence? You can defend yourself if someone jumps you on the street? But I didn't because what I really meant was, Do you think you can handle me? And I knew that question wasn't a good idea.

Instead I reverted to the one Sue Rasmussen hadn't answered.

"But what does it accomplish? What's it for?"

What makes the martial arts *good* for people?

"Do you have any idea how much those trophies cost?" Sternway countered. He must've misunderstood me. "They're the biggest expense we have, by far." He emphasized the words by jabbing the tabletop with his index finger. "Do you know how much it costs to run a decent *dojo*? You need *gis*, gear, belts, wood floors, mirrors, heavy bags, speed bags, *makiwaras*, mats, Wing Chun dummies, *shinais, bos* and *sais*, dressings rooms with showers. None of us could stay in business if we didn't promote the martial arts, attract new students, and generate new interest.

"Mr. Lacone said, 'It takes money to make money,' but he's been wealthy too long. He's forgotten the truth. It takes money to stay alive."

I couldn't argue with that. Maybe he wasn't the right man to answer the question I'd tried to ask. Maybe I needed to talk to Nakahatchi. Or Hong.

But still I hoped that he'd let slip something I needed. I kept my tone casual. "Does that have anything to do with why you haven't joined Martial America?"

Sternway appeared to consider several replies before he said, "If he were closer to his goal, I would. But as matters stand, it's too expensive."

Then he nodded at my plate. "Are you done?"

I held up my hand. "Just one more question."

He waited impassively.

"Are Hong and Nakahatchi serious?" I didn't even try to look innocent. "Aren't they overreacting? I mean, since this is all a game anyway. They seem"—I grinned uncharitably—"too intense for sport karate."

I'd succeeded at last. Sternway pushed back his chair. A hint of darkness disturbed his self-control.

"You haven't been listening, Axbrewder." He could make his voice punch when he wanted to. "*Sifu* Hong and Nakahatchi *sensei* are masters. Either one of them could grind you into dog food with their hands tied. I advise you to believe they're serious. If you don't, you will regret it."

Turning like a blow, he left me where I sat.

Dog food? I wanted to laugh out loud. *Dog* food? He was deluding himself. So far, I hadn't seen anyone here who struck me as a spice mill, never mind an actual meat grinder.

Nevertheless something about the idea must've appealed to me. I was in a better mood as I headed back to the tournament.

7

By midafternoon the tournament was heating up—in more ways than one.

More spectators had arrived. More rings were in use. And they all put out more energy. The adults and teenagers who competed in team sparring showed a real passion for attempting to thump on each other. Sometimes the passion looked like eagerness. The rest of the time, it was plain fear, the kind that makes you overreact because you're trying so hard to pretend you aren't scared.

On top of that, the AC had to work harder, and it was losing ground. Sweat gathered at the base of my spine, and my shirt began to smell like a salad going bad.

And on top of *that*, my nerves still hadn't made the adjustment. I couldn't tune myself to the hall. Watching cost me too much effort. Details distracted me. And all that yelling and pounding tightened the muscles on my scalp until my head ached.

Mostly I kept to the dais. Its elevation enabled me to pick up a general idea of how the IAMA ran team sparring.

Apparently there were eight divisions—brown belt, black belt, advanced, and something called "soft style," all for men, with the same again for women. The silk pajamas had soft style to themselves. The other three divisions wore canvas, most of it white. The exceptions stood out like stains on damask.

As far as I could tell, the silk pajamas fought with no more or less effectiveness than anyone else. But their approach was definitely more flamboyant, with more elaborate stances, bigger arm movements, more spins. Maybe it was supposed to intimidate people.

Teams of four competed head-to-head, one member at a time. They flailed and kicked and yelled like it all meant something. The action didn't stop as often as it did in individual *kumite*. The losers were eliminated, and the winners advanced. Apparently fighters "won" by accumulating points for punches or kicks that satisfied the refs. Breaking the rules produced penalties. Groins and knees were off-limits. Hitting too hard—whatever that meant—and ignoring a ref were definite no-nos. Cumulative points for each team determined the victors.

None of it made sense to me. With all the gear they wore, the contestants might've survived a charging rhino, so how could anyone hit them too hard? But of course I didn't need it to make sense. I just needed to know how the game was played.

The refs issued a lot of warnings. What I saw on the fighters' faces resembled frenzy, the same wildness you see in a horse's eyes right before they take it out and shoot it. Several of them kept attacking after the ref called them apart.

Presumably that was normal—for a karate tournament, anyway. And it wasn't my problem. Ned Gage was the director of referees. If things got out of hand, he could deal with it. Nevertheless the intensity pouring from the rings felt like trouble to me. Without thinking about it, I left the dais to get closer to the action.

After scanning three or four contests from the sidelines, I found the one that bothered me the most.

This match was men's brown belt, and it pitted white against screaming scarlet. At the moment, a gangling teenager in white fought a young man who outsized him by two inches and fifty pounds. The white canvas carried a couple of patches, one the ubiquitous IAMA insignia, the other too small to read. But I couldn't miss his opponent's label. Big yellow letters arcing across the scarlet said, "Nelson Brick's Killer Karate."

Noise inundated all the rings as spectators and teams hollered in every direction, but here it sounded raw and bloodthirsty, like there was something personal at stake. Maybe when the ref declared a winner the losers would be put to death.

Right away I saw why this contest bothered me. The clown in scarlet strutted and thumbed his nose, taunting the hell out of his opponent. Whenever they engaged he said something. I couldn't make out the words, but he was obviously sneering.

The kid grew more and more frantic with every attack. Anger and frustration cramped his punches, and most of his kicks went wild. Every time his opponent scored on him, his face turned a more desperate shade.

The audience loved it.

If I had been the ref, I would've disqualified them both. Sent them home to grow up. But no one here agreed with me. The Brick team encouraged their fighter by jeering at his opponent. The kid's supporters shouted, "Hit him! Hurt him!" Meanwhile the ref called points but not breaks, and ignored everything else.

It ate at my nerves. I resisted an impulse to charge into the ring, sort out the problem myself. But I stayed ready, just in case.

A minute later, the match ended. Killer Karate won by a landslide, thanks mostly to this round. The scarlet pajamas congratulated each other like they'd just won the Battle of Britain. In contrast, none of the white pajamas consoled or commiserated with their thrashed teammate. Instead they seemed to turn their backs on him, like he'd shamed them somehow.

I figured I knew exactly what was going to happen next.

Radiating ego and humiliation, the teams moved away from the ring. Now I could see the second patch on the white pajamas. *Tae Kwon Do Academy*. Master Song Duk Soon's school.

Swaggering with triumph, the clown in scarlet headed for his gear bag, apparently unaware that the kid he'd just crushed was right behind him.

Shame twisted the kid's features like nausea. When his opponent bent to his bag, the kid aimed an elbow at his kidneys, jumping into the blow to get all his weight behind it.

That made it easy for me to catch him by the back of his pajamas and jerk him away before his elbow landed.

"Stop it!" I barked into his face, doing my best drill-instructor imitation. I wanted to break into his dismay fast. "You're out of line!"

Before I could go on, the young Killer sprang up and spun toward me. Yelling even louder than I did, he wheeled a kick at the kid's head.

With me holding him, the kid couldn't protect himself. I heaved him back, turned to cover him with my right shoulder.

When the kick hit me, I staggered, and my arm went into shock. For half a second or so, astonishment paralyzed me. I would've sworn that was just a kick, pure stunt work, all show, but somehow he'd managed to catch me with a baseball bat instead.

Then my brain turned red, and the next thing they knew both

punks hit the floor, Killer scarlet on the bottom, flushed kid next, with me on top, using one knee to hold both of them down.

"I'm going to say it again." Under the circumstances, I thought I sounded remarkably calm. "You're out of line. Both of you. If you want to brawl, take it outside. And I mean *all the way*. Off the hotel grounds.

"Are you children listening to me?"

Let them tear each other apart somewhere public. The cops could sort them out.

A crowd had already gathered. No one under me answered, so I leaned down harder. "I said, are you lis—"

Suddenly I caught a peripheral flash of scarlet, and a blow hit my sternum hard enough to drive me off the pile. Pain tugged across my abdomen, tracing the line of Estobal's bullet. I barely caught my balance as my attacker advanced, ready to club me again.

"No, *you* listen, bub! This is none of your damn business! That twerp tried to hit my guy in the *back*. He was just defending himself!"

The man had a face like permanent apoplexy, complete with bulging eyes and an assertive mustache you could've used to sweep out the hall. He may've been six inches shorter than me, but he outweighed me easily. Every bit of him seemed to swell inside his pajamas. I thought the canvas might tear.

Across all that scarlet he wore a crisp black belt. Yellow letters over his heart identified him as Nelson Brick.

My chest felt numb, and I feared he'd torn open my guts. I wanted the .45 so badly that my good hand ached for it.

Maybe he'd back down if I spit blood at him.

Behind him, the fighters scrambled to their feet. "That's right!" Brick's student yelled. "He was going to hit me while I wasn't looking!"

While I gaped for the breath, I discovered that a man in white stood between me and Brick. Somehow I hadn't seem him arrive—he was just there. He had his back to me, but after my heart thudded a couple of times I figured out that he was Master Song Duk Soon.

"Mr. Brick," he said in a voice like the head of a hammer, "the conduct of your team is disgraceful. He provoked the conflict."

Oh, good. Now I had two crazy instructors on my hands.

None of the *karate-ka* and spectators crowding around seemed likely to back me up. They wanted more action. I was on my own.

Unless I used the cell phone.

"Master," the beaten kid quavered. "He insulted me the whole match. He insulted you. He called Tae Kwon Do 'a toy martial art.' "

Some of the spectators laughed—which made the kid's flush worse. Others muttered disapproval.

As soon as I caught my breath, I'd say, Hell, kid, they're *all* toys. But I wasn't ready yet. I still didn't know how seriously I was hurt.

Master Soon stood with the same explosive ease I'd seen earlier. "The words of a contemptible opponent are equally contemptible," he pronounced. Then he added to Nelson Brick, "Your student is a fool. He repeats what he was taught."

I thought Brick might attack again. He didn't look anywhere near as relaxed as Soon. But then a familiar voice interrupted us.

"All right, everybody," Parker Neill called out, "break it up, break it up." He seemed to disperse the crowd just by flapping his hands. "It's all over. Nothing's wrong. Get ready for your next events."

Ned Gage accompanied him. While Parker waved away the spectators, the head referee placed himself between Soon and Brick.

I was off the hook.

The glint in Gage's eyes looked like humor, but it may've been eagerness. "Master Soon," he said calmly, "Brick *sensei*, your teams are disqualified. I won't allow fighting outside the rings."

Since no one was looking at me now, I probed the pain in my stomach. It wasn't as bad as I'd feared. And I didn't feel any dampness. Apparently my scars had been stretched, not torn.

"Wait a goddamn minute, Gage," Brick blustered. "The whole team? That's not fair. My guy was just talking. He didn't break any rules."

I couldn't tell what Song Duk Soon felt. Whatever it was, he didn't show it.

Gage grinned amiably. "I'm the Director of Referees here. Shall I disqualify your whole school instead?"

"We're going to *win* this event!" Brick protested.

"If I disqualify the whole school," Gage continued, "you'll lose your IAMA membership." He sounded happier by the minute. "You won't get it back until you take one of our seminars on sportsmanship."

To my surprise, Brick looked away. "Where's Sternway?" he demanded. "I'm not going to put up with this.

"And I'm not"—he jabbed a finger in my direction—"going to put up with assholes from the audience interfering when my guys try to defend themselves."

I flexed my fists, working the pain out of my right arm.

Ned Gage widened his grin, matching Master Soon's relaxation. "Mr. Sternway won't help you, Brick *sensei*." Now he made the title sound like mockery. "We all saw what happened. The situation would've been worse if Mr. Axbrewder hadn't intervened so quickly. You owe him an apology."

Parker nodded like a man who'd seen it all before.

"Ha!" Brick snorted. "That'll be the day."

But he didn't go rushing off to find Sternway. I guess he believed Gage in spite of himself. *I* sure as hell believed him. If there hadn't been so many witnesses, I might've kissed his feet.

Still, I wanted some of my own back. Before Brick could move away, I drawled, "Listen, bozo. Maybe you have your own school. Maybe you're a world-class 'martial artist.' But as far as I'm concerned, you're just a fat thug in uncomfortable pajamas. Where I come from, we snack on guys like you. Hit me again, and I'll break your arms."

I'd broken Estobal's neck just hours after he shot me.

"Try it sometime." Brick aimed a nasty glare at me, but it turned hesitant when he saw the look on my face. "By the way," he added roughly, "these aren't pajamas. They're called a *gi*. You should remember that."

Then he reached out and grabbed a handful of his student's canvas. "Come on, boy. You're going to explain to the rest of your team how you got them disqualified."

Jerking the young man along, he stomped away toward a cluster of scarlet *gis* nearby.

The action in the rings continued as if nothing had happened. Yells and padded blows punctuated the tension. Parker Neill shrugged and left. Gage waggled his eyebrows at me like a humorous salute before turning his attention back to the tournament.

I didn't acknowledge either of them. Just for a second, the humiliation facing the young Killer distracted me. Maybe he'd brought it on himself. But he'd been taught by Nelson Brick—and Brick obviously didn't intend to take any responsibility for what his students learned.

By the time I convinced myself to copy Parker's shrug, Master Song Duk Soon had shifted to confront his own student.

The flushed kid stood in front of his Master, practically cowering. Soon said something in a harsher tone than he'd used with Brick. At once the kid dropped to his knees, bowed his head.

"You have disgraced me," Soon announced distinctly. "Remove your belt. You no longer merit it. I will consider how honor may be restored."

He didn't stay to see whether the kid obeyed him. He simply turned his back and left.

The kid had gone stark pale, and his mouth quivered. His hands shook as he untied his belt, folded it carefully, and set it down in front of him. Bowing, he touched his forehead to the belt. When he looked up, his eyes were full of tears.

I left him there myself. I couldn't do anything else for him. The last thing he needed right now was an audience.

I wanted to go after Master Song Duk Soon, tell him what I thought of him. Fortunately both my arm and my guts were feeling better, which allowed me to recover some common sense. That didn't come naturally. Most days I only had common sense when I could channel it from a previous life. But after a couple of deep breaths, I remembered that nothing Soon or Brick did was any of my business. If I tried to throw my weight around with them, I'd just get myself fired.

Parker hadn't gone far. Instead of following Master Soon, I stopped to complain to the Tournament Coordinator.

"Help me out, Parker," I growled under my breath. "Is this normal? Do the teachers always piss on the students around here?" In case he hadn't seen what happened, I explained, "Soon just stripped that kid's belt."

Parker cocked an eyebrow, glanced at me sidelong. "Like I said, Brew." He spread his hands. "True believers.

"It's traditional," he went on before I could object. "Everything the student does reflects on the teacher."

"No shit," I muttered. "His teacher taught him to fight like that. And act like that."

Neill nodded. "And put too much pressure on him. Made winning too important. I know what you're saying.

"What can I tell you?" He scanned the rings while he spoke, keeping an eye on the events. "The arts we study are predominantly Asian. They all downplay individualism and emphasize respect for authority. But it takes different forms in different countries.

"Tae Kwon Do is Korean. So is Master Soon. When a Korean challenges you, he wants to prove his school is better than yours, his style is better, his country is better. The Chinese are more personal. When a Chinese challenges you, he wants to prove his *sifu* is better than yours. If he's a *sifu* himself, then he wants to demonstrate the superiority of what he knows.

"As for the Japanese, they turn everything into spirituality." Parker smiled distantly. "According to Gichin Funakoshi, karate doesn't have anything to do with winning or losing. It's about 'perfection of character.' A Japanese *karate-ka* isn't judged by success or failure. He's supposed to display his best skills with devotion and humility.

"You could say the Koreans care about winning, the Chinese care about looking good, and the Japanese care about not caring."

Then he shrugged. "Those are the stereotypes, anyway. We all know lots of exceptions."

I could think of a few myself. If the Japanese were so all-fired spiritual, why had they spent half a century trying to conquer the world?

Bad leadership, I suppose.

"The real problem here," Parker continued in case I'd missed the point, "is that Master Soon's student isn't Asian. He's obedient because he knows he's supposed to be, and he desperately wants to be accepted. But he doesn't really understand the way he was just treated. He thinks like an individual.

"As for Brick," Neill finished sourly, "he's pure-blood American. It's all ego with him. He isn't as tough as he thinks. If you ever get a chance to compare him with Sternway *sensei*, you'll see the difference right away."

I wasn't convinced. I'd felt Brick's strength—and I had no intention of being impressed by Sternway. But the Tournament Coordinator didn't have to spend his time talking to me, and I wasn't about to repay the courtesy by dissing his *sensei*, so I just thanked him and let him get back to work.

I wanted a change of air to clear my head, so I decided to tell Bernie I needed a break. Get out of the hall for a few minutes. Find someplace where the AC was set on high, maybe lie down on the floor and practice breathing.

When I looked around for the Security Chief, however, I spotted Deborah Messenger across the rings. In fact, she seemed to be staring in my direction. She must've returned while I was concentrating on Brick and Soon.

Suddenly I didn't give a shit about *Killer Karate*, the *Tae Kwon Do Academy*, or their poor abused students.

Since I was supposed to be a dignitary, I didn't rush straight toward her. Instead I started to pick my way through the crowds around the hall.

She turned away as I moved. Oh, well. As long as she didn't leave before I reached her— After a minute or so, I saw her talking to Sternway, Lacone, and Sammy Posten.

OK, she was busy. No need to hurry.

Partway around the walls, I came on Ned Gage. He was watching another round of team *kumite*, but he didn't seem to be engrossed in it, so I stopped to thank him for getting Brick off my case.

He was shorter than Neill, and pudgier. Apparently being a balls-to-the-wall martial artist didn't mean you had to stay slim. Brush-cut hair, a wide mouth, and a mustache that only looked straight when he grinned emphasized the roundness of his face. Judging by the lines on his cheeks and around his eyes, he grinned a lot. If I hadn't already seen him in action, I wouldn't have believed he had enough personal authority to button his blazer. Nevertheless he carried himself with the same relaxation I'd already noticed in men like Sternway and Soon, pliant and worrisome as Semtex.

Raising his eyebrows, he asked, "You all right, Mr. Axbrewder? *I* wouldn't want to let Nelson Brick kick me."

I dismissed the question. "Call me Brew, Mr. Gage. Anyone who gets me out of trouble the way you did doesn't have to be formal."

"Brew." He grinned. "I'm Ned." Then he added, "I was just doing my job. You didn't need rescuing." He looked me up and down quickly. "I suspect you don't let the Bricks of the world kick you twice."

Trying not to think about Deborah Messenger, I grinned back. "Not if I can help it, anyway."

This opportunity was too good to miss, despite my impatience. "Can you spare a minute?" I asked.

He spread his hands. "As many as you want. Until the next crisis." The prospect of another testosterone outbreak obviously didn't trouble him.

"I'm congenitally nosy," I said by way of explanation. "I always want to know why people do what they do." Then I got to the point. "I hear you're a volunteer?"

Ned faked a scowl as he indicated his IAMA patch. "We all are." He sighed heavily. "Such is life." With that gleam in his eyes, he might as well have been laughing.

"Apparently," I drawled. "But I don't get it." I nodded toward the registration table. "From here it looks like you're taking in serious bucks. And I'm told you'll have a bigger crowd tomorrow and Sunday. But you work free. Why do you bother?"

He shrugged off his scowl like it was too much effort. With a sidelong grin, he chuckled, "If I thought you'd believe me, I'd say karate changed my life—which is true, by the way—and I'm expressing my gratitude. But I'm not that unselfish." He met my gaze straight on. "The real reason is, it's fun. All this intensity and seriousness. 'The thrill of agony, the victory of defeat,' " he misquoted sententiously. "It's as good as a circus. And I'm the ringmaster.

"Besides," he added softly, as if he were revealing a great secret, "I don't need the money. I have my own school in LA. I already make 'serious bucks' teaching stuntmen how to fake kung fu and karate for the cameras."

"Well, gosh," I breathed, wide-eyed. Playing along. "What refreshing candor." Then I lowered my voice. "But you can't tell me that Parker Neill and Sue Rasmussen are in it for the fun. He looks like a spectator at his own life. She acts like she's on some kind of Holy Crusade."

I expected him to laugh, but he didn't. Still softly, he advised, "Don't underestimate them, Brew. They're both fine martial artists. They may not be having fun, but they know what they're doing. They volunteer for the obvious reason that Mr. Sternway is their *sensei*. When your *sensei* wants something done, volunteering isn't optional."

I wanted to ask what gave *senseis* so much clout, but he must've assumed that I already knew the answer. "They'd both do it anyway, of course," he went on. "For Parker, this is the world he knows best. Until he gave up competing, he lived on tournaments and adrenaline. Part of what you see in him now is simple letdown. He misses putting himself on the line in the ring.

"And then"—Gage chuckled easily—"well, he's what you might call a 'true believer.' "

The match in front of us ended, allowing us a moment of quiet before other rings took up the slack. I could smell sweat and anxiety despite the laboring AC.

"He used those words himself," I put in. "But he was talking about other people."

The Director of Referees nodded. "I know. He does that. And sometimes he's right. But sometimes he's just projecting.

"He considers himself a better person than he was before he joined Mr. Sternway's *dojo*. For all I know, that's true. I can't see inside him. Or possibly he can't tell the difference between competition endorphins and spiritual growth. The point is that he believes it. If he had his way, everyone would study karate—and all the teachers would be volunteers. The fact that the IAMA is really a business depresses him."

I could imagine how he felt. The mix of dollars and thumping on all sides bothered *me*, and I wasn't involved.

I wanted to move on. But when I scanned the far side of the hall, I couldn't locate Deborah Messenger. Sternway and Lacone must've swept her off somewhere. In the space of about five seconds, my morale sagged like Parker's.

The heat was getting worse. If the AC couldn't cope any better than this now, conditions on Saturday would become positively sulfurous.

With a grimace, I wrestled my attention back to Gage.

"How about Sue? What's her excuse?"

"Oh, she'd volunteer even if her *sensei* didn't run the IAMA," he answered casually. If he caught my lapse, he was too polite to comment on it. "She's ambitious, our Sue." His tone suggested affection as well as amusement. “She wants to be a Power. Lawyer, civic leader, *karate-ka*, you name it. Working tournaments helps her connect with every heavy hitter in this world. She eats lunch with Bill Wallace, does favors for Fumio Demura, knows Chuck Norris by his first name. At the end of the day she can take all that to the bank.”

Leaning toward me, he lowered his voice again. “Rumor also has it that she sleeps with Anson. But you didn’t hear it from me.

“She still competes,” he added less privately. “You might get a chance to see her tomorrow, or Sunday. But watch out. Sometimes her *kata* and *kumite* have so much fire they’ll scorch your clothes if you stand too close.”

I snorted to myself. I’d seen Sue Rasmussen get heated, but I couldn’t picture actual fire.

However, I knew what would happen if I mentioned my doubts. Ned would make some reference to her ripping me apart. Apparently I was expected to consider every third person here some kind of ambulatory bucksaw. In any case, he obviously liked her, and I didn’t want to alienate him. He was more forthcoming than anyone else I’d talked to.

“But she and Parker aren’t having fun,” I remarked as if I wanted confirmation.

His eyes gleamed. “That’s true. Neither of them.”

“And you are,” I prodded.

“Don’t I look like it?” he countered. Then he admitted, “But it’s easier for me. Anson Sternway isn’t *my sensei*. That man is one hell of a fighter, but he’s death on fun.”

He gave me the opening I’d been angling for. I grabbed my chance while I had it.

“How about Mr. Sternway? Why is he involved in all this?”

For the first time, Ned paused to consider what he said. After a moment, he pronounced judiciously, “The IAMA is a valuable organization. It benefits everyone involved. And it was his idea. He deserves what he gets out of it.”

Drawing me with him, he took a couple of steps backward. Apparently he didn’t want to risk being overheard. Almost whispering, he told me, “But down at the bottom, he’s in it for the money. It’s a survival issue. His wife has been bleeding him dry for years. They’re separated now, but that hasn’t made her any less greedy. She’d take every penny he made while he starved to death, as long as the money kept coming after he died."

Aha, I thought. Here was something I could pass on to Marshal Viviter. No wonder Sternway focused so hard on the IAMA's balance sheet. There's nothing like a grasping spouse to make anyone desperate. If he'd been reduced to harassing her, at least he had a reason.

"Thanks," I murmured sincerely. "That helps."

Ned waved my gratitude away. "Don't mention it."

"Too late," I retorted. "I already did." Then I added abruptly, "So how do you know all this?"

Suddenly Gage looked like he might get huffy. "He doesn't hide it." I could feel the edge in his voice. "Ask him yourself."

I raised my hands to ward him off. "No offense. I'm a private investigator. I ask questions like that on automatic pilot. I wasn't implying anything."

Clearly the IAMA Director was a sensitive subject. And I didn't want to make Ned suspicious of my interest. If he mentioned this conversation to Sternway, I could probably kiss my job goodbye.

Ned relaxed visibly. "Forget it. I'm not that easily offended."

Swallowing my relief, I changed the subject. "Then I hope you won't mind one more question. You said karate changed your life." I made a show of incomprehension. "How?"

His laugh told me that the question didn't bother him. "Basically, Brew, I'm just a short round guy in a world full of big biceps and bigger egos. That's an intimidating prospect, let me tell you. For years I survived by keeping a low profile. But now I don't have to get along with any of them. I can laugh whenever I feel like it, instead of when it might placate some muscle-bound hothead who thinks I need an attitude adjustment.

"When an ego like Nelson Brick gets in my face, we both remember that I won Master's *kobudo* here three years in a row." He grinned broadly. "And I didn't work up a sweat doing it."

I did my best to look suitably impressed. "That would've been worth seeing."

He dismissed the idea cheerfully. "Not really. It was fun at the time. It's still fun. I like having the rep. But I wouldn't take it too seriously if I were you. All I did was swing a long stick around the ring for a while."

In a strange way, he was the only *karate-ka* I'd met so far that

I did take seriously. Intuitively I felt sure he'd earned his self-assurance.

Pretending that I didn't want to impose on his good nature, I thanked him again and moved away. The truth was that I preferred to conceal my accumulating gloom. The more questions I asked, the more obvious it became that I didn't understand the martial arts. Or martial artists. They all took safe risks, generated the sensation of danger without any actual hazard, but they acted like it *meant* something.

I felt stupid with heat and lack of sleep. Not to mention loneliness. When Ginny dropped me as her partner, she'd cut off my anchor to the only reality that made sense.

Black belt team *kumite* occupied the rings. Since I didn't have anything else to do, I paid a certain amount of aimless attention. If we had thieves working the room, they were too good for me to spot. And my nerves didn't catch any other alarms.

Now that I'd watched some of the brown belts, I could see that the black belts were definitely better—if "better" was the right word for it. They struck and withdrew faster, with more efficiency and better balance. But they didn't seem to hit as hard. If "better" meant that they sparred more safely, they'd left the brown belts miles behind.

I was tired of safety. If karate was *good* for people—if it made you "a better person"—maybe the time had come for me to go out on a limb by asking *Sifu* Hong why he gave a shit about Nakahatchi's chops. Better yet, I could ask Sternway what made him think it was a good idea to hassle his wife.

Oh, right. That'd be smart.

But the IAMA was being smart by keeping the tournament safe. I'd had about all the smart I could stand.

I must've been praying, although I didn't know it. Like an act of Divine Intervention, the doors near the registration table opened, and Deborah Messenger reappeared. She wasn't more than twenty yards away.

Sternway, Lacone, and Sammy Posten were still with her. The developer beamed on all channels while Posten laughed and Sternway lifted the corners of his mouth like a man who'd forgotten what amusement felt like. Deborah Messenger managed a polite distant smile, but her heart wasn't in it.

As soon as my eyes caught hers, hormones I didn't know I still had hit me like a cattle prod. From the rings, yells assaulted the soundproofing, but I hardly heard them. Trying not to hyperventilate, I sifted through the crowd toward her.

Somehow she detached herself from Posten and the others. By the time I reached her, she was alone.

"Hello, Brew." Her voice barely reached me through the din, but I didn't care. The noise gave me an excuse to stand close to her. "I wondered when I would see you again."

"I didn't." If we hadn't been inundated with blows and heavy breathing, I probably would've sounded too loud, too eager. "I wondered how much longer I'd survive without seeing you again."

She laughed warmly. "And now we'll never know. I suppose I should feel disappointed."

"Do that," I warned her, "and I'll expire where I stand. I'm far too chivalrous to let a lady suffer disappointment in my presence."

She placed a hand like a jolt of electricity on my forearm. "Oh, don't tempt me. Why, it's been"—she laughed again—"*weeks* since I watched a man expire for my sake."

"That's hard to believe." I hoped we were talking about the same thing. "I would've thought you had them lined up around the block."

"Well, of course. But I'm selective." Archly. "I hope you don't think I would allow just any man to expire for me?"

I couldn't think of a retort, so I concentrated on breathing. I didn't want to turn red right in front of her.

With her touch still on my forearm, she shifted closer and asked softly, "Do you have plans for dinner? I need to go back to the office for a while. Sammy and I have been talking business with Anson and Alex, and I'm supposed to write up a report. But I can be here again by six-thirty. Would you like to join me? In The Luxury's elegant coffee shop?"

Too quickly, I said, "Sure." Then I made an attempt to recover some semblance of poise. "I might not be able to hold my breath that long, but I'll borrow a respirator from somewhere."

"Good." She squeezed my arm, then released it. "Don't go looking for me. I'll find you. Just in case I run late."

She had a lot more self-possession than I did. She managed to turn away without staggering once—which I couldn't have done. Hell, I almost fell over just watching her leave.

Come on, Axbrewder, I advised myself sternly. Pull yourself together. Women like that aren't attracted to clowns like you. She must want something. But I couldn't help it. My knees trembled when I started to move again, and the hall seemed to revolve around me on an axis I couldn't identify.

Unsteadily I made my way toward Bernie. He'd hired me. Making outside plans without consulting him wasn't a good idea.

I could've sworn the man was asleep. He'd closed his eyes, and his shoulders rested lightly on the door behind him. Knowing how to nap on his feet was probably a survival skill in his job. But when I said his name, he looked at me without a twitch, and his gaze wasn't any more blurred than usual.

"No offense, Bernie," I said softly, "but have you considered delegating? You're the Chief of Security. You could assign all this standing around to someone else."

"You kidding?" he buzzed. "And miss the excitement?" A moment later he added, "You did good, Axbrewder. Somebody gets hurt outside the rings, and the hotel shares liability."

I shrugged. "Thanks." His good opinion made me uncomfortable. Awkwardly I changed the subject. "I've been invited to have dinner with Ms. Messenger." A triumph of smooth transition. "I wanted to check it out with you before I did it."

Bernie stabbed me with a look. "This isn't a dating service," he snarled—not unpleasantly. "Get laid on your own time."

"Please, Bernie." Was I that obvious? "I'm blushing."

He gathered himself for a stinging retort, so I hurried ahead. "Would it be better if I pretend it's business? It is. Sort of. I want an in with Watchdog. Just in case"—I waved a hand around the tournament—"you know."

In case I did something Watchdog wanted me to account for. Or the tournament led to a better job.

Bernie's jaws worked, chewing nasty sounds to find one that tasted right. Finally he muttered, "Hotel policy. You're allowed to eat. Damn indulgent, if you ask me. Your job's too cushy as it is. But I don't care who you eat *with*."

A moment later, he added, "And stop trying to get on my good side." Loneliness scraped like a raw nerve in his tone. "I told you I don't want to like you too much."

I sighed. "I can't help it, Bernie. It's my nature."

"Fuck your nature," he rasped so that only I could hear him. "Fuck Messenger. Just do your job."

Coming from him, that was the undiluted milk of human kindness.

I wanted to do something for him, but I couldn't think what. He needed friends, and I was just a temporary employee. Besides, I'd spent too many years drunk. I'd lost the knack for friendship.

Lacking any better ideas, I went back to the dais and concentrated on—well, on concentrating.

By degrees the rhythms of the tournament had become easier to read. The competition was continuous, but individual rings conducted events at their own pace. From my elevated perspective, the mass of *karate-ka* and spectators seemed to seethe from place to place as the rings filled and emptied. The ranks of trophies shrank slowly, but the great majority of them, including all the biggest ones, remained where they stood. Fresh as flowers in dew, Sue Rasmussen worked her microphone with relentless enthusiasm. The chops attracted a certain amount of desultory activity, but it didn't amount to much. Masters like Nakahatchi, Hong, Soon, and Gravel counseled or ignored their students. Others emulated Nelson Brick's style of exhortation.

Anson Sternway wandered around the hall like a man with nothing to do, disappearing and reappearing on a schedule all his own, while Parker and Ned smothered disturbances. Some of the time, Sammy Posten shadowed the IAMA Director, but mostly he watched over the chops with an air of ineffectual vigilance. Apparently Alex Lacone had left the hotel. He must've heard the call of money somewhere else.

Gradually I began to see the tournament as something almost physiological, a form of life. I didn't understand it, but I could feel its pulse and respiration, sense its muscles gather and release. If trouble developed, I'd know it.

And somehow the AC held its own against the heat. That helped.

Deborah Messenger had said 6:30, so I didn't start watching

the doors until 5:15. And I didn't actually hold my breath until a little before six. By the time she arrived, I was so focused that I spotted her immediately.

As soon as she caught sight of me, she waved. In a fog of enchantment, as it were, I evaporated from the dais and condensed beside her.

"Mr. Axbrewder." She welcomed me with a smile. "I hope this means we're still on for dinner."

Pretending composure, I replied, "Not unless you stop calling me Mr. Axbrewder." Had I said that before? I couldn't remember. "Makes me sound like your uncle. I prefer Brew."

"So do I," she admitted. Mock-sternly, she added, "And don't let me catch you calling me Ms. Messenger. At least not to my face. Deb is much better."

I made a show of trying it out. "Deb? Deb?" Then I shook my head. "I'm sorry. I need more syllables. Deb is too diminutive." As far as I was concerned, she didn't have a diminutive bone in her body. "Might as well be an acronym. Would you mind Deborah?"

She laughed. "An acronym? For what?"

I shrugged with pleasure. "Who knows? 'Daughter of an Emasculated Bastard'? I've never met your father. 'Dreary Eternal Boredom'? No, that doesn't fit. 'Designed by the Eugenics Board'? Now there's a possibility."

"Enough!" Laughing harder, she waved her hands to stop me. "If you keep this up, I'll lose my professional credibility. Nobody buys insurance from a woman who laughs too much.

"Come on." She gestured me toward the door. "If you insist on charming me off my feet, at least do it in the coffee shop so I can hear you better."

Charming her? *Me?* I wanted to look around, see who she meant. But I wasn't buying insurance from her. I was buying risk. "Lead on," I told her gallantly. "I'll join you as soon as I tell Mr. Appelwait where I'm going."

She already knew that I worked for The Luxury.

Smiling over her shoulder, she moved to the doors. I took about two seconds to catch Bernie's eye and signal my intentions. Then I rejoined her so fast you'd have thought I was pouncing. Unsteadily I accompanied her to the coffee shop.

The place was still generic, but she made it look tawdry as

well. The plastic flowers brandished their artificiality over wilted tablecloths, spotted tumblers, stained flatware, and a ratty carpet bestrewn, as you might say, with crumbs. The neat freak inside me squirmed. I wanted to leave the hotel, go somewhere nicer, but I couldn't afford to stay away from my job that long.

Manfully I set my distaste aside.

Her shining eyes and warm smile made it easy. Under her influence, I forgot all about cleanliness.

For a while I was so befuddled by hormones and longing that I hardly noticed what we did. We must've ordered some food, because eventually we ate something. And she must've asked me a lot of questions, because otherwise why was I talking so much? But none of it caught my attention. Fog filled my head. What was she *doing* here? That's what I wanted to know—an alcoholic's question. What did she have to gain?

We'd been there for half an hour before I achieved the surprising realization that my fist was wrapped around a cup of coffee while she drank red wine. Alcohol usually shouts at me as soon as it enters the room. The fact that I hadn't actually noticed its presence for so long hit me hard enough to shake my brain out of its trance.

She'd been quizzing me about my background. How had I become a private investigator? Why was I in a temporary job like tournament security? Did I enjoy it? What sort of work did I do best? If her manner hadn't been so personal, she could've been conducting an interview.

But one of her questions was, "Are you involved with anyone, Brew?" Apparently this wasn't a *job* interview.

That sharpened my attention in a hurry. "I guess it depends on what you mean by 'involved.' I had a partner for years. And we were definitely involved. But that's changed. We became"—I shrugged awkwardly—"less involved a while ago. And just recently she stopped calling me her partner. I still haven't figured out where I stand with that."

Her lips seemed to moisten themselves. "Do you want to talk about it?"

"Not really." That was honest, anyway. "I'd much rather find out whether *you're* involved with anyone."

She gave me a glistening smile. "Let me think. I had dinner with Sammy once, about a year ago. And Alex—you've met Alex

Lacone, haven't you?—he propositions me whenever we have a minute alone. Does that count?"

I dismissed Posten and Lacone. "No one else? I find that hard to believe. I wasn't actually kidding when I mentioned men lined up around the block." Her pheromones had practically poleaxed me. Surely they affected other males the same way.

"Thank you." Accepting the oblique compliment. "I'll tell you the truth, Brew. I think you've been honest with me, and I want to do the same.

"I'm an ambitious woman. If I have my way, I'll end up running Watchdog Insurance. And—" She hesitated. "Oh, how should I put this? I don't usually talk about it." For a moment she studied the tablecloth. When she raised her eyes again, they were full of complex colors.

"Sex works for me," she said carefully. "I don't mean I'm 'sleeping my way to the top.' But I like sex a lot.

"Oh, it helps me along. The men I want to work with pay more attention because they find me attractive. I'm comfortable with that. But I don't confuse pleasure and ambition. If I find a man attractive, I keep it to myself unless who he is and what he does are irrelevant to my career. When I'm clear on that point—"

She hesitated again, but for a different reason this time. The smile that spread across her face radiated enough heat to make me sweat. "What can I say? I like men who really *are* men.

"And I don't meet many." Chuckling at the expression on my face, she explained, "I think most of them are afraid of me.

"I don't mean of me personally," she added quickly. "I mean of women in general. Or of sex. In public they act like walking erections. But most of them are cowards around women.

"Mr. Sternway is one example," she mentioned in a private murmur. "He's a famous martial artist, respected everywhere. But he lets his wife treat him like dirt." Then she laughed again. "I mean, if you listen to the gossip—which of course I never do."

I tried to play along. "Me neither. Heaven forfend." But I couldn't keep it up. Apparently she thought that I was different somehow. If I let that pass, we'd both regret it.

"But I'm not sure you're right," I countered. "I can't speak for Sternway, so let's take me as an example. I'm not afraid of women. I'm afraid of my*self*. Nothing gets inside me faster than a woman I want." I didn't try to pretend that I wasn't talking about her. "I don't just drape my coat across the mud for a pretty face. I toss in my whole body. And that scares me.

"Maybe," I suggested, "Sternway has the same problem."

In response, her gaze shone as if I'd just said something wonderful. "So I was right about you."

She confused me. "What do you mean?"

"Mr. Private Investigator," she pronounced softly, just for me, "it takes real courage to know what you're afraid of, and admit it. I don't mind fear. Everybody is scared. I'm scared myself." She smiled ruefully. "Or I would be if I were brave enough to tell the truth. But I'm tired of men who hold me responsible."

Behind her assertion I heard loneliness, a deep well of it hidden away where most people never noticed it.

I knew what that felt like.

Mostly in self-defense, I asked, "Since we're being this honest, do you mind if I change the subject?" For once my own gracelessness didn't make me flinch.

"Please do." She flapped her hands in front of her face. "I was about to blush."

I wanted to thank her. Effusively. But if I did, I'd forget my question, so I blundered ahead.

"Tell me more about those chops. I'm no expert on insurance. I know just enough to wonder why Watchdog hasn't insisted on an appraisal. How can you insure them if you don't know what they're worth?"

With no apparent strain, Deborah shifted to a more detached tone. Nevertheless her eyes continued to glow.

"You're right," she answered, "we can't. But we haven't had time to arrange a formal appraisal. Mr. Nakahatchi brought the chops back from Japan only a few days ago. And he doesn't have enough documentation on their provenance to authenticate them.

"Purely as a temporary solution, we've all agreed on a compromise. Until we can have the chops appraised to Watchdog's satisfaction, they're only covered for the current price of the ivory itself. No doubt that undervalues them dramatically. As both exquisite antiques and historical documents, they're worth far more. But at least this way we can insure them. Otherwise Mr. Nakahatchi would have no coverage at all."

Obviously this involved Lacone. Nakahatchi's school was in Martial America, so Lacone couldn't avoid some of the risk.

"Still, I'm worried," Deborah went on. "We'll have our appraisal in a week or so. If the chops turn out to be genuine, Alex's premiums will rise substantially, and Mr. Nakahatchi's will go through the roof. I'm sure Mr. Nakahatchi won't be able to afford his. Even Alex will be in trouble.

"Despite the way he talks about it," she confided, "he's stretched to the limit with Martial America. He needs more schools, and *much* more media attention, to attract the kind of investors who can keep his 'dream' afloat."

Then she finished, "I don't know how any of us will solve that problem, but I'm working on it. In fact, that's the subject of the report I wrote this afternoon. I'm trying to design a deal that gives everyone enough protection to keep them going."

Her answer helped, but I wanted more. Pushing my luck, I asked, "What kind of deal?"

There she pulled back. "I'm sorry, Brew. I can't tell you that." Her smile took the edge off her refusal. "Our clients have a right to a certain amount of confidentiality."

I grinned back. "My mistake." She was right, of course. "It won't happen again."

Unless the chops disappeared. Then I wouldn't give a shit about Watchdog's professional confidentiality.

For a few minutes, we lapsed into ordinary conversation. What did I think of the tournament? Did she enjoy it? How much did I know about the martial arts? Had she ever studied one? But we were just postponing the real issue. I couldn't mistake the undercurrent of intensity in her voice—or my own plain yearning.

Finally she leaned forward and took hold of my hand. Her fingers felt cool and enticing on my overheated skin.

"Brew," she breathed quietly, "there's a reason I asked if you're involved with anyone. I think you know what it is. I'd like you to spend the night with me. I don't know you very well, but so far I really like you. And I'm feeling enough chemistry to set the hotel on fire."

She didn't lack the courage to say what she wanted, I had to give her that. Most of my life I'd been too scared to try it.

With an effort, I shook my head.

"I'd like nothing better. But I can't." Just saying the words left me hoarse. "Not tonight. I don't know where I stand with my partner. My former partner. That takes precedence. We were together for a lot of years." I squeezed Deborah's fingers, then withdrew my hand. "I wouldn't feel right with you while things with her aren't clear."

There I forced myself to stop. If I'd gone on, I might've started to wail. I couldn't remember the last time I'd felt the way I did with her. And I wanted it. I wanted more. Turning my back on it cut into me like a bereavement.

She didn't hide her disappointment. But she didn't turn it against me either. And she didn't try to change my mind. Instead she simply smiled her regret.

"I understand," she murmured. "It's always better to keep things clean."

Before I could think of a response, she signaled for the check. Then while we waited she proceeded to put on a display of self-possession that took my breath away. Instead of the stilted courtesy I expected from her, she covered my losses with a flow of light conversation and easy smiles. In its own way, her air of relaxation was as convincing as Sternway's—and vastly more desirable. I almost believed that she hadn't taken my refusal personally.

When she'd paid the check, and we stood up to leave, she touched my cheek lightly, like a promise that there were no hard feelings.

I still didn't know whether she'd told me the truth about herself.

The idea that maybe she hadn't made me want to weep.

8

Deborah and I parted company in the lobby. She left the hotel—going home, she said. I went back to the tournament.

When I checked in with Bernie, he made a labored reference to speed—or maybe it was quickies—but I hardly heard him. Deprivation of all kinds had caught up with me, and I couldn't shake the impression that I'd wandered into the wrong hall. Or the wrong life.

In my absence, the whole composition of the occasion had changed. The floor had been cleared of chairs, spectators, and contestants, of competition. Maybe they'd been rolled up like rugs and stashed away. Nevertheless the gallery held more people than it had all day, and every foot of space around the walls was crowded, standing room only. An air of anticipation rode the heat upward, accumulating against the ceiling. I felt like I'd blundered into an amphitheater where lions were scheduled to devour every available Christian.

By coincidence I'd arrived in time for the Bill "Superfoot" Wallace demonstration. Judging by the barrage of applause, Sue Rasmussen must've just finished introducing him. Below her, a lean, bandy-legged man took the floor and announced that he and his "opponent" were about to engage in "a battle to the death."

On cue, the audience roared with laughter. Everyone but me knew what to expect.

I suppose I should've been entertained. Or at least impressed. Wallace was fast and flexible enough to amaze sheetrock. He used only one leg—which was probably why they didn't call him "Superfeet"—but he fired kicks with it like rounds from a chain gun. His hapless opponent didn't stand a chance.

In my condition, however, I didn't appreciate the show. Half the time I couldn't even see it. I lacked the moral energy. So I just stood there, glazed positively ceramic, until he was done.

Afterward Rasmussen went into a spiel about all the wonderful events in store over the next two days. Anticipating confusion while so many people surged for the exits, I aimed myself at the chops. But Bernie stopped me.

"You're done, Axbrewder," he buzzed harmlessly. "I haven't seen anybody look this wrecked since the last time I used a mirror. Get some sleep. We can handle it from here." Then he snapped, "Be on time tomorrow." Apparently he didn't want me to think he'd gotten soft.

I think I thanked him. At the time, I wasn't sure. He was right, I didn't have anything left. Saying no to Deborah had used me up. Changing directions, I let the crowd carry me out into the lobby toward Registration, where I picked up the key for a room on Security's account.

The room itself was more generic everything, but I didn't care. I only needed a bed big enough to hold me. As soon as I turned off the lights, the whole world shut down, and I slept like a cadaver.

The next morning, the phone jangled me awake in a rush of panic. Phones do that to me sometimes. I'd let Ginny down somehow, and she was trying to get in touch with me. But it was just my wake-up call.

Nevertheless the jangle left me with a sour lump in the pit of my stomach. Pressure throbbed dully in my temples, hinting at disaster. If something went wrong today, it would probably turn out to be my fault.

Until I reached the shower I forgot that Ginny didn't even know where I was. Unless Marshall told her—

But that, as they say, didn't bear contemplation, so I declined to contemplate it.

Fortunately The Luxury offered an amenity I hadn't noticed the night before—an in-room coffee maker. While it perked, I faced the bathroom mirror stoically and pointed a sandblaster at the fatigue encrusted on my features. My guts hardly hurt at all, and under the bandages my wound was clean, but I swallowed the last of my antibiotics anyway and washed them down with coffee. Then, wishing I owned another suit, a clean one, I got dressed.

I also wished I had my .45. My only weapon was Security's cell phone, and it didn't have enough heft to reassure me.

Oh, well. When I'd consumed every drop of coffee in sight, I left the room and caught an elevator for the lobby.

I was early, so Bernie assigned me to help some of his men carry Nakahatchi's display case from the Manager's safe room, where it'd been stashed overnight, back out to its designated place in the tournament hall. My guts objected, but they didn't give me any real trouble. That was progress. A few days ago I wouldn't have been able to lift my share of the load.

By the time we'd set up the case, Anson Sternway arrived with his entourage—Sue Rasmussen, Ned Gage, and Parker Neill, plus Sammy Posten, Master Song Duk Soon, *Soke* Bob Gravel, Hideo Komatori, and the navy blazers who ran registration. I didn't know what brought Soon and Gravel here so early, but Komatori plainly wanted to check on Nakahatchi's antiques. Posten concentrated on looking important.

Sternway greeted Security and me with a nod, but didn't say anything.

After that Bernie arranged the rest of his troops. Once the registration crew had their paperwork ready, they helped Gage and Neill reset chairs and sign-poles for the rings. Rasmussen erected placards listing the day's events.

My sense of premonition refused to go away. While I strolled along the walls waiting for Bernie, I made a discreet attempt to imitate the poised and easy way the IAMA blazers moved, trying to distract my attention from possible crises. I didn't want to develop expectations, preconceptions, which might get in my way when something actually happened. Nothing hampers intuition like deciding in advance what it's supposed to do.

During the night, the AC had been set on "hard freeze," and now the hall felt like a meat locker. I was tempted to hunch my shoulders and blow on my fingers. But the place would heat up soon enough, so I tried to enjoy the chill while it lasted.

When my boss appeared, I quit faking relaxation and crossed the floor to talk to him.

He scowled at me. "Axbrewder." With his men in place, he was temporarily at loose ends himself. "You needed the sleep. Today you look like you might live."

I tried to thank him, just in case I'd forgotten last night, but he waved it off. "You won't be that lucky again. These gooks always run late. They're supposed to be out of here at nine P.M., but by then they'll be hours behind."

"According to the placards," I observed, just making conversation, "there's another demo tonight. Benny 'the Jet' Urquidez. What're they going to do, make him sit on his hands until midnight?"

Bernie shook his head. "Too many paying spectators. They run the demos on time. Approximately. Then they'll set up the rings again, hold more events." He snorted his version of a laugh. "The spectators go home after the demo. Won't be anybody here except the gooks and the judges. And us. They'll compete in a vacuum.

"Good thing they don't expect Security to supply the applause." The idea seemed to give him an obscure satisfaction.

I nodded. I was in no mood to clap for anyone.

A few minutes later, the hall was ready—rings set up, blazers at the registration table, Security standing petrified watch over the antiques and the doors. Sternway, Rasmussen, and Neill conferred around the record-keeper's laptop while Gage discussed something or other with Soon and Gravel. No one seemed to need Posten's supervision, so he just dithered.

"It's those doors I'm worried about," I remarked to Bernie, pointing across the hall. "Can you cover the service corridors?" They presented the most obvious security risk.

"We spotted you, didn't we?" Bernie countered. Then he admitted, "We're stretched thin. But Max is conscientious. If he's ever missed anything on the monitors, I don't know about it. He'll get a look at anybody who doesn't belong."

So much for the obvious. Nagged by the queasiness in my stomach, I'd fallen into the trap of trying to anticipate trouble, despite my good intentions. Anticipation was Bernie's job. Discovery was mine. Discovery and reaction.

I could think of all kinds of questions to ask people, if I got the chance.

From the dais, Anson Sternway announced his readiness. On cue, the IAMA blazers opened the doors, and the rush began. Like the quick tumult of a flash flood, or the growing roar when a hydroelectric plant opens the spillways, the hall went from hollow quiet to thunder in the space of about thirty seconds. If I hadn't known it was coming, I might've lost my nerve.

Soon I saw that Sue Rasmussen was right. The IAMA World Championships would be a hell of a lot busier today. Crowds inundated the registration table, pounded up onto the bleachers in waves, spilled out across the rings, piled against the walls—men and women in pajamas or warmup suits, torrents of spectators. But no kids this time, except in the gallery. Today was for grownups, "real" martial artists, and everyone took it more seriously. Even the noise had a tearing edge I hadn't heard yesterday. Half the people around me looked like they were going to war.

From the microphone, the master of ceremonies called for judges. I let the human current carry me out into the middle of the floor. Worry burned on my skin like a low-grade infection. Jangling premonitions echoed inside me. Now more than ever I needed to tune my instincts to the jagged rhythms of the tournament, let them warn me when something didn't fit. But I couldn't do it. I was paying the wrong kind of attention.

I missed Ginny.

Distraction, that was the key. Keep the front of the brain busy, let the rest work on its own.

I took the first opportunity I could find. Seeing Parker Neill nearby, I angled in his direction. He stood in the crowd with spectators and contestants frothing past him like water on both sides. I joined him in the eddy.

"Got a minute?" I had to raise my voice against the clamor. "You're probably busy. But I wanted to ask you something yesterday, and I forgot."

"Ask away." He sounded tired—worn down by his longing for competition, if Ned Gage understood him. "By now I don't have a lot to do. Tournament coordination is all preparation." He grimaced. "Today my biggest headache will be deciding how to adjust the schedule when we fall behind."

By way of preamble, I offered, "Well, if you don't mind my ignorance—" But he didn't react, so I forged ahead. "I heard a couple of things that didn't seem to fit the—I don't know what to call it—the 'seriousness of the occasion.' " The alleged quest for *perfection of character*. "One of your competitors was sneering at 'soft styles.' And apparently Nelson Brick's boy called Tae Kwon Do 'a toy martial art.' But I thought—"

I wasn't quite sure how to say what I meant politely.

"You thought," Parker finished for me, "martial artists are supposed to have more respect. Is that it?"

Close enough. I nodded.

"They are," he stated flatly. "Any teacher who doesn't train his students to honor all the martial arts doesn't deserve to *have* students. But in practice—" He shrugged. "It's a complicated problem."

He looked around the hall in case anyone needed him. Then he started to explain. I expected to hear boredom in his voice, the weariness of an expert discussing advanced concepts with a tyro, but I didn't. Instead he gathered animation as he talked. Ned Gage was right about him. Neill was a true believer who needed a chance to express himself.

"For one thing," he told me, "schools and styles are often parochial. Secretive. Some of them think they'll lose their effectiveness if other people know what they do. And some are afraid to admit they can be beat. They teach their students to think their school is the only pure one, or their style is the only one that really works. They concentrate on what they already know. Anything that doesn't come out of their own traditions, they ignore. And they sneer at everything else.

"The result," he pronounced categorically, "is bullshit. Truckloads of it. On one side, some schools refuse to join the IAMA or compete because they believe they'll be corrupted by outside influences. And on the other—

"Nelson Brick is a good example. His students aren't here to learn. They're here because he expects them to prove his style is *better* than anybody else's."

Conviction gleamed in Parker's eyes. "But in fact there *are* no better styles. Or worse ones, either. There are only better and worse martial artists. The styles simply solve different problems, or solve the same problem in different ways."

Around us, the in-rush accumulated toward critical mass. If the ceiling hadn't been so high, the din would've been deafening. Already the temperature had started to climb. Watching vaguely while I listened, I saw several of the masters begin to gather their schools. Nakahatchi sat on one of the bleachers as close as he could get to his display. Hideo Komatori and a group of canvas pajamas attended him like spear-carriers.

Parker lowered his voice confidentially. "That's what makes

Sternway *sensei*'s accomplishments so amazing. I never would've believed that he could get so many schools and martial artists to join the IAMA. And I would have bet money that he couldn't talk Nakahatchi *sensei*, Master Soon, *Sifu* Hong, *Soke* Gravel, and even Brick into joining Martial America."

Then he resumed his explanation. "That's one side of the problem. Nationalism is another—we talked about that yesterday. And then each style has it own personality and philosophy.

"As a crude generalization, you could divide the martial arts into 'hard' and 'soft' styles. Hard styles like Shotokan, Shorin-Ryu, and Muay Thai are ballistic, linear." His tone hinted at fervor. "They're designed to counter your attack with an attack of their own.

"Soft styles—Aikido, Wing Chun, Judo—are circular. They don't counterattack, they redirect. You jump at a hard stylist, and he breaks your ribs. You jump at a soft stylist, and he plants your face in the dirt.

"Obviously," he added, "the best fighters are the ones who can do both."

It *was* obvious—if you accepted the basic proposition that any martial art deserved to be studied at all. But my perspective on violence didn't square with his. I knew from experience that when someone fired a gun at you, you didn't care about whether he was attacking or defending. You cared about how badly you were hit.

Until I saw Hong Fei-Tung settle himself and his phalanx of silk pajamas near the wall as far as he could get from *Essential Shotokan*, I didn't realize that I'd been watching for him. He was on my list. If I couldn't get him to tell me something useful about those chops, I'd have to look for another line of work.

For now, however, I wanted to keep Neill talking. "That doesn't explain why a hard stylist would sneer at soft styles. Or why the IAMA keeps them separate."

Parker nodded. "That's because the soft styles aren't as popular. People like to bang. And soft stylists don't seem to have the personality for self-promotion—or the philosophy. They don't recruit as effectively as, say, Tae Kwon Do does.

"Three quarters of our competitors are hard stylists. So are at least ninety percent of the judges. And most of them aren't qualified to judge anything else. We keep the soft styles separate because we want to give them a fair chance. Otherwise they'll be overwhelmed by sheer numbers—if they aren't alienated by bad judging."

I considered this for a moment, then admitted, "I'm still confused. Isn't Tae Kwon Do a hard style? So why does Brick consider it a toy?"

Neill smiled without much humor. "I said it's complicated. That insult has to do with the difference between a sport and a martial art."

Now he sounded sour, like a man with a mouthful of alum, trying to stifle scorn. "Tae Kwon Do is the Korean national sport. It's backed by their government. And they're"—he sighed—"well, putting it crudely, they're imperialistic. They want worldwide recognition that doesn't confuse them with karate or kung fu.

"They're after the kind of news coverage they can only get from competitions. And they need to attract kids, lots of kids. Of course," he explained unnecessarily, "the two go together. More competitors means more coverage. More coverage means more competitors."

Already the stands were nearly full. Schools gathered in knots, making shoals for the spectators to surge around. Black belts shifted past us on their way to the staging area.

Parker cleared his throat like he wanted to spit. "There's just one catch. To get what they want, they have to demonstrate that Tae Kwon Do is essentially safe. That means rules. Sports require rules. Parents demand rules for their kids." He shrugged. "We have a fair number of rules here.

"But no martial art does that." I heard a tent preacher lurking somewhere in the bushes of his personality. "One way or another, they're all designed to save your life when somebody wants to hurt or kill you. They don't care about rules. If you aren't ready and able to repay any harm that comes your way, you might as well surrender." He made the word sound like an accusation. "So if all your training relies on rules—"

He sighed again, letting some of his enthusiasm go. "That's why boxing isn't a true martial art. Boxers can assume they won't be kicked in the groin or gouged in the eyes. They're protected by rules. That makes them vulnerable."

A sizable crowd had gathered near the roped-off display area, waiting to filter in for a look at the chops. Sammy Posten hovered nearby as if he wanted to strip-search everyone, but he was wasting his time. The crowd defended Nakahatchi's antiques as well as Bernie's guards did. Those chops were in more danger in the Manager's safe room than they were here.

"I hate to agree with Brick," Parker went on in a distant tone, "but sometimes TKD deserves to be called a toy. I've even heard Sternway *sensei* use that term." Right away, however, he added, "Of course, he wasn't talking about Master Soon. His *Tae Kwon Do Academy* still teaches a real martial art."

Up on the dais, Sue Rasmussen stood at her mike sorting papers like she was about to begin mastering the ceremonies. I hurried to ask the question that she and Sternway hadn't answered to my satisfaction.

"But how is that different than what you do? If this tournament depends on rules, isn't it just a toy?"

Then I braced myself, just in case Neill's evangelical streak got the better of him.

He looked around the growing crowd for a moment. When he was ready to respond, he drawled indulgently, "I'm sure it looks that way." I guess he'd decided to spare my life. "You haven't seen much of it. But the difference is real, believe me. When a martial artist competes, he *accepts* the rules, he doesn't *depend* on them. He isn't handicapped by them. If his opponent throws an illegal technique, he deals with it. He isn't at its mercy.

"And he doesn't," Parker stated, "stand around waiting for the ref to call a foul."

Clearly he hadn't taken offense. In his own way, he seemed as secure as Ned Gage. And I understood his point. The distinction made sense.

By then Anson Sternway had walked out into the center of the floor. The tournament was about to start. I thanked Parker quickly and let him go. He gave me a polite smile and moved away.

Half a minute later, Sue called the hall to attention, and everyone jumped upright. Almost in unison, they bowed to His Royal Highness Sternway. A beat behind them, I did the same. He repeated yesterday's response, and a raw ovation answered him like the roar of Romans hungry for carnage. At once Rasmussen launched into her opening spiel and the announcement of events.

Day Two of the IAMA World Championships was underway.

Clenching my fists in my pockets to contain my enthusiasm, I eased out of the way as judges moved to the rings, competitors headed toward the staging area, and spectators jockeyed for positions in the stands.

Briefly I considered going to talk to Hong, then decided against it. There was too much confusion, and I didn't want to shout my questions at him. Better to wait until the tournament settled down, and I could be sure that no one from *Essential Shotokan* might hear me.

Instead I picked my way toward the dais.

Before I got there, I crossed paths with Sammy Posten in middither. However, he made time to grab hold of my arm when the currents of the crowd slapped us together.

"Axbrewder!" I could hardly hear him through the noise, but congested self-importance filled his face. "We need to talk."

I didn't want to hear it. Sadly, being polite was part of the job. Instead of wrenching Posten's fingers, I used the pressure of movement around me as an excuse to twitch my arm loose.

"What about?"

Trying not to look as short as he was, he pushed his face up at me. "I don't like the way you're doing your job."

That didn't surprise me. I had the impression that he didn't like the way *any*one did their jobs. But he'd handed me a chance to practice my snappy repartee, and I didn't want to miss it, so I said, "Huh?"

From the microphone, Sue Rasmussen identified rings for men's brown belt and women's soft style *kata*. On the way to their assignments, competitors, judges, and spectators jostled Posten and me until we practically stood on each other's shoes. I had to scrunch down my chin in order to meet his glare. Would've served him right if I'd drooled in his eyes.

"You're being too obvious," he informed me indignantly. "You aren't here to stop fights. You're here to take up the slack while Security protects Nakahatchi *sensei*'s display. You can't do that if you go around calling attention to yourself."

Fortunately I had enough bulk to make the people behind me shift back a bit. Minding my manners was tough enough without getting a crick in my neck at the same time.

"Oh," I said. "I get it." Axbrewder receiving enlightenment.

"You don't want claims for petty theft. You prefer personal-injury lawsuits." I smiled sweetly.

Minding my manners wasn't one of my best skills.

"Don't be a smart-ass," he snapped. "Those chops are worth as much as a personal-injury settlement any day."

"Mr. Posten." I made an effort to control myself. "This place is packed with people who consider themselves stone killers. You'd need a squad of Navy Seals just to get at those chops." Nakahatchi's antiques simply weren't worth so much trouble. "What's the danger, exactly?"

"Use your imagination," Posten fired back. He was on a mission. "The crowd makes perfect cover. Five guys do it together. One picks a fight like the one you were in. A distraction. Two break the glass, get the chops. The others mess with the guards. In the confusion, no one sees who has the chops. Then they're out of the hall, and we don't have a clue who we're hunting for."

He tried to look triumphant, but he lacked the inches to carry it off.

I peered down at him. He was a typical bureaucrat, rendered stupid by paperwork and illusions of authority. Bernie had Security with radios on all the doors, Max at the screens, the cops a phone call away. No wonder my boss called the Security Adviser "Postal." But I didn't waste time explaining the obvious. Instead I nodded like I saw Posten's point.

"Fine," I conceded, just to see how far he'd go. "Then what? Now the chops are hot. Who's going to fence them? Who handles shit this esoteric?"

Hell, half the people in the country who even knew those chops existed were probably right here.

"I was right," Posten snorted in disgust. "You aren't paying attention. I should never have let Appelwait hire you. We need a man who takes this seriously.

"They don't need a fence," he informed me indignantly. "For the right people, having those chops would be like owning a Gutenberg Bible. Just counting Wing Chun schools, there must be fifty that wouldn't care if the chops are hot, as long as they're authentic. Those schools would put every dime they could scrape together on the table, no questions asked.

"All those five guys need," he concluded, "is access to the IAMA mailing list and a phone."

If I hadn't just spent ten minutes listening to Parker Neill, I probably would've laughed in Posten's face. But "secretive," "parochial" groups can get pretty bizarre. Especially when they're racist as well. Just ask the victims of any militia bombing.

To that extent, at least, Posten might be right. Much as I hated to admit it.

Fewer people thrust around us now. Events were about to begin, and the crowd had started to settle. Rasmussen's announcements didn't produce any added confusion. A breath or two from the AC swirled across my face without cheering me up.

I took the opportunity to steer Posten toward the nearest wall. When we were clear of the aisles and the stands, I told him, "I'm paying more attention than you think, Mr. Posten. And I do have some experience. That display is safe for now. It won't be in any real danger until Nakahatchi takes it home with him."

To *Essential Shotokan*, I pointedly didn't add. To Martial America. A business complex fully insured by Watchdog Insurance.

Posten dropped his head a beat too late to prevent me from seeing the crestfallen look in his eyes. "That's what Deborah says," he muttered. "I say you're both naïve."

But he didn't hassle me anymore. Ego and worry overwhelmed the poor little snot. He actually neglected to lord it over me. Chewing the inside of his cheek anxiously, he wandered away like he'd forgotten I existed.

"Have a nice day," I murmured after him. He was going to give himself an ulcer—if he didn't taste the joys of infarction first.

I knew how he felt.

Worrying myself, I headed for the dais to watch martial artists of every description yell and sweat their way around the rings.

By now half the floor was in use. Brown belts and soft style *kata*, men and women. Thanks to Neill's patience, I found that I could make out at least some of the differences. Not between men and women, but between hard and soft.

In general, the canvas pajamas did whatever they were doing with a kind of compact efficiency. Whenever they turned or spun, they did it on one spot. Otherwise they moved in straight lines punctuated by direct attacks and hard yells. By comparison, the soft stylists were like their silk, flowing and boastful. They made wide sweeps with their arms and legs, jumped and spun in all directions, crouched and sprang in swirls of bright cloth.

To my eye, the silk *katas* were useless as actual fighting. They were dances. They showed off grace, speed, and flexibility, but I couldn't imagine them hurting anyone. If I were attacked that way, I'd probably laugh too hard to fight back.

Now I understood the prejudice against soft styles. If the silk outfits hadn't pretended that they were demonstrating a martial art, I would've been more impressed.

Nevertheless I couldn't shake the impression that I was watching the prelude to a disaster.

I didn't think the hall could hold many more people, but they kept coming. A few still trickled past the registration table, but most of them were spectators. By yesterday's standards, the chops attracted a substantial crowd, presumably because the events the audience cared about hadn't started yet. But the cluster around the display wasn't large or unruly enough to tax Security's abilities. Bernie's blazers maintained order with no detectable difficulty.

Sammy Posten was definitely out of his mind.

From her position of prominence at the mike, Sue Rasmussen volleyed glares in my direction at irregular intervals, but she didn't try to chase me off the dais again. At the moment, Ned Gage was out on the floor, sorting refs and competitors for more events. Parker Neill appeared to be chatting with *Sifu* Hong. Posten had disappeared, at least temporarily.

So far Deborah Messenger hadn't put in an appearance. I didn't have any reason to think she would, but her absence darkened my gloom anyway.

Since she wasn't here, I scanned the hall for Anson Sternway.

Somehow he managed to check his paperwork at the head table, visit Nakahatchi over near the display, talk to other heavyweights around the hall, and supervise registration, all without any apparent movement from place to place. For a while, I entertained myself by trying to keep track of him, but I couldn't do it. Whenever he changed positions, he blended into the crowd so smoothly that I lost sight of him until he stopped somewhere.

It was a hell of a trick. Vaguely I wondered if he did it on purpose. By now it was obvious that some of these martial artists had skills I shouldn't underestimate.

I wanted someone to talk to. But I'd learned as much about karate-related subjects as I could stand for the time being. I needed other kinds of information. Maybe I'd do better if I approached Hong Fei-Tung.

But while I contemplated leaving the dais, I slipped unconsciously into watching one of the *kata* events without actually seeing it. Sort of a Zen thing. Concentration without attention. Or intention. And I discovered a curious thing. If I didn't look for Sternway consciously, I could tell where he was. By an unexpected piece of perceptual conjuring, like narrowing and diffusing my attention simultaneously, I was able to follow his movements peripherally when I couldn't track them directly.

I'd spent the better part of the past twenty-four hours trying to tune my instincts to the pitch and rhythms of the tournament, but I'd gone about it the wrong way. I wasn't used to working in this kind of crowd. With nothing clearly in view except a performance I didn't see, I knew that Sternway was over *there*, and Hong was on *this* side of his clustered students. At the main doors, Master Soon stepped out of the hall for some reason, while Ned Gage made his way toward the head table. And—

Trouble.

—diagonally across from Hong a slim young woman in a nondescript warmup suit dipped one hand into a gear bag that wasn't hers, then straightened up and moved away casually, her hand closed at her side.

My heart forgot a couple of beats. Trying not to be obvious about it, I jerked into focus on her.

Not really a young woman—a girl in her teens. Stringy hair, bland features that deflected notice, dull eyes. Nothing furtive about her, no flush in her cheeks, no rapid glances, no instinctive twitch as she fought an impulse to look behind her.

But now both of her hands were open and empty.

9

I should've whipped out my cell phone right then, called Max, warned Bernie. But I'd been concentrating on her too hard—I hadn't tagged the drop. And she'd already gotten rid of the evidence.

Fortunately I had time. She wasn't done. Her route took her deeper into the crowd instead of back toward the doors.

When a pick and a drop meshed that smoothly, they knew what they were doing. They had experience. And experienced teams typically included three or four picks, all feeding the same drop. Plus a spot, a guy who looked like an innocent bystander to watch for problems, signal warnings, and run interference.

I wanted to do this right, snag the whole team. Pouncing on the girl would accomplish exactly nothing. At the very least, I needed the drop—

But while I spent a couple of minutes failing to identify him, I had time to remember that I wasn't the boss here. This was Bernie's call, not mine.

Trying to look like a dignitary on important business, I took out the phone and dialed Security's preset number.

I wasn't good at the kind of concentration I needed. As soon as I focused on the phone, I lost the girl. While I waited for the connection to go through, I tried to locate her again. For a ragged moment or two, I couldn't find her. Then I did.

The heavy voice that answered said, "Go ahead," like I was supposed to know who he was.

I didn't stand on ceremony. "Axbrewder," I told the phone. "I need to talk to Bernie."

The voice—Max—didn't answer. Instead I heard switches clicking. As soon as the line opened, I said my name again.

"What?" Bernie demanded softly.

The girl had paused like a spectator watching an event. Obviously her drop hadn't circulated back into range yet.

I kept my voice low so that I wouldn't be overheard. "There's a team in the hall. A drop, at least one pick."

I saw Bernie's head jerk. "Where?"

"Teenage girl. Stringy hair. Dull brown warmup suit. To your right." He shifted in that direction. Before he did anything rash, I added, "She's the pick. I haven't made the drop."

He didn't hesitate. "Then we wait."

I nodded to the phone. "If you want to do this right."

"I want the whole team." He was sure. "Especially the drop. I'll take my chances."

I pictured the possibilities. A good team might have three, four, even five picks roughly spaced around the hall, all working in the same direction. The drop would stroll the opposite way, taking wallets, watches, money, whatever from the picks as they passed. And the spot—

Hell, he could be anywhere. The bleachers, probably.

"I'll watch her," I murmured to Bernie. She was my only clue to the drop—unless I managed to identify another pick. "If I still don't have the drop when she reaches me, I'll tag along." I thought hard for a second, then asked, "You want this line kept open?"

"No. If we do this right, there's no hurry.

"We've got the doors." He meant his guards. "You get the drop. And anybody else you're sure about."

"Right." I hung up with my thumb and pocketed the phone.

She was on the move again. Casually, like she lived in karate tournaments, she wandered past Bernie toward Nakahatchi's display. Then she turned to cross the hall in front of the dais.

Scrambling inside, I considered my options. If I tailed her too closely, I'd make myself conspicuous to the drop. And I wouldn't be able to tag any other picks until I knew the drop. But if I stayed back, I might miss him.

I did not want to screw this up.

Concentration, that was the key. The right kind of concentration—the kind I'd used to keep track of Sternway.

I wasn't sure I could do it. I was too tense.

I needed distraction, some way to diffuse my attention, like watching an event without really seeing it.

That gave me an idea.

The girl drifted past me, so close that I could've grabbed her by the hair if I hadn't been faking dignity. She had a gift for looking aimless, vacant, like there wasn't a thought in her head. She'd done this before, too often to be scared by it. Or she knew more than I did about drugs.

I let her go until she began to sift her way among the competitors, spectators, and gear bags that cluttered the edges of the tournament space. Then I retreated to the back of the dais, dropped to the floor, and went after her.

I did my best to look as aimless and vacant as she did, but I didn't succeed. As far as I knew, I didn't have any casual genes.

Karate-ka stretched and warmed up everywhere, spectators applauded over my head from the stands, contestants yelled their lungs out in the rings. Keeping track of her strained my nerves. If I hadn't been so tall, I would've lost her.

But she was moving down the hall toward the place where Hong had set up his encampment.

He sat turned slightly away from me, with his students grouped behind him—a few Chinese, the rest obviously not. He seemed to regard the tournament without interest, as if it were too transitory to impinge on his seamless facade. His features were so smooth that he could've posed for a bust of Buddha. He would've looked ageless if time hadn't marked his stiff short hair and eyebrows with grey.

I paused briefly to pull myself together. Hong Fei-Tung might look as placid as a saint, but I already knew that he had fire hidden inside him. I didn't want to get burned.

Ahead of me, the girl disappeared.

As soon as I panicked, she reappeared. Dammit, she'd probably lifted something from another gear bag, but I'd missed it. Too many people blocked my view—I couldn't see her hands. Then the crowded parted for an instant, and I saw her strolling away with her hands loose at her sides.

Damn and *damn*. I'd missed the drop as well.

But now he had to be between us. And moving toward me. For the next new seconds, at least. Trying not to be obvious about it, I scanned hard.

Three candidates snagged my attention, all acting like they belonged here, all carrying bags that could've held gear or loot. Two of them wore warmup sweats. The other had on a white *gi* with an IAMA patch.

I dismissed the *karate-ka*. In that getup he couldn't escape unobtrusively. And the competition interested him so much that he turned his head to watch every time he heard a yell.

The man right in front of me wasn't a likely candidate either. He wore light blue sweats and the toned whippet look of a sprinter. But he carried his bag wrong, zipped up tight, with his near hand hooked under the strap over his shoulder. He couldn't have accepted a handshake without making a production out of it.

That left a heavyset guy in dingy sweats the color of used bandages. He was only a couple of inches shorter than me, and at least forty pounds heavier, but he carried his bulk like it was made out of polyurethane, light enough to levitate. Dull eyes, a broken nose, jowls he could've used to store food for the winter, brows so full of bone that they gave him a perpetual scowl.

His black vinyl bag had a loose flap instead of a zipper, perfect for slipping things inside quickly. It hung from his right shoulder, with his hand resting on the flap.

He glanced at me unpleasantly as he shifted past, but if he saw anything that worried him, he didn't show it. With any luck I looked too lost, out of my element, to be a threat.

I let him go, didn't so much as turn my head as he went by. I wanted the whole team. If I could keep an eye on him, he might help me tag the other picks.

As casually as I could, I followed the girl toward Hong.

He still gazed out at the tournament vacantly, like he'd been hypnotized into oblivion. But his upright posture gave the impression that he'd starched his spine, and his hands rested on his thighs as if they might clench for blows at any moment.

As a group, his students copied him, but only a few of them looked like they sat in that position easily, and only a couple matched his air of being able to do it all day without strain.

I paused a stride away. Briefly I scanned the hall, practicing diffused concentration until I got a fix on the girl and the drop. Then I turned to Hong Fei-Tung.

I'd already met his temper, and I didn't want to set him off, so I bowed the way I'd seen Sternway bow. Striving to sound respectful, I said, "*Sifu* Hong. May I speak with you? I'd like to ask some questions."

His gaze slid toward me, smooth as oil, and away again. If he remembered meeting me yesterday, he kept it to himself. Instead he glanced at a man seated beside him. At once the man rose to his feet and answered my bow.

Like Hong, he was Asian, but with sharper features. He was obviously younger than his *Sifu*, but his face showed lines Hong's lacked. His smile accounted for some of them, but the creases between his eyebrows made him look like a man who took frowning seriously. The irises of his brown eyes held strange fragments of silver like chips of mica, sharp enough to cut.

"I am T'ang Wen, Mr.—?" He was better at sounding polite than I was.

"Axbrewder," I told him. For good measure, I bowed again. "I met *Sifu* Hong yesterday." Since Hong clearly hadn't mentioned me, I added, "I work with Sternway *sensei* and Mr. Appelwait."

T'ang Wen went on smiling. "Mr. Axbrewder. Perhaps I may be of use?"

Sensing disasters I couldn't identify, I stifled a sarcastic retort. Maybe having a student speak for the teacher was an obscure form of Chinese courtesy—although I suspected that the courtesy was for Hong's benefit rather than mine. Either way, I didn't think I'd gain anything by challenging it.

Instead I said gruffly, "I'm sure you can.

"I hope you'll forgive my ignorance. I've been hired to help make sure nothing"—I glanced deliberately toward Nakahatchi's display—"unpleasant happens here. But I don't know enough. If you'll answer a few questions for me, I may be more effective."

T'ang inclined his head. "If a mere novice in the study of *ch'uan fa* may do so, I will assist you."

In the stands behind their *sifu*, Hong's students had abandoned watching the tournament. Instead they stared at me expectantly, waiting for a chance to take offense. Their distrust was as plain as a wall.

I turned my back on them. I didn't have time for their expectations. I needed to see what went on around me.

"*Ch'uan fa*?" I asked, just to get started.

Anson Sternway now stood on the dais beside the master of ceremonies, consulting with her about something or other.

"Here in the West," T'ang Wen explained, "the Chinese martial arts have come to be called 'kung fu.' " He'd positioned himself so that he could see my face as well as Hong's without standing in front of his teacher. "The term is acceptable, but it is not precise. The Chinese arts are more properly termed *ch'uan fa*, the Way of the Fist. Or perhaps *wushu*, which encompasses all martial discipline." He shrugged delicately. "Like China herself, *ch'uan fa* is little understood elsewhere."

I heard hints in his voice that I wanted to pursue. But he was getting ahead of me. I kept my questions in order.

"So Wing Chun would be an example of *ch'uan fa*?"

"Indeed."

Off to my left, the girl rounded the corner of the hall, still apparently moving with no particular purpose. I'd lost track of the heavyset man, but when I blurred my attention I located him again. He remained on my side of the hall. In another minute he'd cross in front of the dais.

I didn't pause. "How is it different from, say, Shotokan?"

"Wing Chun"—T'ang made it sound like *ving tsun*—"is a separate style from a different country. It has its own philosophy and history." His tone suggested a desire to correct my ignorance gently. "However, *ch'uan fa* and karate are distinguished primarily by time. The Chinese martial arts are far older. They have been developed over centuries rather than decades.

"For example, Wing Chun traces its immediate origins to the mid-seventeen hundreds. The tradition from which it springs may be a millennium older. Shotokan, I believe, was founded less than a century ago. The Japanese master Funakoshi derived it from several Okinawan styles, among them Shorin-Ryu, which in turn grew from China. Tae Kwon Do was also developed from Shorin-Ryu, but more recently.

"Historically speaking, Mr. Axbrewder, karate is the young son of a much older father."

Directly below the dais, the man I tracked passed a younger guy, so close that they brushed shoulders. I was too far away to make out details, but the younger man had lank blond hair hanging onto his forehead and wore an open *gi* top over a black T-shirt with large white letters that said, "NO FEAR." I didn't see him give anything to the heavyset man. But my target's right hand slipped quickly under the flap of his bag and out again.

Now I was sure. He was the drop. The younger man was another pick.

I had to admire the sheer effrontery of a hand-off right under the noses of everyone at the head table—Sue Rasmussen, Sternway, the record-keeper. But the dignitaries were too busy to notice.

"So why was Wing Chun developed?" I asked T'ang Wen. Obliquely I worked my way toward the subject of the chops. "What was wrong with the tradition?"

He treated me to a smile that revealed nothing. "That is an important question, Mr. Axbrewder. I will answer briefly.

"Because of their richness and complexity," he explained, "the older forms of *ch'uan fa* often required decades of dedicated study. As an example, forty years is not considered an unusual span for the mastery of Tai Chi *ch'uan*. In the early seventeen hundreds, however, the Manchurian Qing dynasty challenged the Shaolin temples, which supported the Ming family. This demonstrated the need for a combined style which could be mastered more easily, and therefore be disseminated more widely. Wing Chun was developed at the Northern Shaolin Temple from five older systems for that purpose.

"You may be interested to know that it was devised by a woman, Ng Mui, a Buddhist nun who escaped the Qing destruction of the Temple. This is relevant for obvious reasons. A style intended to be taught easily and widely could not rely on strength or weight for its effectiveness. Rather it required quickness, flexibility, and timing rather than force. With Wing Chun, a small woman might well defeat a large man."

While T'ang spoke, my target passed the display and ambled through the crowd across from me. Reflexively I concentrated on him too hard to see anything else. But when I remembered to widen and blur my awareness, I noticed a matronly woman in a blowzy flower print housedress headed for him. Despite the blur—or because of it—I saw her dip toward a gear bag as if she'd stumbled. Then she righted herself with a bulge in her fist. Two steps later, she nearly collided with the drop. He adjusted the flap of his bag. When she went on by, her hands were empty.

I hardly heard the yelling of the contestants, or Rasmussen's announcements. The events in front of me might as well have been invisible. Tension and worry throbbed in my temples. I had a hard time following T'ang Wen's answers.

I abandoned subtlety. My next question sounded disjointed, but I didn't care.

"Where do the chops fit in all this history?"

Some of the students behind me shifted uncomfortably. T'ang's tone sharpened, giving his voice an undercurrent of anger.

"Our traditions hold that Ng Mui first taught her new system to a young girl named Yim Wing Chun, who had need of its advantages. Subsequently she taught Ng Mui's system to her husband, Leung Bok Chow. When he was convinced of its effectiveness, he began to disseminate the new style, calling it 'Wing Chun' in honor of his wife.

"One of Leung Bok Chow's first students was Leung Len Kwai, a gifted artist. Our traditions say that he carved the essential stances and techniques of Wing Chun into a set of ivory chops in order to preserve the system from later misunderstanding.

"We are Chinese," T'ang Wen finished with a hint of vehemence. "We revere our traditions. For that reason, the chops are priceless to us." Then he added scornfully, "If they are genuine."

Hong Fei-Tung gazed impassively at everything and nothing, as if he'd been sculpted in terra cotta.

My target had stopped moving. A quick check told me that his three picks had done the same. Apparently they'd all decided to watch the tournament. Or they were waiting for a signal—

A signal from their spot. Keep working, or cut and run.

Uncertainty whetted my sense of disaster to a cutting edge. The phone seemed to burn in my pocket.

" 'Priceless,' " I echoed because I had to say something. "And Nakahatchi has them."

Tangible disapproval poured down from Hong's students.

"They do not belong to him," T'ang Wen stated coldly. "He cannot appreciate them. They are Chinese. I do not question the value of Shotokan. But Nakahatchi *sensei* is Japanese. He lacks the centuries of tradition and study from which true appreciation grows."

Out on the floor, Ned Gage adjudicated a dispute between a couple of contestants and the refs. Neill watched nearby, but didn't intervene. Down at the end of the hall, a group of *karate-ka* swung long staffs in elaborate patterns, presumably warming up for a weapons event. Sammy Posten hovered uselessly near the displayed chops. Sternway remained at the head table, master of all he surveyed. He held his right arm crossed over his chest, his right hand on his left shoulder as if to rub a sore muscle.

I gripped the phone in my pocket. During the past half hour, the heat had climbed ahead of the AC. Now it felt stultifying. My arm ached where I'd been kicked yesterday.

Forgetting transitions, I asked roughly, "How do you account for all this misunderstanding of the Chinese and their traditions?"

Alarm made me sound less than sympathetic. Several of the students behind me murmured angrily. T'ang Wen lost his smile. Nevertheless he kept his poise.

"Like the West," he informed me coldly, "Japan has an imperialistic culture. You have more in common with them than with the Chinese. In addition, you have no heritage yourself, and therefore see no value in it. Western practitioners are drawn to that which seems natural to them. You have only to look about you to see the truth of this."

Under other circumstances, I would've asked, And you don't think your contempt for people like us has anything to do with it? Scratch a man who thinks he's being sneered at, and you'll uncover someone who enjoys sneering himself. But I couldn't concentrate on T'ang Wen any longer. I'd run out of time.

Applause spattered the hall as one of the hard style events ended. From the gallery, spectators waved their arms or fists. Rasmussen pointed toward the registration table or the main doors. Sternway lowered his arm. Neill turned away from Gage and the dispute, throwing up his hands in apparent disgust. Posten beckoned like he wanted Bernie's attention, but Bernie ignored him.

Casual as ever, my target moved again. So did his picks. The girl continued the way she'd been going, but both the young man in the NO FEAR T-shirt and the matronly woman changed directions.

They'd seen a signal. They were heading for the doors.

"Excuse me," I murmured to T'ang brusquely. "Something's come up." As I strode away, I snatched out the phone.

Signal, hell. I'd seen a dozen of them. Somehow I wasn't doing my *job*.

The phone rang interminably before Max answered. The line clicked interminably as Max connected me to Bernie's radio. I'd nearly rounded the corner of the hall by the time Bernie's head jerked toward me.

"Yeah?" he rasped.

"They're leaving," I told him urgently. "The drop and three picks. Someone warned them off, I don't know who."

As fast as I could, I described them. My target had almost reached the main doors when I finished.

Bernie didn't hesitate. "I'll take the drop. You get the rest."

Across from me, the heavyset man paused at the main doors as if he could feel Bernie's stare gouge into his back. Then he nodded to the nearest guard, pulled open the door, and left the hall.

I wanted to argue. This guy was too big, too light on his feet. Bernie needed backup. But before I could object, I heard more clicks, and the tone of the connection changed. He must've switched to Security's general channel. I saw tension flash from guard to guard as soon as he spoke again.

"There's a team here. I'm following a suspect outside. Axbrewder's after the others. Hold the doors. Don't let anybody in or out until he says so."

My phone went dead.

Bernie left the hall. I couldn't stop him.

Damn and *damn*. He was the boss, it was his call. But he was making a mistake, I was sure of it. I'd known it the minute I woke up this morning.

Swearing viciously, I shoved the phone into my pocket and forced my legs to slow down. I had to be unobtrusive again. When they couldn't leave by the usual doors, the picks would look for other exits. They might even panic. And the service corridors weren't guarded—

I needed help. Quickly I searched the hall.

For one frightened moment, I couldn't find what I wanted. Master Soon was already gone. Sternway had vanished from the head table while I wasn't looking. Rasmussen stood at the record-keeper's shoulder, consulting about something. Ned Gage and Parker Neill moved toward opposite ends of the hall. Posten had already started to argue with a guard who wouldn't let him outside. Hong appeared to be watching me dispassionately. But I couldn't locate the picks.

Then my head kicked into gear, and I found them.

I had to gamble, so I did.

The kid in the NO FEAR T-shirt could probably run faster than the others. And Ned Gage was closer to me than anyone else I might've trusted.

I angled across the tournament floor to intercept him.

As I approached, he started a smile that fell away when he saw my face.

I didn't give him time to say anything. Hunching, I whispered, "There's a kid, stringy hair, NO FEAR black T-shirt. Over near the display. He's a thief. Don't let him out of here."

Before Gage could react, I wheeled away.

Now I only had to worry about the dull bland girl and the woman who looked like a chaperone for a junior high field trip. On one of my good days, I would've said that I had them outnumbered. But it wasn't, and I was scared. My impulse to hurry had so much force that I could hardly contain it.

Bernie needed me and didn't know it.

Already people had begun to clump at the main doors, wanting out for one reason or another. The girl joined them without any detectable concern. Some of the spectators muttered complaints at the guard, but she didn't join them. As far as I could tell, she was asleep on her feet.

The guard managed to look flustered and determined simultaneously. Trying to be polite about it, he held his ground.

I plowed my way into the crowd until I reached the girl. Smiling, I wrapped my arm around her waist and knotted my fist in the fabric of her warmup suit. If you hadn't seen her quick flinch, you might've thought we were old friends.

"You're coming with me," I told her softly.

She didn't resist. Why should she? She'd gotten rid of the evidence. After one fast glance, she didn't so much as look at me.

Bulk had its advantages. Despite the crowd, I pulled her forward easily until I reached the doors. A few people wanted to know what the hell I thought I was doing, but I ignored them.

The guard nodded to me nervously, peered at the girl, then flicked a question up at my face. Maybe he thought she didn't look like a pick.

I shoved her at him. Reflexively he caught her arms. "Hang on to her," I ordered over the top of her head. "She's one of them. I'll get the others."

"Hey," the girl protested eloquently. "Hey." She may've tried to struggle.

I didn't pay any attention.

Some of the spectators sounded like they were about to get

rude. Facing them, I raised my voice a bit. "Security problem, folks. Nothing to worry about. We'll open the doors in a couple of minutes."

Then I shouldered my way past them and headed for the next set of doors, hunting for a flower print housedress.

She wasn't hard to find. The doors she wanted to use weren't busy, and she stood right in front of them. The guard there was a grandfatherly type with a bad comb-over and pleasant teeth, maybe a few years younger than Bernie, and she was talking to him. Not hassling him. Just the opposite. His attentive smile suggested cronies sharing gossip. When I got close enough, I heard her chuckle comfortably.

I felt a pang of doubt, even though I'd seen her work. She wouldn't have looked less furtive—never mind guilty—if she'd just been anointed by a Bishop. Involuntarily I hesitated.

But the next second at the edge of my vision I saw the NO FEAR kid sprint across the floor toward the service doors—and almost fall on his back when Gage grabbed his arm. At once Gage slipped the kid into a wrist-lock, then walked him in my direction, extracting cooperation with no apparent effort.

That jolted me past my uncertainty. If I was wrong, there was nothing I could do about it now. Bernie needed me.

By my count, he'd already been gone too long.

At the doors, I interrupted the blowzy woman's seduction of the guard by dropping one hand on her shoulder and the other on his. Holding them together, I asked him quietly, "What's standard procedure for dealing with a suspect?"

He gaped at me like I'd asked him to perform a radical mastectomy on her. Apparently he didn't believe Bernie's warning. A nice lady like her, a thief? No way. Hell, in another minute he might've let her go.

Urgency gathered in my chest. I was about to snarl at him, but he managed to jerk his attention back to his job. Swallowing hard, he answered, "Detain them until the cops get here. There's a room we can lock in the Security offices."

The woman put on a perplexed smile and made a show of hoping someone would tell her what was going on.

"Good enough," I snapped. "*This* woman is a suspect." I tightened my grip on her shoulder, just in case. "Do *not* lose her."

Like magic, the junior high chaperone transformed herself

into a yowling harridan. "A *suspect*?" She sounded fierce enough to intimidate the dead. "Of what? Get your fucking hand off me, asshole! I know my rights!" In another second we'd have an audience. "You're *hurting* me! *Get your—!*"

I shut her up by digging in with my fingers until she remembered what *hurting* actually meant.

"Mr. Gage has another one," I informed the guard. "There's a third at the main doors. Get as much help as you need. Lock them up. Don't open the doors until you have all three of them under control. I'm going after Bernie."

I was about to add, Are you *listening*? but he cut me off by wrenching himself out of his confusion. Quickly he snatched the walkie-talkie off his belt, thumbed the toggle, and demanded backup. At the same time, he took hold of the woman's wrist like he didn't ever intend to let go.

A look over my shoulder told me that Gage was close. By now I knew that he could help out if the woman gave too much trouble.

Shifting past the guard as fast as I could, I hauled open the door and left the hall.

Colder air slapped my face, but it didn't help.

Bernie wasn't in the wide hallway between the convention facilities and the main hotel. So where the hell was he? He should've been back by now. He'd had enough time to corral the drop and cook him *break*fast, for God's sake.

The lobby—

But two steps later, another panic hit me. *Damn* Posten. If he was right, if this was a diversion—

I rebounded for the doors like I'd slammed into a wall.

Shoving my head inside, I barked at the guard, "Don't leave the chops alone! No matter what else happens!"

I wasn't sure he heard me. The woman fought him furiously, and he had trouble keeping his grip on her. But Gage caught my eyes and nodded. His wrist-lock supplied just enough pain to make the kid cooperative.

Good enough. I shut the door and headed for the lobby as fast as I could go without running.

Master Soon had left the hall earlier for some reason.

The lobby was practically empty. A few guests lined the registration counter, presumably checking out. Near the doors, a small group of *karate-ka* watched the parking lot, waiting for someone. In the middle of the open floor, Anson Sternway stood with Alex Lacone and Deborah Messenger, his back to me. Lacone's fixed grin, and her artificial animation, made me think that she was explaining the finer points of commercial coverage. As far as I could tell, neither of the men noticed me. But she managed to fling me a bright smile without interrupting herself.

I ignored it. My pulse had kicked into overdrive the instant I saw that Bernie wasn't in the lobby.

Then where—?

If he'd chased the drop out into the parking lot, I could stop worrying. He couldn't have run down a four-year-old, never mind a determined man less than half his age.

Had he already caught his target, taken him to the Security offices? He'd be safe enough there. He'd have backup.

Back into the service corridors? I'd never find him without Max's help. And if his monitors showed any trouble, Max would've called for help by now.

If I were a smart drop, and I wanted to ditch Bernie without an audience of security cameras, hotel staff, and passersby—

In panic I ran for the nearest men's room. Fumbling instinctively at the .45 I didn't have, I smacked open the door and charged inside.

White tile echoed the clash as the door hit the wall and bounced shut behind me. Stressed metal clanged like the clash of ruin, so loud that I thought the mirrors would shatter. The space was big for a men's room, and as generic as the rest of the hotel—six urinals, eight toilet stalls with open privacy doors, at least ten sinks below the mirrors, enough paper towels to mop up Armageddon. The Luxury wanted its guests and visitors to relieve themselves conveniently, if not comfortably.

The room was empty. Except for the echoes. And my thudding heart.

And the legs sticking out under one privacy door.

Thin legs, all bone—too thin for the heavy shoes propped against the tile.

Almost gently, I swung the door all the way open.

He lay sprawled in the stall like he'd been overcome by loneliness, his head on the floor near the commode, one arm draped awkwardly over the toilet paper holder. Dumbly I knelt at his side. I didn't need the lost glaze of his eyes, the pallor of his skin, the trickle of blood drooling past his lips, or the stillness of his abandoned chest to tell me that he was dead.

But there was so *little* blood. It had all drained out of him long ago. Or he'd lost it to the labor of a vexed and failing heart. I wasn't sure how he'd died until I lifted his head and saw the narrow diagonal welt, as bright as a shriek, driven furiously and impossibly deep into his Adam's apple.

He'd been killed. By a blow that crushed his larynx.

Oh, Bernie.

He hadn't even had time to reach for his walkie-talkie. It was still clipped to his belt.

One part of me knelt stunned beside him, nearly unable to breathe, entirely unable to think. He'd been chasing a *drop*, for God's sake, a mere thief—a man with no reason to worry even if he'd been caught red-handed, what with lawyers and bail and good time, and courts overcrowded with far more frightening crimes. No ordinary thug with even a hint of experience, never mind common sense, would commit murder over a bag full of petty theft.

But this one had.

There was nothing ordinary about him. He was a butcher.

While I knelt, however, another part of me—the part that knew its job, and understood how to be angry—had already moved on.

The beige paint on the metal sides of the stall got me started. It showed scratches—

No, they were more than scratches, they were like welts themselves, slashes cut so deep that silver shone through them. And thin, no more than an inch at the widest. One was as long as my forearm, the rest shorter.

Another marked the inside of the privacy door. And when I finally climbed to my feet, I found another outside, on the support between stalls. Something had taken a chip out of the rim of the sink opposite the stall.

I'd seen marks like that before.

10

I took a few seconds to make sure. Then I reached for the phone.

My fingers felt numb, and my hands shook. I was stunned and livid at the same time. If the number I needed hadn't been programmed for me, I might not have been able to dial it.

When Max answered, the shocked part of me stared dumbly at my image in the mirrors—a rumpled suit on a too-big frame, topped by a face like a ghoul's. The other part told him where I was. Then it said, "Bernie's been killed."

Max gasped like an asthma attack. "Shit. Oh, God. Shit."

The part of me that knew its job didn't care.

"Get the cops," I snapped at him. "Then I want one guard, I don't care who. I need him right away. Don't let anyone else in here." Vicious with memory, I added, "And keep an eye on those fucking chops."

I had no authority to give him orders. But he knew I was right. Still gasping, he muttered, "Shit. I'm on it." Then the line clicked dead.

Echoes seemed to hang in the air—the clash of the men's room door, the screech of welts gouged across metal, the fatal rasp of Bernie's crushed throat. I couldn't clear them out of my head. The numb part of me wanted to kneel at Bernie's side again, stay there until help arrived. But I didn't.

Instead I moved woodenly to the men's room door to keep guests and spectators out.

I needed one of Bernie's men. I needed him now. Before the cops got here.

How long would Max take to cover everything?

A tremor spread from the pit of my stomach into my chest and shoulders. I'd caused Bernie's death. Indirectly, innocently, I'd brought him to this. On some level, I knew I wasn't responsible for it. But I took it personally anyway.

The door shifted hard as someone in a hurry put his shoulder to it. I only let it open a crack until I recognized a Hotel Security blazer and badge. Then I stood aside.

The man was relatively young, at least by the standard of hotel security guards, and he'd been running. But he looked tight with muscle, in good shape. Exertion flushed his cheeks, although he didn't pant. Below a crop of blond hair, his pale eyes hinted at frenzy against a background of bravado.

His nametag said, "Wisman."

"Axbrewder?" he demanded urgently. "What the hell—? Where's Bernie?"

He shoved past me when he spotted Bernie's feet. I didn't try to stop him. Still guarding the door, I watched him reach the stall, then go rigid with shock and stumble backward until he hit the sinks.

"Christ," he groaned. For a couple of seconds, I thought he was going to puke. His bravado didn't cover this. As hotel security, his experience and training probably didn't extend past rousting drunks. Violence like this wasn't in his job description.

I didn't give him a chance to think. I needed answers.

"Wisman." I made my voice hard to get his attention. "Did Bernie carry a weapon?"

He turned eyes full of distress and confusion toward me. His mouth hung open. "A weapon—?"

Poor kid. If I'd had time, I might've allowed him a few minutes to pull himself together. But the cops were on their way, and I had no patience for him.

"A weapon," I insisted. "Protection. Something to fight with."

He gaped at me stupidly. "Axbrewder, what're you—? Hotel regulations—"

If Security carried unauthorized weapons, and Watchdog didn't know about them, The Luxury might lose its coverage. The hotel would probably fire every guard in the place.

I heard a siren. It sounded distant, the wail of someone else's crime. But too many walls muffled it. For all I knew, the cops had already reached the portico.

Without transition, the tremors took over. My knees and arms shook. I didn't have a stunned nerve left in my whole body.

"Listen to me." Striding straight for Wisman, I grabbed him

by his lapels and hauled his face up to mine. "I don't give a shit about hotel regulations. I'm not going to cause any trouble."

Abruptly I released his blazer and groped his back until I found what I was looking for—a hard shape like a short stick with a handle at right angles near one end.

"You've got a *tonfa*, for God's sake." In case he needed it. In case a drunk turned ugly on him. Almost shouting, I demanded, "Did Bernie carry a *weapon*?"

He still didn't answer. Maybe he couldn't. I knew his secret now—I could get him in serious trouble.

I took his arm and wrenched him forward until he stood over Bernie's body. I wanted to force him to his knees, make him face Bernie's murder nose-to-nose, but I didn't.

"That wasn't a knife." Even the back of a blade couldn't have smashed Bernie's throat that way, or scarred the walls. "He was killed with some other weapon. *Did he carry—?*"

Wisman heaved against my grasp. "A flik," he answered suddenly. "It's a—"

"I know what a flik is."

Roughly I let him go.

A flik was a short steel rod like a baton, usually about eighteen inches long and an inch thick. Inside it held a tightly coiled steel spring. Very tightly coiled. With a small lump of steel on the end for weight. A release on the handle let the spring out. You swung it the way you would a flail. The flex of the spring and the added weight gave it the force of a cudgel.

Bernie should've been able to handle almost anyone with it. Even that heavyset goon.

Wisman retreated to the sink again. For a minute longer, his brain refused to function. Then he turned, ran some water, and splashed it on his face. When he'd toweled himself dry, some of the frenzy had left his eyes.

"As far as I know," he said hoarsely, "he never used it. The flik. The hotel doesn't need to know about it. The cops can figure it out for themselves."

Absently I muttered, "Let them think the killer brought it with him." I wasn't really listening. "Why not?"

My tone must've warned him that I was thinking about things which hadn't occurred to him. "Why does it matter?" he asked.

"Because," I told him, "it isn't here."

He didn't understand—and I didn't explain.

Why did the killer take the flik? It wasn't his. He had good reason to leave it behind. If the cops caught him, he could tell them Bernie attacked him with it. He got his hands on it and hit back, accidentally killed Bernie in self-defense. Then panicked and ran. Involuntary manslaughter, not murder.

Either he was too stupid to think that clearly. Or he didn't care what he was charged with.

Or he wanted the cops to know that Bernie had been murdered.

Before I could go any further, a couple of uniforms came through the door, and the men's room turned into an official crime scene.

The results looked and sounded like chaos. The cops inspected Bernie's body, talked to their radios, and questioned Wisman and me, all at once. The hotel manager tried to force his way inside, but one of the uniforms blocked the door until Homicide could arrive. I focused on controlling my shakes while I gave simple answers to basic questions. Who was I. Why was I there. What happened. In what order.

Back in my drinking days, I could've done this without trembling at all. Then I'd been afflicted with unsteadiness of another kind. Now I couldn't remember what that felt like.

The bleeding from Bernie's mouth slowed as his body settled, but that didn't make me feel better.

I heard more sirens. Presumably now Carner's finest would keep anyone from leaving the lobby. They might even take a stab at sealing the hotel. Too late, of course. Unless the heavyset guy was stone crazy, he was already gone.

Vaguely I wondered if Sternway had seen anything useful. No doubt he was several times more observant than Lacone.

I didn't let myself think about Deborah Messenger.

And I absolutely did not let myself think about Ginny. Somewhere inside me, her former partner believed that he needed her. But I didn't want to hear it.

Eventually Homicide arrived in the form of a plainclothes sergeant and a staff photographer. When the detective finished his inspection, the photog fired his flash at everything in sight. Each burst wiped color and life out of the room. Soon the blare of light off the mirrors and tile made my head feel like I'd been hit with a flik. Bernie already resembled a specimen pinned down on a pathologist's slide.

Apparently it didn't bother the detective. His name was Edgar Moy, and as far as I could tell his nerves no longer reacted to sensation. Even when he moved, he seemed catatonic. He was a short black man in—of all things—a crumpled trench coat. Untidy stains of grey marked his hair, and his mustache was so thin it might've been drawn on with an eyebrow pencil. He looked at everything sourly, but he didn't give off the kind of compensatory belligerence you usually see in small cops. I guess he'd been short long enough to get used to it.

"Interesting wound," he remarked when he'd finished his inspection. "Any sign of the weapon?" He was asking all of us, the two cops, Wisman, and me.

We shook our heads dutifully. Thanks to the flash, mine felt like it was full of broken glass. He didn't seem to care.

"Who found the body?"

"I did." I wanted to shut my eyes until the photog finished his assault. But even flash and phosphenes couldn't erase the imprinted image of Bernie's corpse. He died again every time the light cut into him.

"And you are?"

I told him, and we started to dance.

It was all routine. I could've choreographed it in my sleep. But he took me through it carefully anyway, just in case I didn't know the steps. When he was done, he knew everything I did about the situation.

Except what I thought about the missing weapon.

"And you're sure," he asked, "you could pick this drop out of a lineup?"

I grinned coldly. "With both hands tied behind my back."

Fortunately the photog was done.

Sergeant Moy considered my forehead for a moment. "You know, Axbrewder," he remarked in a musing tone, "you're swinging without a net here."

I knew what came next, but I didn't help him out. "How so?"

"You don't have a license. And you aren't working for a licensed investigator. You aren't covered."

He wasn't hassling me. I knew that. License or no license, my dealings with The Luxury, the IAMA, and Watchdog were clean.

No, he was warning me not to go after Bernie's killer myself. Without a license, I had no legal standing. Anything I did might be construed as interference.

In his version of the dance, my response should've indicated acquiescence. But instead I asked, "Don't you get too hot in that coat? This town's a sauna."

He didn't smile—or take offense, either. Maybe he didn't know how. "I like the coat. But I don't like to sweat. So I don't put on underwear."

After ordering me to go downtown and look at mug shots—tomorrow at the latest—he turned away, leaving me worried that he already knew me better than I wanted him to. At the door, he spoke to a uniform, issued orders about gathering statements and witnesses. After that he did his waltz with Wisman.

By that time I was practically hopping from foot to foot, I had so *many* things to worry about. I wanted out of the men's room, but Moy hadn't given me permission to leave. Apparently he intended to question his possible witnesses in front of me.

Which may've been a courtesy. He'd warned me off, but he made no effort to shut me out. He hadn't even told me not to call anyone.

As soon as I was sure that no one cared what I did, I withdrew to the back of the men's room. While Moy grilled Wisman, followed by Sternway, Deborah Messenger, and Bernie's second-in-command, I got as much done as I could.

Under the circumstances, Max answered pretty promptly. He told me the chops were safe. The picks had been locked away until the cops were ready for them. Meanwhile the tournament continued as usual. Apparently nothing as minor as a dead security guard interrupted martial artists in their relentless pursuit of trophies. I thanked him, hung up, and called Marshal Viviter.

About the time Sergeant Moy finished with Wisman and started on Anson Sternway, the Professional Investigations receptionist, Beatrix Amity, put me through to her lord and master.

"Good timing, Brew," Viviter said cheerfully. "You caught me between appointments. How's the exciting life of a field operative?"

I was too pissed off for pleasantries, so I told him roughly, "Bernie Appelwait's been killed."

Without transition he turned off the good humor. "At a karate tournament? What the hell's going on there?"

I gave him the concise version. He paused to mutter softly, "Poor old guy. He was an irascible sonofabitch, but I always liked him." Marshal and I had that much in common, anyway. Then he got back to business. "You're in an awkward position there, Brew. What do you need from me?"

Sternway hardly glanced at me while he answered Moy's questions in an unrelieved monotone. He rubbed his left forearm once, then ignored it.

I kept my voice down. "First, do you know a Homicide sergeant named Moy, Edgar Moy?"

"The somnambulist in the trench coat? He's straight, for a cop. And smarter than he looks. Some people think he's lazy because he doesn't close cases quickly. But I'd say he takes his time because he doesn't jump to conclusions."

I'd already heard Moy ask Wisman whether Bernie had any enemies. Until then I hadn't known that the detective was interested enough to consider alternative explanations.

Moy didn't keep Sternway long. When the IAMA director left, Deborah Messenger took his place. She gave me a worried look as she came into the men's room. After that she concentrated on Moy.

To Marshal I said, "He reminded me that this isn't my problem. But I'm not going to drop it. The pieces don't fit."

"You mean," Marshal put in, "why did a guy facing a minor rap like petty theft raise the stakes on himself by committing murder?"

"That," I admitted. "And there's something else."

I didn't risk saying what it was, and Viviter was too clever to ask. Damn him anyway. I wanted to loathe him, but he made it bloody difficult. After a pause, he repeated his earlier question. "How can I help?"

"I don't know if it's possible," I told the phone quietly, "but I want to see the ME's report. And I want to know if Bernie ever had any dealings with Sternway, the IAMA, Alex Lacone, the schools in Martial America, or Watchdog Insurance. I mean, outside his job here."

Again Marshal refrained from questions. "Might be possible," he mused instead. "Or not. I'll let you know.

"Anything else?"

Moy had finished questioning Deborah. Like Wisman and

Sternway, she'd reported that she hadn't seen Bernie go into the men's room. She hadn't seen anyone like the heavyset man. When the detective let her go, she threw me another anxious look, but didn't hesitate on her way out.

Next the uniforms in the lobby admitted Bernie's designated second-in-command, an untidy man named Slade who managed to make his blazer look slept in. I wanted to concentrate on what he said, but I needed one more thing from Marshal.

"Can you give me a direct phone number? In case I have to get in touch with you fast?"

"Sure." He recited a number. "That's my cell phone. It's always on."

Brusquely I thanked him and hung up.

Slade was telling Moy, "You want to talk to Max Harp. He's on monitor duty. If one of our cameras saw it, so did he. But the odds aren't good." Then he added, "Of course, we keep everything on tape, at least for a couple of weeks."

His tone gave off hints of truculence or defensiveness.

Prodded for more, he explained that the Security cameras in the lobby only swept this men's room door at intervals. On top of that, images at the edges were blurred. Even if one of the cameras happened to swing in the right direction at the right time, it focused on more vulnerable locations, like registration and the cashier's desk.

Moy made Slade go over it a couple of times, but I stopped listening. So much for catching the drop on tape.

The detective received the news with his usual enthusiasm. He said, "We'll talk to Mr. Harp," the way he might've said, It's raining off the coast of Bangladesh. "But while you're here, you can help with something else.

"Did Mr. Appelwait have any enemies? Do you know of anyone who might've wanted him out of the way?"

Slade scowled. "Why would he? We're hotel security. It's not the kind of job that makes enemies." Now he sounded bitter, like a man who hadn't forgiven life for wounding his self-importance. But the detective stared at him nervelessly, and he finally conceded, "Some of the men don't like him very much." He may've meant, I don't like him very much. "But we all think he's OK." After a moment, he added, "He's fair with us. And he backs us up when the brass get a twist in their shorts."

"Interesting," Moy observed. He didn't sounded interested. With a shrug, he dismissed the senior guard.

As Slade left, a uniform came in and whispered something to Moy, then withdrew when Moy nodded. Casually the detective turned toward me. "Axbrewder," he inquired numbly, "what's your connection to Ms. Messenger?"

He startled me. I almost retorted, What fucking business is it of yours? But I caught myself in time. Instead I kept my mouth shut, looked confused, and waited for an explanation.

"I've just been told," he said slowly, "that when she heard we wanted to question her, she asked, 'Has anything happened to Brew?' I assume that's you?"

I did my best to shrug, but it felt like a flinch on my shoulders. I didn't know what to make of Deborah's concern.

"There's no connection," I replied as smoothly as I could—which probably meant that I sounded like I wanted to hit him. "I met her for the first time yesterday. We had dinner together. It didn't go anywhere. End of story."

That last assertion was a lie. But the truth had nothing to do with Bernie, or the heavyset man, or my job here. Besides, I didn't trust her reaction. Or mine.

"She didn't find you attractive?" Moy considered the notion. "I can't imagine why." Despite his general catatonia, I thought I saw a spark of humor in his eyes.

Finally the stretcher boys arrived. After Moy signed a couple of forms for the ME, and Bernie was carted out, I was released.

The urgency of my desire to get away had eased a bit. The chops hadn't been touched. Instead of rushing back to the tournament, I wanted to follow Bernie's cart all the way to the ambulance. He deserved at least that much attention. At the same time, I had an impulse to join Moy when he went to question Max.

But I didn't do either one. I'd been sequestered for the better part of an hour—plenty of time for reality to shift on its axis, assume an entirely new bearing.

As I left the men's room, I saw Ginny.

There were dozens of people in the lobby now—cops and hotel staff, curious guests, martial artists, plus Deborah and Ned Gage, who'd presumably helped Security lock up the picks—but I hardly noticed them. The lobby itself was the size of an aircraft hangar, and lit like a playing field, but suddenly it seemed to contract around me, concentrating like the focus of a searchlight. Voices and feet scattered echoes off the tile floor, the glass of the high windows, but they meant nothing to me. I had time to wonder—just for a second—how my life had come to this. Then I went for her like a gale-force wind.

She was here because she cared about me, had to know whether I was all right.

Or because she thought I couldn't cope without her.

Or because she felt guilty—

Her eyes held the hawk I loved, the raptor avid to strike. Her jaw lifted at a combative angle, tightening to knots at the corners. Glints of light as cutting as serrations caught on the edges of her claw. Her purse hung over her shoulder, in easy reach. She could pull her .357 and fire faster than I could spit.

She terrified me. Always had. But none of that mattered now.

With a lifetime's abandonment in my voice, I demanded softly, "What the *fuck* do you think you're doing here?"

She gave me a grin like the arc of a circular saw. "Hello, Brew. It's nice to see you, too."

I was supposed to respond in kind—detached sarcasm, a sardonic bantering tone to blunt the loss. We'd treated each other that way for years, when we didn't know what else to do. But I no longer had it in me.

She'd left me for Marshal—

Clamping a grip onto her left arm above the elbow, I drew her toward the nearest wall. I couldn't afford to make a public spectacle of myself. I wanted to keep my job.

For some reason, she didn't resist, even though she hated being manhandled.

When we reached the wall, I let her go. "I'm not playing here, Fistoulari." She was tall, but I had the weight and inches to loom over her. "If I have to, I'll shout until they can hear me back home. What the—?"

"Calm down." She kept her grin. "You don't have to yell. Marshal told me what happened. The outlines, anyway. I wasn't far away, so I came to see if you need help."

Oh, sure. Like *that* made sense. She wasn't far away. So she came to see if I need help. I wouldn't have believed her if she'd crossed her heart and hoped to die.

In the back of my head, I knew I wasn't *this* angry at her. Not for jerking me around, anyway. Her presence simply gave me an outlet for fury and grief that couldn't do Bernie any good. But I'd spent too many years holding back, and all at once I'd had enough of it.

Clenching my teeth, I rasped softly, "You don't have the *right*. You don't have the right to *ask* me anything, or *offer* me anything, or fucking *tempt* me with anything. I'm not your partner anymore, remember? You ditched me." Somehow I managed not to add, So you could go screw goddamn Marshal Viviter. "You gave up all your rights with me."

That reached her somewhere. Her grin fell away. Gradually the smolder in her grey eyes faded to the softness of ash. She caught her lower lip between her teeth, then released it. For a moment I could see the marks on her skin.

Quietly she said, "This isn't easy for me, either."

I jumped in before she could go on, "I don't want to hear it. You didn't ask me whether I wanted to be ditched. You just did it. I don't *care* whether it's easy for you or not."

Instead of flaring back, she nodded. "You're right."

Which surprised me so much that I took an internal step backward.

"I'm not being consistent," she went on. "I know that. It must be making you crazy. But I feel like I've abandoned you, and I don't like it. That's why I called Marshal. I wanted to know how things were going for you. I guess I was looking for reassurance." She scowled at the idea. "When he told me you had a killing on your hands—" Discomfort lifted her shoulders. "I didn't think. I just came here."

I flinched. Why was it suddenly so impossible to be furious at her? Somehow she'd raised the stakes on me. Again. Now I had to be careful. No matter how I felt.

"All right," I said. "All right." I didn't try to sound calm, but I measured every word. "I can deal with that. I probably would've done the same."

She seemed to appreciate the concession, but I didn't dwell on it. "It's still wrong," I told her flatly.

Her eyes narrowed. Tension in her forearms flexed the hooks of her claw. " 'Wrong'?"

I retreated again. Looking for the truth. Attacking her was a luxury I could no longer afford.

"I mean it's the wrong way to go about it," I said more carefully. "You ditched me for a reason. Maybe it was a good reason." With an effort that twisted my guts, I admitted, "I'm so angry about it because I don't want to admit that you might be right." I hated honesty. Being flayed alive would've been more fun. Nevertheless I didn't stop. "But the fact that I happen to be in the middle of a mess doesn't cancel what you did. You can't have it both ways. You're either in or you're out.

"We both are."

Recognition darkened her gaze. She looked away to hide her distress.

"Maybe I need help here," I went on. "Maybe I don't. But you can't decide that for me." Abruptly a new rush of anger surged through me. Too furious to shout, I finished like the slice of a blade, "You have to wait until I fucking *ask*."

Which I was *not* going to do. I'd kiss Marshal's feet before I'd let her have everything her own way again.

Ginny bit her lower lip so hard that I feared she'd draw blood. Her hand made small broken gestures that didn't go anywhere.

Sighing, she murmured, "I understand."

Deborah had said that last night. I was getting good at rejecting women.

But Ginny wasn't done. In the same tone, she added, "When I want help, I'll ask for it."

Oh, sure. If she'd given me a chance, I might've said something bitter and hurtful—and completely beside the point. She was Ginny by-God Fistoulari, and she loathed herself when she needed help. But she turned her back on me and walked away before I fell victim to my usual charm. Her stride as she crossed the lobby had the harsh precision of a machine press, forcing a new shape on metal too hot to resist. When The Luxury's automatic doors slid shut after her, I felt more alone than I'd ever been in my life.

Sam Drayton had told me that I was stronger than I realized. At the moment I thought he was crazy.

I didn't regret anything I'd said. But I hated it. I hated being the kind of man and having the kind of life that made so much anger necessary.

11

Eventually I started to register my surroundings again. That was a plus. Bernie was still dead. Life didn't stop just because I'd chased Ginny away, amputated the only part of myself I really understood. Presumably Moy would finish asking his questions and leave. He didn't need me for that. But someone ought to help Slade reorganize Security's duty rotation, at least until the night-shift chief arrived to take over. The chops still needed protection. And Sammy Posten would be in a sweat, whether or not Bernie's death caused any insurance problems.

First things first, I told myself. Posten could dither without me. However, Slade might appreciate a show of support.

I scanned the lobby, but didn't find him. No doubt he'd accompanied Moy to question Max. Sternway and Deborah Messenger were gone. I still hadn't spotted Song Duk Soon. Of the people I knew, only Gage remained.

He might've been waiting for me. When I finally noticed him, he ambled in my direction.

"Well, that was exciting." He adjusted his mustache with a grin. "I've been to a lot of tournaments. A few of them were ripped off while I was there. But I've never helped catch a thief before. In fact," he admitted cheerfully, "I didn't know they ever *got* caught." Behind his good humor, he studied me like I'd taken him by surprise. "How did you do it, spot them like that?"

I didn't want to hang around the lobby. If I did, Posten was sure to corner me. Then I'd probably have to stand there while he explained that it'd be my fault if some hypothetical dependent or relative of Bernie's sued Watchdog for "wrongful death." Gesturing for Ned to join me, I headed toward the convention facilities.

"When you judge events here," I countered, "how do you decide who wins? As far as I can tell, all the competitors ever do is yell and wave."

"I can see differences." He chuckled. "I've watched these events a *lot*. And of course," he added nonchalantly, "I've had a certain amount of training."

I nodded. "One way or another, I've caught a lot of people." That was the best answer I could offer him.

Ned accepted it. "Fair enough."

The corridor outside the tournament hall was no more crowded than usual. I felt a small touch of relief when I saw guards still covering the doors. Security hadn't come unglued without Bernie. His men knew their jobs.

I was about to go inside, but Ned stopped me.

"I fly home Monday morning," he said in a confidential tone. "It's likely I won't be out here again until next year. But if you're ever in LA, look me up. Especially if you want work. I've always got room for a man who knows how to catch people."

I might've assumed that he was making fun of me—from my perspective, LA wasn't much closer than Mars—but the business card he pushed into my hand was serious enough to short-circuit my defensiveness. Once I decided to believe him, I said thanks like a good boy.

As I pulled the door open and reentered the tournament, I took an obscure comfort from the fact that Security still functioned. In my bereft state, it gave me an odd sense of kinship.

Once inside, however, I froze for a minute, stunned by the egregious unreality of everything around me. Bernie's murder hadn't changed a thing. Hell, I hadn't changed anything myself. Ranks of spectators still watched or applauded whenever they felt like it. From the rings, *karate-ka* bayed and thrashed at the air while their teammates, teachers, relatives, and antagonists milled around the walls. The dignitaries of this hermetic world sat or talked, taught or passed judgment or negotiated, according to their perceived duties, focused on violence—and oblivious to it. I wanted to scream.

First things first, I reminded myself. Keep doing the job. If Security could go on with no one in charge, so could I.

When I got my legs moving again, I shouldered through the crowd toward Nakahatchi's artifacts, forcing myself to ignore everything else until I'd confirmed that the chops hadn't been disturbed.

Which naturally they hadn't. Posten's paranoia notwithstanding, no one really cared about them.

So why was Bernie dead?

The guard on the display wanted to know more about what had happened. I told him as much as I could without yelling. Then I asked him to pass along a message for me, let Slade know I wanted to talk to him. When he nodded, I faced the tournament again.

Parker Neill and another IAMA blazer awarded trophies in a nearby ring. *Kata* events occupied most of the others. From the head table, Sue Rasmussen blared the names of the winners as Parker presented their trophies. Obviously she didn't care what effect she might have on the concentration of other competitors. Sternway and Alex Lacone stood near her, pretending to bestow benisons on all and sundry. Sternway rubbed absently at his left forearm while he talked.

A glance around the hall didn't locate Deborah for me. Instead I caught sight of Posten. He was heading in my direction with a look of determined hysteria on his unfortunate face.

Hoping to avoid him, I climbed the steps to the dais.

I wasn't much interested in Lacone at the moment, but he spotted me right away and bustled over to shake my hand. "Congratulations, Mr. Axbrewder." While he pumped my arm, he broadcast 50,000 watts of bonhomie in my face—enough radiant energy to slag sheet metal. "By all reports, you were pretty impressive. Mr. Gage painted a glowing picture. Theft has been a problem at these events for years. Maybe now crooks will steer clear of us."

Trying not to sound bitter, I retorted, "I guess Bernie made the right choice when he hired me." Or it would've been, if he'd wanted to end up dead. "Too bad I can't ask him for a reference."

Lacone ignored my tone. His grin left no room on his face for anything else. "Don't worry about that," he advised me in an avuncular way. "We're all aware of your contribution. Why, I wouldn't be surprised if Detective Moy put in a good word for you himself."

"That's gratifying." If I'd felt any more gratified, I would've puked on Lacone's shoes.

Sternway decided to add his congratulations. "Mr. Lacone is right, Brew. You've done well."

"Just my job," I told him through my teeth.

Lacone responded with a few more fulsome remarks, but I decided not to encourage him by paying attention. As soon as he paused, I asked Sternway, "Can I talk to you for a minute?"

His expression didn't shift. "Certainly." He turned to Lacone. "Will you excuse us?"

Lacone smiled us on our way, and Sternway gestured me to the back of the dais.

While I followed, Sue Rasmussen looked in our direction. When I met her gaze, she treated me to a glare of cold fury.

It shocked me like a douse of cold water. Without transition the inside of my head seemed to shift. Suddenly I didn't have any trouble restraining my bitterness. I didn't need it.

From the rear of the dais, we weren't really out of earshot. However, the tournament had enough volume to cover us if we kept our voices down.

Sternway faced me with his usual lack of expression. Riding a wave of pure intuition, I plunged right in.

"Mr. Sternway, you were in the lobby when I went by, but you told Detective Moy that you didn't see anyone head for the men's room. Are you sure?" Playing at helplessness, I added, "I don't know who else to ask."

The IAMA director kept his face closed. "I was talking with Mr. Lacone and Ms. Messenger. It never occurred to me to watch who went to the men's room."

Which was essentially what he'd said to Moy.

"But are you sure?" I asked, still playing. "I would've said that the guy who killed Bernie was pretty easy to spot."

A hint of exasperation tightened Sternway's brows, but I hurried on before he could interrupt. "Heavyset, a bit shorter than me. Dingy sweats—the kind of dingy you get when you don't do much laundry. Light on his feet, hard forehead, fat jowls. Eyes the color of his sweats," and almost that clean.

He was getting tired of me. "As I told Moy—"

I cut in, "I heard you." I wasn't playing now. "But this guy's obviously a fighter. I thought all you martial artists knew each other."

He assessed me for a moment, then stated flatly, "You don't believe me."

"I didn't say that. I just don't have anything else to go on.

You're the king of this little world. I would've thought that being observant was a requirement of the job."

He didn't hesitate. "Axbrewder, this tournament, any tournament, is filled with people I know and people I don't. I can't be expected to recognize them all."

I didn't hesitate either. "OK, forget the sweats. How about people you know that aren't here? Have you met anyone who matches that description?"

Sternway opened his mouth, then caught himself. His gaze wandered briefly, looking for something. Inspiration? A memory? "Perhaps—" he murmured. "I'm not sure." He massaged his left forearm. "I'll have to think about it."

When he faced me again, he'd recovered his exasperation. "I hope you aren't wasting my time with this. Your question doesn't make sense. None of the people I know here fit your description. If I know a man who does, he isn't here. So he—"

I had no more idea than Sternway did what my question meant, but I didn't worry about it. Intuition is like that. Making sense was someone else's job—usually Ginny's. Before he could finish, I countered like I knew what I was doing, "Or you didn't notice him."

That stopped him. After a moment's consideration, he nodded. "I'll think about it. That's the best I can offer."

If I hadn't disliked his manner so much, I might've said thanks. But I didn't. Instead I changed the subject.

"So how did you hurt your arm?"

I wanted to catch him off balance, but I must've been dreaming. He was HRH Anson Sternway, Mr. Shorin-Ryu 8th-*dan* on his own turf, and he didn't so much as blink.

"A stupid accident." He glanced at his forearm. "I was walking behind the dais"—he indicated the floor below us—"and tripped on one of the wires." A tangle of leads and power cords for the microphones and laptops sprawled in plain sight. "When I fell, I hit my arm on the edge where we're standing."

I didn't have any reason to doubt him, so I replied piously, "I hope you didn't tear your blazer."

He showed me the fabric. "Apparently not."

I might've responded with some empty remark about expensive blazers being worth what they cost, but he distracted me by staring abruptly into my eyes. "Why do you care?"

I smiled insincerely. "I don't. I was just curious." Since I couldn't threaten his balance, I tried to keep him on his toes instead. "Part of my job. I get paid to notice things."

His gaze didn't waver. "You seem to be good at it."

Well, shit. If that constituted keeping him on his toes, I needed to find some other line of work. Nevertheless I still felt strangely lucid, defended by a sense of intuition that I didn't try to explain.

"Some days," I admitted. In a more confidential tone, I added, "I sure noticed that look Sue gave me."

A chink in his armor at last. He actually frowned, and a suggestion of darkness gathered in his eyes. "What look?"

Mentally I thanked Ned Gage for the hint. Grinning all over my face, I shrugged. "I think she likes me."

For a second I thought HRH might go so far as to insult me. Put the commoner in his place. He stopped himself, however, before he revealed anything as human as indignation.

"I didn't see it," he told me coldly. Then he turned back toward Lacone.

Still grinning, I headed in the opposite direction—and nearly collided with Sammy Posten. So much for being paid to notice things. He must've been hovering there for several minutes, waiting to pounce, but I hadn't registered his presence.

"Mr. Posten." Instead of groaning, I gave him a look of malicious good humor. "It's your turn to congratulate me. Looks like I just saved you a few bucks."

I didn't expect him to care about that, and for once I was right. "Chump change," he snorted. "I have bigger concerns."

"Such as?"

"Such as Nakahatchi *sensei*'s chops. They're vulnerable. Even you have to admit that now."

I frowned. "Excuse me? I must've missed something." Actually I agreed with him, but I didn't want to show it. "I just caught a small team of petty thieves. And I've seen dozens of clowns just like them. You can take it to the bank that none of them gives a shit about that display."

Watchdog's Senior Security Adviser bristled like a porcupine. "You aren't paying attention, Axbrewder." His problem was, he didn't have a quill to his name. "You're doing your job, I'll give you that. But you don't see the implications.

"Everyone I talk to seems to think no one is stupid enough to try to steal from 'martial artists.' The chops are safe because they're surrounded by fighters who can cut down trees with their bare hands."

He was surrounded by them himself, but he didn't seem aware of the fact.

"That's bullshit," he informed me hotly. "You've just demonstrated it. These 'martial artists' couldn't spot a thief with a telescope. What's wrong with them? If you can do it, why can't they?"

Before I could attempt a reply, he finished, "How safe do you think those chops will be when Nakahatchi *sensei* takes them home?"

The poor deluded man looked positively triumphant, like he'd just scored in my face. Apparently he didn't remember that I'd made the same point myself earlier.

This was getting out of hand. Even I couldn't imagine what he gained by insulting every *karate-ka* within earshot. No wonder Bernie had liked him so much.

"Mr. Posten"—I meant *Postal*—"let me explain something. How shall I put this?" I wrapped one hand around his biceps and dug in a bit to emphasize my advantages. "I don't care. It's not my job.

"I was hired by The Luxury and the IAMA for this tournament. If those chops are endangered while they're here," I said sententiously, "I'll die defending them." Like *that* was going to happen. "But if you're worried about after the tournament, tell someone else." I had Lacone in mind, but I wasn't about to say so. "It's not my problem."

Just for a second, I tightened my grip—giving him something to remember me by. Then I turned away. I didn't particularly want to watch his reaction.

But he surprised me. Instead of swearing abuse at me, he demanded, "What would it take to make it your problem?"

I took another step or two while I fought down an impulse to wheel on him and shout, Tell me why Bernie was killed! Tell me what it has to do with those damn chops! Don't let that poor old man be dead just because he made the mistake of cornering a moron.

When I had myself under control, I looked at Posten over my shoulder and grinned again. "A paycheck," I answered succinctly.

Three more strides took me to the edge of the dais. From there I went down the steps and back into the crowd.

My hands were trembling again.

Why *was* Bernie dead? I couldn't get my mind around the idea of an experienced drop so brain-dead that he killed a security guard to escape a petty larceny rap—and then took the flik so that no sane cop would suspect him of killing in self-defense.

I knew the answer. I just didn't know it. On some intuitive level, I already had a picture of what must've happened. Unfortunately that level didn't deign to communicate with the rest of my brain.

Bernie must've been killed by a man with something more to hide than a gear-bag full of evidence.

He'd been killed because—

I couldn't get it. It remained out of sight, teasing me like the first phosphene hints of a migraine.

Well, damn. I wanted to club my forehead with my fists, but I knew from long experience that you can't make intuition work by pounding on it. I had to leave it alone, relax if I could, and just wait for it.

The tremors in my hands made the bare idea laughable.

Since I wasn't likely to relax, I did the next thing. I went looking for Deborah Messenger.

I didn't find her, of course. She must've left after the cops questioned her. I had to make do without her.

And Ginny.

It wasn't easy, but eventually I found a little calm. My hands still shook, but I stopped sweating despite the steadily rising heat. The yelling and effort in the rings seemed to pass over my head. *Karate-ka* celebrated victory or trudged away in defeat without requiring my attention. My sense of impending disaster had already come to fruition, and I didn't expect more. Not immediately. Meanwhile I was just marking time, waiting for intuition or events to give me what I needed.

The sound of my phone almost surprised me.

I put my back to the wall to block out at least some of the background noise. "Yes?"

Slade's voice asked, "Axbrewder? You wanted to talk to me?"

The connection's lousy acoustics made him sound wrung out, squeezed dry by self-pity.

I snapped back into focus. First things first. "What's been going on?" I countered. "Did Max tell Moy anything? Is there anything on the tapes?"

"Shit," Slade muttered. "I told him it wouldn't do any good, but of course he didn't listen to me. We had to go over those tapes frame by frame. That damn detective thinks he's being careful, but I say he just didn't want to go do any real work."

Apparently Slade didn't care why I wanted to know.

"But you didn't find anything?"

He snorted, "No. The camera sweeps only cover that part of the lobby every forty-five seconds. And when they do, they don't show anybody who looks like your description."

"I understand," I said, mostly because I thought it might give him a sense of accomplishment. Then I asked, "Did Moy take the tapes?" He could get Carner Police Department's lab to bring up better resolution than Max's monitors. If he wanted to go to that much trouble.

"Yeah." Slade didn't try to hide his scorn. "For all the good it's going to do him."

I didn't pursue it. Instead I put on my best Uncle Axbrewder tone. "Thanks, Slade. You have a lot to deal with. Is there any way I can help?"

He swore. "I wish you could keep fucking Postal from chewing on my ass. But I don't think you can." Then he sighed. "Just watch those chops. We're shorthanded. On top of everything else, they expect me to do Bernie's paperwork."

"Count on it." I gave him a sour grin he couldn't see. "If some asshole tries to get at the display, I'll make him eat it."

"You do that."

Before he hung up, I explained that I had to go look at mug shots tomorrow. Sourly he gave his consent.

I put the phone away.

The tournament sounded louder than I remembered. Sue Rasmussen must've made an exciting announcement.

I couldn't call Marshall again. I hadn't given him enough time. And I didn't want him to think I was hysterical.

Grimly I went back to marking time.

By degrees the ranks of trophies dwindled. I still hadn't seen any of the hard and soft stylists go head-to-head. Presumably that would happen on Sunday, when the "grand championships" would be decided in each category of age and rank regardless of style. In the vaguest possible way, I looked forward to it. After what T'ang Wen had told me, I wanted to see whether the soft styles were really as useless as they appeared.

Ginny was gone. I had no leverage with Moy. I'd already refused Deborah Messenger. And I was stuck here. I needed this job.

Fortunately by midafternoon the ebb and flow of the tournament gave me another shot at Parker Neill. I found him near the display, apparently watching events while he waited for something that might require his attention. By way of greeting, he took a turn bronzing my laurels, so I decided to risk a question that might interest Marshal.

"Got a minute?" All this courtesy made me sound positively unctuous.

Against the weight of his habitual sag, he lifted his vague nose to smile at me. "Sure. For all I know, I've got twenty."

I smiled back to disguise what I had in mind. "Maybe you can satisfy my curiosity. There's a rumor going around"—I flapped a hand at the hall to indicate no particular source—"that Anson Sternway and Sue Rasmussen are in bed together."

Suddenly I couldn't remember where I'd gotten the impression that Parker was plump. His flesh seemed to lift and tighten until it fit him like Spandex. Unexpected lightness almost raised him off the ground.

"Listen to me, Axbrewder." A curdling glare filled his face with threats.

With the index finger of his right hand, he reached out and touched me lightly over my heart.

Or it should've been lightly. He didn't put any force into it that I could see. But when he tapped me I felt a jab of pain as if he'd hammered an awl between my ribs. For an instant I couldn't breathe.

No one touches me. Not like that.

Reacting on instinct, I flung a punch at his head.

I'd always thought I was fast, but my fist didn't get anywhere near him. He slapped it aside effortlessly.

And he didn't give me a second chance. All at once he stood right in front of me, too close for blows. If I wanted a fight, I'd have to grapple with him.

What was left of my lucidity yelled at me to stop. Somehow I did.

Spectators and contestants sifted past us, but they seemed insubstantial, beyond notice. No one looked at the chops.

While I hunted for breath, Neill said coldly, "Anson Sternway is my *sensei*. Do you have any idea what that means? I respect him. Absolutely. Unconditionally. He taught me—he *made* me who I am. I don't listen to *rumors* about him."

I sneaked a little air into my lungs. "Doesn't it bother you," I wheezed, "that he's only in it for the money?"

Then I froze, too furious to restrain myself in any other way if he decided to poke me again.

But he surprised me by dropping his gaze. The way he sagged back into himself told me that I'd hurt him. "You don't understand," he said in a low mumble. "He and his wife are separated. He wants a divorce, but she's fighting him. He needs money."

Before I could come up with a flashy retort, he wandered away like he'd forgotten what he was doing. For a moment he looked like he'd never moved lightly in his life. Then a swirl of the crowd came between us, and I couldn't watch him anymore.

Glowering, I rubbed my chest. How had he *done* that? With just one finger? I felt like I'd been impaled on a piece of rebar.

Sternway was Sue Rasmussen's *sensei* as well. Maybe that explained the look of hate she'd given me. Maybe in karate the students were supposed to be so loyal that they went crazy.

"You all right?" Ned inquired. Somehow he'd arrived beside me without attracting my attention.

I cleared my lungs. "I think so."

He laughed quietly. "That's good. If you'd taken another swing at him, we'd have to scrape you up with a shovel."

I was mad enough to argue the point. Parker had caught me by surprise. That wouldn't happen again. But I'd lived with myself long enough to recognize my own chagrin when it masqueraded as anger. Swallowing a lump of bile, I asked ruefully, "Was it that obvious?"

Ned dismissed my ego with a grin. "Don't worry about it. I'm sure I'm not the only one who noticed. But being as how this is a karate tournament and all, everybody else probably thinks you were playing."

Then he added, "You want to tell me about it?"

I was still too angry to let it go. "You're wrong about him," I pronounced distinctly.

Ned raised his eyebrows. "Who? Parker?"

I nodded. "He doesn't sag like that because he isn't competing. His disappointment runs a whole lot deeper."

In an obscure way, I knew how Neill felt. My own disappointment had been downright abysmal for years.

Gage considered the idea for a moment. "You may be right. But I'm not even going to ask. I've said it before, he's a true believer. True believers have that problem. They get disappointed.

"Don't lose my card," he ordered as he moved away. He may've said it to reassure me.

It didn't help. Everyone here seemed to know too much about me. From Sam Drayton I expected it. From relative strangers like Ned and Parker and maybe even Sue Rasmussen, it made me squirm.

Sourly I wondered how far a true believer would go for a *sensei* who needed money.

I also wondered how much money Sternway actually needed.

While my back was turned, the tournament had continued piling on volume. And the heat had grown worse. I felt it leaning down on me from the high ceiling despite the AC, spreading a sheen of sweat across my ribs until my shirt stuck to my skin under my jacket. Still the people in my vicinity seemed like shadows, denatured of substance by their detachment from Bernie's death. The yelling in the rings and the applause from the stands sounded like the feverish hunger of ghosts.

Haunted by unreality, I tried to recover my lost lucidity. But it was gone now. The lingering ache in my chest seemed to block it somehow. Between my stomach and my heart, I had too many vulnerable spots.

I couldn't imagine how Security endured this kind of work. The Luxury's guards must've spent most of their lives asleep.

Which explained why Bernie had insisted on chasing down the drop himself. He'd simply wanted to inject a little meaning into his job. It wasn't my fault that he was dead. He'd taken the risk because he'd needed it more than he needed backup.

Somehow that notion failed to improve my morale.

Around me the tournament trudged along with no end in sight, mechanically grinding losers away and leaving winners behind. As far as I could tell, the whole process was nothing more than an exercise in self-congratulation. Every trophy that Sternway and his retinue handed out increased the IAMA's importance. The size and number of the trophies conferred validation, and publicity was all that separated martial artists from ordinary thugs.

The only flaw in this caustic view was that Neill had nearly broken a rib for me with one light touch, thereby forcing me to recognize that I tended to underestimate the people here.

At the rate I was going, I'd make a great candidate for the Council on Depression's annual poster child.

When someone laid a hand on my shoulder, I wheeled around as if that were the last straw, and if I didn't start savaging people who touched me I'd never be myself again. Full of ire and self-disgust, I came *this close* to splashing napalm all over Deborah Messenger.

She flinched, her eyes wide with fright. "I startled you," she said quickly. "I'm sorry."

Suddenly being myself again didn't seem like such a plus.

She must've gone home to change after her discussion with Sternway and Lacone. Now she wore a casual white cotton shirt, tight beige shorts that showed off her long legs, and a pair of cute sneakers. She looked like a dream—the kind I used to have before alcohol and loathing soaked them out of me.

Stumbling over my consternation, I tried to apologize. "No, please," I assured her, "it's my fault." I held up my hands like I thought that might placate her. "I shouldn't have turned on you like that. You just caught me in a particularly rotten mood."

She smiled tentatively. "Are you all right? It must've been terrible, finding Mr. Appelwait's body like that. You looked so upset." Residual fright made her talk in a rush. "I wanted to ask how you were, but you seemed like you didn't want to talk to me. Then you had a fight with that woman—" Her voice trailed off.

"Ginny Fistoulari," I told her more abruptly than I intended. "My former partner."

She nodded like I'd confirmed a guess. "I had to go back to the office to finish some business," she went on. "I wasn't sure I should come here again. But I finally asked myself"—her smile grew stronger—"what's the worst that could happen? You could tell me to get lost. I wouldn't enjoy that, but I've survived worse." Then she frowned. "I *liked* Mr. Appelwait. And I hated that detective, Sergeant Moy. I don't think he cares."

While she talked, I guided her through the crowd until we reached the comparative privacy of the wall. As her nervousness wound down, I took a chance by saying, "I'm glad you came. I'm sorry I gave you the impression I might not want to see you. I had a lot on my mind."

"I'm sure you did," she put in quickly. "Please don't—" With an effort, she caught herself. "I'll tell you what, Brew." This time her smile was so clear that you could've used it to land aircraft. "I'll stop apologizing if you'll talk to me."

I ached to put my arms around her, and the strain of swallowing the impulse made me sound hoarse. "You don't have anything to apologize for. Of course I'll talk to you."

A brick wall probably could've said the same with better grace.

Still smiling, she said, "OK, then. If you don't mind—" By degrees she turned serious. "I still don't really know what happened to Mr. Appelwait. Can you tell me?"

I cleared my throat. No question about it, I wanted to tell *someone*. But I wasn't sure how much I could afford to say. "There isn't a lot," I admitted. "We had a team working the hall, three picks and a drop." Being cautious, I didn't mention the spot. "They're—"

"I know what they are," she assured me. "I've talked to a lot of cops since I starting working for Watchdog."

That made the explanation easier. "They began to leave," I went on. "I think they caught me watching them. Bernie told me to corral the spots. He went after the drop. The evidence." I couldn't keep a grimace off my face. "Once Security had the picks, I tried to catch up with him. But I was too late.

"He must've cornered the drop in the men's room. That's what it looked like, anyway." As soon as I said the words, an intuitive alarm went off in the back of my head, but I didn't know what it meant. "Apparently the drop decided to fight his way out."

A definite alarm. Something I'd just said wasn't right.

Deborah shuddered delicately, then looked at me hard. "Do you think the cops will find him?"

"No." Suddenly I knew I was right.

"Why not?"

"Because," I said like reading it off the inside of my skull, "they're looking for the wrong man.

"There was someone else in the men's room. Someone Bernie knew." Someone working with the drop. The spot? "He killed"—murdered—"Bernie to shut him up."

She stared at me in surprise and shock. "Who?"

I shrugged bitterly. "If I knew that, I wouldn't feel so useless."

Who could possibly have considered Bernie worth killing? What in God's name was going *on*?

Song Duk Soon had left the hall ahead of Bernie and the drop.

There wasn't anything to kill for here. Even the chops weren't that precious.

I didn't understand it. Nevertheless my instincts had told me the truth. About that I felt no doubt whatsoever.

Luckily Deborah didn't ask if I'd said any of this to Moy. Instead she inquired, "So what are you going to do?"

That was easier. "Turn it over to Marshal Viviter. I'm stuck here for the duration. And he has resources I don't. I'll tackle it myself when this"—I indicated the tournament—"is over."

She opened her mouth to say something. Whatever it was, however, she thought better of it. She chewed her lower lip for a moment, looking embarrassed. Then she surprised me by asking awkwardly, "Mr. Viviter? Not Ms. Fistoulari? You used to be partners." Her gaze fell away from mine. "She wouldn't have come here if she didn't want to help."

I damn near fell over. Without thinking, I said, "She wasn't here to help. She came because she thought I needed rescue—"

Abruptly I bit myself off. Last night I'd refused Deborah. Now she sounded like she might be giving me a second chance. If I wanted to take advantage of it, I couldn't very well hold Ginny responsible.

"Deborah—" My voice shook like my hands. I had to whisper to control it. "Last night I said I needed things with her to be clear. Now they are. That makes it my turn."

My turn to risk—

"I don't know you very well. But I really like you." I couldn't help quoting her. I didn't know what else to do. "I'd like you to spend the night with me." Then I added, "If you still want to."

After that I held my breath.

When Deborah raised her eyes again, they were full of caution. "Don't jerk me around, Brew," she murmured softly. "I can take care of myself, but I still feel things. I didn't enjoy being turned down."

I knew how she felt. And I was in no position to make promises.

"I don't have a crystal ball." I stopped trying to steady my voice. "I don't know whether you'll get jerked around or not. But my situation is different now. That's what Ginny and I were fighting about. We agreed to go our separate ways.

"And I'm glad." Which was true, as far as it went. "All those grey areas were driving me crazy.

"I don't want to jerk you around," I finished. "I want you to say yes."

Deborah didn't hesitate. Or speak. Instead she gave me a smile that made the whole inside of my chest ring like a gong.

12

The tournament ran until nearly midnight, but I hardly noticed what happened. Winners and losers, trophies, grievances, triumphs, even Benny "the Jet" Urquidez's sparring demonstration—none of it made the remotest impression on me. I didn't forget Bernie, not for a second. But the rest of my attention was fixed elsewhere.

Deborah and I may've slept that night, I wasn't sure. I couldn't pretend that I understood her. Her presence mystified me entirely. But she'd told me the truth about one thing, at least. She definitely enjoyed sex. That night we did things I'd never imagined. She found responses in me that I didn't know I had.

Yet when my wake-up call came I positively bounced out of bed. While we made ready to face the day, I wore a loony grin I couldn't get rid of. I would've felt like a complete idiot if she hadn't looked as pleased and satisfied as I was.

Faking discretion, we said a businesslike goodbye after breakfast. I promised I'd call her on Monday, and finally tore myself away to head for the tournament hall. But she ran after me, caught my arm, and put her mouth to my ear.

In a quick whisper, she told me, "I think you're going to get good news today."

Then she left like she knew exactly what effect she had on me.

I ached to go after her, but I had a job to do. Somehow I made myself return to it.

In the back of my head, a tune repeated itself like a litany of pleasure, although I couldn't remember the name of the song—or any of the words.

The routine of the tournament hadn't changed. When we'd retrieved the display from the manager's safe room, IAMA blazers opened the doors for registration and spectators. Today, however, the audience significantly outnumbered the competitors. Originally only "championships" or "grand championships" had been scheduled—which obviously drew the biggest crowds—but a revised listing indicated a backlog of unfinished events from the previous day. I'd probably be stuck here until midnight. Again.

Sighing, I proceeded to ignore the problem. All I had to do was keep an eye on the chops, watch for more picks, and wait out the day. By tomorrow I'd be able to collect my paycheck. Then I could get serious about hunting for Bernie's killer.

Marshal would've been proud of me. With that tune on its endless loop in my head, I was actively polite to everyone I encountered. I even watched some of the events like I enjoyed them. And today the gradually building heat didn't bother me. I was uncharacteristically immune to petty vexations.

Ginny wouldn't have recognized me.

Sometime around noon, the "Masters' *Kata*" got underway. Since Sue Rasmussen had advised me not to miss it, I observed it from the vantage of the dais.

Along the edge of a ring nearby, seven so-called masters knelt while an eighth bowed to the judges. At this level, apparently, the IAMA no longer distinguished between hard and soft styles. Two men and a woman wore silk pajamas, the rest canvas. The man going first was Song Duk Soon. Among the others I recognized Hong Fei-Tung, *Soke* Bob Gravel, whom I'd met briefly on Friday, Nelson Brick, and—to my surprise—Parker Neill.

Brick I thought I understood. He'd suffered a blow to his ego earlier, so he wanted to recoup. But why was Parker there? I'd assumed that the dignitaries didn't compete, if only to avoid any appearance of favoritism. Certainly there were no official blazers among the judges. In fact, I only recognized one of them.

Nakahatchi.

I wondered why he chose to judge instead of competing.

Glancing around for someone to ask, I spotted Ned Gage. He saw me beckon and joined me on the dais as Master Soon sprang into motion.

Soon knew how to put on a show, I had to give him that. From a cold start, he practically exploded into dramatic blows, leaping spins, and kicks so high they might've been aimed at the ceiling. The fury of his yells tugged at my guts. Some of his kicks seemed to leave streaks of flame across my vision, as if they'd ignited the air for an instant.

At the end, he passed without transition from violent exertion to stillness. He wasn't sweating—as far as I could tell, he wasn't even breathing hard. Smoothly he bowed to the judges, then retreated from the ring, bowed to his fellow masters, and knelt alone opposite them.

I applauded dutifully. Like the rest of the audience, Ned showed more enthusiasm. For a second there, he looked like he might cheer.

The woman in silk was already on her way into the ring, so I asked Ned quickly, "Why is Parker competing?"

Ned grinned. "I think you upset him yesterday," he whispered. "He wants to prove something. Maybe he needs to remind himself he's still alive.

"Of course"—humor gleamed in Ned's eyes—"he won't win. None of the judges want to look like they're sucking up to the IAMA."

"Surely he knows that," I objected. "What's he going to prove?"

Ned chuckled. "You'll see when it's his turn."

The woman in silk began before I could ask another question.

In sharp contrast to Soon's *kata*, hers seemed to be formed entirely of silk. It was a graceful flowing dance, full of sweeping arms and legs, deep crouches and whirling leaps, but I didn't see one honest blow. Maybe she planned to frustrate her imaginary opponent by smothering him in her clothes. Her approach sure as hell wouldn't do him any other harm.

The applause this time was more spotty. Stylists in silk cheered uproariously as she knelt beside Soon. Other reactions were distinctly tepid.

"Someday," I murmured to Ned, "I'll have to ask you what *that* was for."

"I'll need at least an hour." He chuckled again. "And even then I probably won't convince myself I understand it."

"Who is she?"

"Sai Ma. She calls her style 'Flying Crane.' Other than that, I don't know a thing about it."

Flying Crane, forsooth. No wonder I was so impressed.

Brick went next. If appearances counted, he immediately began killing people left and right. I heard every exhalation, hard as a punch. Hell, I practically heard his *gi* tear with each attack. He didn't move with anything like Soon's speed, or the woman's, but his knuckles strained into his blows, his kicks went off like gunshots, and his eyes glared white whenever he yelled. If he put any more effort into it, he'd rupture himself.

When he finally bowed to the judges, he splashed sweat onto the carpet.

The audience loved it, but Ned was less polite. "That and two bucks," he told me confidentially, "will get him a cup of coffee. He couldn't handle a real fight. He'd wear himself out posturing."

I wasn't sure I agreed. If Brick ever decided to kick me again, I didn't intend to stand still for it. But Gage was the expert here. I kept my opinions to myself.

After those three rounds, the judges showed their score cards to the record-keeper. Nakahatchi, I noticed, had given Sai Ma his highest marks.

During the pause, I asked Ned why Nakahatchi wasn't competing.

Ned shrugged. "You'll have to ask him. But I can tell you why *Sifu* Hong is."

"OK," I said, just being helpful. "Why?"

"Because Nakahatchi *sensei* offered to be one of the judges. *Sifu* Hong wants to intimidate him, at least metaphorically. Nakahatchi *sensei*'s ownership of those chops costs every Wing Chun stylist here face." Ned gave me a laughing glance. "In case you hadn't figured that part out for yourself."

I had, actually. After T'ang Wen's explanations, even I couldn't miss it. But I didn't waste time saying so.

"What about the scoring? Why do you think Nakahatchi rated Sai Ma so highly?"

Ned shrugged. "I'm guessing here, but I'd say it was face again. Nakahatchi *sensei* is sensitive about the chops. He wants to compliment the soft stylists. He'll probably rate *Sifu* Hong even higher." He frowned his disapproval. "On the other side, Tae Kwon Do and Shotokan have a lot in common. They both grew out of Okinawan styles, primarily Shorin-Ryu and Sheri-Ryu. Nakahatchi *sensei* may have downgraded Master Soon because he doesn't approve of the direction the Koreans have taken.

"Personally, I would've done the opposite. I wouldn't challenge Master Soon on a bet." Then he grinned fiercely. "But I'd love to find out what Sai Ma is made of."

He could have her. I preferred Deborah.

From then on, the scoring took place at the end of each *kata*. Another hard stylist went next. Then came Parker's turn.

Surprisingly, he no longer sagged. Even his skin looked taut, as if he'd condensed himself to pure force. Instead of competing with Soon's speed, Sai Ma's flow, or Brick's exertion, he shifted through the steps of his *kata* slowly, with the effortless solidity of a boulder and the precision of a javelin. Each of his strikes etched itself against the air, marked in place by the acid snap of his *gi*. Wherever he set his feet, they seemed to put down roots. From start to finish, he conveyed the impression that he'd transformed himself by turns into both an irresistible force and an immovable object.

"Wow," Ned breathed through the applause. "See what I mean?"

I nodded in spite of myself. If I moved that slowly, I couldn't hit a blind four-year-old. And yet— Parker had definitely proved something. I just didn't know what to call it.

Whatever it was, the judges liked it.

Another *ch'uan fa kata* followed. This one made marginally more sense than Sai Ma's, but neither the spectators nor the judges were impressed.

Next *Soke* Bob Gravel took the ring. He was a slight man with greying hair and a flare of keenness in his pale eyes. A patch on his *gi* said *Malaysian Fighting Arts.* Before he began, I asked Ned what *soke* meant. "Founder," he told me. Apparently Gravel taught a style which he'd designed himself, based on a number of Malaysian arts with names I didn't know—Arnis, Silat, Kali, Muay Thai.

Certainly his *kata* looked like nothing I'd seen before. All of his stances were either deep cross-legged crouches or upright assaults. Occasionally he waved his arms like Sai Ma, but more often he did nasty things with his elbows. He pumped his knees a lot, pawed several kicks, and swung his legs in long sweeps that torqued his hips into impossible positions.

By the end of his performance, I knew I could take him—if you gave me a loaded shotgun and a good head start. More than anyone I'd seen so far, he convinced me that he was dangerous.

By degrees I was being forced to revise my opinion of the martial arts. Despite my prejudices, I had to acknowledge that some of these people knew a thing or two about real violence.

When *Sifu* Hong took the ring, I almost stopped breathing.

On one level, his *kata* resembled what I'd seen from the other soft stylists. As soon as he began, however, I found that I couldn't watch him in those terms. He made me believe that he performed a fight against actual opponents. Somehow every movement—every punch, kick, grab, jump, block—created antagonists in the air around him. Everything he did instantly demonstrated its purpose by forcing me to visualize the attack it countered, the body it struck, the blow it avoided. While his *kata* lasted, I understood everything about it. No part of it was flamboyant or wasted. Even his smallest gestures and shifts were charged with intent. They all had use.

I hardly heard the ovation he received. Astonishment left me practically deaf. I felt like I'd just witnessed the birth of a religion—the moment when violence was transfigured by skill and devotion into something ineffable, almost sublime.

Minutes seemed to pass before I noticed Ned gazing at me with a question in his eyes.

Involuntarily I reached out and braced myself on his shoulder. "I think," I mumbled while I turned my back on the ring, "I need to sit down."

"Don't you want to see who wins?"

I shook my head. Still leaning on him, I retreated to the back of the dais. There I seated myself heavily and dropped my legs over the edge.

"Brew?" Ned asked. "You all right?"

"Yes." I sighed. "No." Then I made an effort to pull myself together. "I just realized something."

Ned sat down companionably beside me. "I know what you mean. *Sifu* Hong is amazing."

I shook my head again. "Something else." Of course Hong *was* amazing. But I'd been gripped by a perception that resembled ecstasy, a moment of intuition so acute that it might as well have been metaphysical.

"Like what?"

I took a deep breath and held it until the pressure grew strong enough to steady me. Then I let it out. When it was all gone, and my lungs were clear, I told him, "I haven't been taking those chops seriously enough. They're worth killing for."

They were the Body of Christ, priceless to true believers everywhere. Entire crusades had been fought for less.

If they were genuine.

Ned frowned. "And you got that from watching *Sifu* Hong?"

I tried to explain. "I thought they were just antiques. Worth only what collectors decide to pay. But that *kata*—" Words couldn't convey what I'd seen. "They aren't antiques. They're religious icons. The kind of thing people venerate."

And kill for. Bernie was dead because of them.

Someone else would be next. The killer wouldn't stop until he got what he wanted.

Ned laughed. "Then there's nothing to worry about. We'll be done here by midnight. After that the chops aren't your problem."

Sure, I thought. Not my problem.

The killing had already begun. That made it my problem.

Grimacing, I replied dishonestly, "And I say, thank God. Otherwise I'd feel morally bound to give myself an ulcer."

I wanted to deflect him from the truth. If I didn't, he might get in the killer's way somehow. I didn't want his blood on my conscience.

A minute later, Sue Rasmussen announced the Masters' *Kata* Champion. Soon won, with Gravel second and Hong third. Apparently prejudice against the soft styles was alive and well at the IAMA World Championships.

"Judges." Ned dismissed the results with the back of his hand. "Go figure." Then he told me privately, "But I was right about one thing. I saw the scores before you turned away. Nakahatchi *sensei* gave his best marks to *Sifu* Hong."

Somehow I wasn't surprised. Nakahatchi may've been trying to keep himself alive.

Ned went back to his duties, but I stayed put for a while, feeling dazed and essentially stupid. Eventually, however, I summoned the will to resume my own responsibilities. I didn't think the chops were in any immediate danger, so I went looking for an opportunity to talk to someone from *Essential Shotokan*.

Trying not to be obvious about it, I made an oblique approach to the spot where Nakahatchi had set up his enclave. He sat a bit above me, surrounded by students. The dullness in his eyes made him appear to slump even though his actual posture was erect. Once again his thin hair and the lines beside his mouth gave me the impression that his face was war torn in some way, strewn with the casualties of an old conflict. Despite my need for information, I felt suddenly reluctant to approach him.

I was still reeling from the effects of the Masters' *katas*.

Fortunately I recognized one of his people, Hideo Komatori. We'd been introduced Friday morning. That gave me an opening.

"Mr. Komatori." Unsure of the real thing, I produced an ersatz bow. "Axbrewder. We met briefly on Friday."

Like his *sensei*, he wore white canvas, but his black belt showed less wear. As he stood to return my bow, I saw that he was considerably taller than Nakahatchi—which still left him a hand shorter than I was. I couldn't tell his age. Mid-thirties? To my eye, Asian faces disguised their years. He carried himself with the lightness I'd learned to expect from serious martial artists, back straight, hands ready. But he smiled like he was sincerely willing to talk to me.

Stepping down from the risers, he shook my hand. "Mr. Axbrewder. You're well? You enjoy the tournament?"

Until he stood right in front of me, I didn't notice the scar that ran from his forehead down through his left eyebrow into his cheek. It was so old and pale that I could only make it out when the light caught it.

"It's a job," I answered. "That changes how I look at it." Then I asked, "Would you mind answering a few questions?"

He opened his hands as if to show that they held nothing. "You've spoken to others far more advanced than I. What remains that I might answer?"

Observant fellow. Like Nakahatchi, he knew why I was here.

"Part of my job," I replied, "is to protect your display. I'd like to understand what makes it so important." I had no idea what Nakahatchi's agenda might be. "As you say, I've talked to several people. But they all have their own perspectives. How do you see the situation?"

From his seat Nakahatchi watched me as if he were too Zen to shoo off a cockroach, never mind squash the pest.

Komatori looked politely quizzical. "You want to understand the significance of the chops to Nakahatchi *sensei*?"

"That, too," I admitted. "But I'd also like to know how he got them in the first place. And I'm curious how he plans to guard them after the tournament."

Which wasn't any of my business, but I didn't care.

"Axbrewder-*san*"—apparently *san* came more naturally to him than *mister*—"you'll understand that the chops were put in my master's care quite recently. Indeed, we're concerned about their safety. Perhaps you'll consent to advise us?"

Involuntarily I smiled. He couldn't have told me to keep my nose out of *Essential Shotokan*'s affairs more courteously if he'd asked Miss Manners to translate for him.

I didn't try to match him. Cheerfully rude, I countered, "Not without getting paid for it." Then I conceded, still smiling, "I mean, I couldn't say anything useful unless I analyzed your security, saw where you're planning to keep the display, and knew how much you can afford to spend on improvements."

By tomorrow I'd be off the payroll. And I had other things to do.

Komatori withdrew the question with exquisite grace. "As you say."

I wasn't accustomed to dealing with manners like his. "Still," I observed, trying not to lose my way, "you've been thinking about your security. You must anticipate trouble."

He treated me to a sample of Asian inscrutability. "It's always wise to consider trouble."

"Sure. But you must be worried about something specific. Break-ins? General burglary?" If so, it was Lacone's problem—and Watchdog's—not Nakahatchi's. As long as the chops had been adequately insured. "Or don't you trust your neighbors?"

Lacone had told me that Soon's *Tae Kwon Do Academy*, Gravel's *Malaysian Fighting Arts*, and Hong's *Traditional Wing Chun* occupied Martial America alongside *Essential Shotokan*. He'd mentioned two or three other schools, but they hadn't moved in yet.

"Axbrewder-*san*," Komatori replied, "is this your first experience among martial artists?" He indicated the tournament with a discreet gesture.

I nodded.

"Yet you must be aware," he went on, "that Western cultures differ from Eastern in many ways. For example, they understand honor differently.

"You're an honorable man." Giving me the benefit of the doubt. "Nakahatchi *sensei* is honorable as well. Would you prefer death to dishonesty? There West and East may be similar. But would you prefer death to disrespect?"

He let his question hang delicately in the air.

That was too subtle. "Humor me, Mr. Komatori. I'm Western. Assume I *don't* understand."

His tone hinted at a sigh. "To a man like my master, your question is disrespectful. To answer it would be dishonorable."

In other words, he wouldn't say anything that might sound critical of another school.

"Thanks," I growled. "Now I get it. I think."

"As you say," he responded, "your duties don't require you to consider these matters."

The infernally courteous sonofabitch may've been making excuses for me.

If I didn't get something concrete from him soon, I'd have to tear my hair. Groping for a crack in his demeanor, I tried a different approach.

"Maybe this will help me understand. Why didn't your *sensei* compete in the Masters' *Kata*? Was that about honor too?"

Or was it just public relations? Maybe Nakahatchi thought that sitting in judgment on the event would do more to promote his school than trying to win it.

But if Komatori's demeanor had any cracks, that sure as hell wasn't one of them. "Indeed so," he answered smoothly. "Competitions test individual excellence. My master wanted to express his respect for those who chose to test themselves.

"Yet competition holds no true place in the study of the martial arts. Funakoshi *sensei*, the founder of Shotokan, once wrote, 'The ultimate aim of the art of karate lies not in victory or defeat, but in the perfection of the character of its participants.' " As if that settled the matter, Komatori concluded. "My master has no need to test his excellence."

Nakahatchi gazed down on us with the detached and benevolent sorrow of a *santo*. Apparently he was too busy becoming perfect to take the risks Hong and Soon did.

So much martial piety got on my nerves. Maybe I was just too Western—or grubby—to understand all these refinements. I considered my options for a moment. But I found that I couldn't just walk away, so I girded up my loins, as a guy I knew used to say, and made one more attempt.

"There's something else I'd like to ask you, if you don't consider it disrespectful. How does your *sensei* happen to own those chops?"

How did a Japanese *karate-ka* in the US gain possession of what might well be a Chinese national treasure?

I hoped that Komatori might squirm a bit, but he didn't. "A common misconception, Axbrewder-*san*," he assured me. "My master doesn't own the chops. He holds them in trust.

"Less than a month ago, he visited his own *sensei*, Mato Hakatani, in Japan. When he returned, he brought the chops here. They were placed in his care by Hakatani *sensei*, who purchased them many years ago from a perhaps disreputable dealer in Chinese antiquities." Komatori's manner conveyed refined distaste. "Since he purchased them, Hakatani *sensei* has been troubled in his mind. They were sold as genuine, but at a price much below their apparent worth. What's to be done with them? What's the course of honor?

"If genuine, they're of inestimable value to the Wing Chun schools of China. To make a gift of them would be fitting. But there are many Wing Chun schools, many traditions. Which should Hakatani *sensei* choose? He doesn't wish to slight any style or tradition.

"Also there's the problem of governments. They're inclined to claim such gifts as national treasures. The intended recipients might never see them."

Komatori paused briefly, then added, "And if they aren't genuine— Making a gift of them might be considered as an insult."

I thought he was chewing more than he could bite off. But he didn't ask my opinion, and I didn't offer it. Instead I suggested, "Surely you can authenticate them somehow? That would solve at least one of your problems."

He nodded. "That's why Hakatani *sensei* wanted the chops brought here. Of course, the necessary expertise is available in both China and Japan. But Hakatani *sensei* feared that any Chinese"—for an instant Komatori's tone suggested discomfort—"or Japanese authority might be tainted by self-interest. Personal or national gain might inspire a false judgment. In this country, my master may find an authority whose assessment supports confidence."

It was my turn to nod, so I did. Antiques appraisers weren't thick on the ground, but they weren't exactly scarce either. In Carner, the Land of Recreational Income, there had to be a few who could date the chops accurately—and wouldn't give a shit about their status as icons.

But Komatori hadn't finished. "In addition," he said, "Hakatani *sensei* is elderly. He no longer feels able to guard the chops effectively. As a mark of esteem, he gave them to Nakahatchi *sensei*.

"Finally, Hakatani *sensei* believes that if the chops are genuine, they're too precious to be held privately. Such a treasure must be shared. In Carner, *karate-ka* from coast to coast will be able to see the display."

I understood the sentiment, but I wasn't persuaded. "Maybe so. But the more people you let in, the greater the risks.

"Which means," I added sharply, "your teacher is in deep shit if anything happens."

Again Komatori didn't hesitate. Instead he replied with another display of inscrutability, "If the chops were lost, and my master could not recover them, he would end his life."

That sounded like craziness to me, honor exaggerated to the point of fanaticism. Nevertheless it fit the intuitive picture I'd picked up from *Sifu* Hong's *kata*. Under the right circumstances, there was no limit to the amount of blood those chops might cost.

If I heard much more of this, I'd go crazy myself. "Well, thanks, Mr. Komatori," I muttered. "I'll let you go now. I've taken too much of your time."

He made a deprecating gesture. "Please, Axbrewder-*san*. Your interest honors us."

Nakahatchi nodded as if in assent. Giving us his blessing.

That did it. I positively could not stomach so much courtesy. Leaning toward Hideo confidentially, I asked, "Then tell me one more thing. How did you come by that scar?"

Like it was any of my business.

But he still refused to take anything I said amiss. "A training accident," he answered. His smile hinted at self-mockery. "When I was younger."

I raised my eyebrows. "You train with live blades?"

I'd spent my life surrounded by people who took things amiss.

He shrugged gently. "Only when the student suffers from arrogance."

In other words, his benign and insufferable teacher had taught him a lesson that nearly cost him an eye.

Charming. I was so impressed I wanted to retch.

As I walked away, I itched to wash my hands of this tournament, the IAMA, and all martial artists. I was wasting my time here. I wanted to go after Bernie's killer. That crime, at least, I could hope to understand. Intuitively, irrationally, I believed that it was linked to the chops. But I also believed that it had nothing to do with Nakahatchi's and Komatori's refined notions of honor and politeness.

Regardless of what I wanted, however, I still had a job to do. The tournament continued to trudge along, doling out trophies like communion wafers, and I was being paid to act diligent until all of the IAMA's elect had received their validation.

Too fed up to watch any more events, I spent my time chewing on the question of how I proposed to track down the heavyset man.

My only connection to Bernie's killer.

Unfortunately I was in Carner, not Puerta del Sol—entirely out of my element. I didn't know the city, hadn't spent years among the lost men and women who frequented Carner's shadows and angles and alleys. Those benighted souls almost certainly knew what was really going on. At home I could've found the drop just by asking around. Here I had no idea who to approach.

Much as I hated the prospect, I'd need Marshal's help. Or Detective Moy's.

To pacify my chagrin, I left the tournament to go look at Moy's mug shot. With no success. An hour and a half later, I was back. Apparently no one had missed me.

Time passed. Events ended. Trophies were awarded. New events began. And eventually Sue Rasmussen announced a supper break, during which the IAMA functionaries would clear the floor for Fumio Demura's demonstration. The Grand Championships would follow when the rings had been reset.

I considered taking the opportunity to call Marshal, but I decided against it. He might not appreciate hearing from me on a

Sunday evening, when—I couldn't help thinking this—he was probably alone with Ginny. And he might not be able to answer my questions until Monday anyway. So I ate a quick meal in the coffee shop, braced myself to endure five or six more wasted hours, and went back to the tournament hall.

By then the night-shift Security team was on duty. I spent a few minutes talking with The Luxury's Deputy Chief of Security, pretending to find out what he wanted me to do, but really just determining where and when I could pick up my paycheck. Then I moved up onto the dais to watch Demura and his students on the off chance that I might see something I understood.

As usual, the demonstration started late.

And it started without me. While Rasmussen proclaimed the presence of the famous teacher, much-published author, and noted Hollywood fight choreographer and stunt double Fumio Demura *sensei*, Alex Lacone arrived, trailing Sammy Posten like a dinghy in his wake. Broadcasting enthusiasm on all bandwidths, he practically bounded up to the dais, consulted briefly with Anson Sternway, then beckoned for me.

"Mr. Axbrewder," he boomed. "Just the man I want to see."

Rasmussen covered her mike and asked him to lower his voice. Somehow she contrived to sound pleasant about it, despite her disaffection for me.

Lacone replied with an unrepentant grin and drew me to the back of the dais. From there he dropped like a sack of cement to the floor. Posten followed by sitting on the edge of the platform, reaching his legs downward, and scooting his butt awkwardly off the dais. Sternway sprang down lightly. I managed to join them without falling over.

The knot in my stomach told me that I knew what they wanted.

If Lacone were actually glad to see me, he was the only one. Sternway greeted me with a flat gaze and an unrevealing nod. Posten muttered my name ungraciously, but didn't say anything else.

On the other side of the dais, the spectators erupted with laughter and applause. The four of us ignored them.

"Mr. Axbrewder," the developer began, "we're all impressed with the way you handled things yesterday. I said so at the time. You know what you're doing, and that's a fact. *I* wouldn't have spotted those crooks if they were the only people in the room."

That wasn't what I would've called high praise, but I kept my mouth shut.

"As you know," he went on, "we have a problem. That is to say, Sammy and I do. It's the same problem you were hired for this weekend. Nakahatchi *sensei*'s antiques."

Damn it anyway. The sonofabitch was about to offer me a job.

The spectators cheered. Demura must've had them eating out of his hand.

"When the tournament ends," Lacone explained unnecessarily, "the display goes back to *Essential Shotokan*. Until then, it's covered by The Luxury's insurance, and the IAMA's. But after that it's my problem. I'll have to provide adequate insurance."

Two days ago I would've been glad to hear it. Now I wasn't sure how I felt.

"Watchdog and I had a deal worked out," Lacone continued. "It was exorbitant"—he winked at Posten to show that he was kidding—"but my bean counters told me I could afford it. Unfortunately," he sighed, smiling on a rueful wavelength, "Watchdog now thinks they underestimated the risks involved.

"I guess we all assumed that surrounding the display with martial artists would protect it pretty well. But we learned yesterday"—he put on a show of being tactful—"how should I put this? Martial artists don't have the right kind of expertise. They didn't spot those crooks. You did."

His grin radiated enough heat to raise blisters as he forged ahead. "After you demonstrated the realities of the situation, Watchdog decided—and I have to agree—we need to reconsider our position. Meaning no disrespect to Nakahatchi *sensei*, or any other school in Martial America, that display needs better protection."

By which he meant that Watchdog, in the person of Paranoid Posten, had reneged on the earlier agreement. Posten had panicked yesterday, and now Watchdog intended to raise Lacone's rates.

The developer beamed radioactive sincerity at me. "After tonight, Mr. Axbrewder, I want you to take on the same job you've had this weekend. Keeping an eye on those antiques." He winked conspicuously. "I think I can guarantee I pay better."

He ought to. By my standards, I was already getting paid pretty well. But Lacone wouldn't do this unless hiring security got him a substantial break from Watchdog. Knowing insurance companies—not to mention developers—I was sure that he'd save a hell of a lot more than he offered me.

Posten's expression suggested reluctant agreement. Yesterday I'd made the mistake of telling him that the chops would be in more danger once they reached *Essential Shotokan*.

Now was my chance. All I had to say was, Thanks, but no thanks, I have other commitments. But I couldn't focus on it. I was too busy wondering why Sternway had tagged along. Posten's presence I understood, but what did the IAMA have to do with Lacone's problems? Hell, hadn't Sternway repeatedly declined to join Martial America?

If I was right, the drop wasn't my only link to Bernie's killer. The chops were involved somehow.

Trying to think, I stalled for time. "Mr. Lacone, I'm a private investigator, not a security guard. Frankly, I took this job because I need the work. But I'm not bragging when I say I'm wasted here. The money The Luxury and the IAMA saved by hiring me is trivial compared to what I cost."

Posten nodded in the background.

Firmly, I concluded, "If you're looking for someone to walk through the building every night punching a time-clock, you could spend less and get better service."

The audience applauded on cue. Sternway appeared to watch the rest of us without paying any attention.

But Lacone acted like I'd said just what he wanted to hear. With a happy grin, he replied, "That exactly why I think you're the man for the job. We already hire a security service, but all they do is patrol the parking lot and check the doors. A determined crook could get past them easily.

"And—"

There he stopped. Instead of continuing, he deferred unexpectedly to Sternway.

HRH knew what Lacone wanted him to say. "The situation is delicate, Brew," he explained. "As you know, *Traditional Wing Chun* is also located in Martial America, and *Sifu* Hong believes strongly that the chops should belong to him. And there are other rivalries. Master Soon's *Tae Kwon Do Academy* is jealous as well. The chops are irrelevant to Tae Kwon Do itself. But men like

Master Soon resent the status those chops confer. They consider it undeserved."

"In other words—" Lacone put in.

"In other words," I interrupted, "you're more worried about problems inside Martial America than outside. That's why you think you need someone like me."

Someone with no martial loyalties.

Master Soon had left the hall ahead of the drop.

"I recommended you," Sternway remarked for reasons that weren't clear to me. Why the fuck did *he* care?

And just like that, without warning, I was hooked. Instead of rejecting Lacone's offer, I put my head into the trap.

"All right," I said, even though the very idea scared me. "How about this? You can hire me for a week, as a consultant. I'll analyze your security, suggest ways to improve it. At the same time, I'll poke around where people don't want me. Look into their backgrounds, their connections, see what I can turn up.

"You'll pay me twice what I'm making now. Give me the keys to the building, let me do the job my way. And after a week we'll both decide whether we want to keep it up."

Then, because I didn't like Posten and didn't know how far I could trust Deborah, I added, "If that's acceptable to Watchdog, of course."

Posten acquiesced, scowling like a man with indigestion.

Lacone didn't hesitate. "When can you start?"

"After lunch tomorrow. Say around one-thirty?" That would give me time to take care of at least some of my own affairs.

The developer stuck out his hand. "It's a deal."

We shook on it.

Sternway consulted the air as if the rest of us weren't present.

I wanted to get this over with. "In that case, let's meet here at one-thirty. If Nakahatchi leaves the display in the manager's safe room until then, we can escort it back to Martial America. When it's in place, you can show me around, make sure I understand what's involved."

"Fine, fine." Lacone beamed in all directions. "Whatever you say. One-thirty it is."

Wrapping an arm around Sammy's shoulders, he drew the Senior Security Adviser with him toward the end of the platform.

Before HRH could join them, I said in the same tone I'd used on Lacone, "Mr. Sternway, I've got a couple of questions."

Apparently he wanted to seem affable. "I thought we were on a first-name basis, Brew. Call me Anson."

He kept changing the rules. One minute I was Axbrewder-with-disdain, the next I was colleague-Brew. I couldn't keep up with his vagaries, so I avoided the issue.

Bluntly I told him, "I don't understand why you're involved in all this. I thought you wanted no part of Martial America."

I'd just been hired to poke around where people might not want me.

He frowned without much conviction. "I must have given you the wrong impression. I'd like nothing better than to see Martial America succeed. If it does, it will benefit the martial arts generally, as well as promoting its member schools. In fact, I persuaded three schools to relocate there. I'll join them as soon as the complex makes enough money to support lower rents."

I raised my eyebrows skeptically.

"I've been involved with Martial America from the beginning," he went on. "I helped design the building. Mr. Lacone needed the advice of a martial artist. I served as his consultant."

Just to be sure I'd read him right, I asked, "Did you volunteer?"

"Of course not." His tone said, You must be joking. "Mr. Lacone hired me."

So that was about money too, not some hypothetical benefit to the martial arts.

"Did you also get paid for persuading those three schools?"

I half expected him to take offense, but he was too sure of himself for that. "Certainly," he said as if the answer were self-evident. "Time and effort cost money, Brew. You know that as well as I do. Considering what Mr Lacone hopes to accomplish with Martial America, my involvement is a perfectly normal expense. And I would say it's necessary. He won't succeed without me."

Thus spake HRH, Director of the IAMA. Probably I should've responded by bowing my head to the floor. But I didn't. Instead I grabbed my opportunity to ask a different kind of question.

"I've heard that you call Tae Kwon Do 'a toy martial art'. What's that all about?"

In an instant his manner changed. He seemed to condense in front of me, gather for an explosion. At the same time his stance lifted as if he'd grown suddenly lighter. Without transition he became a shout of danger.

"Perhaps I should have been more discreet," he pronounced, frowning. "I assume you'll respect my confidence."

I nodded like he could trust me implicitly. I wasn't eager to get hit by Parker Neill's teacher.

He studied me for a moment. Then he risked answering my question.

"Master Soon is a fine martial artist, but he can't deny or alter the fact that TKD deserves to be called a toy. It has become the Korean national sport. When a martial art becomes a sport, it loses its seriousness, its credibility."

"Because sports are controlled by rules," I put it just to make Sternway think I understood, "and real martial artists know there aren't any."

"Exactly." The sense of threat he radiated began to ease.

"But if Soon is such a fine martial artist," I continued, "he must feel tarnished by what's being done to his art. He must want to regain face."

"Exactly," Sternway repeated. But abruptly he seemed to lose interest. Or maybe I'd touched a nerve. He cocked his head like he was listening to Demura's audience, then informed me brusquely, "I have to go, Brew. We'll be starting more events in a minute."

I didn't try to keep him. "Thanks for your time."

He pretended to make a polite departure, but his heart obviously wasn't in it. In seconds he left me alone with the leads and cables that connected the IAMA to its fans and adherents.

I'd missed Fumio Demura's demonstration completely.

13

Shortly before midnight, we put the chops away. When the night-shift Security chief had reclaimed the cell phone and confirmed arrangements to pay me, I left The Luxury and slogged across the asphalt to my waiting car.

I half-expected to find the Subaru melted on its wheels. If it felt as drained as I did— But apparently it was made of sterner stuff. The engine caught without much coaxing. The headlights fixed the parking lot with a walleyed glare. Even the AC almost worked.

For a minute or two, I leaned my forehead on the steering wheel, just trying to remember who I was. Then I retrieved the .45 and tucked it into my belt, shoulder holster and all. Anchored by its ambiguous familiarity, I drove back to the apartment.

Like a coward, I hoped Ginny wouldn't be there. I didn't feel real enough to face her. In the past twenty-four hours, I'd lost track of myself. Deborah Messenger, Alex Lacone. Parker Neill and Anson Sternway. Bernie. As far as I could tell, I'd become a figment of someone else's imagination.

While I drove, however, I decided that accepting Lacone's offer made my kind of sense. I wasn't the right man for the job—I lacked the mindset and experience of a good "security consultant." But it would keep me in contact with the chops. And that in turn might lead me to Bernie's killer.

He hadn't been murdered to protect a gear-bag full of pilfered loot. *That* I was sure of. The real stakes were a whole lot higher.

Deborah, on the other hand—

Wouldn't Ginny consider that a betrayal? I sure as hell felt betrayed every time she turned to another man. I *still* wanted to eviscerate Marshal Viviter, even though he treated me like we were friends.

I'd told Deborah that things were finally clear between Ginny and me, but obviously they weren't clear enough to relieve my umbilical fear of Ginny's reactions. When I saw through the window that someone had left a light on in the apartment living room, my heart nearly collapsed.

I parked the Subaru anyway, but for a while I couldn't get out of the car. Damn it, I'd made things as clear as I could. Hadn't I? We weren't partners anymore. In any way. I'd practically etched it on the floor of the hotel lobby.

Things were clear enough, but *I* wasn't.

I didn't understand Deborah Messenger. I didn't trust her, or how I felt about her, or what we did together.

I might've sat there for hours, but eventually self-disgust made me move. Taking the reins of my life between my teeth, I locked the Subaru for the night and let myself into the apartment.

Ginny sat in an armchair near the phone, pretending to read a magazine. Fully dressed, like she was about to go out—or had just come in. Purse beside her on the floor. Eyes so sharp you'd think she'd used a whetstone on them. I knew she was only pretending to read because she had the pages of the magazine clamped in her claw hard enough to tear them.

"Brew." She sounded unnaturally casual, but her gaze went straight through me. "It's good to see you."

Usually when I felt this bad around her I said something nasty. Fighting the impulse, I turned away to relock the door. Next I shrugged off my jacket, pulled the .45 in its holster out of my belt, and slumped almost prostrate on the couch.

That was as close as I could come to letting down my defenses.

She didn't say anything else until I finally faced her. Then, with the same eerie lack of intensity, she asked, "Are you all right?"

"Ginny—" I covered my face with my hands, rubbed at the stubble on my cheeks. For several heartbeats I held my breath. As I let it out, I dragged down my hands. "You're scaring me. You sound too calm. What's going on here?"

She smiled thinly, as if she'd recognized something about herself that she didn't like. "It seems to me," she answered from a distance, "we've already spent enough time yelling at each other. I don't want to do that anymore."

I tried again. "Ginny—" But she went on without me.

"We aren't partners. And you're right," she conceded, "I decided that without consulting you. I told myself I didn't care how you felt about it. But I was wrong. On both counts. We have a lot of history. That doesn't change just because we've forgotten how to get along." Her gaze searched me like a scalpel. "You're still important to me. And I"—she spread her good hand—"owe you something better than an apology."

She was going to break my heart. As recently as yesterday, I would've snarled, As important as Marshal? But not tonight.

Tonight I faced her and waited.

"Brew—" Abruptly she looked down. Her hair swung forward to veil her expression. "I can't be your partner. Not now. I can't stand what that does to us. But I'm not going to move out. And I don't want you to. I'd rather"—she shrugged helplessly—"muddle through this together somehow."

I didn't think I could bear it. I wanted to sneer or yell, hit her with the most hurtful thing I could think of. Nevertheless the sheer difficulty of what she offered restrained me.

I was at least equally responsible for ruining our relationship. I owed it to her to risk as much as she did. Hell, I owed it to myself.

Instead of lashing out, I said bleakly, "Don't go that far until I've been honest with you. You have a right to know where you stand with me."

Even if the truth drove her away. I had to take the chance—

The time I'd caught her in bed with another man, I'd hit her. Actually *hit* her. And that had cost me something I couldn't retrieve. I'd been letting people put their hands on me ever since. If I had to hurt her now, I wanted to do it openly, instead of leaving her at the mercy of an accidental discovery.

Sam Drayton had told me, *You're stronger than you realize.*

"I met a woman at the tournament," I told her. "She seems to like me." The words made me want to weep. "We spent the night together last night."

The magazine fell from Ginny's grip. She'd torn through all the pages. Her eyes avoided me behind her hair.

For the second time, I held my breath. I could feel myself start to die, as if I'd amputated the thing that made my heart beat.

Cruelly far away, she murmured, "I'm glad."

That shocked me. " 'Glad'?" The word came out like a croak. "Are you sure?"

Slowly she raised her head to show me another slight smile that resembled recognition. "Well—" Then her mouth twisted. "Glad enough for government work, anyway."

That was more consideration than I'd ever given her.

A moment later she asked like a sigh, "And you're all right now?" Ruefully she admitted, "Tonight I can't tell."

I shrugged against the back of the couch, trying to adjust my heart so it would fit in my chest. "I've got a new job, if that's what you mean." Obviously it wasn't. But I didn't know how else to tell her what she needed to hear. "I should be able to pay my share of the bills."

I meant to stay, if she did.

She nodded. Apparently she could accept whatever I had the strength to offer.

She sat where she was for a minute or two, her eyes shrouded. Then she pushed herself to her feet. "I'm going to bed," she informed me quietly. "I need to get an early start tomorrow."

As did I. But I let her go without saying so.

Someday, I promised myself, *some*day I was going to ask about her job with Marshal. I was going to let her see that I wanted to know. But not now. For the time being it was enough that we'd survived.

Maybe tomorrow—

I didn't get the chance then, however. When she said early, she meant *early*. By the time I'd lugged my carcass out of bed, she was already gone. Which may've been just as well, under the circumstances. I had plenty of other things to think about.

So I thought about them without making much progress while I showered, shaved, put on clean clothes, ate breakfast, started a load of laundry, tidied the apartment, and finally wedged myself back into the Subaru. By nine o'clock I was back at The Luxury, heading for the Security office. Despite Carner's unrelieved heat, I wore my rather limp suit jacket to conceal the .45 under my arm.

Slade was on duty, holding down Bernie's desk until The Luxury named a successor. His manner didn't inspire confidence, but eventually he managed to steer me through some final paperwork and hand me a check.

It was the biggest check I'd seen with my name on it in years.

Nevertheless I didn't pause to congratulate myself. First things first. From The Luxury I went to a bank and exchanged the check for cash. Then I used my map to locate a cellular phone store.

With a phone I could get to work.

Sitting in the Subaru with the engine running and the AC on high, I called Professional Investigations and asked for Marshal.

Beatrix Amity greeted me like I'd never been rude to her in my life. "Just a moment, Mr. Axbrewder. Mr. Viviter asked me to put you through. I'll just make sure he's available."

Which reminded me that I still didn't know what the hell he got out of being so nice to me. My rather bitter theory that he was just doing Ginny a favor had started to look pretty tattered.

He kept me waiting for five minutes or so. Then he came on the line. "Brew?" The connection made him sound less sincere than usual. "Sorry to keep you waiting. I thought I'd hear from you, but I was in the middle of something when you called."

I also didn't know why he bothered to apologize. I was just riding his coattails—I didn't actually work for him. He owed me nothing.

"I've got time," I told him brusquely. That was as close as I could come to courtesy on short notice—at least with him. "Did you get anything?"

"Tut tut." Despite my phone's inadequacies, I heard a grin in his tone. "I've already talked to you about your manners." Then he went on more seriously, "And if *you* don't have any legal standing in this case, *I* certainly don't. Why do you assume I can get anything?"

"Because you like Bernie," I retorted. "And because you know there's something wrong about his death."

Deliberately I didn't add, And because I asked you. That means something to you. For the same reason you got me a job.

"Like *why* he's dead," Marshal observed.

"But there's more," I continued. "Whoever did it took the weapon." Briefly I told him about Bernie's flik—and my decision not to inform Moy.

He considered that for a long moment. "You're saying," he pronounced softly, "he didn't accidentally end up dead. You're saying he was murdered."

"I'm not sure about premeditation," I added. "Unless Bernie had skeletons in his closet—" I let the idea hang. "But the goon who did it isn't even trying to pretend self-defense. As far as I'm concerned, that spells 'intention.' "

And a desire to make the intention known.

Marshal got the point. His manner turned businesslike.

"You asked several questions about Bernie," he said more briskly. "Past dealings with Watchdog or Lacone, and so on. I can't begin to answer them unless I assign someone to dig into it—and I still wouldn't have any standing.

"But—" He paused for effect, then admitted, "Luckily Moy owes me a couple of favors. I have a copy of the ME's report."

Sweat ran down my ribs despite the AC. "And—?"

Now Moy knew I wasn't going to leave Bernie's death alone.

"Death consistent with being hacked in the throat with a thin blunt object. Crushed larynx, asphyxiation. No surprise there.

"Flecks of enamel paint in the wound. Again, no surprise."

The marks I'd seen on the walls of the stall must've been made while Bernie fought for his life. While he still had a grip on the flik. Its coils would've picked up a lot of paint.

"Also," Marshal went on, "fibers of dark blue cloth. From a navy blazer, apparently. Which by coincidence," he remarked sourly, "is what Bernie was wearing at the time."

I practically held my breath. "Did the ME match those fibers to Bernie's blazer?"

I heard pages flip. "Doesn't say so here."

"*Damn* it." In frustration I rapped the steering wheel with the knuckles of one fist. "That's sloppy."

"You're in a charitable mood this morning." Marshal wasn't amused. "Have you forgotten who didn't tell Moy about the flik?"

I swore again—to myself this time. Moy didn't know Bernie had been killed with his own weapon. The detective had no reason to think those fibers might've come from someone else's blazer.

Every guard at The Luxury, as well as everyone who worked the tournament for the IAMA, wore a navy blazer. Not to mention the inevitable dozen or so spectators. For three days those blazers had been as common as gear-bags.

Groping, I asked, "What about bruises? Other marks on the body? Anything that suggests where the fibers came from?"

I meant, Anything other than my own bad judgment?

"Let me see," Marshal murmured. More pages flipped. Then

he reported, "Contusions on the knuckles of the right hand. More flecks of paint." Bernie must've struck his hand while defending himself. "Bruises around the right wrist." Made when his assailant grabbed him to take away the flik. "And a deep one on the left cheek." A blow to stun him. "The ME says the bruises occurred immediately before death. None match the death wound. They weren't made by the same weapon.

"In other words, still no surprises. At least for us." After a moment, Marshal added with less sarcasm, "If I were Moy, I'd want to know which hand the assailant used. The ME doesn't say."

Oh, perfect. *That* was genuinely sloppy. It made a difference. Left hand to right wrist, right hand free to strike. A punch to the cheek, snatch the flik, and swing. Bernie could've been killed in one motion. Continued action—possible accident or miscalculation. But right hand to right wrist, left hand out of range. Especially in a restroom stall. In that case, Bernie must've been killed by a separate motion. His assailant had to switch hands in order to strike. Which implied a greater degree of intention.

Before I could complain, however, Marshal said, "In fact, I think I'll mention that to Moy. Professional curiosity, and so on. I was going to call him anyway"—a grin sparkled in his voice—"thank him for his generosity. Who knows? A question like that may make him look at the case harder."

Damn Marshal Viviter, anyway. He got harder to dislike every day. If I actually had to stop hating him, I'd probably go crackers. Crushed Saltines all the way.

Ginny'd left me for a better man. Just as I'd always feared.

Chagrin made me crabby—chagrin and ego. Instead of thanking him, I demanded abruptly, "Are you going to research Bernie?" I may've sounded just a touch ungracious.

Another man—a lesser man—would've snapped back, but Marshal didn't give me that satisfaction. "You still haven't told me why," he countered reasonably.

Of course I hadn't. I wasn't exactly proud of relying on him like this. Nevertheless I owed him. He'd already given me more help than I had any right to. And I had nowhere else to turn.

Swallowing my pride—or at least my defensiveness—I answered him as well as I could.

"Bernie wasn't killed by the drop. Over a few watches and

wallets? I don't think so. There was someone else in the restroom. Someone with a hell of a lot more to lose." Or to gain. "Don't ask me what. Or why he and the drop were together. All I'm sure of is that Bernie recognized him, and he didn't want Bernie to identify him."

I sighed, thinking of the Security Chief's fragile corpse, the sheer pointlessness of his death. "The only thing worth killing for at the tournament," I explained, "were those antiques. But maybe there's something in Bernie's past. Something that connects him to someone at the tournament indirectly."

Marshal didn't say anything for a moment. Then he reached a decision. "All right," he announced firmly. "I'll look into it. But there's only so much I can do without legal standing.

"In the meantime, what have you got for me?"

I couldn't help noticing that he agreed to what I wanted before he asked for anything back. No *quid pro quo.*

Ashamed of myself, I made an effort to tone down my sarcasm. "Not much. But I've picked up a couple of things that seem to be common knowledge in karate circles.

"One is that Sternway is hard up for money. He's obsessive about it. The IAMA people I talked to blame his wife. They think she's taking him to the cleaners."

"That sounds like her, frankly," Marshal remarked.

I didn't stop there. "Also he may be having an affair with a lawyer named Sue Rasmussen. I'm told she's one of his students." I hesitated, then added, "I don't think she likes me."

Marshal replied with a humorless chuckle. "Really?" Then he said more seriously, "Now there's a nice ethical question for you.

"Mai Sternway has hired us for protection because she thinks her husband is stalking her. She wants us to prove it's him, which will improve her bargaining position. But does that mean we're obliged to give her other kinds of information she could use against him?"

I was in no mood for his scruples. I was still kicking myself because I hadn't told Moy about the flik. And Marshal had a gift for making me feel inadequate. With more than my usual charm, I countered, "Surely you aren't asking *me*?"

He groaned. "No, Brew. It was rhetorical. I'm just thinking aloud."

Gritting my teeth, I forced myself to say, "I may be able to help you more later. I've got another job. Lacone wants me to baby-sit those chops for a while, earn him a break on his insurance rates. I start this afternoon.

"Since I'll be working for him instead of the IAMA or Anson Sternway, I'll have fewer constraints." Fewer scruples of my own. "And he acts like he's ready to elope with Sternway. He may let something interesting slip."

"Well, good for you." Despite my rudeness, Marshal sounded sincere. "You must've made my referral look pretty good. Even if Alex has already married Anson, he's still a businessman. He wouldn't hire you simply because I recommended you."

I could taste Saltines. They were in my future somewhere, waiting for my resistance to crumble.

But he wasn't done. "For some odd reason, Brew," he commented, "you inspire confidence. God knows how. If you were any more irritable, you'd be arrested as a public nuisance. But after just three days of relative drudgery, you get offered a job that could be real work. And you convince me to spend money and manpower on a case that doesn't belong to either of us.

"Just one word of advice." Like flipping a switch, he reassumed his professional detachment. "Don't treat Alex the way you do me. He doesn't really need you—and he's accustomed to a bit more sucking up."

Viviter hung up without asking for my phone number. No doubt Beatrix had it on her caller ID.

The Subaru had started to overheat. The squirrels caged under the hood needed more rpms to stand the strain of the AC.

I knew exactly how they felt. I had so much sweat on my face that I couldn't keep my sunglasses up. And I de*tested* Saltines. Instead of pausing to brush the crumbs out of my head, I pulled out of my parking space while I dialed Deborah's private number at Watchdog.

Marshal had that effect on me, made me feel like I needed to prove something.

In the wrong frame of mind, my brain full of inappropriate clutter, I pretended that I knew how to navigate in Carner while my call went through to Deborah.

When the phone jammed against my ear said, "This is Deborah

Messenger," I nearly drove off the road. She sounded just as brisk and professional as Marshal Viviter, but her voice was still the same one I'd heard laughing and crooning and gasping less than thirty-six hours ago.

I had to haul the Subaru away from a collision before I could answer, "Deborah. It's Brew."

"Brew! Are you all right? You sound—" She may've heard the near miss in my tone.

I struggled to relax. "Don't ask. It's too embarrassing to explain. I'm fine." As fine as sweat, adrenaline, and crushed crackers allowed. Since I didn't want to discuss my driving, I lunged at the first topic I could think of. "I guess you knew Lacone was going to offer me a job."

She accepted the shift smoothly. "I wasn't sure. Sometimes men like Alex won't take advice from a woman." She laughed deep in her throat. "On the other hand, he doesn't like Sammy much—and Sammy doesn't like you. That may have influenced him a bit."

Apparently she'd urged Lacone to hire me. I wasn't sure how I felt about that, so I stayed away from it.

"Anyway," I went on, "I start this afternoon. Right now I'm lost somewhere in Carner. Don't take it personally if I sound distracted. I don't know this place yet."

She chuckled into my ear. "You didn't get lost Saturday night."

For a moment I actively blushed. "It's amazing what comes back to you when you're inspired," I muttered awkwardly.

" 'Inspired.' " I heard her glowing through the connection. "I like that."

I gripped the steering wheel hard enough to leave impressions of my fingerprints. "Maybe you'll still like it the next time. When can I see you again?"

I had to ask. My hormones didn't leave me much choice.

What could she possibly gain from me?

"Let me check my schedule." The clicking of a keyboard carried to my phone. She must've used a computer to keep track of her duties. "Damn. Not tonight. I'll be at a seminar all evening." More clicking. "How about dinner tomorrow?"

"Just tell me where and when."

She did. Not having a hand free, I didn't write any of it down. I didn't need to—I was in no danger of forgetting.

"Good," I said when she'd given me directions. "That's a long wait, but I can probably keep my legs crossed until then."

She chuckled again. "See that you do."

If this kept up, I'd drive into the side of a building. Somehow I forced myself to change the subject.

"In the meantime"—I cleared my throat—"how do you plan to get Nakahatchi's chops appraised? If you don't mind my asking."

After yesterday, I was sure that Posten would insist on speeding up the process.

Deborah took my abruptness in stride. "No, I don't mind. You're on our side.

"We're in touch with an appraiser from New York. Rather well-known. He's agreed to fly out next week—for a substantial fee, of course."

I veered for a freeway ramp with my usual liquid grace. "You mean there's no one local?" In sports-rich Carner?

"Well, there is," she admitted. "A man named Carliss Swilley. He sells Oriental antiques. And he offers an appraisal service. He's an odious little pedant, but he has good credentials.

"However"—she sighed mock-seriously—"Watchdog's home offices are in New York. *Nat*urally they don't think an authority from mere Carner has enough credibility to suit them."

Naturally. Even in Puerta del Sol, New Yorkers were famous for their cosmopolitan outlook on the rest of the country. But around here people probably resented it more.

"I get the picture. But I think it's a bad idea to wait that long. Bad for you, bad for Lacone." Not to mention bad for Nakahatchi. "You need some kind of appraisal on paper right away. Even if the home offices insist on redoing it next week."

Deborah was silent for a long moment. When she spoke again, I could barely hear her through the freeway noise.

"You think something might happen to the chops."

She didn't point out the obvious fact that I hadn't even seen Martial America yet. Or that she and Posten together probably had ten times my experience with this kind of security. For some reason she seemed to trust me.

"I do," I answered. "But I can't explain it. I mean, there's nothing to explain. It's just a hunch. All I'm sure of is that Bernie wasn't killed by a petty thief. So why is he dead?

"As far as I know, he wasn't protecting anything valuable enough to kill for except those chops."

"I don't see the connection." I heard a frown in her voice.

"I don't either," I conceded.

She thought a bit longer, then said, "All right. I'm sure Sammy will back me on this. He's had the twitches ever since Saturday. I'll get back to you when I have something concrete."

"Thanks," I said sincerely. She hadn't lost her power to make me twang. "You can reach me on my cell phone." I recited the number. When she said she had it, I shifted back to Bernie.

"But of course it might not have anything to do with the chops. Bernie may've been killed for something he knew, or was involved in. Can you tell me if he ever had any dealings with Lacone, or Martial America, or Nakahatchi? Watchdog? Anson Sternway? The IAMA? Outside his job, I mean."

I wasn't asking her to violate professional confidentiality. As she'd said, we were on the same side. Basically.

"Funny you should ask," she replied like it wasn't funny at all. "I was thinking about that earlier. I guess," she explained, "Bernie's death upset me more than I realized."

I started to say that I knew what she meant, but she went on, "There's nothing in our computer about him other than the reports he filed for The Luxury on security issues and claims. Our records go back fifteen years, which is as long as we've been in business. In that time, he never had a policy with us, he wasn't used as a reference, his name doesn't show up on any other reports. And that includes our work with Martial America and the IAMA.

"So the short answer is no, he didn't have any dealings with Watchdog."

For some reason I wasn't surprised. Those chops had begun to haunt me. "How about Lacone?" I asked without much hope. "Sternway? Nakahatchi?"

Deborah sighed. "I wouldn't know. I could always ask Alex, of course." She didn't try to hide her distaste. "He'd like it if I wanted something from him. But we don't usually talk to Mr. Sternway. Sue Rasmussen handles insurance for the IAMA. And we're in roughly the same position with Mr. Nakahatchi. We provide his liability coverage, but Mr. Komatori takes care of it for him."

Damn. I missed Puerta del Sol. At home I would've known exactly who to approach for information. Spend a couple of hours trolling dark bars and wasted shelters, buy cautious drinks for grizzled and weary Chicanos, Mestizos, Indians, ruined former Anglos—dealers in seamy knowledge—and I would've learned everything I needed about Bernie's private life. If he'd had one.

But not here. Here I'd have to do it the hard way.

Which wasn't Deborah's problem. "Oh, well," I responded regretfully. "So much for that idea. Don't worry about it. I should get plenty of chances to talk to Lacone and everyone else in the next few days."

She changed gears so fast that I nearly dropped the phone. "I don't mind," she drawled. "Alex probably won't tell me anything useful unless I let him fondle me. But that might be fun. I'll just imagine your reaction. I can see you now, gnashing your teeth while he slides his hands into my blouse—"

"*Stop* it!" I croaked. "You'll cause a pile-up. I'm driving badly enough as it is."

She gave me the throaty laugh that made me want to tear her clothes off. Somehow I kept the Subaru on the road.

For a couple of minutes we chatted about other things. I had about a dozen questions I wanted to pursue, most of which could be summed up in one. Why me? But I was already lost in a tangle of freeways, and every mile I drove threatened to make the problem worse. I needed to get out my map, regain my bearings.

Manfully I said goodbye and hung up the phone.

My ear burned for twenty minutes afterward.

14

Once I'd figured out where I was, I decided I had time for one more chore, so I tacked and hauled my way back to Acme Cars Cheap, where I exchanged the Subaru for a battered Plymouth van with no back seats, an industrial-strength air conditioner, and almost enough leg room. When the air in the Plymouth had finally cooled enough to dry my skin, I located the nearest fast-food joint—a Burger Boutique, forsooth—ate a quick meal, and returned to The Luxury Hotel and Convention Center.

I arrived twenty minutes early, but Anson Sternway appeared less than five minutes later, wearing his usual lack of expression.

He'd traded in his dignitary clothes, including the blazer, for casual grey slacks and a white cotton shirt with long sleeves, but he still moved like an ambulatory vial of nitroglycerin. Neither of us offered to shake hands. We'd already done that.

Just being polite, I asked, "What brings you here?" Since nothing I said ever made an impression on him anyway, I tried a leaden joke. "Returning to the scene of the crime?"

He didn't react. Maybe he didn't get it. "Mr. Lacone can't be here," he told me flatly. "He has other commitments, so he asked me to show you around Martial America."

I raised my eyebrows. "Do you run this kind of errand for him often?" I would've assumed that the Director of the IAMA had better things to do.

He shrugged slightly. "I'm on retainer with Martial America. Mr. Lacone pays for my time." Then he added, "He'd like a call from you this afternoon." Effortlessly he produced a business card and handed it to me. "You can use his private line. He wants your assessment of Martial America's security."

Marshal had already warned me twice, so I didn't ask, Is there *any*thing you won't do for a few bucks? Instead I said, "Thanks," and pocketed the card.

We waited together in silence for a while. HRH seemed too superior for small talk. I had plenty of new questions for him, but I wasn't sure that I could get through them before *Essential Shotokan*'s people arrived.

Sure enough, a few minutes later Hideo Komatori and three other men parked their run-down Dodge station wagon under the portico. If I hadn't talked to him yesterday, I might not've recognized him. He seemed like an entirely different person in a lightweight seersucker suit, sky blue shirt, and bolo tie. Through the glass of the main doors, he only reminded me of himself by his upright posture and easy carriage.

Once he entered the lobby, of course, I could see his scar.

His companions also wore suits that looked too warm—not to mention formal—for Carner's climate. Two of them were young, hardly more than teenagers. The third was considerably older, maybe forty-five. They all walked self-consciously erect, too aware of being emissaries for *Essential Shotokan* to match Komatori's air of comfort.

He was the only Asian among them—and the only one who wasn't sweating. Apparently the Dodge sported Subaru-quality AC.

From a distance of ten feet, they paused to bow carefully to Sternway. His bow in return probably should've looked casual, but by comparison it seemed negligent. However, it didn't bother Komatori. Amiably he moved closer to shake Sternway's hand. His companions stayed where they were.

"Komatori-*san*." Sternway's greeting sounded marginally warmer than the one he'd given me.

"Sternway *sensei*," Komatori answered respectfully. "You honor us."

Sternway spread his hands. "The honor is mine. I'm pleased to help Mr. Axbrewder protect Nakahatchi *sensei*'s treasure."

On cue Komatori turned to me, bowed, and offered his hand. "Axbrewder-*san*. I'm relieved by your involvement. Now the chops will be safe. Please tell us how we may assist you."

I shook his hand easily enough. "Call me Brew. 'Axbrewder-*san*' takes too long." But after that I had to scramble to get up to speed. All this politeness left me behind.

Fortunately Komatori gave me a moment to think by introducing the men with him—all students of Nakahatchi's. They bowed fulsomely to Sternway, took turns shaking my hand. By then I was ready.

"There won't be any trouble," I said to Komatori, projecting confidence with all my might, "but we've got three cars, so we can take an extra precaution. We'll load the display into your wagon. Mr. Sternway can lead us to Martial America. You'll follow him, I'll follow you.

"That's overkill, I know." I wasn't even a little bit worried about an attempt on the chops in broad daylight. "But we might as well get in the habit of being careful."

I couldn't read Sternway's expression, but he agreed with a nod. Komatori acted duly respectful, and the students seemed gratified that their responsibility for these priceless artifacts was being taken so seriously. Together we swung into action, in a manner of speaking.

After I'd signed out the display from the hotel manager's safe room, transferring liability from The Luxury to Martial America and Nakahatchi, Komatori and his men loaded it reverently into the Dodge. Sternway brought his car, a middle-aged Camaro with more muscle than brains, around to the portico and took the lead. When I had the Plymouth in position, we headed out.

Sternway led us in a stately procession. If we'd had our headlights on, you would've thought we'd missed the turnoff for a funeral. What we were doing seemed at once grave and ludicrous, packed with significance to the people involved, and more than a bit overwrought from any other perspective. Rather like the tournament in that respect. Or the martial arts themselves.

For forty-five minutes or so we wandered through an indistinguishable assortment of Carner's schools, stadiums, athletic supply warehouses, shopping centers, playing fields, and suburbs, all of which looked like they'd been cloned from various sections of Indianapolis. I felt profoundly lost, despite my map. I needed shadows, darkness, buildings undermined by age, streets pocked with use like smallpox—a city inhabited by loneliness, secrets, and disrepair. A city where Bernie's death made sense. Even sunglasses couldn't protect me from so much newness and light.

Unfortunately I had to cope anyway.

Alex Lacone's "dream" sat on a lot big enough to hold a couple of Puerta del Sol's high schools. From a distance it resembled a suite of professional buildings designed for doctors and dentists. I wouldn't have recognized our destination if a mall-style marquee lettered in hubris hadn't proclaimed:

Martial America
National Center for the Martial Arts

You couldn't miss the exaggeration. Despite the size of the lot, there were only two buildings. The rest of the area stood empty, unfinished. Half of it hadn't even been paved.

Nevertheless Lacone had put up a good front. Strips of lawn punctuated by young sycamore trees and glistening with recent water edged the lot on all sides. When the trees grew a bit bigger, they'd help disguise the limitations of the development. In the meantime, the marquee positively shone with self-confidence, and light poles like spires marked the boundaries of the pavement.

The square buildings themselves didn't exactly dominate the horizon—they were only three stories high—but they made a striking impression. For one thing, their concrete walls were so white they must've been polished like teeth twice a week. And in so much eye-straining white the tinted glass of the long double display windows on the ground level and the smaller windows above looked deep and dark, almost black—as inviting as shadows, or as forbidding. In addition, the levels of the buildings were offset from each other so that the second story extended in one direction and the third in another. And they didn't sit squarely on their side of the lot. Instead they'd been placed at angles so that they met and mated at one corner of each ground floor but not at the upper levels.

One advantage of their orientation, I saw as I followed Sternway and the Dodge into the parking lot, was that it diminished the prominence of any particular side. A square setting would've favored the sides that happened to face the street and the parking lot. But as they were, Lacone could at least pretend to touchy martial arts egos that all his locations were equally desirable.

This mattered because each side housed a different school. A sign over the display windows on the left wall of the nearer building announced *Essential Shotokan*, with Master Soon's *Tae Kwon Do Academy* on the right. An identical sign identified *Malaysian Fighting Arts* in the next building.

Twenty or thirty other cars occupied the lot, but the sheer size of the space made them look like they'd been abandoned. I wasn't convinced that even Carner could supply enough schools and students to make Lacone's "dream" come alive.

Bracing myself, I climbed out into the heat to join Sternway and Komatori.

"Here it is," Sternway told me unnecessarily. Despite his unrevealing demeanor, I thought I detected a note of complacency in his voice.

Encouraging him to talk, I asked, "Whose idea was it to angle the buildings like this?" I wanted him in a forthcoming mood.

"Mine," he admitted. "But most of my suggestions involved the *dojos* themselves."

Then he directed my attention to the unfinished lot. "Mr. Lacone's plans include at least four more buildings like these, two or more on each side, with a tournament facility, museum, and stores in the center."

Lacone had described *a hall-of-fame-style museum* and *a complete education center, repository, and promotional outfit.* Plus a variety of martial arts suppliers.

And all of it *white* enough to blind a solar astronomer.

"As you can see," Sternway continued, "he has a long way to go. But he has the space and the enthusiasm, and I believe he can raise the money. If he attracts enough prominent schools, that will call attention to the development.

"In turn, Martial America's success will benefit the martial arts all across the country." HRH sounded like he was reading this speech off a particularly dull brochure. "Carner will become a Mecca for masters and students everywhere."

Just for something to say, I remarked, "He's ambitious."

Sternway regarded me through a pair of mirrored sunglasses that hid his eyes. "Every man worth knowing is."

That was debatable, as they say, but I didn't bother. I was sweating again—I wanted to get out of the sun.

Fortunately the students had already opened the back of the station wagon to off-load the display. Hideo Komatori joined them, and they raised the case between them as if it were sacred—or full of gelignite. Sternway and I followed them almost respectfully as they approached *Essential Shotokan.*

Its only entrance stood under an awning between the long

dark windows. The heavy oak door had been carved with symbols and *kanji* which probably conveyed meaning to martial artists, but which told me nothing. Komatori produced a key, and I held the door open while we went in.

I found myself facing a stairway to the second floor in a hallway which ran back toward the center of the building. Both the stairs and the hall sported beige indoor/outdoor carpeting that absorbed sound. On either side, wide entryways like portals supplied access to large rooms.

Immediately Sternway started to act like a tour guide.

"On this level all the buildings have the same layout. To the right is the main *dojo*." That room went all the way to the far wall of building, and was roughly half as deep as it was long. "Notice the raised hardwood floor and the mirrors."

I could hardly help noticing. Even under fluorescent lights the floor seemed to glow, polished by hours of bare feet and care. Reflecting in the floor-length mirrors, which covered every foot of wall not already taken up by windows or doors, that glow appeared to fill the entire room.

"Hardwood is the best training surface," Sternway explained, "because it flexes slightly, gives a bit of cushioning. Of course," he remarked by the way, "when *Gracie Brothers Jujitsu* moves in, their floor will be covered with wrestling mats." Then he resumed his lecture. "The mirrors help students watch and correct their own techniques.

"No one is here now because *Essential Shotokan* doesn't hold classes during the early afternoon." He seemed sure of his facts without consulting Komatori. "Nakahatchi *sensei* teaches advanced seminars in the morning. But from 4:00 until 10:00 the *dojo* will be in use almost continuously."

When I'd seen enough—which took me about four seconds—HRH beckoned me to consider the room on the left. "This *dojo*," he told me like I couldn't have guessed on my own, "is primarily for equipment training."

It also had a hardwood floor, but instead of mirrors its walls were lined with heavy bags, speed bags, uppercut bags, stretching and weight machines, thick vertical wooden boards with padding at their ends—*makiwara*, Sternway called them—and rows of shelves for focus mitts and a bewildering variety of other pads.

"Bathrooms and changing rooms are at the end of this hallway. The door at the back of each *dojo* leads there."

Komatori and his students waited patiently through all this. Which wasn't easy—that display was heavy. As soon as Sternway paused, I asked Hideo where the chops would be kept.

A nod of his head indicated the stairs. "You will see, Brew-*san*." Apparently that was as close as he could come to calling me Brew.

Starting upward, Sternway continued his practiced spiel. While he talked, he rubbed absently at his left forearm.

"The second floor has a large room that can be used for lectures or meetings, or for screening videos. There are also two apartments for masters or students who wish to live here. Nakahatchi *sensei* and Komatori-*san* both do."

"What about the other masters?" I meant Gravel, Hong, and Soon.

"Master Soon and *Sifu* Hong live in their *dojos. Soke* Gravel has his own home, so two of his senior students use his apartments."

We reached the top of the stairs and turned right to move in the opposite direction. On the left, another stairway continued upward. Ahead was another door, a smaller version of the one that faced the outside world. It wasn't locked. Sternway swung it open without knocking and led the rest of us through.

This was obviously the conference room. Instead of windows, it had the kind of indirect lights that put people at ease, blond veneer paneling designed to look expensive, and a warmer rendition of the ground floor carpet. But it didn't contain any tables, lecterns, or video screens. Wooden folding chairs lined along the walls were the only furniture. In the center of each side wall, another carved door interrupted those lines.

Komatori and his helpers carted the case into the center of the room, folded out its legs, and set it carefully upright. The older student straightened his back with a muffled groan, but his younger companions did their best to pretend that they could've carried the display all day.

"You're going to keep the chops here?" I asked Komatori. The idea didn't exactly lift my heart.

He must've heard the doubt in my voice. "Yes, Brew-*san*. Is this not a proper place?"

"It's the best spot available," Sternway put in promptly. I guess he wasn't interested in my qualms. "It's easily accessible. The chops are an important historical resource, and Nakahatchi *sensei* doesn't want to conceal them. But it's only open when the school holds classes. Everyone in the *dojos* can keep watch."

I'd already seen how *karate-ka* kept watch, but I didn't object. Instead I pointed at the ceiling. "What's up there?"

Sternway shook his head. "That isn't a useful option. Mr. Lacone customizes the third floors to suit the needs of individual schools. Some want storage space or more apartments. Others like to add a private *dojo*, or a martial arts library. Nakahatchi *sensei* has both, as well as guest quarters for visiting masters. He likes a measure of seclusion. Setting up the display would disrupt the school."

Hideo Komatori nodded polite agreement.

That sounded plausible enough, but I wanted to object anyway. Security would definitely be a problem here. However, I kept it to myself. I worked for Lacone. The inadequacy of Nakahatchi's arrangements were none of Sternway's business.

When I didn't argue, he finished his disquisition. "As I've said, each school determines its own use for the third floors. Master Soon and *Sifu* Hong have included small equipment and supply stores. *Soke* Gravel maintains a collection of Malaysian weapons for training. The possibilities are as diverse as the martial arts themselves."

I wondered how long he'd been giving this particular pep talk. He delivered it like Holy Writ.

"And all of this was your idea?"

"In essence, yes. As I've said, Mr. Lacone has no background in the martial arts."

I still didn't understand why Sternway hadn't moved into Martial America himself. He sure seemed proud of it, despite his flat demeanor. And he certainly could've cut a favorable deal with Lacone.

But I didn't think that HRH would tell me the truth in front of witnesses, so I changed directions.

"What about keys?" I asked Komatori. "How many are there? Who has them?"

Compared to Sternway, Komatori sounded like a model of openness. "When we entered our lease, Brew-*san*, Mr. Lacone provided two keys. Two more have been made. Nakahatchi *sensei* retains two for himself and his wife. I've been entrusted with one. And Aronson-*san*"—he indicated the older man behind him—"also has a key. He's our senior student."

I raised my eyebrows involuntarily. Nakahatchi had a wife? He hadn't struck me as a married man. Too ascetic, maybe. Or too full of sorrow.

"I assume you're talking about keys to the front door. What about others? These apartments? The conference room?"

Komatori frowned as if the question surprised him. "There are none. We haven't needed them."

I stared at him. "You mean to tell me one key opens every door here?"

He offered another of his delicate shrugs. "And the doors above us as well. In addition, there are the fire exits."

They needed a key to use the fire exits? I swallowed a sour laugh. Carner's building inspectors couldn't, could not, have approved that. Hell, Watchdog couldn't have approved it.

Was this another of Sternway's bright ideas?

I didn't ask that. Instead I demanded, "Which are where?"

"I'll show you," Komatori offered mildly.

"In a minute." I definitely wanted to see the fire exits. But I was reluctant to make a production out of it in front of HRH. Still none of his business. And I had a different question for my tour guide.

"Anson, Mr. Komatori says there are only four keys. But you unlocked the front door. Where did you get yours?"

He gave me a look that might've been veiled contempt. "My apologies. I forgot. This is for you." He took a heavy Schlage key from his pocket and handed it to me. "It's a master key for both buildings. Mr. Lacone keeps it for obvious reasons. The terms of the lease allow tenants to re-key any locks they wish, with the exception of the fire exits. In an emergency he must be able to let the fire department or the police inside."

Unfortunately that part made sense. Of course Lacone had a master key. Later I'd ask him how many there were. And who had them.

"Shall we look at the fire exits now?" Sternway went on. "Or would you prefer to see the top floor first?"

Itching to get rid of him, I responded, "I'll go upstairs later."

His condescension gave me hives. "And I'm sure Mr. Komatori can show me the fire exits. You must be a busy man, Anson. There's no need for you to hang around."

This time I saw contempt clearly in his eyes. "Mr. Lacone pays for my time. When you're finished here, I'll take you around to the other schools." He tried to sound helpful, but he couldn't carry it off. "You aren't known here. An introduction from me may make your job easier."

He meant that it might lend me a bit of credibility—which I was prepared to do without. On the other hand, his company would enable me to ask other questions.

"Thanks," I murmured with no appreciable sincerity. "That'll be fine."

So Komatori showed us the fire exits. He dismissed his carters, then took Sternway and me back to the head of the stairs from the first floor. There he opened a door in the wall under the upward staircase. I'd taken it for the door of a utility closet when we'd passed it earlier—it had no lock—but it let us into a short corridor running toward the center of the building.

The corridor ended at an iron fire door with a big red EXIT sign over it and a bar-latch instead of a knob. As soon as I saw it, I understood the keys. It was a self-locking door. Push the bar on this side and it opened. From the other side you needed a key to get in.

"The latch is wired to an alarm," Sternway explained, "as well as to the fire department. But it isn't active while the *dojos* are in use. At night each school sets its own alarm once the students have left."

Well, they were *supposed* to, anyway. Whether they actually did it or not was another matter.

Komatori opened the door and bowed us through.

Beyond the door I found myself on a railed metal catwalk bolted to the unpainted cinderblock wall of a large utility well. The well was a square hole roughly twenty feet on a side that reached from the ground floor of the building to its roof. Conduits and ducts of various sizes growing out of a cluster of boilers, furnaces, air-conditioning units, emergency generators, water mains, and circuit-breaker boxes below me stretched to the ceiling, where the vents continued through a grillwork skylight covering the shaft. At the moment most of the illumination came from the skylight, but permanent floodlamps in all four walls kept the catwalks constantly lit.

After the relative comfort inside, the utility well felt like a sauna. All that machinery put out enough heat to incubate virus strains, and through the skylight the sun baked the cinder-block walls. Without transition my skin started to ooze sweat. If I had to stay in here long I'd have fungi growing under my arms.

The catwalk made a circuit of the entire shaft, connecting fire doors in each of the walls. An identical catwalk and doors hung overhead, accessed from the third floor. Diagonally across from me on both sides, ladders surrounded by safety cages provided a way upward as well as down to ground level.

Komatori let the fire door swing shut behind him. It hit its frame with a solid thunk like the sound of a marble slab dropping into place over a tomb. The catwalk shook slightly, complaining at its bolts.

Stubbornly officious, Sternway called my attention to the key-hole in the door. "Each school can use its fire exits at will, but they can't be opened from this side without the appropriate key. This provides security as well as privacy."

Well, duh, I thought. Hit me over the head with it, why don't you. "I take it," I drawled, "you don't trust the schools to respect each other's privacy."

Komatori looked faintly shocked, but I wasn't talking to him.

Sternway considered me expressionlessly for a moment. Then, instead of answering, he said, "Komatori-*san*, thank you for your assistance. I'll show Mr. Axbrewder the rest of the fire escape route. Then we'll visit the other schools.

"Please tell Nakahatchi *sensei* that I honor his willingness to share the chops. I'll give him any assistance he may need. Also I'm sure Mr. Axbrewder will have some useful suggestions for the display's safety."

HRH didn't want anyone else to hear what he was about to say.

Plainly dismissed, Komatori gave a respectful bow. Sternway replied in kind, and Komatori fished out his key to let himself back into *Essential Shotokan*. The thud as the door closed raised an empty echo from the walls. The noise gave me the odd impression that I'd gotten myself into more trouble than I could handle.

With my palm, I wiped a sheet of sweat off my forehead. "That was subtle," I remarked.

Sternway snorted. "As subtle as your question, Axbrewder."

I'd succeeded in exasperating him at last.

I replied with a grin like a grimace. "But in my case it's part of my job. I'm supposed to ask tactless questions, insult people, piss them off. Kick over the anthill and watch what squirms out." Feeling malicious—he had that effect on me—I added, "You'd be amazed at what I've already learned."

He studied me from under lowered eyelids. Suddenly I felt that I was in danger. His usual ominous relaxation seemed to concentrate—strain for release like compressed napalm, hungry to erupt in fire. His tension only lasted for a moment, however. He'd changed his mind about something. Or simply lost interest.

"I doubt it." His disdain was unmistakable.

I didn't realize that I'd been holding my breath until I tried to tell him he hadn't answered my question. Under my jacket, my shirt stuck to my back.

Fortunately he repeated it for me. "Do I trust these schools to respect each other's privacy? Of course. But I don't trust them to respect each other."

Trying to be unobtrusive about it, I let the air out of my lungs and took another deep breath.

"Historically," he explained, "martial arts schools attract students and grow by demonstrating their superiority over other schools. In China particularly, that tradition goes back centuries. Often masters would travel great distances to test their skills against other masters with stronger reputations. Battles between schools were not uncommon."

Which went a long way toward explaining tournaments.

"My concern for Martial America is that proximity will make the schools jealous of each other. It will bring out their competitiveness, as well as threatening their secrets. If they try to resolve their differences by fighting, people might be hurt—or possibly killed."

I finally started breathing normally again. Sternway seemed to become less and less dangerous as he spoke.

"And the more schools Martial America draws," he added, "the worse the danger will become. Especially if they're as aggressive as, say, *Killer Karate.*

"Then, of course"—he allowed himself a sigh—"the problem is exacerbated by the fact that Nakahatchi *sensei* owns a set of possibly genuine antique Wing Chun chops.

"This distresses *Sifu* Hong and his entire school, for obvious reasons. But it also disturbs Master Soon. It draws attention away from his *Tae Kwon Do Academy*." Sternway attempted a humorless smile. "You might say that Nakahatchi *sensei* has up-staged him. He's indignant about it."

He paused briefly, then said, "That presents a problem for me as well as for Martial America. The IAMA exists, among other reasons, to promote a sense of mutual cooperation, understanding, and support among all the martial arts. And Martial America in particular has the potential to foster a sense of community which can only benefit the martial arts."

I got the point. "Unless it degenerates into a war zone first," I muttered sourly.

He nodded.

"Sounds like quite a dream," I commented. To my surprise, I found him more sympathetic when he wasn't acting like a hereditary monarch—or talking about money. "I'm surprised you got this far with it. How did you manage to convince even four schools to share a location like this?"

He offered me another unconvincing smile. "It helped that *Essential Shotokan* and *Malaysian Fighting Arts* aren't especially competitive. If I could find a few more schools like them, a few more masters like Nakahatchi *sensei* and *Soke* Gravel, Martial America would be further along."

That was an excuse, not an answer. I stared at him and waited for more.

He glanced around the well. "I suppose I could say that I can be eloquent when the occasion warrants. But you might not believe me." Then he faced me squarely. "On the other hand, you may not believe the truth either."

"Try me." Whatever the "truth" was, I wanted to hear it.

He considered the question for a few more seconds before he conceded. "Very well.

"The truth, Brew, is that I have credibility as well as authority in the martial arts. Legitimate eighth-*dans* aren't as common as you might think. I've been known and honored nationally and internationally for a number of years. And the excellence of my students supports my reputation. Men like *Sifu* Hong and Master Soon listen to me because I've earned their respect. They wish to show that they deserve to stand with me."

Now I didn't find him sympathetic at all. He sounded like an advocate for the Divine Right of Kings. He was HRH Anson Sternway, descended from the mind of God. Therefore less exalted mortals had no choice but to worship at his feet.

My skepticism must've showed on my face. Abruptly Sternway's manner changed. He leaned toward me almost confidentially. "Tell you what, Brew. Let me take you out to a place I know tonight. Say around ten. I'll show you how I earned respect."

My eyebrows jumped. What was he trying to do, educate me or intimidate me? Either way, I wasn't sure I wanted to be on the receiving end.

But Deborah couldn't see me until tomorrow night, and I didn't have any other plans—

Suddenly I missed Ginny. Or missed the way I felt when we worked together. She'd always been the boss, which somehow relieved my inclination to second-guess myself. If I could rely on her for strategy, I could choose my own tactics.

Stalling for time, I tried to change directions, put the pressure back on Sternway.

"Tell me something else first," I countered. "How well did you know Bernie Appelwait?"

He glared surprise at the question. "I hardly knew him at all." Hints of irritation leaked past the general flatness of his tone. "We've held our World Championships at The Luxury for six years now. We've had the same dealings with hotel Security every year. Aside from that, he's a stranger to me."

Inspired, as you might say, by his displeasure, I pursued the issue. "But the IAMA must have security issues occasionally. You didn't hire Bernie for anything? Ask him to do a job in his spare time? Consult with him?"

HRH shook his head sharply.

"Well, did you ever teach him? He probably studied self-defense somewhere." His flik conveyed that impression. It wasn't a weapon most people knew about. "How about with you? Or maybe he's related to one of your students?"

Fuming, Sternway tried to interrupt, but I kept going.

"Or maybe it had to do with money?" I was having fun now. "You talk about how hard it is to make a living in the martial arts. Security people sometimes have connections they don't talk about on the job." I was stretching, but I didn't care. Only the congestion gathering in Sternway's face mattered to me. "Did you ever need a loan shark? Or protection from a loan shark? You might've asked Bernie—"

He cut me off like a splash of acid. "What do you think, Axbrewder? *Say* it. Do you think I had something to do with his death?" At his sides, his fingers twitched, eager to form fists. His voice struck echoes off the hard surfaces of the shaft, resonance complicated by concrete and iron. "Do you think I *profit* from the death of a tired old security guard at a second-rate convention hotel?

"If you consider me insane, say so. I'll stop wasting time with you."

When he burned like that, as expectant as a blasting cap, his students probably wet themselves. For some reason, however, he didn't scare me now. Instead I experienced a moment of unadulterated bliss. The sonofabitch was human after all. I could piss him off.

Happily I grinned at him. "I'll take that as a no."

"I hope so." He measured me like he was gauging how hard I'd go down. "You're being absurd. And insulting."

I shrugged, still grinning. "Just doing my job."

He aimed his ire at me for a moment longer. Then he seemed to think better of it. He turned away, gazed out over the utility well. He still looked like an explosion poised to happen, but gradually the imminence eased out of him.

Sounding flat again, he pronounced, "Kicking over anthills is a job for children."

And just like that my little bliss popped like a soggy firecracker, doused in sweat. Suddenly making him angry stopped being fun. I hadn't realized that I was so transparent.

Maybe I owed him a little less intransigence.

Sighing to myself, I asked, "Where do you want to meet?"

"Meet?" His frown said, What the hell are you talking about? Obviously he'd forgotten his invitation.

"You offered to show me how you earned respect." I tried to sound deferential, but I wasn't much good at it.

He nodded. "You'll come with me." Apparently he considered that good news. All at once he resumed his usual expressionlessness. "We can meet in the parking lot here." Almost smiling, he added, "This may help you understand martial artists."

Before I could say anything, he asked, "Shall we finish the tour?"

Since there weren't any other anthills in sight, I shrugged. "Sure." Then I let him lead me along the catwalk toward the nearest ladder.

By then my feet were so damp that I squished when I walked.

The catwalk complained again as we moved, hinting at the screech of tortured metal. But it didn't pull loose from the wall or collapse under us. I wasn't that lucky.

15

All in all, it reminded me how dependent I'd become on Ginny. She and I'd balanced each other. When I kicked over anthills, she put the pieces together that made it worthwhile. And when she went to tear out someone's throat, I kept her in check.

Without her I felt just about as childish as Sternway thought I was.

But I had nothing else to work with, so I paid attention while my guide showed me the rest of the fire escape route. When I'd followed him down the ladder to the ground level, I discovered four more fire doors there, one for each school, and an open corridor in a corner of the well that presumably led out of the building.

With my master key, I unlocked *Essential Shotokan*'s door and found that it opened into a room lined with lockers, obviously one of the changing rooms Sternway had mentioned earlier. Like locker rooms everywhere, it smelled damply of sweat, anxiety, Tiger Balm, and rotting jockstraps. Men's or women's, I couldn't tell. According to Ginny, they both smelled the same.

Satisfied, I let the door swing shut, and Sternway took me to the exit along a corridor lit by a couple more floodlamps. Fortunately the air here was a bit cooler. If I'd stayed in the utility well much longer, I might've started to drip skin.

Right angles to accommodate the design of the *dojos* on either side blocked the view ahead, but the corridor tended generally toward one of the corners of the building, and in a moment we reached the exit, which turned out to be a small room built into the intersection of this building and the next one. Heavy glass doors with bar-latches gave us an exit on either side. Sternway chose the door away from the parking lot, and we stepped out into the glare of Carner's afternoon.

I felt a wash of relief, like I'd escaped being boiled for dinner by cannibals. Despite the pressure of the sun, some of my sweat started to evaporate, cooling my overheated emotions. I practically staggered with a kind of giddiness as I confirmed that my key worked on the glass door.

Sternway watched until I was finished. Moisture darkened his shirt under his arms, but other than that he hardly looked damp at all. Maybe he'd reached 8th *dan* in Shorin-ryu by being so tough that he almost didn't need to sweat.

"What do you think?" he asked when I'd put the key away.

I was still off balance. "About what?"

He studied me without blinking. "Are the chops safe?"

I wiped my face dry with both hands. "Not unless you confiscate every set of lock picks in the city." Maybe I hadn't escaped after all. Maybe I was just being cooled off to garnish a salad. "And not if there's a fire."

An entire team of rock climbers couldn't get the display case down that ladder. Not without rope.

Sternway didn't glance away. "What will you tell Mr. Lacone?"

Apparently he always called the developer "Mr. Lacone." Maybe he worshipped Lacone's money.

I treated my tour guide to a false grin. "I'll have to think about it." I wasn't about to tell him what I really had in mind, so I mentioned something that was too obvious to miss. "At the very least, I'll want him to install a heavy bolt on the inside of that conference room door. Or I'll advise Nakahatchi to do it."

Sternway gave an almost subliminal shrug. Without comment he moved off along the side of the building we'd just left.

I dug out my sunglasses and followed dutifully.

Almost immediately we reached the entrance to *Traditional Wing Chun*. Under the shelter of its awning, I found that it'd been customized to resemble the portal of a Chinese temple. It had a heavy red door and frame, with a gracefully curved red lintel and brass door handles in the shape of a circle. Stamped or molded into the brass was an image that reminded me vaguely of one of the chops—a stylized figure holding a long staff over its head, apparently levitating.

Sternway pulled the door open and went inside.

I joined him, grateful to get back into the air-conditioning.

The main *dojo* to my right was in use. T'ang Wen, the man

who'd talked to me about *ch'uan fa* the other day, stood in the middle of the floor, leading half a dozen barefoot men and women in silk pajamas through a sequence of movements as rigidly stylized and implausible as *kabuki* theater. Nevertheless T'ang and his class focused on the pattern as if it were a matter of life and death. None of them seemed aware of our arrival.

"We'll wait until they're done." Sternway kept his voice low, apparently out of respect for training-in-progress.

That was fine with me. I needed to cool down anyway.

The pattern took another minute or two to complete. Then T'ang bowed to his students, his left hand cupped over his right fist in front of him—a different bow than the one Sternway used. At once he beckoned a student to take his place, and left them to practice while he came to greet us.

In the doorway he and Sternway bowed at each other. "Sternway *sensei*," he said quietly. "You honor us. How may I serve you?"

Despite the lines on his face and the sharpness of his features, I couldn't read his expression. He was a man who smiled easily, however, and he wasn't smiling now. The silver chips in his eyes seemed to concentrate on Sternway like hints of distrust.

"Mr. T'ang," Sternway replied. "I believe you've met Mr. Axbrewder?"

He must've noticed us together on Saturday, before Bernie was killed.

"Indeed." T'ang turned to me and offered his hand. "Mr. Axbrewder." While we shook, he smiled. "Have you come to learn more of Wing Chun? New students are welcome at any time, although I suggest one of our beginning classes. Training such as this"—he indicated the group behind him—"is difficult without an introduction to the movements and their meaning."

This seemed like a particularly good time to practice my manners, so I said, "Not right away, thanks. Maybe later. Mr. Sternway is just showing me around Martial America."

T'ang Wen's face revealed nothing.

"That's right," Sternway put in. "Mr. Axbrewder has been hired to improve security for the building. I'd like to present him to *Sifu* Hong."

Something in T'ang's eyes withdrew, dulling their silver edge, but his tone remained bland. "*Sifu* Hong is upstairs," he answered. "If you will excuse me, I will see if he may be disturbed."

"Certainly," Anson replied with his usual lack of warmth. "Thank you."

T'ang bowed again, stepped past us into the hallway, and moved smoothly up the stairs out of sight.

Sternway had already explained some of the undercurrents here. Probably no one at *Traditional Wing Chun* would welcome what I was doing for Watchdog and Martial America—and for Nakahatchi.

While we waited, HRH glanced around briefly, making sure he wouldn't be overheard. Then he remarked, "The Chinese are too flamboyant." He seemed to think that he was answering a question I hadn't known how to ask. "Half of what you see in kung fu is just for show. Wing Chun isn't a bad style, but even here"—he indicated the *dojo*—"there's too much posturing."

He also considered Tae Kwon Do a *toy martial art.* Apparently he was just full of respect for his fellow martial artists.

"They've had a lot of time to work on it," I objected mildly. Centuries, in fact, if what I'd been told was accurate. "They must think it's good for something."

I wanted to see how far he'd go.

"It's intended to distract and intimidate," Sternway replied. "To defeat an opponent mentally as well as physically. Rather like a gorilla beating its chest." He gave me a cold smile. "But chest-beating only works against another gorilla." Then he added pedantically—just in case I'd missed the point—"The most common criticism of Wing Chun is that it isn't effective against other, more direct styles."

Apparently he was willing to go pretty far.

T'ang Wen spent more time upstairs than I expected. If all he had to do was tell Hong we were here, he'd have gotten a response faster from the Oracle at Delphi. Nevertheless Sternway didn't show any impatience, so I kept mine to myself.

Finally T'ang came down the stairs. Alone. A frown he didn't try to disguise gripped his features—and he was definitely a man who took frowning seriously.

Nevertheless I had to admire his relaxation. The silver in his irises gave his stare a flaying edge, but his shoulders and arms stayed loose, perfectly at ease.

"Mr. Sternway," he announced softly, "my master is disturbed that you would insult us in this way."

My eyebrows jumped involuntarily. Insult—? But Sternway's poise didn't flicker. Like commenting on the weather, he replied, "This saddens me, Mr. T'ang. *Sifu* Hong holds my deepest respect, and I meant no offense. How may I make amends?"

"Insult?" I asked aloud. "What insult?"

They both ignored me. Still softly, T'ang told Sternway, "Take this man from here." He flicked a hand toward me. "While he remains, the offense grows."

I opened my mouth to object—I wanted to know how I'd suddenly become the enemy—but Sternway spoke first.

"I would prefer," he stated, "to account for my actions to *Sifu* Hong in person."

"My master does not wish to hear any justification." T'ang's frown turned the lines of his face to bone. "For myself, I ask you to comply before the insult becomes unpardonable."

"Oh, come off it," I put in. "I haven't even be*gun* to insult you. Don't treat me like I'm not here. If I've done something to offend your 'master,' tell me what it is. *I'll* account for—"

So quickly that I didn't even see him move, T'ang flung a blow at my face. His fist stopped a quarter of an inch from my nose and hung there, motionless, as if the air had frozen solid around it. I could've counted the hairs on the backs of his fingers—

Before I could blink, the fist disappeared, slapped down by Sternway's palm.

He and T'ang faced each other as if neither of them had twitched a muscle.

"We'll comply," Sternway said quietly. "I'll return later to speak of this with *Sifu* Hong."

Forcing myself to breathe, I took a step back, out of range. "Like hell we will." If T'ang swung at me again, I wanted to see it coming. "I'm here to do a job. I've been hired by the owner of the building, which he has the right to do. I'm being paid good money to help protect those chops, and I'm not going to back down because of some 'insult' I don't understand."

At last T'ang faced me. The silver in his eyes seemed to cut right into me. Softly, venomously, he said, "You were hired to protect the chops from us."

Wearing his indignation like a fright mask, he wheeled away

and reentered the *dojo.* While I stared after him, he resumed teaching his class. When his students yelled with him, they sounded livid, enraged by his ire.

I turned on Sternway. "Did you expect that?" Hong's reaction—and T'ang's—hadn't surprised him. And he hadn't asked for an explanation.

"Outside, Axbrewder." He took hold of my arm, tugged at me to move.

I ripped out of his grip. "I said—"

He interrupted me. "What do you think you gain by making the situation worse? Is this another anthill? Will it help you do your job?"

Without giving me a chance to answer, he strode out of the building. Dissociating himself from me—

Damn right I gained something. *Protect the chops from us.* I hadn't known Hong thought that way. But I needed more.

I caught up with Sternway on the sidewalk. I couldn't see his eyes—he'd already put on his sunglasses—but his manner revealed nothing. He might've been waiting for me to use the bathroom.

"All right." I couldn't keep the tension out of my voice. "I'm outside." Carner's hard glare attacked my vision. Heat seemed to drum inside my skull. "Answer the question. Did you expect that?"

Did you set me up?

"No." His tone might as well have been a mask. He hid everything behind it. "I was trying to prevent it.

"I knew it could happen," he went on. "And I was sure it would if I left you to handle *Sifu* Hong on your own. Your way of talking to people—" He shrugged. "I'd hoped that I might be able to defuse his distrust before it gathered strength."

"Well, you were wrong," I snorted. "So what do you think I should do now?" Did he imagine that I could do my job without being accepted by the people who used the building? "I'd like to hear any other good ideas you've got."

"It's simple." HRH sounded entirely unperturbed. "We'll finish visiting the other schools. Then you can go do whatever it is you do, and I'll return here to pour oil on the waters. I'm sure I can persuade *Sifu* Hong to be more reasonable."

I paused for a moment, considering my options. Then I said, "No," and headed back into *Traditional Wing Chun.*

He barked my name after me, but I ignored it. Security for Martial America was my job, not his. And I was tired of trailing along behind him like an overgrown puppy.

Inside the big red door, I didn't hang around for T'ang Wen to notice me. Instead I went straight for the stairs and strode up them two at a time. By the time I'd climbed halfway, I heard my name again, this time from T'ang, but I didn't stop.

So far *Traditional Wing Chun* was laid out exactly like *Essential Shotokan.* At the top of the stairs I doubled back toward the door of the conference room. It was shut, but not locked.

In the conference room, unfortunately, I had to guess which of the apartments Hong occupied. Nameplates on the doors would've come in handy, but there weren't any. And since the lights were off, the only illumination came from the open door behind me. What I could see of the carpet looked equally worn in front of both apartments.

T'ang Wen solved the problem by catching up with me before I risked flipping a coin. I feared that he'd hit me, so I spun around before he got close enough, pointing one finger straight at his face as if I thought I could stop him with it.

"Keep your distance." I suppressed as much of my tension as I could. "I'm sure you can tear me apart with one arm in a sling." Actually I would've liked to see him try, but right then didn't seem like a good time for a testosterone contest. "But I'm not here to cause trouble."

With the light behind him, shadows hid his expression. I couldn't tell anything from his face. Nevertheless he took me seriously enough to stop moving. "Mr. Axbrewder," he informed me heavily, "you *are* trouble."

I couldn't argue with that. Instead I said, "There's been a misunderstanding. I want to clear it up." I groped quickly for the right phrase, then finished, "I'm here to give *Sifu* Hong face."

"You?" T'ang's voice was poised like his body, ready to attack, but waiting. "You are Western, cultureless and uncouth. What do you know of face?"

Good question. I wondered if he realized just how good. Maybe he could see Ginny and Bernie and my dead brother in my eyes. Maybe he could smell old booze in my sweat—

"I know enough," I told him. "Enough to understand that I need to talk to *Sifu* Hong in person."

"Then speak to me, *gwailo*," he countered. "Give *me* face. I will convey your thoughts to my master."

I shook my head. "It doesn't work that way. I can't correct the problem with you. You aren't the one who's been insulted."

Maybe *I* was. I didn't know what *gwailo* meant.

"We will hear him, Wen," Hong Fei-Tung said at my back. He'd opened his door and entered the conference room so quietly that I hadn't heard him. Hell, I hadn't even felt his presence in the air. "Then I will determine whether his words have merit."

I couldn't be sure, but I thought I heard a touch of reprimand in the *sifu*'s tone.

Without hesitation or protest, T'ang Wen bowed to his master, left hand over right fist, and withdrew a step.

I turned toward Hong.

Dim light from the doorway fell on his face, making it look like terra cotta worn smooth and flat by time. He couldn't have gazed at me more impassively without being dead, but his eyes granted me a warning glimpse of the intensity I'd seen in him outside The Luxury, when he'd taken his first look at the chops.

I didn't need Sternway or even T'ang to tell me that I had to be careful now. Very careful. I'd already struck a spark from T'ang. From Hong I might get the full conflagration.

"*Sifu* Hong." My breath caught high up in my chest. My nerves remembered how they'd felt when Parker Neill had poked me. I mimed one of Sternway's bows while I tried to make my diaphragm work.

He didn't bow back. Within his silk robe his body remained unnaturally still. Not even respiration stirred the fabric.

With as much ease as I could muster, I began, "You'll have to forgive me. As Mr. T'ang just remarked, I'm Western. I don't know all the appropriate forms and courtesies. No matter what I do or say now, I'm going to seem crude."

Deliberately I refrained from pointing out that he should be used to it by now. He'd been living here long enough. He must know how to get along with us uncultured, couthless Occidentals.

"I don't have any personal experience with this," I continued abruptly, "but I'm told that as a school *Traditional Wing Chun* is widely respected. As the school's *sifu*, you're held in high esteem. Everyone I've talked to says so," even Anson Sternway in his ungiving fashion, "and I have no reason to doubt them. You're regarded as a man of honor."

At my shoulder, T'ang breathed harshly, "To say so is to suggest that the opposite is possible."

I ignored him to concentrate on Hong. "Mr. Lacone and Sternway *sensei* haven't insulted you by hiring me to protect the chops. They hired me to give you face."

"You speak," T'ang put in, "but you say nothing. Sternway and others believe my master will attempt to reclaim the chops. They will call it theft, although the chops are rightfully Chinese. You are the hand of their distrust. You oppose my master for an action he has not committed and does not contemplate."

This time I answered T'ang. "Now you're insulting *me*." But I kept my eyes fixed on Hong. "Do you think *I* have no honor?

"Your master is an honorable man. Of *course* he won't do anything dishonorable. But the police don't understand honor. They understand greed. And national pride." Never mind bigotry. "Not honor."

Then I appealed directly to Hong. "*Sifu*, if anything happens to the chops, whose voice will defend your honor to the police? Whose but mine? They'll assume you had something to do with it. They'll have to. Distrust is their job.

"But *I'm* responsible for security here now. The safety of the chops is *my* problem. And if I fail to protect them, then I'm responsible for discovering the truth about what happened to them.

"That's called honor where I come from.

"You don't have any reason to resent me," I finished. "The simple fact that I'm here protects you. My presence gives you face."

Which, as I was acutely aware, was only one way to look at it. Naturally T'ang had a different perspective.

Bitter as bile, he demanded, "Do you wish my master to believe that those *gwailo* Sternway and Lacone hired you as a sign of their respect? He is not such a fool. He—"

"Enough, Wen," *Sifu* Hong interrupted softly. His gaze never left mine. No expression touched his flat features. "This country is not China. Here men may perform work without sharing the purposes of their masters."

On my own behalf, I explained, "I don't work for Sternway

sensei. I work for Mr. Lacone. He's in the profit business. He wouldn't do anything to insult you. He doesn't want to lose a respected school"—a paying lessee—"like *Traditional Wing Chun.* And he certainly doesn't want anything to happen to the chops. That would damage his plans for Martial America."

After that I couldn't think of any way to make myself clearer, so I shut up.

T'ang shifted restively behind my shoulder, but didn't say any more.

His master studied me for a moment longer. Then he nodded crisply, like an acknowledgment.

"Mr. Axbrewder," he announced, "I have heard you. We will not speak of this again. Events will reveal their meaning as they unfold."

In other words, I was dismissed. He was willing to suspend judgment, at least temporarily. Maybe he expected me to count my blessings and just go away.

Fortunately he didn't stop there. "While you remain in the service of Mr. Lacone," he continued, "you are welcome here. If you wish our assistance, if you desire to learn more of Wing Chun, or if you require any knowledge that is ours to share, please name your need to T'ang Wen."

Before I could open my mouth to thank him, he turned away. The weak light from the doorway made his short grey hair look like an iron skullcap, ascetic and impregnable. He might've been walking off a battlefield as he stepped into his apartment and closed the door, leaving me with T'ang.

Apparently he'd just given *me* face.

At any rate, he'd accepted my protestations. But I didn't grasp why they'd been necessary in the first place.

T'ang cleared his throat. He sounded uncomfortable doing it, but when I turned to look at him his face was shrouded in shadow, his reactions hidden.

"Are you content, Mr. Axbrewder? I will do what I can to satisfy you."

The words suggested more than one meaning. What kind of *satisfaction* did he have in mind?

"I'll think of something," I muttered. Then I winced at my own gracelessness. Trying to make amends, I admitted, "This is all new to me. I'm a little baffled at the moment."

T'ang stood in silence, apparently waiting for me to frame a question. But I didn't speak.

Even taking into account my ignorance of China, and of Chinese psychology, I couldn't get my head around the idea that my presence was an insult. As far as I could tell, he and Hong had reached that conclusion from another dimension, bypassing ordinary reality altogether.

It must've come from somewhere.

I wanted an explanation. But I didn't know how to ask for it politely. Stalling, I indicated the lighted hall beyond the conference room and started in that direction. T'ang joined me smoothly.

I didn't say anything until I could see better. When he'd closed the conference room door, I studied his face for a moment, looking for remnants of hostility, but I didn't find any.

Maybe now I could stop worrying that he might hit me.

"I do have a couple of questions," I told him while my muscles loosened. "Is *Traditional Wing Chun* a new school? Have you always been located here?"

"No, Mr. Axbrewder." Now T'ang sounded like the man I'd talked to at the tournament, accessible and at ease. He'd already taken Hong's attitude to heart. "My master came to this country from Hong Kong twenty years ago. For a time he visited other Wing Chun masters in various cities, considering possibilities. When he had determined that Carner was suitable, he opened his doors to students."

Which must've been long before Lacone started dreaming about Martial America.

"As he prospered," T'ang went on, "he invited more and more of his family to join him from Hong Kong and China. My paternal grandfather was my master's uncle by marriage. My parents were among the first to accept my master's invitation, and I began study with him fifteen years ago."

Presumably Sternway was still fuming on the sidewalk, so I started toward the stairs. I wouldn't exactly grieve over it if he got fed up and left. On the other hand, he might have an answer for questions I didn't know how to ask T'ang. What he'd told me outside no longer seemed adequate.

As T'ang accompanied me, I observed, "After that many years, *Sifu* Hong must've been pretty well established. What made him decide to move into this building?"

That was as close as I could get to what I really wanted to know.

The subject didn't produce any discomfort. "Sternway *sensei* is widely known," T'ang answered calmly. "Association with him is beneficial. In addition, my master considers that the goals of the IAMA, and of Martial America, are worthy. He believes the time for exclusiveness in the martial arts has passed, and he favors open cooperation among the many styles for the benefit of all.

"Also"—from the head of the stairs T'ang gestured toward the *dojos* below us—"the facilities are excellent.

"When Sternway *sensei* asked the martial artists of Carner to consider this location, my master was the first to agree." Pride showed in his voice. "I was given the honor of signing the first lease in his name."

Which sure didn't make it sound like T'ang or Hong distrusted Lacone. Something must've changed relatively recently.

T'ang and I descended the stairs. To keep him talking while I tried to think of a different approach, I asked, "How long was *Traditional Wing Chun* alone here?"

An innocent question, I would've said. But apparently I'd plucked an unexpected nerve. T'ang stopped so abruptly that my momentum carried me a couple of steps past him before I could turn to find out what was wrong.

His eyes were almost level with mine. Their silver hinted at incandescence.

"We were not," he pronounced distinctly. "When Nakahatchi *sensei* learned that my master had agreed, he signed a lease with an earlier date of occupation."

I blinked. "Nakahatchi was already here when you moved in?"

"Yes," T'ang stated. "He had been uncertain of his own decision. But when he learned of my master's, he made arrangements to place himself first."

"Why bother? What's the point?"

T'ang shrugged disdainfully. "He is Japanese. The Japanese seek precedence over the Chinese in all things."

Oh, good. More racial stereotyping. Just what we needed.

I wanted to retort, Gosh, are you *sure*? Maybe it didn't have anything to do with Hong. Maybe Nakahatchi's previous lease just expired before yours and he had to move earlier.

Maybe you're just a narrow-minded little bigot, and everything you say is horseshit.

But I knew myself too well. Once I got started, I probably wouldn't stop until everyone in the damn building knew how I felt. I was supposed to be *polite* here. Martial America needed less hostility, not more.

Practically biting my tongue, I moved on down the stairs and headed for the front door. T'ang followed a few paces behind me.

Nevertheless I had no intention of letting good manners interfere with my other priorities. When we reached the door, I put my back to it and confronted T'ang. Without transition, I asked, "Did you know the man who was killed at the tournament? Bernie Appelwait?"

That touched no nerves at all. T'ang looked mildly surprised, but I didn't pick up the slightest vibration of unease as he replied, "His death is disturbing and shameful, Mr. Axbrewder. My master hopes that his killer will be apprehended quickly. We both knew him by name, and we saw him in the course of his duties during Sternway *sensei*'s tournaments. But I have never spoken with him, and my master has made no mention of such a conversation."

"You don't have any students related to him? You didn't consult him about security at your former *dojo*?"

Perplexity tightened on T'ang's brows. "Indeed no."

"Is it possible," I went on, "that *Sifu* Hong might've had dealings with him you wouldn't know about?" Trying to be polite, I didn't mention things like loan sharks.

T'ang shook his head. "Mr. Axbrewder, Hong Fei-Tung is my *sifu*. I do not ask such questions. But I do not believe it is possible. My duties include all business transactions for *Traditional Wing Chun*. About my master's personal concerns I know nothing.

"However"—he smiled delicately—"we are Chinese. We need no assistance in matters of money."

Oh, well. I hadn't actually expected anything as far-fetched and simple as a direct connection between Bernie and this school or the chops. But I had to check.

That left Lacone. And Nakahatchi.

With visions of Sternway's indignation dancing like sugar plums in my head, I thanked T'ang Wen, told him that I'd get in touch if I needed anything else, and let myself out.

I found HRH waiting right where I'd left him. His white shirt caught so much sunlight that it seemed to blur around him, enclosing him like flame. Expecting trouble, I braced myself for another flare of his exasperated condescension.

But he almost knocked me off stride with a lukewarm smile. "How did it go?" he asked in a tone of polite disinterest. He didn't sound impatient—and certainly not angry. I couldn't see his eyes behind his sunglasses.

What the hell—? I stared at him. "Fine."

He nodded like he hadn't expected anything else. "That's good." Then he added, "While you were inside, I talked to Master Soon and *Soke* Gravel, so you're covered there. You can introduce yourself whenever you have time, but they know why you're here now. I'm sure they'll cooperate with you."

I had the vague impression that I'd left my mouth open. For a moment I couldn't think of a thing to say.

"As far as I'm concerned," Sternway said evenly, "we're done for today. Unless you have more questions?"

In self-defense I put on my own sunglasses and tried to kick my brain back into motion. With an effort, I admitted, "There's still a lot I don't understand about martial artists. And martial arts schools." Grabbing the first detail that occurred to me, I asked, "Do T'ang and Komatori really handle all the business for their schools?"

Sternway nodded. "I believe so, yes. It's a traditional arrangement. The highest ranking student takes care of the practical side of running a school, freeing the master to concentrate on higher matters. I may have mentioned that Sue Rasmussen fills the same role for me."

"That's it?" I insisted. "Tradition?"

He smiled coldly. "As I say, it's a traditional arrangement. But naturally common sense prevails. If the senior student isn't capable—" He shrugged. "As it happens, both Mr. T'ang and Mr. Komatori are more fully acclimated to this country than their masters. Wen's family moved here from Hong Kong when he was quite young. And Hideo was born in the US, although I think his parents are still Japanese citizens."

I considered that briefly. "Then I guess I need to talk to either Komatori or Rasmussen."

"Why?" Sternway may've been genuinely curious.

"Apparently," I explained, "Hong feels insulted by the fact that Nakahatchi moved into Martial America ahead of him. I'd like to know why Nakahatchi did that."

Just how deep did the friction between *Essential Shotokan* and *Traditional Wing Chun* run?

"I can't help you." Sternway's interest seemed to dissipate. "Sue handles the leases. That's one of the services the IAMA offers its members. I wasn't involved."

Which was another detail that didn't seem to fit. He wasn't mad at me for going back into *Traditional Wing Chun* without him. And he didn't know about Hong's history with Nakahatchi. Considering all the things he *did* know—

For a heartbeat or two I tried to look like I accepted his answer. Then I changed the subject.

"You mentioned T'ang's family. He told me that *Sifu* Hong has been inviting his relatives to join him here for years. Do you happen to know how many of them he has in Carner?"

All at once Sternway resumed his majesty. A muscle in his cheek gave his mouth a condescending twist.

"*Sifu* Hong isn't a gossip, Brew," he replied, unnecessarily patient. "He doesn't chat with me about such things. But the last rumor I heard put the number around fifty."

I gaped behind my sunglasses. *Fifty*— That would make one hell of a support system for a man who wanted to steal and hide a set of antique Wing Chun chops. Stories about triads flared through my head, Hong Kong gangs as bloody-minded as the Russian Mafia, with just as much reach.

If Hong didn't actually have all the honor I'd given him credit for—

Ah, shit. This damn job was getting messier by the hour.

Sternway gazed at me, blank as a sphinx. "Are we done here?"

I jerked back into focus on him. "Just one more question." My voice was harsher than I intended. "You expected trouble from Hong. Earlier you said you wanted to introduce me so that you 'could defuse his distrust.' But why would he distrust any of us? It can't have anything to do with me personally. He doesn't know me. He must have a problem of some kind with you. Or Mr. Lacone.

"If you actually want me to do my job, you'd better tell me what's really going on here."

For a moment HRH seemed to study me behind his sunglasses. Then he barked a humorless laugh. "No, Brew. This isn't another anthill. This time you're scuffing your shoes on bare dirt.

"Haven't you learned anything about the tensions that inevitably exist between martial arts styles? Are you completely ignorant of Japanese and Chinese history? In one form or another, they've been at war with each other for centuries. Despite vastly superior numbers, China has usually lost. What do you think it means to *Sifu* Hong that a traditional enemy, a traditionally *victorious* enemy, holds a precious piece of his own heritage?

"You disappoint me, do you know that? You should be able to understand that *Sifu* Hong doesn't distrust me or Mr. Lacone or the IAMA. He distrusts and resents Nakahatchi *sensei*."

That, apparently, was his final word on the subject. He turned away without saying goodbye and headed for the parking lot. The way he moved, fluid and fatal, made me think of nitroglycerin flowing downhill.

I probably should've believed him. Hell, I was just as ignorant as he accused me of being.

But I didn't. Instead I felt like he'd granted me a small epiphany, an intuitive glimpse into the heart of a city I didn't understand. Suddenly I saw how Carner's night dwellers flourished in a place so full of light. Sunglasses. They carried pieces of darkness with them everywhere.

I didn't believe Anson Sternway for a variety of reasons. He wasn't pissed off after I'd kept him waiting so long. He was sure that Hong resented Nakahatchi, but he claimed he didn't know anything about their personal history.

And he kept so much of himself hidden.

16

For a while I stood where I was, asking myself, What would Ginny do? What would *any* smart person do? But nothing dramatic occurred to me, so I just did what came naturally.

Leaving *Malaysian Fighting Arts* and *Tae Kwon Do Academy* for tomorrow—despite Master Soon's curious absence during Bernie's murder—I went back to my rented Plymouth, fired it up, and cranked the AC as high as it would go. While the air cooled, I used my cell phone to call information and get Bernie's home number and address.

The address turned out to be an apartment building of some kind. When I tried the number, no one answered. Which wasn't a surprise—he'd given me the distinct impression that he lived alone. And the cops had had plenty of time to finish with the place. After five rings a phone machine delivered an announcement in Bernie's querulous voice, but I didn't leave a message.

Instead I dug out my map.

I found his address maybe five miles diagonally across Carner from Martial America, in a small neighborhood where all the streets had kitsch-cowboy names like Quirt, Rowel, Stirrup, and Lariat. It sounded like the kind of blue-collar neighborhood people chose when they couldn't afford anything better. I planned a route, then kicked the Plymouth into gear.

Once I was out of the parking lot, I dialed the number I'd been given for Alex Lacone.

It must've been his private line—he answered it himself. I could hear him beaming as he said, "Lacone here. I don't recognize your caller ID."

"Axbrewder, Mr. Lacone. I picked up a cell phone this morning so we could keep in touch."

"Brew." His tone shifted to a warmer channel. "How's it going? Did Anson take care of everything for you? Are those chops safely tucked away?"

I leaned into the blast from the AC, still trying to cool down. "Everything's fine so far." I hadn't asked him to call me Brew. He must've picked it up from Sternway. Or Deborah. "Mr. Sternway gave me this number and your skeleton key. The chops have been delivered to *Essential Shotokan*. I've had a tour of the building, and paid a visit to *Sifu* Hong. Tomorrow I'll drop in on Master Soon and *Soke* Gravel."

"Good, good." He'd tuned his enthusiasm to an all-approval station. "Sounds like you've made a real start."

Before I could express an opinion about that, he went on, "How does it look so far, Brew? We agreed on a week for a full report, but naturally I'm curious about your preliminary reactions. How much worrying should I do right now?"

I could've told him, but I wanted to deflect him a bit, maybe disturb his balance some. "One question first, Mr. Lacone," I countered. "This skeleton key—how many other copies are there?"

"Two, I believe," he replied without hesitation. "We keep one handy in case we need to send out someone for emergency repairs. And of course it's available for the police, the fire department, the paramedics, that sort of thing. The other is in our office strongbox. Just as a precaution."

"And you're sure you have your copies? They haven't been misplaced or borrowed?" I meant stolen.

"I'll check."

The phone picked up a clicking sound like an intercom switch. Then I heard Lacone ask, "Cassie, do you have the keys for Martial America?"

A woman's voice somewhere in the background answered. It seemed to quaver a little. "I have one of them here, Mr. Lacone. The other is in the strongbox."

"Good, good." I guess he liked saying that. Without prompting, he continued, "Has anyone used them recently?"

"Not since we made the copy you gave to Mr. Sternway."

"Thank you, Cassie." The clicking sound came again.

"Cassandra Hightower," Lacone explained to me. "My personal assistant. She hasn't made a mistake since the Roosevelt administration." He chuckled. "That's *Teddy* Roosevelt." Then he added, "She'll give you any help you need if I'm not available."

I nodded at the windshield, trying not to get lost. "Glad to hear it." Maybe I could stop worrying about skeleton keys.

Lord knows I had plenty of other worries.

"You asked for a preliminary opinion, Mr. Lacone," I went on. "The way I see it, right now the chops would be safer if you just left them in the parking lot. That way no one would think they're worth anything."

For a moment, he offered me a shocked silence. Then he murmured, "Oh, my." Which was a big improvement on *good, good.* "That seems harsh."

"I don't think so." I didn't want to drag the conversation out. Carner's convulsive rush hour had begun to gather around me, and I needed to concentrate on my driving. "I'm sure you remember how the locks are keyed. Each *dojo* just has one. The same key fits the front door, the fire exits, the apartments, the conference room." Plus whatever was on the third floor. "Anyone with a copy of *Essential Shotokan*'s key can get at the chops at any time, day or night."

I could feel him getting ready to object, but I forestalled him by saying, "I assume that Nakahatchi *sensei* has been sensible about copies. I'm told there are only four. But those aren't complicated locks, Mr. Lacone. Anyone with a set of picks can open them. And you can buy picks almost anywhere." Including mail order. "Along with instructions. In effect, anyone at all can get at the chops.

"As matters stand, you'd better pray that Nakahatchi *sensei* and Mr. Komatori are light sleepers, because that's all the protection you've got."

Sammy Posten could've told Lacone exactly the same thing. He didn't need me. But I kept that to myself.

Lacone breathed, "Oh, my," again. This time I didn't hear any imminent objections.

"It's a simple problem, really, Mr. Lacone," I explained. "That building was designed for public use, not to secure valuable antiques. Any place like it would have the same problems."

After a long moment's consideration, he asked, "What do you suggest?" For once he didn't sound like he was smiling.

"Two things to start with," I replied promptly. "First, install a couple of heavy bolts on the inside of the conference room door. And I don't mean deadbolts you can open with a key. I'm talking about old-fashioned sliding bolts set top-and-bottom so that they anchor the door to both the lintel and the floor.

"Then hire an electronic security firm to put motion sensors in the hall outside the conference room. And set pressure plates under the carpet in front of the door. Have them all wired to an arming switch in Nakahatchi's apartment—or Komatori's.

"It'll be an inconvenience," I admitted. "They'll have to remember to shoot the bolts and arm the sensors when they lock up for the night. But that's trivial compared to the cost of insuring those chops. And I'm sure Watchdog will approve.

"I'll have more for you when I've studied the building"—I meant the schools—"and done some research. But bolts and some electronic security will cover you for now."

Unless a thief tried to get in through one of the apartment windows—which seemed implausible to me. In Carner's heat, no one left windows open. And both apartments were occupied.

The developer's silence gave me the impression that he wasn't happy. "What kind of research?" he asked reluctantly.

"I want to talk to someone who handles security for a museum. He'll know more than I do about protecting valuables in a public building."

He may've been worried about what my suggestions would cost.

Apparently I was right. "I believe," he pronounced after another pause, "my present insurance covers me until the chops are appraised." In other words, this was Watchdog's problem, not his—at least for now. "I'm sure I can get those bolts installed in a day or two. But motion sensors and pressure plates sound expensive. I don't want to spend that kind of money if I don't have to."

For instance, if the chops turned out to be counterfeit—

"That's your call, Mr. Lacone," I put in unsympathetically. "You're paying me to give you advice, not to stand guard on the display personally. I'll protect them as well as I can. But I can't be there twenty-four hours a day."

"I understand, Brew, I understand." His bonhomie sounded a trifle forced. "Of course I want your advice." A beat later, he asked, "How much would those sensors and plates run me?"

I shrugged at the windshield. "You'll have to get an estimate from an electronic security professional. I don't have the expertise to install them, so I don't buy them myself."

I refrained from adding that it was silly to wait a couple of days before putting in bolts. I'd made my suggestions. If he chose not to take them seriously, that was his business.

And I also didn't mention that I'd already urged Deborah Messenger to arrange a preliminary appraisal. She could deal with him when she was ready. The bad news didn't have to come from me.

"Well, I'll give it some thought," Lacone announced as if that constituted reaching a decision. By degrees he recovered his smiling tone. "In the meantime, Cassie will fill out a work order. We'll talk again soon."

Before he could finish dismissing me, I put in, "Just one or two more questions, Mr. Lacone."

"Of course," he sighed. He seemed to be losing his enthusiasm for me. "Go ahead."

I offered the traffic and the street signs a hard grin. "I had a small problem at *Traditional Wing Chun* this afternoon. Nothing serious—just a misunderstanding. But it took me by surprise.

"*Sifu* Hong seemed to think that you hired me to protect the chops from *him*."

"He did?" Lacone asked. "I'm astonished, Brew." He sounded astonished. "Where would he get such an idea? It's preposterous. I have nothing but the greatest respect for him. Men like him—and Nakahatchi *sensei*—and Anson Sternway—they give me faith in my dreams for Martial America."

Sincerity wasn't his strong point, that was plain. But he came close enough to satisfy me, at least for the time being. He had good reason to keep his schools happy, if he could.

"I'll tell him you said so. That should relieve his mind."

Then, deliberately abrupt—hoping to catch him off-guard—I asked, "How well did you know Bernie Appelwait?"

"Bernie—?" For a moment he seemed unable to place the name. Then he said, "Oh, that security guard. The one who got killed.

"I didn't know him at all. Just his name. He worked at the tournament. Didn't he hire you to help guard the chops? I think I may have shaken his hand once.

"Why do you ask?"

Instead of answering, I countered, "What about your assistant? Maybe she remembers him."

"I can't imagine why she would," he said dubiously. But he

clicked his intercom anyway. "Cassie, does the name 'Bernie Appelwait' mean anything to you?"

"Of course, Mr. Lacone. He was the Chief of Security at The Luxury Hotel and Convention Center." Maybe she really hadn't made a mistake in decades. "At one time you considered hiring him to provide security for Martial America. But you didn't want to pay as much as he earned at The Luxury. Eventually you concluded that the buildings didn't require full-time security."

"Ah, yes," he conceded. "Now I remember. Thank you, Cassie." Another distinct click silenced the intercom.

"Invaluable woman," he muttered. "I don't know how she does it." He didn't sound pleased. "But she's right, of course. We talked about hiring full-time security—this was months ago. But security firms cost an arm and a leg. Someone suggested a hotel security guard might be less expensive. I may have mentioned Mr. Appelwait myself, poor man. But when I learned what The Luxury pays an employee with his seniority—" The phone connection conveyed a shrug. "Eventually we discarded the idea."

"Who is 'we,' Mr. Lacone?"

"Let me think. Sammy Posten, naturally. Anson." He paused briefly. "Oh, and Mike Piangi. He's the Vice President for Commercial Loans over at Carner National Bank and Trust."

In fact, they were exactly the people with whom he might've been expected to discuss security for Martial America. As my employer he was certainly forthcoming, I had to give him that.

I'd baffled him, however, and he wanted an explanation. "What's this all about, Brew?"

"I have no idea, Mr. Lacone," I admitted honestly enough. "All I know is that Bernie was killed while he was responsible for the chops. That's a pretty remote connection, obviously. But if I want to earn what you're paying me, I have to look into every conceivable hint of trouble, no matter how implausible it seems."

Which was why I needed to know where Hong's knee-jerk distrust came from.

"Fair enough." He had his smile tuned to a stronger signal now. Maybe he thought that every potential threat I identified and blocked reduced the eventual cost of long-term security. "You're doing a fine job, Brew. Keep up the good work."

That made it easy to get off the phone. When we'd said goodbye, I hung up.

By then I was nearly lost again. The accumulating traffic demanded my attention, which made me feel that I'd wandered off my route. And on top of that, I was not in a good mood.

The chops had been in Bernie's care when he was killed. Lacone had mentioned Bernie's name to his business associates. As connections went, those weren't just remote, they were bloody intangible. Which left me pretty much right where I'd started—clueless. If I didn't find something useful at Bernie's apartment, I'd have a hell of a time tracing his killer.

Unless the killer cut his way through more innocent bystanders to reach the chops— A man who didn't mind hacking down a frail old security guard wouldn't stop until he got what he really wanted.

Involuntarily I shuddered, and my guts squirmed. For a moment or two, sweat blurred my vision, despite the Plymouth's AC. If this kept up, I'd find myself in the kind of black funk that positively begged for booze.

Luckily I hadn't missed any turns. By now rush hour had clogged itself down to a thin trickle, but that made spotting street signs easy. Stoplights and hostile drivers clotted my route, but eventually I reached Bernie's neighborhood.

His apartment turned out to be upstairs in a brick four-plex on a block full of identical buildings with narrow strips of lawn like dog runs between them and exactly one unconvincing sycamore in each front yard. Some of the flower beds against the walls showed more care than others, but they all seemed to hold the identical gardenias and peonies. On the inside, Bernie's building sported carpeting like Astroturf, designed to hide dirt and stains, and planters occupied by forlorn plastic palm fronds. It was well lit, however, like the rest of Carner, with uncompromising fluorescent bulbs partially humanized by frosted shades.

A staircase took me up to a landing with a numbered steel door on each side. I knocked on Bernie's—just in case the cops, a relative, or some fiduciary friend happened to be there—but there was no answer. When I hadn't heard anything for a minute or so, I jimmied the door and let myself in.

Someone had left a light on in the living room. With my back to the door, I glanced around. The living room ran half the length of the building, but that didn't make it large. And it was crowded with furnishings—a couple of spavined bookcases, an old pre-remote TV, a cracked Naugahyde recliner, a couch with defeated springs, a sturdy little workbench littered with tools and glue, and four assorted end tables, all set around an ersatz Oriental rug. The whole space including the rug looked neglected, abandoned to depression and dust—with the exception of the framed photographs on the walls, and the wine bottles and jugs of various sizes carefully positioned on their sides in delicate stands on every available surface.

Bottles and jugs with wooden sailing ships inside them. I counted eighteen.

The photographs were all of the same woman, middle-aged, tending to fat, with nondescript hair, a wide forehead, small brown eyes too far apart—and a smile so utterly and entirely seraphic that it wrung my heart. It beamed like a blessing out of every frame, warming everything she saw.

I knew intuitively who she was, without a scrap of actual identification. Bernie's wife. Dead for a number of years now, if the condition of the rug were any indication.

Every day he'd worked his twelve-hour shift at The Luxury. And every night he'd taken refuge here under her loving gaze, meticulously building ships in bottles because she was gone and he was alone.

I found more in the kitchen, some jaunty, others trudging against forgotten winds. And more in the bedroom. Even in the bathroom. Ships in bottles and pictures of his wife were the only decorations he'd cared to have around him.

I had a lump in my throat I couldn't swallow as I started searching his apartment.

If the cops had been here ahead of me, they were neat as hell about it. I didn't find any disturbed dust to indicate that something had been moved, any of the usual scrap of police investigations in the wastebaskets. Which meant that whoever had the job of putting Bernie's "affairs" in order and disposing of his "effects" hadn't been here yet. Maybe he'd died intestate, so uncared-for that the residue of his life would just sit here until his landlord evicted it.

In the end, I didn't have to do much searching. I found everything that interested me, including his address book, neatly organized in a filing cabinet in one of the bedroom closets.

Everything except a will. But that didn't mean much. The cops might've taken it to deliver to some lawyer or agency.

Assuming the cops had been here, they must've copied what they wanted out of his address book. That made my job easier, but I still didn't like it. It suggested that Edgar Moy wasn't taking this investigation very seriously.

A quick scan of Bernie's financial records didn't supply any surprises. I was no CPA, but the numbers looked about right for a man who'd worked steadily and spent very little—no unexplained infusions of cash, no unidentified expenditures. Rent aside, his biggest monthly expense was a payment to a nursing home.

The address book made my eyes ache when I looked at it. It was relatively empty compared to others I'd seen, and every blank space seemed to describe a life of emotional poverty. It gave me the phone number for the nursing home, however, along with a collection of other numbers, some self-explanatory, others just labeled with the names of people I didn't know.

My stomach complained to remind me that I hadn't eaten for a while, but I figured its objections were mostly an excuse to stop what I was doing, so I ignored it. Feeling like an intruder, I helped myself to a tall glass from one of the kitchen cabinets and filled it with water. Then I sat down on the couch—the recliner was so obviously his that I didn't want to violate it—and started to make phone calls.

Talking to the nursing home turned out to be the worst of the lot. Bernie's sister, Maureen Appelwait, lived there, alone in the world except for her link with her brother, supported by him while she drifted in and out of Alzheimer's, and no one had told her that he was dead. I caught her between lucidity and confusion, apparently trying to go in both directions at once, and my news didn't help. She cried some, forgot what I'd told her a few times, demanded details I loathed giving her. But in the gaps she revealed a little bit about his life.

He was her only brother. They had a sister, Florence, who'd passed away five years ago—or was it three? Eight? One night while she slept her heart had simply stopped. His wife, Alyse—Maureen spelled and pronounced it for me, "ah-LEASE"—died fifteen years ago, killed by a misdiagnosed kidney cancer. He was devastated, just devastated. The three women had been *such* friends, Florence and Maureen never married, Alyse couldn't have children, they and poor Bernie had given each other the only family they had, and what was the name of that nice doctor who told her she was doing fine, just fine? Was it yesterday? Or maybe when she moved into the nursing home?

I listened to her for half an hour. Not once did she ask what would happen to her without Bernie to pay the bills. If she had, I couldn't have answered.

After I hung up, I gulped down the glass of water. Then I got off the couch, located Bernie's vacuum cleaner—a wheezy upright nearly as old as I was—and cleaned the hell out of the rug. I didn't stop until I could push a damp finger down into the nap and not pick up anything.

By then evening had become full dark outside. Night stained the windows black, and shadows leaked in past the shades, or under the front door, until they filled the apartment, crowding it with questions. Trying to keep Bernie's loneliness at bay, I switched on more lights and went back to work.

Fortunately the rest of my calls were easier. There were a few that I wanted to postpone because I had no legal standing—a law office, a bank, an insurance agency, The Luxury's day-shift manager. For a wonder, I managed to catch most of the others at home. The majority worked for The Luxury, primarily on Bernie's shift. Two were neighbors. The ones left over turned out to be either acquaintances of Bernie's—the kind of acquaintances you share a beer with occasionally and don't tell anything personal—or friends of Alyse's.

One way or another, they all told the same story. Bernie Appelwait was exactly what he looked like, an aging security guard grown isolated and short-tempered since the death of his dear wife. He could've retired a while back, rested on his pension, but he wanted to keep busy. Since he did good work, The Luxury let him stay.

Alyse's friends made *tsk*-ing sounds, emitted little gusts of sympathy and sadness, but they didn't have anything new to add. And what you might loosely call Bernie's drinking buddies contributed even less. Mostly they were just surprised to hear that it was possible for a hotel security guard to get killed on the job.

After a couple of hours continuously on the phone, I'd learned nothing that helped me do anything except fume. The picture emerging under Alyse's poignant gaze was pretty much the one I'd expected—and dreaded.

Bernie hadn't been killed because he was Bernie Appelwait. Or even because he was The Luxury's Chief of Security. He'd been killed because he happened to be in the wrong place at the wrong time.

To that extent, it was a senseless crime. And senseless crimes were always the hardest to solve. Always. They lacked the motivation that linked killer and victim in simpler murders. Like a drive-by shooting, they revealed a great deal about the killer, and very little about the victim.

Typically killers like that escaped clean unless they left an eyewitness or some definitive circumstantial evidence behind.

Nevertheless I was sure that Bernie's death could be explained. My nerves insisted on it, and I believed them.

He'd died because he could identify his killer. And, somehow, because of the chops.

On that happy note, I probably should've relocked the apartment and driven away. Found myself something to eat on the off chance that raising my blood sugar would lift my mood. But the sheer effort which Bernie had put into his ship building seemed to require more of me. And from her pictures Alyse smiled glowingly, like a woman sure in her heart that I wouldn't let her down.

I checked the time. In a little more than an hour, I was supposed to meet Anson Sternway back at Martial America.

Groaning at the offense to my bedraggled pride, I dialed Marshal Viviter's cell phone number.

I didn't know what he did with his off hours—or rather I thought I knew way too much about what he did with them—so I feared that he wouldn't answer. But he picked up after the second ring.

"Viviter."

He didn't sound like I'd interrupted him in the middle of anything really compulsory.

"Marshal." A complex relief blunted the edge that usually came into my voice when I talked to him. "It's Brew."

"Brew," he acknowledged. "You never quit, do you."

"You forget I don't know anyone in Carner." I tried to keep it light. "Who else am I going to talk to?"

"So talk." He hesitated fractionally, then asked, "Are you all right? You sound—"

He didn't specify how I sounded.

Instead of answering his question, I said, "I'm in Bernie's apartment."

"Really? That's called 'breaking and entering,' Brew."

"Tell me about it some other time," I retorted. "I don't work for you, so it's not your worry."

Abruptly I stopped. With the phone clamped hard to my head, I paused to kick myself for being snide to a man who hadn't actually done anything except help me.

Through my teeth, I muttered, "Sorry about that. The strain must be getting to me."

He didn't respond. I took a deep breath and started again.

"I know I asked you to research Bernie's past. But I didn't know how much you could accomplish without a client to represent, and I had some time, so I came here.

"I've been through his papers." Compounding the misdemeanor. "And I've called a bunch of his friends and relatives. Here's the short version. He was involved in absolutely nothing that might explain why he was killed. If he hadn't walked into that restroom right when he did, he'd still be alive."

Pure fucking bad luck.

"For a man who just met him three days ago," Marshal observed, "you're taking this pretty hard."

I wanted to pull the phone away from my ear and beat myself on the head with it. "You haven't seen this apartment," I countered. "It's so damn *lonely*—" My throat closed.

"And you aren't?" he asked quietly. "Come on, Brew. You knew from the start that it probably didn't have anything to do with him. If he hadn't been pugnacious and independent enough to go into that restroom alone, he'd still be alive. You're grasping at straws. If Bernie was involved in something that got him killed, you might not have to feel so sorry for him.

"Or—"

Again he didn't specify.

And again I didn't ask. I didn't want to risk hearing him say that he thought I was just feeling sorry for myself.

Changing the subject hard, I asked, "Have you heard anything new from Moy? Has the ME figured out which hand left that bruise on Bernie's wrist?"

Marshal had no trouble keeping up with me. "You're going to love this," he said in a completely different tone. "He was so taken with the question that he called back to tell me the answer." Cops never called private investigators back. That was a law. "The ME says the bruise was made with the assailant's right hand. The bruise on the left cheek looks like it was made backhand, with the left fist. It's about the right size and shape for that. He now speculates that the assailant grabbed the right wrist with his right hand and swung his left fist across the left cheek."

For some reason, Marshal didn't remind me that the ME and Moy didn't know about the flik because I hadn't mentioned it.

Staring at ships in bottles, I asked, "What about those fibers?" The ones pounded into Bernie's throat. "Does the ME know yet if they came from Bernie's blazer?"

"That's not his department." Somehow Marshal managed to sound like he wasn't making an effort to be patient. "The blazer and the fibers are at the lab now. But I'm sure Moy only went that far because he liked my question about the wrist bruise. He thinks this one's too obvious. He won't ask the lab to hurry on it."

That, too, was my fault. No doubt the detective assumed that the killer used his own weapon. Moy had no reason to think the fibers could've come from some other blazer.

"He ought to take a closer look," I growled in my own defense. "*I* didn't see any spots on Bernie's blazer that looked like fibers were torn off."

"Brew—" Marshal began.

I heard the warning in his tone. "Don't say it," I snapped. "I'll *tell* him. I'll call him in the morning."

Then I sighed. Marshal probably deserved an explanation. Wearily I said, "I only kept my mouth shut because Wisman asked me to."

"Wisman?"

"One of The Luxury's security guards. They aren't supposed to carry weapons. Hotel policy. He thought he'd get in trouble if anyone found out about Bernie's flik. The dumb kid had a *tonfa* hidden under his jacket. I guess I wanted him to trust me. At the time, anyway. We were supposed to be working together."

Viviter considered this for a moment. Finally he pronounced, "I understand. No harm, no foul, as they say. Even if you'd betrayed Wisman's little secret right away, the lab wouldn't have started on those fibers until the ME was done. We wouldn't be much closer to an answer than we are now."

Damn it, the sonofabitch had no *business* treating me so gently. But I knew perfectly well why I hated his attitude with such vehemence, and it had nothing to do with him. His only real fault was that he reminded me too much of the man I wished I were.

Still grasping at straws, I changed directions again. "While you had him on the phone, did Moy happen to mention whether Bernie left a will?"

Marshal chuckled at that. "He shouldn't have, but he did. Just trying to get me off his back.

"It seems Bernie left a respectable estate. Nothing excessive for a senior security guard who knew how to save, but respectable. He left it all to his sister Maureen. No other bequests."

I thought about Maureen Appelwait in her nursing home, and wondered if she'd forgotten—again—that her brother was dead. "*Damn* it," I groaned. "I don't like this."

"It doesn't have to be fair," Marshal said in my ear. "If you wanted fair, you should've gone into accounting."

I took the phone away from my head and stared at it for a while. In a funny way, I thought I *had* gone into accounting. Wasn't that what private investigators did? Account for things?

Who would account for Bernie, if I didn't? Alyse didn't seem to have any other volunteers handy. But I was too tired to explain myself to Marshal.

When I lifted the phone to my ear again, I heard him saying, "Brew? Brew?"

"Sorry," I muttered. "I had to think for a minute."

"You worry me," he retorted a bit stiffly, "you know that? Nobody recovers from a gut wound in only a month, and yet here you are, wearing yourself out over a man you hardly knew. I admit his death doesn't make sense. But most crimes don't. And this one isn't your problem. It's Moy's. He can handle it better than you can. He has the resources to track it down. You don't.

"Take my advice, Brew. Go home. Get some rest. Concentrate on keeping Alex Lacone happy."

Actually I disagreed with him. Most crimes did make sense. Maybe they all did. They might look random or gratuitous from the outside, but on the inside they all had their own logic. People did what they did for reasons. Crazy reasons, sometimes, stupid or malicious reasons, careless reasons, misguided—but reasons. The man who'd killed Bernie and taken the flik had reasons. They just didn't involve Bernie personally.

Before I hung up, I said, "I appreciate what you're doing for me, Marshal. I know I don't sound like it. I suppose that's because I don't understand you." Or because I thought I did—and I hated it. "But you've already done more than I had a right to ask for, and I want to say thanks."

He replied with a snorting noise. "In other words, no, you won't take my advice. OK. You're a big boy now. You can probably make your own decisions. What *are* you going to do?"

I shrugged at the nearest sailing ship. "I have a date with Sternway. He wants to show me where he gets his credibility in the martial arts.

"One way or another," I added aimlessly, "all Lacone's plans for Martial America seem to depend on Sternway's credibility."

"Brew—" Marshal stopped himself, then started again. "Have you still got that cannon you showed me the other day?"

"Sure." I carried it like a weight on my heart. I'd killed my brother with it. Without it I felt incomplete. "Why?"

"Just a precaution." He sounded a bit too casual for my taste. "I've heard rumors about Sternway's nights out."

Apprehension crawled like a line of ants across my belly. "Such as?"

"Such as rumors, that's all," Marshal replied tartly. "I couldn't guess whether they're true or not." His tone lightened for a moment. "Tomorrow you'll be able to tell me." Then he seemed to bear down. "Just don't let him talk you into anything that strikes you as odd."

Odd? I muttered to myself. Anson Sternway? No shit.

Aloud I said, "I'm safe then. The way I feel tonight, he couldn't talk me into buying him a drink."

With evident relief, Marshal replied, "Good."

After that he reminded me to call him when I'd talked to Moy. Finally we managed to hang up.

Staring vacantly at the ceiling, I thought, Rumors? Oh, joy.

So far I hadn't liked anything that working for Lacone had gotten me into.

17

I might've just sat there for an hour or two, drinking the occasional glass of water and hating Bernie's death, but it was obvious that I couldn't. While I'd been on the phone, Alyse's smile had taken on an expectant tinge. Didn't I have places to go? she appeared to ask kindly. Questions to ask? Ideas to pursue? Or maybe behind her angelic beam she just looked worried.

And I was running out of time.

I felt too tired to eat anything. Just climbing to my feet and leaving Bernie's apartment without cleaning it some more seemed to exhaust my reserves of willpower and tough-mindedness. By the time I reached the Plymouth, I ached to sprawl on the floor behind the seats and take a nap.

So I decided to act like a grown-up for a change. If nothing else, I needed to shore up my nerves for one of Sternway's "nights out." Ignoring the steady nag of my watch, I pulled out of Bernie's neighborhood and went cruising for another fast-food joint. I didn't start to pick my way across Carner toward Martial America until I'd visited the drive-through of a generic chicken place and taken plenty of napkins to absorb the grease.

Luckily the drive was comparatively easy. Blazing streetlamps, incandescent car dealerships, and halogen-scorched malls notwithstanding, this part of Carner was almost deserted now. Unless they attended some sporting event, the city's regular denizens must've retreated to their homes. No doubt they all yearned for some space where they could actually turn off the lights. As a result, the streets were almost empty, and I hauled into Martial America's parking lot only ten minutes late.

By then I had enough heartburn to power a nuclear submarine, and the effects of Bernie's loneliness had sunk into the marrow of my bones. I was in no danger of letting Sternway talk me into *any*thing.

Lights showed in the upper windows of *Essential Shotokan*, but the *dojo* below, like the rest of that building, was dark. *Malaysian Fighting Arts'* training spaces were apparently still in use, although I didn't hear any yells.

The IAMA director waited for me beside his Camaro, standing with his arms crossed in a pose that would've looked rigid on anyone else. He'd changed his white shirt and slacks for a light grey sweatshirt and warmup pants. On his feet he wore boat moccasins with no socks. Shadows cast from the nearest light pole concealed his expression.

I parked the Plymouth in line with Sternway's car and got out. Just for a second, the night air felt inexplicably cold. Then stored heat from the concrete pushed the sensation away. Familiar sweat gathered at my temples as I walked toward him.

He nodded a greeting. "Glad you could make it." His tone might've meant anything.

I peered at him, but even close up I couldn't read his face. He looked as unapproachable as a stone idol. "Am I overdressed?" I asked. "You didn't tell me you were going to change."

"It doesn't matter," he replied distantly. "No one cares." He gestured me toward the Camaro. "Shall we go?"

I shook my head. "I'll follow you. That way I can drive myself home afterward." I didn't want to be stuck with him if he decided to do something *odd.*

"Suit yourself." With an indifferent shrug, he reached for the door of his car.

Suit myself. Fine. "Just one thing," I put in. "A question I forgot to ask earlier."

He dropped his hand. "Yes?"

"I've been wondering. What's the real reason you haven't moved into Martial America? Wouldn't you be in a better position to keep the peace if you were there when trouble started?"

He tilted his head, and a flash from the light pole gleamed in his eyes. "Possibly." The subject didn't interest him. "Or I might be caught in the middle. I could lose my leverage with both sides."

"But it might be worth the risk," I insisted. "Lacone sounds like he's willing to cut quite a deal for you."

Sternway made a small sound like a sigh. "He's in the business of making money, Brew. Generosity would reduce his income."

Then he appeared to rally his attention. "In fact," he went on more strongly, "Mr. Lacone has offered me very favorable terms. But there are strings attached. If I stake the future of my school on the success of Martial America, I'll be damaged if his dream fails. In order to protect myself, I'll have to continue working on his behalf whether he pays me for my efforts or not. You could say that I'll be trapped into serving as his consultant and promoter for free.

"I'm better off independent of Martial America."

As he spoke, I felt the kind of satisfaction you get when you find a jigsaw piece that fits. One section of the puzzle he presented came into focus.

Earlier he'd made a sympathetic speech about how the IAMA existed *to promote a sense of mutual cooperation, understanding, and support among all the martial arts.* And how Martial America had *the potential to foster a sense of community which can only benefit the martial arts.* At the time, I hadn't known what to make of his professed idealism. Now I did.

It was bullshit. Huckster talk. What he really cared about was getting his hands on Lacone's money.

Without warning I began looking forward to whatever he planned to show me tonight. I wanted to know now he *earned respect* in the martial arts world. His credibility obviously didn't derive from innate moral authority.

"Fair enough." I grinned at him with my teeth. "That answers my question.

"I'm ready when you are."

He considered me for a moment longer. His gaze reflected sharp slivers of light like surgical probes. Then in silence he turned back to the Camaro, opened the door, and got in.

I followed his example. A minute later we were on our way, leaving behind the sections of Carner that I'd started to know.

The night sky, rendered featureless by Carner's ubiquitous artificial illumination, didn't help my general disorientation. Before long, however, I developed the vague impression that we were heading approximately downtown.

Marshal's warnings squirmed at the back of my mind. I felt an unexpected impulse to call Ginny, let her know what I was doing. As if we were still partners—

I needed to get over that somehow.

Sternway led me onto one of the freeways, then off again

before I could identify it. We spent a mile or two on Vista Boulevard, a divided street arched over with louring elms. When we left it, we seemed to pass almost immediately into a zone where the city fathers begrudged spending money. Their commitment to excessive lighting remained, but the quality of the illumination shifted, grew colder and more fluorescent, less habitable. Unnatural white lay on the walls of the buildings and the cracked pavement of the sidewalks, turning them the color of desiccated bone. At the corners, shadows deepened and spread, forming swatches and pools of real darkness. Defying Carner's expenditure of electricity, night found its way into the city's unprotected alleys and doorways and gutters. Grit and dispossessed scraps of paper fluttered occasionally in broken gusts of wind.

The streets narrowed as Sternway led me between squat bars, pawn shops, and porn joints that looked like the fallen sections of some larger hulk. Neon signs and advertisements in crass colors flickered over the sidewalks, but most of them had letters or pieces missing, and dirt and neglect dulled the rest.

Without signaling, the Camaro turned left into an alley crowded with shadows that seemed to swallow the Plymouth's beams. Barely able to see, I crept along behind Sternway's taillights like a sailor who'd wandered into a Sargasso, walls of storm looming on either side. We passed a series of unlit doors, some broken and gaping, others slumped on their hinges like homeless souls. Then his brake lights flared, and the alley opened into a small parking lot like an abandoned scrap yard.

A dozen or so cars nearly filled the space, but Sternway wedged his Camaro into a gap against one wall. I eased the van in behind him close enough to tap his bumper. This way, I thought grimly, he couldn't abandon me here no matter what happened.

When I stepped out, I smelled refuse, rotted kitchen scraps, piss, and the lingering reek of vomit. But behind those odors hung an unexpected athletic scent, the distinctive scent of sweat, Tiger Balm, and pain.

Despite my disorientation, I felt suddenly that I'd arrived in a world I understood. I couldn't so much as guess what this grubby place had to do with Sternway's famous martial credibility, but I knew beyond doubt that the language spoken here would be furtive and hostile, as familiar as the midnight patois of Puerta del Sol.

Sternway locked the Camaro and joined me. A stretch of lamplight from the street lay across the middle of the yard, revealing him clearly as he passed through it. The disinterest he'd conveyed outside Martial America was gone. Now he reminded me of a lit fuse, primed with secret excitement—sparking toward detonation.

"Where are we?" I asked.

"It doesn't have a name. That's why we couldn't meet here." He drew me into motion behind him. "You might not have been able to find it. And they wouldn't let you in without me."

I wasn't at all surprised.

Almost hurrying now, he approached a door in one of the side walls. This door was metal, heavy as a lid, with a closed shutter at the level of his face. He knocked crisply three times, raising a muted echo from the frame. After a heartbeat or two, the shutter clattered open. From the small window, light and cigarette smoke spilled outward.

Framed in the opening, a blunt face with what appeared to be dragon's claws tattooed around the eyes glared at us. The eyes focused on Sternway and dropped slightly in recognition. Then they shifted to me.

"Friend of mine," Sternway volunteered insincerely.

A voice like a gravel sifter issued from the door. "He carrying?"

Sternway glanced at me and nodded. "Looks like it."

"Tell him to leave it."

The shutter crashed shut.

My *friend* considered me as if he expected me to comply automatically. Until then I hadn't realized that he knew I had a weapon. When I frowned, he said in a casual tone, "Put your gun in the van, Brew. They won't let you in with it." He looked almost happy. "You don't want to argue with the bouncers here."

The hell I didn't. From inside the door I heard muffled sounds like screams. He might as well have asked me to walk into a fire fight unarmed.

I wasn't sure I knew how to face trouble without the .45.

Unfortunately I couldn't imagine an alternative that didn't involve turning my back and driving away. After a moment's hesitation, I shrugged, returned to the Plymouth, and stashed my gun in its holster under the seat. There I hesitated again. In some other life, I would've called Ginny for backup, but that wasn't an option now. Instead I took the phone out of my jacket and slipped it into a pants pocket. Leaving my jacket on the seat, I relocked the van and strode back toward Sternway.

Even then the night air felt too warm to be natural. The surrounding walls seemed to retain something more than the sun's heat.

Sternway nodded his approval and immediately repeated his knock. This time the shutter stayed closed. But the door scraped outward, pushed by a hand the size of a Christmas fruitcake.

At once the shrouded din inside resolved itself into shouts of encouragement, scorn, and exertion, combined with the flat thud of blows. Behind the stink of cigarettes and cheap cigars, the athletic odor sharpened.

In the doorway a man with a recidivist's skull, bulging forearms, and at least fifty pounds he didn't need acknowledged Sternway, but didn't step out of our way. Instead he studied me. He wore a black muscle shirt and torn jeans held up by a length of heavy chain. From the neckline of his shirt protruded the tattooed head of a Chinese-style dragon with scaled forelegs that reached up along his neck and face until the claws circled his eyes. Chewing tobacco stained his lips a sickly red.

Deliberately he scowled at my pants.

Swallowing stomach acid, I suggested politely, "Make up your mind, asshole. I can get sneered at anywhere. I don't need to stand here for your benefit."

He ignored me. To Sternway he said, "Left pocket."

There was a distinct bulge in the left pocket of my pants.

"Cell phone," Sternway answered cheerfully.

The bouncer shifted his wad. "You know the rules. He calls the cops, you're both history."

Heavily he retreated from the doorway to let us in.

Sternway practically bounded over the threshold. I followed with less enthusiasm.

As I passed him, the bouncer said, gravel-on-metal, "Watch your back, motherfucker."

I smiled. "Don't worry about me. I'm already impressed. I

didn't know it was possible to say 'motherfucker' without moving your lips."

Apparently he didn't care whether I was impressed or not. Dismissing me with a contemptuous snort, he turned away to slam the door. It clanged shut like the door of a cell.

When I was sure he didn't mean to watch my back for me, I went after Sternway.

He paused to let me catch up. Then he warned me softly, "I hope you're as tough as you talk, Brew. If you keep that up, you'll have to prove it."

I wanted to laugh in his face. Less than twenty-four hours after Muy Estobal shot me, I'd killed him with nothing but my arms and my weight. Thugs like that bouncer didn't scare me. I'd been defending myself in Puerta del Sol's rathole bars, derelict parks, and littered alleys for years. Under pressure I've been known to throw filing cabinets around like paperweights.

On the other hand, my chest still felt tender where Parker Neill had poked me. And I couldn't pretend, even to myself, that I'd regained all my strength. Hell, my torn guts hadn't really stopped bothering me until a few days ago.

And I knew what beatings felt like. I'd taken my share.

Instead of laughing, I told Sternway, "I'll try to keep my mouth shut."

He nodded and turned away.

A doorway to the left let us into a corridor with lockers lining one wall. Roughly half of them were locked. The rest may've been empty. The force of a falling body somewhere ahead made their doors rattle.

Sternway stopped at a combination lock halfway down the row, dialed the locker open, and took out sparring gear—foam hand- and foot-pads, a mouthpiece, a protective cup. I'd seen similar equipment everywhere at the tournament.

Shit, I thought. It's a fight club. What fun.

He meant to show me that he deserved *respect* by pounding the by-products out of a roomful of drunken brawlers.

No wonder the damn place didn't have a name. It had to be illegal. Especially if people put money on the bouts—and I was sure they did, knowing Sternway. Even more so if it served booze.

He gave me a sharp glance to gauge my reaction, then stowed his wallet and keys in the locker. When he'd kicked his moccasins in as well, he replaced the lock and spun the dial.

Lithe and quick, he continued along the corridor. Past the row of lockers, he pushed open the door to what must've been a changing room, judging by the concentrations of Tiger Balm and battered weariness in the air. "Restrooms here if you need them," he informed me as he went in.

I shook my head. Instead of following, I moved forward to take a look at what I was getting into.

After half a dozen paces, the corridor reached a room with decor like a black hole, large enough to house a popular dance club and bar. At once the noise seemed to swell like a mushroom cloud, enhanced by the hard linoleum floor and cinderblock walls. Through a haze of smoke that obscured the ceiling, I saw maybe as many as fifty tables crowded around all four sides of a raised boxing ring, complete with ropes and corner poles. Streaks and splotches that looked like old blood decorated the canvas.

At the moment the ring was empty.

Small groups of men occasionally accompanied by women occupied folding chairs at most of the tables. Some of the women looked like they were trolling for muscular companionship. The rest had apparently come to cheer on their husbands, boyfriends, or pimps.

Ashtrays and drinks, mostly beer, littered the tabletops, but the room didn't sport a bar, and at first I didn't see where the booze came from. Then off to my right an unmarked door with no knob or handle swung open, and a couple of waitresses came in wearing what looked like the cast-off remains of can-can costumes. They carried trays packed to the rims with bottles, glasses, and cans. For a second I wondered how they re-opened the door from this side, but then I noticed a hasp on the inside of the door hinged to extend past the frame. That prevented the door from closing completely.

Clever, I muttered to myself. A bar pretending it was separate from the fight club supplied the booze. Shut the door, snap on a padlock, and tell the cops you don't have anything to do with what's on the other side. And of course the patrons of the fight club would claim that they brought all their drinks with them.

Nothing illegal there. The cops couldn't prove otherwise unless they staged an undercover raid. Which might get a little risky without guns, considering the fight club's clientele.

I scanned the room for a couple of minutes, forming an impression of the men at the tables. Some of them had the bulging stocky look of ex-pugs and prizefighter wannabes. Others carried leaner frames and sleeker muscles that reminded me of the black belts I'd seen spar at the tournament. A certain number had obviously come just to watch and bet. They were too full of beer, or otherwise larded with dissipation, to be mistaken for fighters themselves. And a small handful, almost dapper compared to the rest of the crowd, had the characteristic air, at once avid and detached, of bookies and punters, here to set odds, back favorites, meet bets, and generally stir money around the room so that plenty of it ended up in their pockets.

Four bouncers circulated between the tables, usually in the general vicinity of the waitresses—just making sure the patrons didn't stiff anyone. Like the thug at the front door, a couple of them wore thick chains somewhere handy. The others apparently relied on bulk, threatening faces, and a manly indifference to pain to make them effective.

In the far corner, a steel door sealed the room, imitating a fire exit. After a moment, I decided that it had to be a second, maybe more private, entrance. There weren't enough cars in the parking lot to account for all the people here.

From where I stood, I didn't see anyone who looked familiar, from the tournament or anywhere else. Maybe Sternway was an exception—maybe most *karate-ka* didn't play this game. Or maybe they were just more choosy about where they played it.

For a moment or two, I felt positively cheerful. Inside these walls—if nowhere else in Carner—I knew exactly what was going on.

Before long Sternway arrived at my shoulder. He wore his footpads, carried his gloves and mouthpiece. From there he moved into the crowd and took a chair at an empty table close to the ring. As soon as I joined him, he leaned forward.

"Works like this," he told me in a primed whisper. "Challenger gets into the ring. Anybody who wants to. Guy who won the last bout gets first chance to accept. If he refuses, somebody else can accept. Again, anybody.

"No rules, no time limit. Gear optional. Bout's over when one of them surrenders. Or can't get up."

"No rules?" I stared at him. "You mean biting is OK?"

He grinned sharply. "If you can get away with it."

I'd never seen him grin before. It made him look feral. Predatory as a polecat.

In one smooth motion, he left the table. After a quick pause with one of the punters, he headed for the ring, flowing easily between the ropes. At once a halfhearted shout of recognition went up from the room, a mixture of leaden cheers and groans. Obviously most of the crowd knew him. And, just as obviously, some of them weren't glad to see him.

I watched with a sort of bemused dismay as he pulled on and secured his hand-pads, waiting for an opponent. The sonofabitch was *serious*. He wanted me to shiver in my little booties whenever I looked at him, purportedly so that I'd understand why men like Nakahatchi, Hong, and Soon let him tell them what to do, and he didn't care who he beat up to achieve his desired effect.

His eagerness suggested that he was in no danger of getting beat up himself.

Apparently the former "victor" refused Sternway's challenge. For a minute or two he gazed around the room, looking for candidates. Then a chair behind me scraped the floor, and a man headed for the ring. He was naked to the waist, and in the clouded light he looked like he'd been spit out by a rock crusher and glued back together again. He moved with the lumbering inevitability of a landslide, but as far as I could tell his only real qualifications seemed to be arms the size of axletrees and enough scar tissue to deaden the impact of a piled river.

He didn't have gloves, foot-gear, or a mouthpiece. Maybe he didn't even wear a cup.

A couple of dozen people shouted approval when he climbed into the ring. While he faced the crowd and turned in a circle to let everyone get a look at him, activity flurried briefly around the bookies and punters. The little I could overhear suggested that the impromptu book was against him, 3-1.

Sternway would have to earn his money the hard way.

A waitress with a wasted syphilitic face arrived to ask me what I wanted. Instead of telling the truth, I ordered a club soda. She took my money disdainfully, didn't offer me any change.

When the betting subsided, Sternway and his opponent squared off.

In spite of myself, I was impressed—not for the first time—with Sternway's dangerous ease. He couldn't have looked more relaxed without falling asleep, but instead of slumping he seemed to lift, grow lighter, until his feet hardly touched the canvas. In contrast, the other man looked solid enough, dense enough, to leave dents with every step.

Hoarse cheers spattered around the room as scar-tissue-and-rocks started forward.

He didn't get far. In the middle of his second stride, Sternway lunged into a punch so fast that I hardly saw it hit. Then somehow the same motion carried Sternway into the air for a flying kick that rocked his opponent's head. A second later he was out of range again, floating as if he hadn't moved at all.

His feral grin seemed to fill his whole face.

But the scarred man wasn't discouraged. Maybe Sternway's pads softened the blows. Shaking his head to clear it, he charged headlong at the IAMA director.

That much force would've driven a Volkswagen into the ropes, but Sternway stepped aside. As his opponent went by, he flicked an elbow casually at the bigger man's shoulder. The blow looked as light as a kiss, but it snatched a roar of pain or frustration from the big man.

He started to turn like he wanted to charge again. Sternway stopped him with a kick on the top of his calf that collapsed him to his knees. Before he could try to stand, or even get his hands up, Sternway hit him three times in the face, blows as loud as shots. Then Sternway drifted happily back out of range.

To my chagrin, I realized that I'd been holding my breath. Almost involuntarily I identified with the scarred man. He fought the way I did. I wanted him to shrug off his hurts and keep going.

If he landed one punch, he'd knock the damn joy off Sternway's face.

Obediently he regained his feet and went back to work.

This time, however, he didn't charge. Instead he advanced more cautiously, looking for a chance to grab or strike. For a while he and Sternway circled each other like dogs in the preliminary stages of a dominance contest.

Then a look of calculation came into Sternway's eyes, hinting at a pre-planned attack. In the process he offered his opponent an opening I could've hit from where I sat.

Thinking, Don't do it, that's what he wants, I watched the bigger man go for the opening with a roundhouse hard enough to powder cinderblocks.

Again Sternway shifted out of the way. All according to plan. While the punch extended the bigger man's arm, Sternway flicked another elbow at the exposed shoulder.

The same shoulder he'd hit before. In the same spot.

When the bigger man recovered from his swing, he couldn't lift that arm anymore. Couldn't even hold it out in front of him. His fingers seemed to writhe with a life of their own, autonomically, no longer under his control.

His supporters groaned and swore disgustedly. Money changed hands as a few spectators paid off.

Ignoring everything else, Sternway drifted around the ring like he was gamboling inside.

His opponent bared his teeth and moved to attack again, but I didn't want to watch. While Sternway systematically reduced the bigger man to rubble, I made a show of looking for the waitress. Actually I was trying to think of an excuse to leave.

Eventually Sternway's opponent lay on the canvas, still conscious, not obviously bleeding, but as slack as a man with a broken neck.

As the bouncers removed him, a movement behind them caught my eye. The alleged fire exit opened and closed. The ring blocked my view, but I thought I spotted the top of a head enter the room. Then it dropped out of sight as the new arrival took a seat.

I felt a sudden tingling in my guts—the first cold touch of premonition, intuitive alarm.

Acting detached, Sternway left the ring and headed for the punter who held his bet. Then he returned to my table. For the moment, at least, he'd hidden away his eagerness. Only a smolder of it showed in his eyes as he sat down.

He wasn't sweating. Hell, he wasn't even breathing hard. Apparently he found no-rules fighting about as aerobic—not to mention stressful—as a walk in the park.

He leaned toward me to say something, but the waitress interrupted him with my drink. He ordered a diet Coke, paid her out of his winnings. Judging by his wad of bills, I guessed he'd just made a couple of hundred bucks.

"Feel like trying it?" he asked. The noise in the room covered his tone, but it sounded like a taunt nevertheless.

I gave him a grin as sharp as I could make it. "This is your idea of fun, not mine. When I'm in the mood for excitement"—I pretended to laugh—"I lie down until I feel better."

His upper lip hinted at a sneer, but he didn't argue.

By then another challenger approached the ring. The pang in my stomach tightened as I recognized the bouncer who'd let us in.

I looked a question at Sternway. The fight club could lose control of its patrons if it let the bouncers get pounded.

He shrugged. The issue didn't interest him.

Deliberately I asked, "You going to take him on?"

He didn't answer.

The tattooed bouncer climbed between the ropes like a man with a mission and planted himself in the ring. His eyes in their claws glared right at Sternway and me. I assumed—or hoped—that he wanted to know if Sternway accepted his challenge. But before Sternway could react, the man's gravel-sifter voice grated out, "Not you. Him." He pointed straight at me. "I want *you*, motherfucker."

I might as well have had a spotlight on me. Suddenly every head in the room turned in my direction. Tension or anticipation spattered through the smoke like overheated oil.

Sternway made a sound like the bark of a raptor. "Up to you," he told me. "You have the stones for it?"

On some other occasion, I might've said, Fuck you, and gone home. But not this time. The premonition clutching at my insides didn't let me.

The room held dangers I couldn't identify.

"I said I *want* you!" the bouncer announced. Just in case I hadn't understood him.

I still had no clue what I was looking for, but I got to my feet anyway.

A few men shouted approval when they noticed my size. Sounds of interest scattered through the room. Bookies and punters went to work. But I ignored everything around me.

For the first time since I'd sat down, I could see past the ring to the people at the far tables.

"I'm new at this," I said, pitching my voice to carry. "Let me see if I've got it straight." I spoke to the bouncer, but I hardly glanced at him. Past his bulk I scrutinized every face that wasn't turned away or hidden. "No rules. Is that right? And we go at it until one of us surrenders?"

"That's right, motherfucker," my challenger snarled. Maybe he thought his tattoo made him an actual dragon.

Casually Sternway offered, "Or until one of you can't continue."

At first I saw nothing beyond the ring except more people, none of them distinguishable from the rest of the club's patrons. They regarded me with a kind of conflicted hunger, a desire composed of bloodthirstiness, greed, and scorn. Some of them didn't care who won, as long as fighters got hurt. Others scurried around inside themselves, trying to calculate odds for and against.

But then the man I didn't know I was looking for raised his head, and suddenly everyone else seemed to recede, leaving him alone across the canvas from me, isolated by lights and smoke and butchery.

A big man, dull eyes floating above a heavyset frame. Jowls like fanny packs strapped to his jaws. A forehead suited for battering down doors. A pile of debris instead of a nose.

I answered the bouncer without paying any attention to him. "Fine. I surrender. You win."

I wasn't sure that the heavyset man had actually focused on me yet. Hell, I wasn't sure that he'd gotten a good enough look at me the other day to recognize me now. But I turned away quickly, just in case.

While the tattoo roared obscenities, and his disgusted audience volleyed contempt at my head, I ducked down to tell Sternway, "I think I'll go puke." Throwing as much chaff in his eyes as I could. "If I'm not back in a couple minutes, order me a stomach pump. And some Valium."

Then I headed for the restroom.

It was a tactical decision, and I hated it already. Bernie's death burned holes in my gut. I wanted to go after that thieving goon now, right *now*, drop him where he sat before he could so much as think about trying to get away. In an earlier life—as recently as two months ago—I wouldn't have hesitated.

But I didn't have all my strength back. When the cops found out that I'd been withholding information, I'd be in trouble. And I wasn't after the heavyset man himself. I only cared about him because he could lead me to my real target.

Also I didn't have the .45.

In other words, I was afraid. Which I hated to admit, even to myself. But at the tournament he'd moved with Sternway's *plastique* lightness—and I'd just watched Sternway demonstrate what that ease meant.

Hounded by expletives and raspberries, I pushed into the changing room and let the door swing shut behind me. At once the smells of effort and aching muscles replaced the club's cigarette stink. Gripping the cell phone, I checked the stalls, urinals, and showers to be sure I was alone. Then I dialed 911 and chewed the inside of my cheek while I waited for the dispatcher.

The phone hadn't stopped ringing when it was snatched out of my hand with enough force to jolt my head.

Instinctively I turned and pitched a fist that would've caught Sternway dead in the face if he hadn't been lightyears too fast for me. He flicked my punch away with his fingers like he'd seen it coming for the past week.

At the same time, he canceled my call.

"What the hell's the matter with you?" he demanded almost cheerfully. "Don't you listen to *anybody*? If you call the cops, we're both history." He must've heard me dial only three digits. "And I do *not* mean barred from the club. We'll be left in so many pieces nobody will ever identify them."

A shiver of cold fury gathered in my stomach. As if I hadn't just tried to clobber him and failed, I held out my hand. "My phone." Deliberately I snapped my fingers. "Give it back. Or explain to Detective Moy why you're obstructing his investigation."

Sternway returned my gaze with an air of vague amusement. No doubt he could've killed me with one hand. And I believed him about the danger. If a bouncer caught me calling the cops, I'd be in serious shit. But at the moment I didn't give a damn.

I stared him down anyway.

"The goon Bernie followed into the men's room is here." I put all the acid I had into it, every scalding drop of heartburn and grief. "Moy wants him for murder.

"He didn't do it. That's obvious. But he knows who did."

I hoped that was a punch Sternway hadn't seen coming.

A muscle at the corner of his jaw twitched. He didn't betray any other reaction.

"Moy is a cop," I flung at him. "He's going to think you and that asshole are in this together, *so give me the damn phone.*"

Just for a second, I thought he would drive his hand right through me and pull out my heart. But then his head made a small movement like a nod. Half smiling to himself, he looked away so that he wouldn't have to watch while he dropped the phone into my hand.

"It's your funeral, Axbrewder," he said softly. "Don't expect me to back you up. Not here."

With a gentle shrug, he left the room.

Abruptly its smell seemed to shift. Now the odor of Tiger Balm and bruises felt more threatening than the rank hunger of the fight club. Hurrying because I was scared—and because I didn't want the goon to get away—I went to the door and braced my back against it while I re-dialed. Then I held my breath.

When the dispatcher answered—a woman's voice—I didn't give her time to ask questions. "Just listen," I told her. "My name is Axbrewder. Get a message to Sergeant Edgar Moy. He's investigating a murder at The Luxury, and I've spotted his suspect. He better get here fast. I don't think I can handle him myself."

Quickly I gave her the best directions I could. Five seconds later, the phone back in my pocket, I headed for the ring to find out whether the heavyset man was still there.

Now no one noticed me. For all I knew, the whole club had forgotten I existed. A new fight transfixed the room. The tattooed bouncer had found an opponent, one of the lean fast men who looked like he'd styled his body after a greyhound. At the moment the lean fool was getting killed. He could scarcely stand, and as soon as the bouncer found a handhold that dragon would start to crush bones.

The heavyset man remained in his seat, observing the fighters with a look that resembled clinical detachment.

For a heartbeat or two, relief left me woozy, and the smoke almost smelled good to me. Finally, I thought. A break. Now I can get somewhere.

Trying to stay calm, I found my way back to Sternway's table and sat down.

He hardly glanced at me. "Satisfied?" Maybe the fight interested him somehow.

I waited for a pause in the grunt-and-slap of the struggle, the halfhearted encouragement and disgust from the spectators, then said, "Ask me later. Moy isn't here yet."

A moment later I heard the unmistakable sound of bones breaking, the sharp anguish of the bone itself muffled and moistened by battered flesh. I looked up just in time to see the bouncer fold his opponent's elbow in several different directions at the same time. The lean man squealed once, like a horse with a shattered leg. Then the bouncer punched him to the canvas, and he stopped complaining. For a few seconds I wasn't sure that he was still alive. But eventually he coughed, splashing blood across his cheek, and then I saw his chest shudder with pain as he breathed.

I didn't realize that I was on my feet until the bouncer faced me and pointed at his opponent, "That's *you*, motherfucker!" he snarled over the crowd. "He took your place!"

After a few ragged heartbeats, I managed to sit back down.

"Dickless bastard!" the tattoo offered viciously. "Left your cock in your momma and never got it back. You like watching what you can't have?"

I didn't take him up on it. Under other circumstances, I might've thought I had something to prove. But at the moment I did *not* need to get my back broken while the heavyset man disappeared into the night.

I'd given him a good look at me. If he recognized me from the tournament—

Sternway leered contemptuously, but I ignored him the same way I ignored the jibes and catcalls around me. I had too many other things to worry about.

While the dragon tattoo stomped around the ring, waving his arms and demanding a new challenger, another bouncer and a stricken woman, a wife or girlfriend, got the lean man off the canvas. "What happens now?" I asked Sternway.

He shrugged dismissively. "He gets left outside. If she doesn't have a phone, the bar next door calls an ambulance." A cold smile stretched his mouth. "It's reported as 'gang-related violence.' If either of them mentions this place, he doesn't make it out of the hospital. Maybe she doesn't either."

He paused for a moment, then added as if I'd asked for a justification, "He knew what could happen. He's got nothing to bitch about. If he didn't tell her the rules, that's his problem."

Oh, sure, I thought. Fine. All clean and tidy. If you made it sound any prettier, you could set it to music.

Grinning over my teeth, I muttered back, "I can see why you like it here. All this honest brutality probably makes you feel right at home."

Briefly his mouth twisted, but he didn't say anything.

The next instant I forgot all about Anson Sternway as the heavyset man rose from his seat.

Carrying his gear, my target climbed into the ring so easily that he practically wafted.

I wasn't sure, but I thought I caught a glimpse of consternation in the bouncer's eyes.

At once the room about went crazy as everyone with a spare buck scrambled to place bets. By the time the action around the bookies and punters subsided, the odds were 3-2 against the dragon tattoo. Which would've suprised me if I hadn't see that look in his eyes. Everything else about him proclaimed that he could stand up to a howitzer shell at point-blank range.

In a kind of nauseated suspense, I watched the goon pull on his hand- and foot-pads and turn to face the bouncer. On all sides of the ring, men hollered and whistled, brandished their fists and pounded the tables, as if they expected a bloodbath. Two or three women raised their breasts like they were offering themselves as trophies.

I hated it, but I wasn't much better myself. My own lust squirmed in my stomach, throbbed in my bones. The heavyset man had something to do with Bernie's death, he could lead me to the killer, and I wanted him hurt—damaged enough to make him docile.

The bouncer and my target didn't waste time posturing. Without warning they flung themselves at each other with a shock that made my guts lurch.

Right away the tattoo tried to grapple, secure a hold so that he could put his bulk to work. But the goon ducked under his arms and drove uppercuts into his ribs, rapid and staccato, a sound like pounding beef. Then the heavyset man danced clear.

If the bouncer were hurt, he didn't show it. Instead those uppercuts had shaken the consternation from his eyes. Now they bulged in the dragon's claws, porcine with rage, and a beast's predatory roar stretched his jaws.

His opponent's dull gaze suggested boredom. The goon carried his knuckled forehead and loose jowls with an air of weightless negligence, as if he already knew exactly how the fight would end.

The fighters jumped at each other again. The tattoo swung a wide punch that would've stunned a gorilla, but the goon surged inside the blow. Before the bouncer could react, the goon delivered an elbow strike that rocked the bigger man's head, staggered him.

The crowd responded with a howl that made no distinction between approval and outrage.

Again the heavyset man eluded a grab and drifted away.

Snarling deep in his throat, the bouncer slapped himself hard a couple of times to clear his head. Then he went back to the attack. But this time he didn't charge. Instead he shifted a step or two from side to side as he advanced. He wanted to back his opponent toward the corner pole, trap him there long enough to get a grip on him.

An urge to cough rose in my throat—tension, cigarette smoke, and heartburn working together. I fought it down.

My target let the bouncer herd him backward a few feet at a time until he was deep in the corner, hemmed in by the ropes. Blind intuition warned me that he was luring his opponent after him. If I'd been the bouncer's trainer, I would've screamed at him to retreat, keep to the center of the ring where he could maneuver. But his supporters didn't see what I saw—or didn't care. The entire room squalled at him to press his apparent advantage.

Then the heavyset man struck his audience silent with an attack so sudden that it hardly registered on me until it ended. In the space between one heartbeat and the next, he seemed to lift into the air, drawn upward by the rising force of his left knee.

And when he reached the apex of his jump, his right leg lashed out like the snap of a whip, catching the bouncer under his jaw and cracking his head back hard enough to splinter his spine.

Or *some*one's spine, anyway. Mine, for instance. The dragon tattoo rocked with the blow, staggered backward a step. But he simply had too much muscle to go down that easily.

Which the dull-eyed goon must've known. Without so much as a flicker of hesitation, he landed in a long crouch—right knee compressed under him, left leg extended behind—that dropped him below the bouncer's reach. In virtually the same motion, he drove forward again, heaving off the spring of his right leg to ram his left knee into his opponent's belly with the force of a sawed-off shotgun.

The bouncer doubled over with a gasp that seemed to expel every atom of oxygen from his lungs.

Now the heavyset man paused for a fraction of a second—just long enough to adjust his position. Then he swung his thick right leg up in an arc around the bouncer until it stretched almost straight for the ceiling. From there his heel slashed downward, hammering with all his weight and muscle behind it onto the base of the bouncer's neck.

The bouncer collapsed flat on the canvas as if every hard thing in his body had been smashed to jelly.

A spasm of coughing I couldn't control ripped through my throat hard enough to make my eyes tear. For a moment while I coughed I thought I saw the bouncer try to rise, jerked upward by the autonomic misfiring of his nerves. When I was able to blink my sight clear, however, I saw that he hadn't moved. Shallow respiration stirred him slightly. A couple of his fingers twitched—the involuntary sign language of pain. But he was out cold.

Around the room, people yelled hoarse triumph or disgust, but I ignored them. I already had enough disgust of my own—and way too much alarm. If Moy didn't get here soon, with enough men—not to mention guns—I might have to tackle the goon myself. Or let him walk away. And I was no match for him. Coughing tugged at my guts like Muy Estobal's bullet. If I went up against that thug alone, I wouldn't stand a chance.

I hadn't given the 911 dispatcher very good directions.

My target stood untouched by the noise like a man who didn't care what had just happened. After a minute or so while bettors counted their winnings or cursed their luck, another bouncer got into the ring to check on the dragon tattoo. With a little rough persuasion, the tattoo finally lifted his head, tried to lever his arms under him. The other bouncer offered to support him, but he shook off help and gradually worked his way upright one joint and muscle at a time. Staggering, he struggled between the ropes and down to the floor on his own.

From the tray of the nearest waitress, he grabbed a beer and chugged it. Then he shambled toward the back of the room as if he considered himself fit for duty.

He didn't once look at his opponent.

The heavyset man remained in the ring, but no one accepted his challenge. Still coughing, I watched him scan the room for a volunteer, but when he turned toward my table I ducked my head. If he hadn't recognized me yet, I didn't want him to do so now.

My heart lurched painfully when he said, "You. Big guy." Despite his battered face, he had a voice like slow silk, liquid and threatening. "I don't like the way you look at me. Get up here."

I glanced aside at Sternway, but he concentrated on the goon. His face held no expression of any kind.

I nudged his arm. "Moy isn't here yet," I breathed between muffled coughs. "It's your turn. Challenge him. Keep him busy."

Sternway shifted toward me slowly, regarded me as if for a moment he'd forgotten I existed. Swallowing unnamed emotions, he asked, "*That's* who you spotted at the tournament? I didn't realize—" Abruptly he leaned closer. "Shit, Brew," he whispered, "that's Turf Hardshorn. This is the only place I've ever seen him.

"I don't know his real name. They call him 'Turf' because he always 'plants' his opponents."

The man in the ring said something I didn't hear. Probably a mortal insult.

"So challenge him already," I told Sternway tensely.

Earn the right to sneer at me.

"Are you crazy?" he retorted, still whispering. "Didn't you watch—?" He pulled back a few inches. "He's the only fighter I know who scares me. I'd rather take on that bouncer blindfolded."

I couldn't read the look in his eyes. He may've been challenging me himself. Daring me to call him a coward—

I certainly hadn't earned *that* right.

The heavyset man raised his voice. "You with the cough. I'm *talking* to you. Don't you have any guts? Or maybe you're an undercover cop." He waved his hands in front of his face. "You stink like a cop. I can smell it from here."

Shit. Oh, shit. With just a few words, he'd shifted the whole club against me. If I didn't do something about it—fast—I'd be lucky to get out of here with only a few crushed bones. A couple of men were already on their way out of their chairs, spitting hostility as they rose. The bouncers moved to block the exits. Everyone else glared all kinds of murder in my direction.

"Back me up," I hissed under my breath at Sternway. Although he'd already said that he wouldn't. "Unless you want Bernie's killer to get away."

Then I raised my face to the ring.

Baring my teeth like the grin of a fright mask, I leaned back in my chair and spread my arms. "Well, if those are my only choices," I drawled so that the whole room could hear me, "I guess I'm just gutless."

"I don't think so," the goon replied smoothly. "I think you're a cop. You want to bust us all and make yourself a hero."

Half the fighters in my vicinity looked like they were about to jump me. I heaved a dramatic sigh and climbed heavily to my feet. "In that case—" Deliberately I faked insolence to disguise the fact that I knew I was about to get killed. Unless Sternway actually did back me up. "Since we're doing all this thinking anyway, *I* think we should take it outside. That way"—I rolled my eyes—"if I'm a cop I can't bust anyone else. And if I *am* a cop, you won't have to worry about witnesses."

I had the small satisfaction of hearing Sternway groan quietly, seeing the goon tilt back his head in surprise. But it didn't last long. A heartbeat later my challenger smiled. "I like it," he answered, slick as silk. "Let's go."

Slowly, taunting me, he stripped the pads from his hands and feet. Then he vaulted lightly over the ropes, dropped to the floor, and headed for the exit in the far corner of the room.

I didn't have any choice. I had to follow him. Denying myself so much as a glance at Sternway, I started to pick my way between the tables in the same direction.

I wanted the .45. More than that, I wanted Ginny. I'd walked into worse trouble than this when I knew she had my back. Or when she needed me to cover her. Without her I felt truncated in some profound way, almost unmanned—

Unfortunately my target didn't give a shit how I felt. Sternway probably didn't. Bernie and Alyse were past caring, and Ginny had walked out on our partnership. Moy wasn't here. No one gave a flying fuck at the moon about any of this, except me.

I wasn't sure that the crowd would let me go, but they did. Men and women fired obscenities as I passed, and one clown actually tried to spit at me—without much success—but none of them got in my way.

Like Jesus lugging his cross up Golgotha, too doomed for any kind of rescue, I crossed the room toward the far exit.

My target pulled the metal door open and let it swing shut after him. The dark outside seemed to swallow him before the door closed.

Before I could try to catch up with him, the bouncer with the dragon tattoo planted himself in front of me.

"Not that way, motherfucker," he grated. "*You* use the fucking front door."

The fury in his eyes suggested that he blamed me for the beating he'd just taken. He wouldn't have been in the ring at all if he hadn't wanted to repay my sarcasm. I'd created this whole mess myself when I'd first entered the club.

If the heavyset man escaped now, I might never find him again. A goon with a name like "Turf Hardshorn" wasn't likely to have a published phone number, or even a steady address.

I moved straight at the bouncer like he wasn't there.

Eagerly he spread his arms, stepped forward to meet me.

Hurrying too much to think or hesitate, I aimed both my arms under his right and heaved them up and around, sweeping his arm past me. Then I braced my left hand behind his shoulder and shoved as hard as I could.

I got lucky. He'd pushed forward to counter my sweep, and his own momentum helped me send him headlong into a cluster of seated spectators.

Before he could disentangle himself from fallen chairs and sprawling patrons, I reached the door.

Then I was out in a service alley. Light from the street limned the edges of the buildings, but their shadows obscured the alley, filling it with darkness. A stink as thick as syrup told me that I stood near an untended Dumpster before my eyes adjusted enough to discern the outlines of its bulk between me and the street. Dimly I made out darker shapes that resembled litter and trash cans. Rectangles of midnight in the opposite building suggested sealed doorways, boarded windows. Other than that I couldn't see a thing.

My target might've been right behind me, waiting for the perfect moment to break my back, and I wouldn't have known he was there. Until the door to the club opened again, letting out a wash of illumination, and Sternway stepped into the alley, I was blind in every way that mattered.

Fuck. Fuck and damn.

In the brief moment before the door closed again, I saw what I feared most. Sternway and I were alone. The heavyset man had already fled. Or hidden somewhere.

Which told me that he'd definitely recognized me. Whether he'd killed Bernie or not, he had no intention of getting caught.

The information did me no good whatsoever.

"Shit." The rank air aggravated my throat, triggered another coughing spasm. I had to wheeze for several seconds before I could tell Sternway, "He got away."

"You sure?" Sternway answered out of the gloom. He sounded unnaturally casual. "I've seen him fight before. I don't think you scare him that much."

Shit again. Apart from the distant reflections from the street, I might as well have had my eyes shut. Sternway was right. That goon didn't fear me at all. And I was the only witness who could connect him to Bernie and The Luxury—

Darkness this thick might conceal him anywhere in the alley.

Sternway had come this far with me. I guess that meant I could trust him.

I wanted to be near a wall, protect myself from attack on at least one side. Involuntarily curling my fingers around the butt of a gun I didn't have, I moved softly toward the Dumpster.

"What is this, a game?" I rasped loudly. I couldn't sound as casual as Sternway, and didn't try. Instead I covered my pounding heart and ragged breath with harshness. "You can't just step up and fight? We have to play hide-and-seek first?"

"Great idea, Brew," Sternway snorted, scorn as thick as the reek of garbage. "Piss him off even more. Who knows? He may forget he can tear out your liver with both hands tied behind him.

"This isn't a goddamn anthill."

I'd never heard him swear before. He was trying hard to warn me, but I didn't know how to heed him.

"Maybe," I muttered, mostly to myself. "Maybe not." I reached the Dumpster, felt the rough iron with one palm, then set my back against it. It felt impossibly cold. I didn't think anything in Carner ever cooled down that much. "Depends on what crawls out."

Without warning the darkness seemed to swirl and solidify, concentrate into a swift shape. I barely got my forearms up in time to prevent a blow from clanging my head off the side of the Dumpster.

I'd been hit that hard before. Bullets carried about the same punch. And once Muy Estobal had given me a beating that damn near crippled me. But still— When it happened, it wasn't something you could brace yourself for, or hope to absorb. My arms would've been equally effective against a wrecking ball.

A series of hits so quick that I couldn't distinguish them from each other drove between my forearms, dug into my floating ribs, slammed at my scarcely healed guts. By the third or fourth impact their force was all that kept me upright, nailed to the Dumpster when every clenched or rigid thing inside me had already been shocked into pudding. As soon as the hitting stopped, I folded helplessly to the pavement.

The fall didn't hurt. I had the sensation that I'd simply floated to the ground, drifting and curling from side to side like a sheet of paper in a slight breeze.

Some detached part of my brain imagined fancifully that as soon as I struck the cement I'd roll sideways, hauling up my knees and arms to ward off more blows. Surely there were more blows coming, I didn't doubt that for an instant. My assailant had no reason to stop. Why should he? I wasn't dead yet. Hell, I hadn't even been damaged as much as humanly possible.

He didn't stop. I heard more punches, heavy as sandbags,

emphasized by grunts of effort and the skittering slap of fast bare feet. For some reason, however, none of them seemed to touch me, despite the fact that I lay sprawled on my face, still pretending that soon I would start to roll, prepare to defend myself.

I wasn't being hit at all.

Somehow I wedged my arms under me and managed to heave my head off the pavement.

The darkness of the alley seemed deeper than it had a few seconds or minutes go. Or maybe I'd just forgotten how to see. A strange dance of gloom—obscurity wrapping and blowing around itself—may've been taking place a short distance in front of me. Or not. Maybe the dance was inside my head.

Nevertheless the sounds of battle continued. Expelled breath. Punished flesh. Still nothing struck me.

By degrees I understood that Sternway had come to my rescue.

Anson Sternway, who usually made my nerves squall with dislike. Who had told me, *He's the only fighter here who scares me.* Who had no detectable reason to care what happened to me.

HRH Anson fucking Sternway was about to get himself killed because I'd asked him to back me up. Because I'd made myself a target by taunting the bouncer at the front door.

That I felt.

Wobbling like a drunk, I got my legs under me and stumbled upright.

The effort hurt as if parts of my body had been violently removed, but it cleared my vision a bit. Swirl after swirl, the dark dance resolved itself into two shapes hurling everything they had at each other. I couldn't tell which was which. Gasps and sodden thuds seemed to arise from everywhere in the alley at once.

Sternway was fighting my fight. Gritting my teeth, I leaned what was left of me into motion.

I intended to put a stop to it. By falling on both of them, if I had to.

Out of the confused struggle, an unidentifiable voice gasped words between the blows. I heard them one at a time, registered them as discrete events. When I finally put them together, they said, "What the fuck are you doing?"

The next instant, one of the fighters let out a raw howl like the *kiais* I'd heard at the tournament. At the same time, he swung a fist like a sledgehammer into the other man's throat.

The sharp wet crack of a crushed larynx stopped me like I'd been punched in the chest. When one of the obscured shapes went down, I nearly fell with him.

From somewhere nearby, a location I couldn't identify, it might've been anywhere in the alley, Sternway's voice panted, "I shouldn't have been able to do that." Despite his exertions, he sounded entirely calm. "My night vision must be better than his. I've seen him counter attacks like that a dozen times."

He may've been justifying himself—

Crumbling to my knees beside the downed fighter, I groped at him until I reached his slack jowls and the liquid pulp of his larynx. Blood still oozed from the tears in his throat, but I couldn't find a pulse at his carotid artery, or in his wrist. As soon as I touched his chest, I knew he was gone. I'd handled enough corpses in my life to recognize the limp defeated feel of lifeless skin and muscles.

What the fuck are you doing?

When he left, he'd taken my only link to Bernie's killer with him.

18

Baffled and beaten, I bowed my head over Turf Hardshorn's body. For a while I couldn't think. Hell, I could hardly feel. I hurt too badly. A persistent ringing troubled my ears. Parts of my chest felt like they'd died a while ago.

"He's dead," I muttered hoarsely. I had to acknowledge the loss somehow.

"I know," Sternway said in the background. "I felt his windpipe go." A moment later he added unnecessarily, "He would've done the same to you if I hadn't stopped him."

What the fuck are you doing?

I couldn't imagine what to do next.

But I couldn't just kneel there until the end of time. My duties didn't end with this death. The fact that I'd failed Bernie tonight—and Alyse—didn't give me the right to surrender. It just meant that I'd have to try harder.

Which was a conclusion I'd grown accustomed to over the years.

Fumbling through the pain in my ribs and stomach and head, I got one hand on the cell phone and called 911.

Sternway said my name, but I had no energy to spare for him.

I'd go mad if Moy had ignored my summons.

When I told the dispatcher who I was, she instructed me to hold on. In fifteen seconds she connected me to Detective Moy.

"Axbrewder, where the hell are you?" He sounded bored despite the high-pitched whine in my ears. "Those were some shitty directions you left for me."

Apparently I wasn't the only one who'd been left. Since any information I produced now was bound to be worse, I forced myself to my feet and handed the phone to Sternway.

"Tell him where we are."

Some of the dead patches along my ribs contracted. Others spread out like oil spills.

Through the obscurity, Sternway's shape gave off the charged impression of a man with something important to say, but he didn't hesitate. He identified himself to the phone, said a few things that must've made sense to Moy. By the time he hung up, I could see red and blue lights strobing on the sides of the buildings.

The detective had been that close— If I hadn't given him shitty directions, he might've been able to rescue me.

That was usually Ginny's job.

The ringing took on a vague resemblance to music. I thought I recognized the animal husbandry section from Handel's *Messiah.* All we like sheep.

Sternway poked the phone at me. "Axbrewder," he said again. "We need to talk."

Vaguely I accepted the phone, put it away. "About?"

"I backed you up." He pitched his voice so that it wouldn't carry. "Now it's your turn. Don't say anything about the club."

I stared at him past a shroud of darkness. For a moment I couldn't think of a response. He wanted to protect his peculiar taste in recreation—I understood that—but the distortion of his priorities confused me anyway.

Boy, do we like sheep.

Finally I murmured, "Ask me something I can do. Moy needs to know. Now, tonight. He has to trace Hardshorn. Get his real name, find out where he lives, where he works, who his friends are, anything." Otherwise the link to Bernie's killer would vanish forever. "That means he needs to question people right away."

Behind us, car doors slammed. Guided by flashlights, three men headed into the alley. They didn't appear to be hurrying.

"I saved your life," Sternway insisted.

What the fuck are you doing?

I nodded at the gloom. "And I owe you. But I need Moy. I can't handle all this alone."

Despite the groaning protests of my ribs and arms, I braced myself to interfere if he tried to leave. I knew I couldn't stop him, but I intended to make an issue out of it nonetheless.

Fortunately he didn't move.

A minute later, the flashlights came around the end of the Dumpster. Edgar Moy and a couple of CPD uniforms incarnated themselves out of the shadows. The street cops weren't familiar to me, but Moy seemed unchanged, trench coat and all. Languidly he held his flashlight so that we could see his face, with its pencil-stroke mustache, nerveless cheeks, and sour eyes. The grey in his hair made him look like he'd just emerged from a dustbin.

"Axbrewder." He sounded too far away to do me any good. "Mr. Sternway." Then he aimed his flashlight at the pavement. "Who's the corpse?"

I told him. Gradually the ringing in my ears lost its weird resemblance to music. Now it sounded more like a drill bit running too hot.

I missed the sheep.

"Isn't that a coincidence," he observed rhetorically. "Two days ago he kills a security guard at The Luxury, and already you've tracked him down." His skepticism had all the subtlety of an interrogation with a rubber hose. "Even though it's none of your business.

"Which one of you heroes whacked him?"

Sternway donned his regalia, in a manner of speaking—HRH complete with pomp and circumstance. "It wasn't like that, Sergeant," he answered stiffly. "Axbrewder recognized him inside." He indicated the door to the club. "We didn't want to lose him, so we followed him when he left. He attacked Axbrewder suddenly. Axbrewder fell, and I joined the struggle. While we fought, I struck him in the throat. His larynx was crushed.

"I didn't expect that. I've seen him fight before. I had no idea of beating him. I simply hoped to stay alive until help arrived."

With imperial ease, he made his explanation sound like a complaint against the cops, as if Hardshorn might somehow still be alive if Moy had done his job properly.

The uniforms put on a show of inspecting the body—probably just staying out of Moy's way. Then one of them wandered back to the cruiser to call in the lab boys and photogs. The other studied the nooks and corners of the alley for no apparent reason.

Moy turned his head toward me at a quizzical angle. "That right, Axbrewder?"

I nodded. "Justifiable manslaughter." I tried not to sound bitter. "I couldn't handle him. I'd be dead now if Mr. Sternway hadn't jumped in."

"Fascinating." He didn't sounded fascinated. "Where's your

weapon? I thought all you private investigators carried guns. You looked half-naked without one on Saturday."

"I left it in my car." He'd started to piss me off. And the whine at the edge of my hearing didn't help. I wanted to straighten my back so that I could tower over him, but my ribs rejected the idea. The dead parts of my chest refused to flex.

"So by pure chance," Moy went on, "you and Mr. Sternway were out together when you spotted the alleged killer of a hotel security guard. Compounding the coincidence, he's a man Mr. Sternway has seen fight before, a man he knows well enough to identify by name, but didn't see at the tournament. And now he's dead.

"Do I have it right so far?"

He didn't expect an answer. Without conviction, he added, "Give me one more providential fluke, and I'm a happy man. I can hardly wait to find out what law-abiding citizens like yourselves do when you're out together. If I hear you were trolling for suspects, I'll expire with bliss."

His sarcasm laid too many of my nerves bare. "So far," I put in harshly. "Almost. The 'alleged' part is right, anyway."

Then I waited for him to pay some actual attention.

"Go on," he prompted incuriously.

"That"—I pointed a rigid finger at Hardshorn's body—"is the drop I spotted working the tournament. I don't make that kind of mistake," although God knows I'd already made a shitload of others. "But he didn't kill Bernie."

" 'Bernie'?" Moy seemed momentarily amused. "Are you referring to Bernard Appelwait, The Luxury security guard? I didn't get the impression you knew him that well."

I couldn't match his tone, but I managed to let some of the drill bit into my voice.

"I like to be on a first-name basis with people who end up dead because I didn't do my job well enough. I knew Hardshorn was dangerous as soon as I saw him. And Bernie was an old man. He shouldn't have gone after Hardshorn alone—and he sure as hell should not have gone into that restroom alone. If I'd been faster," or clearer, or maybe just smarter, "he wouldn't have."

Moy shrugged. "And now you're taking it personally." My appetite for chagrin didn't pique him. "You've already made that obvious." A reference to Marshal's phone calls. "But you haven't quite mentioned what you and Mr. Sternway were doing here in the first place. And you still haven't told me why you think this limp sucker didn't kill Mr. Appelwait." His tone smiled. "Unless I've missed something."

Gritting my teeth, I dragged myself a bit more upright. The deadness in my chest resisted every movement, and at least half a dozen ribs squalled objections. Maybe some of them were broken—I couldn't tell yet.

"I left something out on Saturday." The drill bit whined hotter. "The murder weapon. The missing flik." If Moy hadn't recognized the marks on the stall, or the slash across Bernie's throat, he deserved a demotion. "It was Bernie's."

At least now I had Moy's attention.

"Wisman asked me not to tell you. The Luxury doesn't allow weapons, but Bernie wasn't the only guard carrying one anyway. Wisman thought there would be trouble with the hotel.

"At the time, I didn't see any harm in it. Now—" I lifted my shoulders painfully. "Now I've had a chance to think."

"Fascinating," Moy remarked again. He sounded like he wanted to add, All this and Heaven, too. Take me now, O Lord. But I didn't give him a chance.

"I asked myself what kind of petty thief kills a security guard with his own weapon and then takes it. I couldn't come up with an answer.

"And there was someone missing. The spot. Any good team has a spot. Someone to watch for trouble. Someone who warned Hardshorn to get out of the hall.

"So I asked myself, what if Hardshorn wasn't alone in the restroom? What if his spot was there, too, when Bernie came in?" Maybe they'd met to hand off the evidence, make it harder to track. "Then it almost makes sense. The spot knew I'd identified Hardshorn, but the only threat he faced himself was Bernie.

"Which wasn't necessarily a big deal," a danger worth killing to avoid. "They didn't have to slaughter him. As long as they got away, it didn't much matter if they left him alive. You weren't likely to catch them."

If the cops—any cops—were good at catching that kind of crook, the whole world would be a different place.

I couldn't see Sternway's face, but his shape in the shadows conveyed concentration, intensity, as if he took all this more seriously than Moy did.

"Unless—?" Moy offered helpfully.

I tried to pull a deep breath past my ribs. They didn't approve.

"Unless," I sighed thinly, "the spot was someone Bernie knew. Someone who wouldn't have a prayer if Bernie identified him. Someone who couldn't hide from it, or bluff it out, or confuse the issue. *Then* it makes sense. Even taking the flik makes sense"—well, almost—"because it confuses what happened."

Moy waited for me to go on, but I was finished. Probably I wouldn't be able to stay on my feet much longer. The whine in my ears had finally started to recede, but some of the dead patches on my chest continued oozing larger. If they spread much farther, I wouldn't be able to breathe.

After a moment the detective nodded. "All right, Axbrewder. That's withholding information and obstructing a police investigation. Do you have any other secrets you'd like to come clean about before I go into my Outraged Officer of the Law dog-and-pony show?"

Judging by his tone, he wasn't pissed off. I would've taken that as good news, if I'd had the energy.

Briefly I considered telling him that I'd been to Bernie's apartment. But then I decided it was none of his damn business. It was between me and Alyse.

What the fuck are you doing?

For some reason, Hardshorn's last words ran on and on in my head, repeating themselves like a mantra. They could've meant anything.

I shook my head. "Don't you have enough on me already?"

By then the second uniform had returned from the cruiser. He and his partner had finished an inspection of the alley, and were waiting for Moy at the door to the club.

"Warner," he told them, "Hanson, I'm officially furious at this low-rent private fuckup. I've just nailed his ears to the side of that Dumpster. You both heard me. We wouldn't want the lieutenant to think I'm getting soft."

They chuckled dutifully, but their hearts weren't in it.

The detective turned back to me. "Did you understand me, Axbrewder? You've just been napalmed. If you don't keep your nose clean, I'll come back and scatter the ashes."

If his black skin hadn't hidden his face in the dark, I might've seen humor glint from his eyes.

There was nothing I could say, but he clearly didn't expect a response. Pointing at the door, he asked Sternway, "Is that the only way in?"

Apparently Sternway had reconciled himself to the possibility that he might lose his hobby. Maybe his victory over Hardshorn consoled him. "That's the back," he answered expressionlessly. "I'll show you around to the front."

Moy paused him with one hand. "Backup?" he asked Warner or Hanson.

One of them replied, "They're sending a couple of units. Should be here any time."

"Good.

"You've got this door," Moy instructed them. "No one leaves until we're done. I'll wait at the front."

Then he beckoned for Sternway to lead the way.

As the IAMA director started past the Dumpster, Moy took hold of my arm, tugged me into a slow walk. I didn't have the heart to shrug him off.

"Are you all right?" he inquired privately.

That wasn't a question I could answer simply, so I avoided it. "I've had worse beatings," I told him. "I'll heal."

I could tell by his grip on my arm that he wanted to pry. Just what I needed right then, a cop with good instincts. Marshal had warned me that Moy's boredom, his air of indifference, was just camouflage. After a moment, however, he seemed to let his curiosity about me go. His hand slid off my arm.

Still keeping his voice low, he shifted his ground. "What am I going to find in there?"

Beyond the Dumpster, the light improved. Now I could see the street at the end of the alley. Sternway strode on ahead, leading us out of darkness like a prophet.

I opened my hands instead of trying another shrug. "It's a fight club. Sternway seems to like no-rules sparring.

"Those chops," I explained, "the antiques at the tournament. They've been moved to Martial America. The developer, Alex Lacone, hired me to keep them safe. Sternway is a consultant to Martial America. He gave me the tour this afternoon. While we were talking, he invited me here. He wanted me to see for myself why martial artists treat him like the Second Coming of Bruce Lee."

As far as I was concerned, my encounter with Turf Hardshorn was coincidental entirely.

Moy considered this while we rounded the front of the building and headed for the alley where Sternway and I had parked. Or maybe he just wondered how much sleep he'd get tonight. In the distance ahead, I saw a couple of cruisers come briskly down the street, no lights or sirens. They may've thought they were incognito. As Moy and I followed our guide toward the cul-de-sac parking lot, he changed the subject again.

"You're done here, Axbrewder. Go to an emergency room. Get Sternway to drive you. I owe your buddy Viviter more than a couple of favors. If you collapse from internal bleeding, I'll feel like I've let him down." A moment later he added sardonically, "I love your theory about Appelwait's killer. But it's just a theory. You're supposed to be an investigator. Show me some evidence."

For a mercy, the parts of my chest that felt slain had stopped spreading. Unfortunately this seemed to aggravate my bruises. Or were they torn muscles? Cracked ribs? They sent out small licking tendrils of pain like flame on splashed gasoline.

On the plus side, I could hear almost normally.

If the lab ever tested those fibers from Bernie's throat, Moy would get all the evidence he needed.

Despite my chest, I would've preferred crawling home to a ride with HRH. "You might need Sternway," I said speciously. He'd saved my life, hadn't he? "When I get to my car, I can sit down. That'll help. And I have a phone. I can call someone."

Moy grunted noncommittally. As if the question related to needing Sternway, he asked, "What should we look for in there?"

Navy blazers? Not likely.

"You figure it out," I sighed between tongues of fire. He knew the drill as well as I did. "I'm too tired."

By then we'd reached the hidden parking lot. I leaned against the Plymouth for a minute, mustering my strength. Sternway waited for us a few yards closer to the club's front door.

Before he left me there, Moy suggested, "Be a good boy, Axbrewder." He may've smiled. "Keep your nose clean. If you're lucky, some day you'll make a nice pet for an older woman who doesn't know any better."

Sure thing, Sergeant, I muttered in silence as he moved off. That's sounds great. I can hardly wait.

I put off getting into the van because I didn't actually want to go. I couldn't stay on my feet well enough to help interrogate the club's patrons, that was obvious. Nevertheless I wanted to *be* there. I wanted to hear everything Moy dug up. Otherwise I might never know what it was. I'd already drawn on Marshal's favors pretty hard. They wouldn't stretch to cover releasing the results of an official interrogation. Presumably-innocent bystanders had rights that mere cadavers like Bernie lacked.

But Moy had already granted me more leeway than the law allowed. And I was in no shape to push my luck. If sitting down didn't clear my head, I might not be able to drive. I sure as hell didn't have what it would take to pay attention while the detective and his uniforms did their jobs.

Bowing to the inevitable, as they say, I groped out my keys and contrived to climb into the van. Once I'd turned the ignition, and the Plymouth sputtered to life, I let myself sag onto the steering wheel and rest for a while. Then I hit the lights, mostly to let Moy know that I was being a good boy, and considered the puzzle of getting a vehicle this size back out to the street.

Behind me, four more uniforms followed their flashlights into the alley. I let them catch up with Moy and Sternway before I began to inch the Plymouth tortuously around so that I wouldn't have to escape the cul-de-sac in reverse.

By the time I'd completed that inelegant maneuver, Moy had flashed his badge at the shutter in the metal door, and he and his men had taken Sternway inside.

Oh, well. So much for Indomitable Mick Axbrewder, the Private Investigator Who Never Says Die. I actually murmured "die" to myself for a couple of minutes, "die die die," like a chant, while I swayed along the alley to the street. Obviously losing my mind. But after that I tried to concentrate on the road. I didn't want to drive like a drunk as I strove to triangulate on my apartment.

The thought of an emergency room didn't hold much appeal. As I left the vicinity of the fight club, some disgruntled pugilist was probably saying, Turf Hardshorn? Shit, yes, I know him. But

I wasn't there to hear it. An emergency room would immobilize my chest and even give me drugs, but that wouldn't make me feel any better.

What the fuck are you doing?

Anson Sternway had saved my life.

If there'd been a nice warm womb handy, I would've squeezed into it somehow.

Naturally I wanted a drink. But I knew better. Booze didn't soften the slings and arrows of outrageous and so on. It just validated self-pity.

More by Divine Intervention than Inspiration, I eventually found my way into a part of Carner I recognized, where the streets and buildings were so brightly lit that they looked like bleached neoprene, and all-night "sports emporiums" offered their wares on every third corner. After that, it was only a matter of time until I located the apartment.

A glow in the window announced that Ginny had left a light on for me. Or she was still up.

I couldn't imagine how I felt about that.

By stages, I parked the van, locked it, and carried myself to the door of our apartment.

It wasn't locked. She hadn't gone to bed yet.

For all I knew, she wasn't alone.

To my own surprise, I found that I didn't actually care. Bracing one arm on the frame, I opened the door and let myself in.

She sat in the armchair by the phone, with a magazine she hadn't opened on the end table beside her. Her gunmetal gaze, as direct and uncomplicated as pistol fire, caught me before I'd crossed the threshold. Without appearing to move at all, she gained her feet and came forward. But when she reached me, she didn't say anything, or offer to help. Instead she simply closed the door after me while I moved to the couch and tried to sit down without wincing. Then she went back to her chair. Her eyes never left my face.

I closed my own for a minute, rested my head on the back of the couch. By now I could tell that my ribs weren't broken. Unconvincingly I muttered, "I didn't expect to find you up. Is anything wrong?"

"Brew, you look terrible." She sounded like she'd gone into another room. Or maybe my hearing had turned fuzzy. Before I could think of a snappy retort, she added, "But in a good way."

I lifted my head to stare at her. If she were poking fun at me— She looked serious, however. She even said, "I'm serious," as if I'd accused her of insulting me. "I've seen you look terrible before. This is different."

I blinked, gaping like she'd lapsed into glossolalia. But the straight focus of her gaze didn't waver, and after a while I leaned back again. She could see something that eluded me, so I decided to ignore it.

"I took a beating tonight," I told her. "My own damn fault. I made about three too many bad decisions in a row."

"And?" she inquired carefully.

"And nothing. I got what I deserved."

Maybe she'd discovered intuition in my absence. Instead of demanding an explanation, she dropped the subject. With no change in her tone, she remarked, "I was hoping we could talk tonight."

"Why?" She had Marshal, didn't she? Why did she want to talk to *me*?

"I'm used to working with you," she said as if I'd responded reasonably. "You help me think. Marshal gave me a case, and I can't make sense out of it."

This time I didn't gape at her. Tentatively I lowered my head to the arm of the couch, then gritted my confusion long enough to drag my feet off the floor and stretch out my legs. But even in that position I didn't have enough support to sustain me.

Marshal had given her a case—and she wanted *me* to help her think?

While various hurts quarreled in my chest, I tried to understand myself. Somewhere deep inside—so deep that ordinarily I could pretend that it didn't exist—I ached to talk to her myself. Did I help her think? I knew exactly what that was like.

If she wanted to bridge the rift between us, the least I could do was let her try.

"I'm not really all here," I admitted. "I hurt too much. But I'll give it a shot. Maybe I'll come up with something."

"Good."

I received the distinct impression that she leaned forward sharply in her chair—that she was eager or anxious in ways that didn't have much to do with her case—but I didn't turn my head toward her. In fact, I kept my eyes shut so that I wouldn't catch even a glimpse of her. If I let the look on her face distract me, I might not hear what she said.

"Professional Investigations," she began, "has a client named Mai Sternway," and my heart sank so fast that I hardly heard what came next. "She hired us to protect her from her husband, Anson."

That unconscionable bastard, I thought—meaning Marshal. He hadn't sent me to Bernie by chance. Or out of undifferentiated goodwill. And it was no accident that he'd been so helpful since. He'd set me up because he wanted me to feed him dirt about Sternway—he'd admitted that. But not for his own sake. He'd done it for Ginny.

Without being obvious about it, he intended to maneuver us into working together.

"They're separated," she was saying, "and she wants a divorce. But she's been getting threatening phone calls. And that's not all. Rocks have been thrown through her windows. Once her tires were slashed while she was out shopping. Buckets of shit have been smeared on her doors, front and back."

Damn it to hell. What kind of man assigned cases so that he could force his girlfriend to deal with her former partner?

"Mai says her husband's doing it," she continued. "She claims he wants to scare her so she won't demand what's rightfully hers.

"I'm supposed to protect her, but so far I haven't been very effective."

A man who considered their partnership too valuable to lose.

A man who didn't think of her as his girlfriend.

I wanted to howl, but my insides hurt too much.

Unfortunately it was my turn to say something. For a moment I put my hands over my face to keep my eyes shut. Then I pulled them down again. I hardly knew what we were talking about.

"The calls," I ventured. "She recognizes his voice?"

"No." Ginny spoke as if we sat in the dark together—carefully, distinctly, unsure of the distance between us. "He's muffled his voice somehow. But she's sure it's him."

"And you believe her?"

"I answer her phone when I'm with her. Those are definitely

threatening calls. Sometimes they're obscene. The voice is muffled, but it's male. She played me a tape he left behind. One of those pocket recorders, just reminders to himself. I can't tell if it's the same voice."

That wasn't what I'd asked, but I let it pass temporarily.

"I assume you've covered all the obvious stuff." I could go that far without understanding the conversation. "Caller ID. Traces. ID blockers."

She may've nodded. I didn't open my eyes to check.

"He moves around. Most of the numbers have turned out to be pay phones. The rest are in bars and nightclubs. None of them belong to Sternway. Or his karate school. Or that organization he runs, the IAMA. An ID blocker shows up every once in a while. I don't have the equipment to crack it." She was referring to a piece of electronics that could hold a connection open long enough to trace even after the ID-blocked number hung up. "So far Marshal's source at the phone company hasn't reported any results."

Striving to focus past a chest full of old grievances, I asked unnecessarily, "Sternway doesn't have a blocker on his home phone?"

"If he does," she stated, "he only turns it on when he's harassing Mai."

Vaguely I wondered where he found the time. I'd have thought he was too busy to hassle anyone who wasn't standing right in front of him.

"How's she taking it?"

Ginny let some of her studious neutrality drop. "Mad as hell. That woman is a refined, cultivated harridan. She looks like one of those frail creatures who gets the vapors. She even dresses that way. A china doll too delicate to trim her own fingernails. But she doesn't act like it.

"She wants his blood, as much of it as she can get. And she has a scream that can bleed you dry at thirty yards. Of course, I don't know what *he's* like. But he must've had a death wish when he married her.

"And by the way," Ginny added, "Mai lives pretty high. I didn't know karate honchos made the kind of money she spends. Unless one of them inherited bucks, they've both been in trouble for years."

By degrees I found myself starting to relax. As long as I kept my eyes shut and concentrated on Ginny's voice, I could let Marshal Viviter and Turf Hardshorn drift away into the background. If I didn't distract myself by sitting up—or arguing with her—I might be of some use after all.

"If it means anything," I offered through the phosphene dance inside my eyelids, "the people I've met around Sternway think that Mai wants to castrate him financially. Presumably that's the story he tells.

"But he's"—I searched the dark for an adequate description—"complicated. I've seen quite a bit of him, especially today, but I can't tell you if he's the kind of asshole who bullies his wife. In the martial arts world, he's Mr. Hell-on-Wheels. Impressive sonofabitch. The beating I got tonight—" I tried a shrug, but it hurt too much to complete. "It would've been worse," a lot worse, "but he rescued me. Jumped in there and killed the clown who was trying to kill me."

Ginny might've reacted to that information, but I kept going.

"On the other hand, you couldn't call him a nice guy and feel comfortable. The way he talks, you'd think he sees everything in terms of money. Money and fighting. If he actually believes in anything—or cares about anybody—he keeps it to himself."

She considered that for a moment. "None of which makes him an abusive husband," she concluded.

I nodded, just a slight shift of the muscles to show myself that I was still alive.

What the fuck are you doing?

If she'd been there in the alley, I would've asked her if I'd heard Hardshorn right. In my condition, I may've missed something. The clangor in my ears had confused the details.

"You didn't answer my question a minute ago," I observed casually. "I get the impression you don't believe Mai's story."

Ginny snorted. "Most men would have a hard time living up to an image as black as the one she paints." Then she admitted, "But it's more than that. I'm not convinced he could do what she accuses him of without being in at least two places at once. She got calls this weekend while he was at that tournament, but none of the numbers were from The Luxury. And if he slashed her tires when she says he did, he got back to his school at about the speed of light. I checked."

For no particular reason, I asked, "She get any calls Saturday afternoon?"

For an instant Ginny's tone hardened. "You mean while I was at The Luxury?" She may've thought that I meant she'd been derelict to Mai when she'd come to check on me. "She says not.

"Why?"

I couldn't tell her. I didn't know. Intuition suggested the question. The rest of me just groped for patterns.

"So you think she's faking it," I prompted.

"I'm starting to." Slowly Ginny's voice unclenched. "I'm not there twenty-four hours a day. For all I know, she threw the rocks and dumped the shit herself. And she could hire the phone calls. I'm starting to wonder if she retained Professional Investigations to help her make Anson look bad, corroborate her story, so she can crucify him in the divorce.

"I can't see how the pieces fit any other way."

Without thinking about it, I said, "If the calls don't stop now, you're probably right."

Her silence sounded like, Huh? so I went on, "I don't know how smart Sternway is, but I'll bet he's pretty clever. Like I said, I've been around him a lot.

"And I'm there because Marshal recommended me. Sternway knows that, of course. He can assume that I talk to Marshal. Also he probably knows that Mai hired Professional Investigations. Marshal could confirm some of her accusations by checking with me.

"Presumably Sternway can't know I share an apartment with Mai's protection. But he doesn't have to be Heisenberg to realize that I could be a danger to him.

"If he's making the calls, he'll stop now. He'll want me for an alibi."

"So if the calls keep coming," Ginny finished for me, "they aren't from him."

I didn't try another nod. While I could still talk without thinking, I said, "If I were you, I'd search her house. Sometime when she isn't there. Really dig into it."

Right away, I felt her bristle. I could read her with my eyes closed. She sat eight feet away, but the nerves in my skin were sensitive to her abrupt ire.

"What in hell for? You don't think maybe that violates our client-investigator relationship?"

More ethical questions. "Sure it does." What else was I going to say? "But you might find something interesting."

Prying wasn't actually unethical. It was her job. Ethics only came into it if she learned something that affected her decisions.

Besides, she'd never hesitated to research her own clients before.

But apparently she didn't see it that way this time. "Like what?" she demanded.

Suddenly I was angry. Too much lurked beneath the surface, waiting for one of us to make a mistake. It wore me out.

"Ginny," I sighed, "if I knew that, I wouldn't be lying here like this. I'd be fucking *prescient*, and goons like Turf Hardshorn wouldn't lay a hand on me."

" 'Turf Hardshorn'?" she echoed. " 'Turf'?"

I didn't stop. "If you think she hired someone to make those calls, maybe you can find out who. Hell, even crazy people fill out their checkbook registers. Or maybe she keeps buckets of shit hidden away somewhere, just in case. *I* don't know.

"You said you wanted to talk to me. If I had a better suggestion, I'd say so."

For a minute she didn't respond. A couple of cars went by outside, muffled and fuming. My pulse yearned in my chest.

Then she muttered, "*Damn* it, Brew, I hate it when you do that."

I heard a familiar exasperation in her voice, the kind that meant she wasn't seriously angry. Not at me, anyway.

"Do what?" I countered.

"Make those leaps. I can't follow them. And you're right *way* too often. Half the time when you're around I feel like I've had a lobotomy without noticing it."

All at once the pressure in the room evaporated. I had the giddy sensation that someone had lifted a set of free weights off me. Despite our difficulties, she was by God *trying* to get along with me.

I felt so relieved that I about lost consciousness.

For a while I didn't say anything. Instead of trying to make sense out of her, I concentrated on letting my aches and disappointments recede into the couch. With my eyes closed, I could almost imagine what it might feel like to be at peace.

But Ginny wasn't done. When she'd chewed her exasperation small enough to swallow, she said in the same careful tone she'd used earlier, "So tell me. How does it happen that you're spending so much time with Anson Sternway?"

I knew what she had in mind as soon as she said the words. Bridging a rift like ours wasn't something that you could tackle on just one side. You had to work for the middle from both ends. She'd made a start. Now she was asking me to do my part.

And I wanted to respond. I'd been wanting her to back me up for hours now.

Probably I should've told her about Bernie. That was what mattered to me most. And if nothing else it would explain how I got myself beat up. But I couldn't. Somehow the way Alyse Appelwait had looked at me prevented it. Between us there was nothing at stake except how I felt about her husband.

Nevertheless Ginny had opened a door for me, and I didn't mean to let it swing shut.

"It's like this," I began. "After the tournament, a developer named Alex Lacone hired me to improve security for his current project, a development he calls Martial America. It's a karate complex—he's got four schools so far, and he's trying for more. Sternway's his martial arts consultant.

"The problem is those chops, the antiques at the tournament." Belatedly it occurred to me that Marshal might not have told Ginny anything about my job. After all, he hadn't revealed much about hers to me. "They're either priceless or just valuable, depending on whether or not they're genuine."

Too drained to go into detail, I gave her a brief background sketch of the chops, the tournament, and Lacone's insurance dilemma. Then I explained, "The chops haven't been authenticated yet. That's supposed to happen soon. The insurance company has a local expert in mind to appraise them."

Wearily I added, "I've already spent enough time at Martial America to know that Lacone's security stinks. Sternway gave me the tour this afternoon."

My sense of fatigue grew. And the more I said, the worse it became. For some reason, answering Ginny's question was harder than it had any right to be. Instead of continuing, I wanted to concentrate on my pains and confusion until they seemed big enough to excuse my failure to match her.

Probably I would've felt safer that way. Hadn't I spent most of our years together convincing myself that I couldn't hold up my end? I'd liked calling her my partner, but actually she'd been my boss. The one who made the decisions, took the responsibility. Kept me on my feet.

If I wanted a partner, I'd have to earn one.

Deliberately I opened my eyes and took a good look at the ceiling. When I'd located—or imagined—a small collection of spider webs that I'd missed in my various cleaning frenzies, I leaned my bulk off the couch, braced myself, and stood up.

"Brew—?" Uncertainty and concern complicated Ginny's gaze. The tension in her arms and shoulders made her look like she wanted to come help me stand. The effort of restraining herself sent slivers of reflection off the curve of her claw.

"I'll be right back." I intended my expression to be reassuring, but it didn't feel that way.

Stiffly I lumbered past her to the kitchen, where I moistened a couple of paper towels and picked up a broom. Then, rather like a sailboat navigating against too much wind, I tacked and hauled my way back into the living room.

"But security isn't the real issue," I resumed. "Lacone will install obvious things like better locks and alarms as soon as the insurance company insists on them." I hardly sounded audible to myself, but Ginny looked like she could hear me. "And whether or not the chops are genuine is secondary right now. The actual problem is that the chops are hot."

With a bit more effort than the job should've entailed, I draped the paper towels over the end of the broom. While Ginny stared, I angled toward the corner where I'd seen the spider webs.

"Hot as in stolen," I explained. "And emotionally hot. One of the schools is Chinese. Their *sifu* considers the chops a national treasure, ripped off in a kind of cultural rape. He's practically quivering with outrage because right now the chops belong to a Japanese *sensei* in the same building.

"Both schools seem to think those chops are about *honor*—personal, stylistic, national. And Sternway tells me that martial arts schools have a tradition of solving problems by beating the shit out of each other. Reclaiming their honor by main force."

In spite of my ribs, I stabbed damp towels at the offending

webs. Sir Axbrewder in his armor, jousting with the Black Knight of Imperfect Cleanliness.

"On top of which"—in retribution, my bruises made me groan—"he talks like another school in the same building can't tell the difference between honor and ego. *They're* outraged because the chops give more 'face' than they've got. Sternway has spent hours trying to warn me about the likelihood of a three-way explosion—although he can't say it in so many words because Lacone pays him to promote Martial America."

Panting weakly, I lowered the broom. Maybe I'd imagined the spider webs. Smudges on the towels, however, indicated that I'd cleaned *some*thing.

Patiently Ginny waited for me to go on. Her face wore the kind of expression you'd expect from a psychiatrist while a patient with multiple personalities argued with himselves.

I needed to get to the point before I fell down.

"But it's more complicated than that," I told the end of the broom. At least to me. "I spotted a team of thieves working the tournament. We rounded up the picks. The security guard who got killed"—I could go that far without tarnishing my pledge to the Appelwaits—"was trying to catch the drop."

Abruptly I shambled back to the kitchen. When I'd disposed of the towels and stashed the broom, I returned to the couch. Sitting down because I didn't want to collapse headlong, I said thinly, "That just doesn't make sense to me." I told her why. Then I added, "Since it doesn't make sense anyway, I can't shake the idea that there was something else going on. Something I missed.

"The only things worth killing for at that tournament—and I mean the *only* things—were those chops."

And whoever did it wouldn't stop until he had them, no matter how many people he had to kill.

Ginny waited until she was sure I was done. Then she suggested in a quiet voice, "Another one of your leaps."

"Maybe," I admitted.

She paused briefly before asking, "Does this have anything to do with getting beat up?"

I sighed as my sense of defeat renewed its grip. "Turf Hardshorn was the drop."

She whistled through her teeth. "And now he's dead. Cute." I could almost hear her brain shuttle like a sewing machine on full throttle, stitching together pieces of the story that I hadn't bothered to mention. After another pause, she announced flatly, "You'll never know what he thought he was doing."

I almost countered, Not unless you trace that ID blocker. But I stopped myself in time. The idea had jumped into my head with the unmotivated inevitability of a post-hypnotic suggestion, and I didn't trust it. Sometimes intuition betrayed me. On occasion I'd pushed it so hard that it just went crazy.

What the fuck are you doing?

I wasn't ready to trust myself that far yet.

She went on stitching. "So you have to make some assumptions. It's hard to believe he could be stupid enough to call attention to himself at that club if he killed the security guard. That seems to confirm your theory about another man in the restroom.

"You can also assume"—she hesitated momentarily—"this other man still wants the chops. If you don't get your hands on him, he might kill someone else."

Then she shook her head. "I'm sorry, Brew." Her jaw tightened as if she were worried about my reaction. "I don't get it. I can see why you think Hardshorn wasn't alone in the restroom. But the rest of it—I don't see how you can assume the chops were involved."

When she said it that way, it sounded pretty implausible. I hadn't mentioned my conviction that Bernie had recognized his killer. That the killer had a hell of lot more to lose than a bag full of petty theft.

I also hadn't mentioned the flik.

Stubbornly I kept Bernie to myself.

She gave me another minute, just in case I wanted to come clean. Deliberately she aimed her broken nose and her hawk's gaze off to one side so that I wouldn't have to face anything I preferred to avoid. In a vague way, I found myself wondering what had changed for her since I'd first contacted Marshal. Her attitude toward me had shifted in the past few days, and I didn't know why. But we still weren't on terms that would've allowed me to ask.

Finally she flicked a glance at me, then looked away again.

"You didn't ask for my advice." She'd resumed her neutral tone. Most of the tension had eased from her shoulders, but her claw still caught the light unsteadily. "But I say, take it a step at a time. Maybe there's something you can do to defuse the problems in Martial America."

True, I hadn't asked. But that didn't stop me. "Like what?"

"Have you considered getting the—what did you call him?—the *sifu* of that Chinese school to authenticate the chops?"

I stared at her.

"If he decides they're fakes," she explained, "he might relax. And even if he thinks they're genuine, he might take being consulted as a sign of respect. It might give him 'face.' That could tone down his outrage."

Damn. My jaw dropped involuntarily, and I couldn't stop staring. How did she *do* that?

Now I remembered why I'd always thought she was wonderful.

She met my stare. "Well?"

Somehow I swallowed my astonishment. "That," I said hoarsely, "is a horrible idea."

"Why?"

"Because I didn't think of it. And it might work. I don't see how Hong can turn it down. He's too serious to pass it up. The only tricky part—" I swallowed again. "I'll have to convince the Japanese *sensei* to go along with it."

But I didn't actually think he'd object.

"Virginia H. Fistoulari." A helpless grin twisted my bruises. "If I'd come up with that one myself, I'd call it brilliant."

Ginny clicked her claw once or twice. Her eyes smoldered humorously. "You don't have to. 'Brilliant' is my middle name."

"Really?" I knew for a fact that her middle name was Harriet. "I thought the *H* stood for 'hacksaw.' "

This time she grinned back. "That's what you're supposed to think."

"Well, damn. I wish you hadn't told me. Now I'll be up half the night, trying to figure out how many *H*'s 'brilliant' has."

"No, you won't." Abruptly she stood up, cocked her fist on her hip like an indignant schoolmarm. "If you don't put yourself to bed im*medi*ately, I'll club you unconscious. I said you look terrible in a good way, but you still look terrible."

I did what she told me. I had a lot of work ahead of me—if I could get back out of bed in the morning. And taking her orders still felt as natural as sunshine. Muttering complaints I didn't mean, I climbed off the couch and lurched toward my bedroom.

As soon as I got my clothes off and stretched out, I plunged into sleep like a fall off a tall building.

19

During the night, patterns took shape inside me. Strands of inference that had nothing to do with my conscious mind wove toward a conclusion, unseen. By the time my alarm went off, I knew beyond all reason or argument that the chops were the key to Bernie's death.

And that the man with Hardshorn in The Luxury restroom wouldn't hesitate to kill again.

How I'd reached that conviction I couldn't guess. I tried to understand it as I stumbled into the bathroom, but both the reasoning and the implications eluded me. A cold shower didn't help. Neither did shaving. And the deep bruises across my ribs only confused the issue. All I knew for sure was that I'd better get to work before more people died for being in the wrong place at the wrong time.

I hated intuition when it worked this way. It seemed to do more harm than good. I had no idea who to protect. Or who to protect against. The more I thought about it, the more it eroded my confidence.

Fortunately that effect was counterbalanced by last night's talk with Ginny. Somehow we'd begun to repair the damage we'd inflicted on each other. Maybe I was finally starting to accept her relationship with Marshal. Or to accept that she had a right to it, whether I liked it or not.

Also my torso and arms didn't hurt as badly as I'd expected. Hardshorn had hit me hard enough to flatten a utility shed, but the emotional impact of the blows didn't linger, despite my bruises.

The fact that Ginny and I could talk to each other now meant more to me than almost any number of battered ribs.

She'd left the apartment before I got up, depriving me of a chance to see what her new attitude looked like in the light of day. I didn't fret over it, however. I had plenty of other things to worry about.

Since I didn't own a second suit, I put on contrasting slacks and a clean shirt. While I cooked breakfast, I sorted through some of the clutter in my head, which in turn enabled me to make a decision or two. By the time I'd eaten, washed the dishes, extracted a few phone numbers from directory assistance, and holstered the .45 under my jacket, I was approximately ready to face the day.

Outside the sun had already sunk its teeth into Carner's concrete. The Plymouth smelled vaguely of sweat, baked vinyl, and yearning. It didn't want to start, but on the third try it limped to life. When the AC had circulated enough stale heat to begin cooling, I headed for Martial America.

Piously hoping that I wouldn't get lost, I attempted a route that didn't rely on Carner's freeways. I wanted to make some calls along the way, and I figured I'd be safer on surface roads.

First things first. Before anything else, I called Marshal's cell phone. When he answered, I said, "Thanks for the warning," even though I hadn't profited from it much.

"Brew?" he asked.

"I now know the truth," I announced. The street I'd picked seemed to lead in the right direction. "I can tell you whatever you want to know about 'Sternway's nights out.' "

Marshal wasn't amused. "Does this mean," he demanded crisply, "you've decided to dispense with politeness entirely? It's customary to identify yourself when you call. In case you hadn't noticed, cell phones make it tough to recognize voices."

"Oh, don't be so touchy." His reaction surprised me, but I didn't take it seriously. "I call Lacone 'sir' whenever I talk to him. How much politeness do you think I can stand?"

Apparently my attitude made him madder. "For someone who doesn't work for me, you presume a lot, Axbrewder."

Instead of snapping back, I admitted, "I know. It's because I don't have anywhere else to turn." Also because I couldn't figure him out. "Bernie's death got a whole lot messier last night, and I need to take it out on *some*one."

"Is that why you told Ginny to search Mai Sternway's house?" he retorted. "You're trying to 'take it out on someone'?"

Oh, shit. She'd already talked to him. That shocked me momentarily, although it shouldn't have. I was accustomed to thinking of her as the boss, answerable only to her client.

"It's just a hunch," I sighed. "I can't explain it. I simply had the feeling that she might learn something useful."

"Mai Sternway is a *client*," he informed me stiffly. "She pays good money for loyalty, discretion, and—"

I cut him off. "And stupidity? Get off it, Marshal. I didn't tell Ginny to do anything disloyal. Or indiscreet. I just reminded her that any good investigator tries to know as much as possible about the client. If nothing else," I pointed out with more sarcasm than the situation required, "it might help prevent this particular client from setting you up.

"Why don't you stop complaining and tell me what's really bothering you?"

"I don't know you that well," he fired back. But then he paused. For a few seconds my phone didn't pick up anything except occasional static. When he spoke again, he'd put most of his vexation aside.

"OK, I'll say this much. I told Ginny to go ahead, search the house. Not because I think it's a good idea. I don't. But I think I might be getting complacent. You've only been working here since Friday, and already you know more about Anson Sternway than I do. That pisses me off."

And, I added for him, searching Mai's house hadn't occurred to him. He'd gotten into the habit of taking his clients at their word. Carner was too rich, making money came too easily. How many years had passed since he'd been reminded that trusting his clients might be fatal?

Ginny and I, on the other hand—

I couldn't think of anything else to say, so I answered the question he hadn't asked.

"He goes to a fight club, where he and a bunch of other blood lovers pound each other into the canvas. Last night one of them was a goon they called Turf Hardshorn. He attacked me. Probably would've killed me, but Sternway did him first.

"He's the drop Bernie followed into that men's room."

Marshal whistled surprise through his teeth—which told me that Ginny had kept her mouth shut about my business.

"Presumably," I explained, "he attacked me because he recognized me from the tournament." Then I went on, "Moy showed up eventually. He stayed to go through the club, find out what he could about Hardshorn, but he didn't encourage me to join him. I'll call him later. Maybe he'll tell me if he learned anything.

"He might," I insisted as if Marshal had objected. "For some reason, he keeps giving me the benefit of the doubt."

Marshal muttered something I couldn't hear. Then he aimed his voice into the phone again.

"So the goon who did Bernie is out of the picture. How does that make his death 'messier'?"

"Because," I answered, "it still doesn't make sense, and I've lost my only lead." I'd already described my theory that Hardshorn wasn't Bernie's killer.

Marshal paused to consider the problem. After a moment, he asked, "Who else could it have been? Who else had enough at stake to kill for it?"

"How the hell should I know?" His question cut too close to intuitive convictions I couldn't understand and didn't trust. "No one has any real connection to those chops except Hong and Nakahatchi, and they never left the hall."

Neither had Sue Rasmussen and Ned Gage. Or Komatori and T'ang. Or Bernie's guards. Only Master Soon was absent at the right time.

That left me with way too many other possibilities, and no viable way to winnow the list.

"I see the problem," Marshal admitted. "What do you hope to get from Moy?"

"Anything at all about Hardshorn. Who he is, where he worked, where he lived, who his friends were."

I meant, Anything that might suggest a link to the chops, or to someone at the tournament. Or to Bernie.

Marshal seemed to accept that. "How can I help?"

"Keep after Moy about those fibers they found in Bernie's neck," I told him. "If they didn't come from his blazer—"

"There must have been someone else in the restroom," he finished for me. "Someone wearing a similar blazer."

Right. Someone wearing a blazer. And a contusion. If Bernie hit him hard enough to leave fibers in the flik, he'd have a bruise on him somewhere.

"Consider it done," Marshal promised. "Moy has already told me too much to stop talking now."

"Thanks." I was sincere, but I couldn't leave it there. Feeling grateful to him still made me uncomfortable. Only half joking, I added, "You know I hate you, don't you?"

I couldn't imagine why he was willing to do so much for me.

He laughed humorlessly. "You don't exactly hide it. I just don't know why you bother."

The line clicked dead. I put the phone down to concentrate on my route for a minute or two. I was already floundering in too many directions at once. I did *not* need to get lost on my way to Martial America.

Originally I'd assumed that Marshal was nice to me for Ginny's sake. Because he was fucking her. But that quaint notion no longer seemed adequate. It didn't explain why he'd thrown Ginny and me together over the Sternways.

And it didn't account for the distinct modulation of Ginny's manner toward me.

Just to be on the safe side, I checked my map. It indicated that I was right on track.

In my condition, the mere idea felt like a cruel joke.

Sighing to myself, I picked up the phone and dialed the number on Edgar Moy's card.

He didn't sound surprised to hear from me. And he told me without prodding that the driver's license in Hardshorn's wallet identified him as "James M. Hardshorn," address withheld pending investigation. The wallet also contained nearly fifteen hundred bucks in cash, but no credit cards or other information—in particular, no conveniently incriminating phone numbers, addresses, or contacts.

If Moy had learned anything useful last night, he kept it to himself. Instead he told me in a bored tone which might've masked humor or irritation that no one had admitted knowing Hardshorn outside the fight club. Several patrons reported watching him fight several times. A couple of fighters said that they'd taken him on. None of them had ever seen him lose.

They'd said the same of Anson Sternway. Apparently Sternway and Hardshorn had never tackled each other. According to one of the bouncers, the two were establishing their reputations so that when they finally fought the winner would make as much money as possible.

Ah, hell. I thanked the detective and hung up. I still didn't know whether he took my theory about Bernie's killer seriously, but I figured I'd better leave that subject to Marshal. He'd known Moy a lot longer than I had.

So far I hadn't accomplished a thing for Bernie—or Alyse. So what? *Take it a step at a time.* No one ever cracked a case by standing still.

Despite—or maybe because of—my floundering sensation, I called Deborah Messenger next.

I was on a roll of sorts. Like Marshal and Sergeant Moy, she answered her phone right away.

"Deborah," I said, "it's Brew," just to prove that I could benefit from Marshal's advice. "Are we still on for tonight?"

She laughed with pleasure. "Let me put it this way. If you're calling to cancel, I'll buy a voodoo doll and stick pins in it until you change your mind."

I grinned into the phone. "Don't worry. I wouldn't miss it."

How else could I hope to find out what she was up to?

"In that case," she said like nibbling on my ear, "this must be a business call. I'll try to act like a professional." Her tone gave the remark a provocative frisson.

"I suppose one of us had better." Without transition my grip turned slick on the wheel. I could hardly hold onto the phone. "Otherwise I might drive into a pole."

She laughed again. "Flatterer."

I swallowed at the sudden lump of desire in my throat. "But you're right, it's business.

"Has Watchdog decided to get the chops appraised?"

"If you can call what corporations do 'deciding,' " she told me, "yes. The home offices still aren't willing to rely on a local appraisal. Their expert will fly out from New York next week as scheduled. But they agree that getting a temporary evaluation here might be a good idea.

"Sammy talked them into it. Those crooks at the tournament really spooked him. He's convinced himself that more of them are lining up on the sidewalk." I pictured her rolling her eyes. "He can be pretty hysterical, as I'm sure you've noticed, but he knows how to play company politics. I'll bring Carliss Swilley out to Martial America around eleven this morning, if that suits you." Politely she added, "I've already called *Essential Shotokan.*"

I checked my watch automatically. "Eleven is fine. Any excuse to see you before this evening works for me." I hesitated, then forged ahead. "I've got an idea I want to try."

As soon as I said it, I felt like I'd stepped off a cliff. Suddenly I'd committed myself to intuitions I couldn't name, possibilities I didn't want to face.

But Deborah didn't know that. "Does Martial America have a restroom we can lock?" She sounded like she was licking her lips.

"It's not that kind of idea." I wedged the phone at my ear with my shoulder, scrubbed both palms on my pants. "I thought it might be interesting to ask *Sifu* Hong's opinion of the chops."

She took a moment to change gears. "Is he an authority?"

"Probably not in the way you mean." I continued falling. "But he's a moral authority. If I can tell him that Watchdog Insurance and Alex Lacone value his opinion, it might relax his hostility a bit." Certainly it might make my job easier by defusing some of his personal distrust. "And who knows? It may give Posten ammunition to use on your home offices."

Deborah paused to consider the idea. After a few seconds, she answered slowly, "Brew, I have to be sure I understand what you're asking." She sounded dubious. "Do you want us to offer *Sifu* Hong an appraiser's fee? Because if you do—"

"No," I put in, "nothing that official. I just want to be able to tell him that I speak for Watchdog as well as Lacone when I ask for his cooperation."

Lacone wouldn't object. Anything to keep the peace.

"Oh, that's no problem." Her relief was evident. "You can use my name. And Sammy's. I'll make sure he doesn't get huffy about it. The homes offices won't complain. Since they aren't excited about the idea of a local appraisal, even a temporary one, they'll welcome a second opinion. If the two don't match, they can feel smug about insisting on their own expert. And if *Sifu* Hong agrees with Mr. Swilley, that only strengthens Watchdog's position."

She didn't add, In case something happens to the chops this week. She didn't need to. Instead she said, "Don't worry about Mr. Swilley. I'll smooth his feathers before we arrive."

"Deborah Messenger, you're a sweetheart." The danger that Swilley might take offense hadn't occurred to me. "On top of being the sexiest lady I've met in many a long year."

In a throaty whisper, she told me, "Check the restrooms." Then she hung up before I had a chance to make a fool of myself by dropping the phone.

Damn. The van's AC couldn't push out enough cold air to keep me from sweating. What was I getting myself into? Last night I'd liked the idea of consulting Hong. Now without warning it scared the crap out of me.

Deborah's attitude, her incomprehensible eagerness, no longer worried me. I couldn't think about it. Somewhere in the back of my head, a small voice whimpered wordlessly, like an illiterate mute trying to warn against imminent violence.

I did *not* trust my instincts. Not this time. Not without some kind of evidence to back them up. The back of my head had leaped out over an abyss, and I couldn't see the other side.

Until I understood what my nerves wanted to tell me, I couldn't do anything except fall—and pray that I latched onto something solid enough to stop me before I smeared my body all over the rocks at the bottom.

Trembling, I forced myself to check the street signs, confirm that I wasn't lost. *Take it a step at a time.* What else could I do? When my forehead finally stopped dripping, I dug out the listings I'd acquired from directory assistance. *Take it*— Carefully I dialed the number for *Essential Shotokan.*

It rang until I was about to give up. Then a male voice answered, "*Essential Shotokan.* I am Hideo Komatori."

"Mr. Komatori." I couldn't account for all this good luck with phone calls. "It's Brew. Good morning."

"Brew-*san.* Please excuse my delay. I was meditating." Underneath his usual reserve, Komatori sounded pleasantly considerate. "It is indeed a good morning.

"How may I be of service?"

"I was hoping—"

Abruptly I stomped on the brake to avoid a Corvette convertible veering recklessly into my lane. In his muscle shirt and shorts, the driver had the cut look of a professional poster boy. His hair kept him too busy to bother steering.

Somehow I avoided swearing into the phone.

"Sorry," I told Komatori. "Bad driver." The guy had enough hair to get tangled in it when he moved his hands. "I was hoping I could speak to Nakahatchi *sensei*."

"I'm sorry, Brew-*san*," Komatori answered. "My master doesn't use telephones. I'm sure he'll speak with you in person, if you wish. Or could I speak with him on your behalf?"

I almost climbed the back of the 'vette before I realized what I was doing. "He doesn't use telephones?"

Komatori laughed politely. "I'm afraid not. He distrusts the modern world in many of its forms. In particular, he believes that telephones allow men to avoid responsibility for their words and actions. He may be right. I've often thought that we all lie more easily over the phone than in person. Don't you agree?"

Deliberately I receded from the poster boy. "But he lets you give him messages?"

"He doesn't hold me accountable for their content."

"Well," I said after a moment, "I'll take your advice on this one. I think you've already had a call from Deborah Messenger? Watchdog Insurance?"

"Indeed," Hideo replied promptly. "She mentioned a Mr. Carliss Swilley, who has been retained to authenticate the chops. My master knows nothing of this Mr. Swilley, but of course he has no objection. For various reasons, he's deeply concerned to determine whether or not the chops are genuine. He's been troubled on this point, and he welcomes anyone who might resolve the matter."

I nodded at the phone, then remembered that Komatori couldn't see me. "I'm glad to hear it." Then I plunged on, still falling. "Do you think he'd object to letting *Sifu* Hong inspect the chops? Should I ask him in person?"

Again Komatori gave a reserved laugh. "Ordinarily I shouldn't speak for my master. It isn't considered proper. But in this case, I know his thoughts. He would be honored by a visit from *Sifu* Hong, for that purpose or any other. I'm not betraying a confidence, Brew-*san*, when I say that he would have invited *Sifu* Hong himself, but to do so seemed indelicate."

" 'Indelicate'?" Feeling confused, I checked my map again. I was definitely getting lost *some*where.

"*Sifu* Hong has made his anger evident. Naturally it must be respected. To invite him here might be seen as an attempt to placate him. That would be an affront."

"I still don't—"

"Ah, but if the invitation comes from *you*, Brew-*san*," Komatori pronounced, "the problem evaporates. It grants *Sifu* Hong face, it allows this *dojo* to show respect for an esteemed master, and it preserves Nakahatchi *sensei*'s stature, so that he may offer *Sifu* Hong courtesy rather than placation."

Mentally I threw up my hands. It was clear that "good manners" to men like Komatori and T'ang, Nakahatchi and Hong, meant something entirely different than they did to Marshal—something deeper, more definitive. I couldn't claim that I understood it.

"Maybe," I said reluctantly. "Maybe not. *Sifu* Hong has at least one grievance that won't go away just because the invitation comes from me."

Hideo waited while I dredged up what T'ang told me yesterday.

"There's no graceful way to say this," I went on. "I guess it has to do with face. Apparently *Sifu* Hong believes that Nakahatchi *sensei* upstaged him. *Traditional Wing Chun* signed the first lease with Martial America, but *Essential Shotokan* moved in first. *Sifu* Hong seems to think your *sensei* did that deliberately. To eclipse him in some way."

Feeling too awkward to frame a direct question, I shut up.

I couldn't read Komatori's silence. Maybe I'd insulted him. Or maybe he was just considering his answer.

After a long moment, he replied, "Perhaps I can understand how *Sifu* Hong might have received that impression. There's no tradition of personal communication between masters. Schools such as ours have always kept to themselves.

"But I can tell you plainly, Brew-*san*, that *Sifu* Hong is mistaken about this. Like his school, ours once occupied another location in Carner. My master didn't want to move. We'd been there for several years, and he felt a loyalty to the owner. When the time came to renew our lease, however, we learned that his loyalty wasn't reciprocated. The owner raised our rent considerably, more than we could afford, and we needed to find a new location rather quickly. Mr. Lacone offered us favorable terms and immediate availability.

"In retrospect," Komatori admitted, "it seems unfortunate that we moved in before *Traditional Wing Chun*." Then he added, "But I assure you—and you can assure *Sifu* Hong—that my master's decision was entirely pragmatic. It had nothing to do with a desire for precedence. We didn't learn that *Sifu* Hong had signed the first lease until both schools were in place."

"You mean Mr. Sternway didn't mention it?" I asked more sharply than I intended. I would've expected Sternway to use every argument he could muster on Lacone's behalf, including school loyalty and national pride.

But Hideo didn't hesitate. "Indeed not," he stated firmly. "That would have been indelicate."

And Sternway knew how much Nakahatchi valued delicacy? Maybe he did.

"Then how did you find out?" I pursued. "Since there's no 'tradition of personal communication.' "

Now Komatori paused. "I'm not sure," he said slowly. "I believe Ms. Rasmussen mentioned it. We consult often. But"—his tone conveyed a smile—"I'm not confident of my memory."

Good ol' Sue Rasmussen. That gave me another reason to talk to her. I mean, aside from the fact that she hated me.

"What do you consult about?"

Komatori had his answer ready. "Insurance and liability. Leases. Publicity. Tournaments and seminars. She and I talk to each other at least twice a month."

Which made sense. The same was probably true for T'ang Wen. Still another reason to give her a call. *Some*one must've planted the idea that I'd been hired because Lacone and Watchdog didn't trust Hong.

"All right," I sighed. "I'll deal with that when I talk to *Sifu* Hong. But I think you've given me what I need. Thanks."

"I hope I've been of service." Hideo sounded sincere. "My master desires to relieve the tensions between our schools."

"Well—" I thought for a moment. "Assuming I can talk *Sifu* Hong into this, does eleven suit you? Since we're all concerned about face, I don't know who should get precedence, Mr. Swilley or *Sifu* Hong. I'd rather deliver them together."

"That will be fine." Komatori's tone conveyed confidence.

So now all I had to do was convince Hong, and my fall would be complete. I didn't understand *that* either.

Where was the danger? My guts churned with an almost metaphysical alarm, as if I'd put someone at risk, someone I ought to protect. But who?

"Brew-*san*?" the phone asked my silence. Apparently I'd been distracted longer than I realized.

"Sorry again," I murmured while I dredged my attention back to the present.

"Another bad driver?"

"Unfortunately no," I admitted. "The back of my brain has been trying to tell me something, but I can't seem to hear it."

"Do you meditate?" Komatori inquired. "Perhaps your receptiveness is cluttered in some way. To still your mind is to hear yourself more clearly."

I made an effort to dismiss the notion without sounding dismissive. "I'm sure you're right." I already knew my receptiveness was cluttered. "But until I have time to still my mind, there's another question you might be able to answer for me."

"Certainly."

I checked my bearings quickly, then asked, "Have you, or Nakahatchi *sensei*, or *Essential Shotokan* ever had any kind of contact with the security guard who was killed on Saturday?"

" 'Contact,' Brew-*san*?" Komatori countered. "What do you mean? My master and I have been introduced to him at the tournaments. Perhaps some of our students also knew him by name. Is that what you wish to know?"

"Not really. I was thinking more of contact outside the hotel. Was he ever a student of yours? Did he ever do any security work for you on the side? Arrange loans—or help pay them off? For you or any of your students?"

Komatori fell silent long enough to make me think that my cell phone had lost the connection. Then he said quietly, "You bewilder me, Brew-*san*. I don't understand why you ask these questions." Then he added more firmly, "However, I'm sure that your reasons are excellent.

"Naturally I can't speak for the private lives of our students. But to the best of my knowledge, none of us has had any contact with the unfortunate Mr. Appelwait outside the hotel. Certainly my master and I haven't."

And that was the truth, at least as far as I was concerned. Nothing about him set off any alarms in my head. If I needed to, I was prepared to gamble on his honesty.

In any case, I'd already given up on the far-fetched notion that Bernie's death had anything to do with Bernie himself. He hadn't brought it on himself through past indiscretions or unfortunate connections. He was dead, purely and simply, because he'd caught someone in that men's room who considered his identity worth murder to protect.

So I told Komatori again, "I'm sorry. I don't mean to confuse you. There's just something about Bernie's death that doesn't make sense. I've been groping for any information I can get about his life. Who he knew. Who he did business with. What kind of business it was. Just in case," I finished with a shrug that nearly made me drop the phone, "the cops miss anything."

"Ah." Hideo's sigh seemed to convey more comprehension than he was entitled to. "I respect your concern. If any other questions occur to you, please ask them."

"I will." He could count on that, anyway.

When we'd agreed to meet on the ground floor of *Essential Shotokan* a few minutes before 11:00, we hung up.

I didn't need to check my watch. The clock outside a nearby bank told me that the time was about 9:30. I had either a lot more time than I needed or nowhere near enough, depending on how Hong reacted. Since I still didn't know why the idea of asking him to evaluate the chops scared me, I took a couple of deep breaths and dialed the number for *Traditional Wing Chun*.

As it happened, directory assistance had a listing for Hong Fei-Tung, but I didn't want to call him directly. I'd be in a stronger position if I played by his rules, made an appointment through T'ang Wen.

My luck with phone calls held. T'ang answered after the third ring.

His reserve as he greeted me had a different quality than Komatori's, an instructed feel—the sound of a student acting on his teacher's wishes instead of his own. When I asked if *Sifu* Hong might be willing to talk to me in, say, fifteen minutes, he replied that he'd have to consult with his master. Then he put the phone down and left me hanging for almost two miles.

I wasn't more than ten blocks from Martial America when T'ang returned with the information that *Sifu* Hong had graciously consented to see me. Since I couldn't grasp Komatori's distinction between "courtesy" and "placation," I thanked T'ang with more enthusiasm than I actually felt, on the theory that it was better for a *gwailo* to sound too humble than not humble enough. Then I concentrated on trying to control the inarticulate clatter of panic in the back of my head.

Damn it. What was the *problem* here? Why did my guts believe that I'd just made a mistake which would haunt me for years?

Hideo had suggested meditation. As soon as I'd wheeled the van into one of Martial America's abundant parking spaces, I tried to do just that. Close my eyes behind my sunglasses, relax into the background mutter of the Plymouth's engine, empty the stale alarm from the pit of my stomach. Unclutter my "receptiveness." The thought of involving Hong with the chops frightened me for some reason, an intuitive reason. I needed to know what it was. Otherwise I'd have to ignore it. In rational terms, Ginny's suggestion made perfect sense.

Was I putting Hong at risk in some way that I couldn't imagine? Was that possible?

What could threaten a man who knew as much about fighting as Hong did?

No answers occurred to me. Instead of opening a door to the back of my head, my efforts simply made me sweat. Apparently meditation wasn't something you could just jump into on the spur of moment. Or maybe I didn't have a meditative personality.

In disgust, I turned off the van, locked it, and headed toward *Traditional Wing Chun*.

The *dojo*'s ornamental door was open, but all the lights were off, and I didn't find anyone on the ground floor. Since manners were so important here, I didn't go upstairs unescorted. Instead I did my best to look patient while I waited for someone to greet me.

T'ang kept me standing there for a few minutes—long enough to make his delay obvious, but not enough to justify a complaint. When he reached the bottom of the stairs, he gave me a bow just on the polite side of brusque.

"Mr. Axbrewder." I thought I heard veiled anger. The silver in his eyes had the whetted look of a fighting blade. "Your desire to speak with my master again surprises me. He has shown you great condescension. Are you not satisfied?"

Something had changed since yesterday. T'ang had had the better part of a day to gnaw on his own ego. Maybe he now resented his master's comparative open-mindedness with me.

Or maybe not. Maybe he had a new problem.

Under other circumstances, I would've said something snotty to provoke him, just to gauge his reaction. Snot being my stock-in-trade and all. But today I had too much at stake.

With a bow of my own, I replied as blandly as I could, "I want to ask *Sifu* Hong a favor, Mr. T'ang. He's in a position to give me some real help, if he's so inclined. His generosity yesterday makes me hope that he'll agree."

"Generosity" was such a nice word for it, I thought, compared to "condescension."

Unfortunately I'd already lost the courtesy competition. T'ang's air of umbrage intensified as he demanded, "And what is this 'favor'?"

Then I had it—I knew what his problem was. I'd committed a breach of *dojo* etiquette. Yesterday Hong had instructed me, *If you wish our assistance, please name your need to T'ang Wen.* But I hadn't complied. I'd been so concerned with my fears that I'd forgotten Hong's restrictions.

In other words, I was now denying T'ang Wen face.

And I couldn't think of a way to back down gracefully, not without sacrificing my own face. Nevertheless I had to soften the insult *some*how. If I didn't, there would never be peace in Martial America.

I spread my hands. "Forgive me, Mr. T'ang." I didn't have to fake the chagrin in my tone. "Naturally"—ha!—"I remember that *Sifu* Hong told me to speak with you. But my proposal touches on his honor, and I wouldn't consider myself honorable if I spoke of it with anyone else.

"There's another matter, however," I added before he could react, "that I should leave with you. I'm sure you'll bring it to *Sifu* Hong's attention more appropriately than I could."

If that didn't mollify him, I didn't know what else to try.

T'ang lowered his eyes, masking irritation. But I hadn't left him any useful recourse. After a moment he said like a sigh, "Name this matter, Mr. Axbrewder."

Almost sighing myself, I told him, "I talked to Mr. Komatori about the timing of *Essential Shotokan*'s lease. He said, first, that Nakahatchi *sensei* moved in when he did because he was being forced out by his previous landlord, and, second, that he didn't learn your master had signed the first lease until after both schools were in place."

I didn't point out the obvious conclusion. If T'ang couldn't see it for himself, I was wasting my breath.

"Do you believe this?" he retorted suspiciously.

"Why would he lie?" I countered. "Nakahatchi *sensei* has the reputation of an honorable man. And Mr. Komatori says that Sternway *sensei*"—deliberately I emphasized Sternway's martial stature—"never mentioned *Sifu* Hong's business or decisions when he persuaded Nakahatchi *sensei* to move here. Isn't Sternway *sensei* also an honorable man?"

Again I hadn't left T'ang any recourse. He couldn't argue without insulting Sternway—and so far I hadn't met one martial artist who would've gone that far.

For a moment he studied my midsection as if he imagined the pleasure of punching me, maybe rupturing an organ or two. Then he conceded without any particular grace, "As you say. I will convey this to my master at a suitable time."

"Thank you, Mr. T'ang," I said firmly. Still on my best behavior. Then, remembering something else Komatori said, I went on, "Before we go upstairs, may I ask you a question?"

T'ang lifted his head. The silver in his eyes had lost its edge, which apparently indicated that he'd recovered his self-possession. Only a slight frown complicated his expression.

"My master instructed that you should ask me if you have any questions."

Like a man picking his way through a minefield, I began, "Yesterday you seemed to think that I'd been hired to protect the chops from someone in *Traditional Wing Chun*. The idea upset me—which is my only excuse for reacting so rudely.

"Of course, you don't know me. But I have to say, I'm still confused by your reaction. Have Sternway *sensei* or Mr. Lacone given you any reason to think that they don't trust and respect you?"

T'ang Wen squirmed. Again he dropped his gaze, hid what was in his eyes. Uncomfortably he answered, "We were given reason."

I let my tone sharpen. "You implied a minute ago that you consider Sternway *sensei* honorable. What has Mr. Lacone done to make you suspicious?"

T'ang stayed hidden behind the mask of his face. "He himself has done nothing. He is a polite and cooperative landlord, as such things are measured in this country."

"Then where did you get the idea—?"

Abruptly he looked up, gave me a straight thrust of silver. "Mr. Sternway's associate. Ms. Rasmussen."

That cut seemed to bite deeper than it should have. "She said that I'd been hired to protect the chops from you?"

"She did not say it," he stated flatly. "It was present in her words."

"Let me guess." I scrambled inside. "She's also the one who told you that Nakahatchi *sensei* moved here ahead of you to claim precedence. She didn't say it. 'It was present in her words.' "

T'ang replied with a curt nod.

Damn and *damn*. Sue Rasmussen, the cutthroat cheerleader, was going out of her way to plant trouble for Martial America. Rather odd behavior for a woman who slept with Lacone's ambassador. What was she trying to do? Undermine Sternway so that she could take over the IAMA?

Instincts whispered in my ears, offering me hints too breathy and obscure to be deciphered. Sue Rasmussen wanted to seed distrust in Martial America? Sue *Rasmussen*?

Marking time while I tried to think, I murmured aimlessly, "That's interesting." If I'd had the sense God gave plankton, I would've turned on my heel right then and walked out of the building, without saying another word to anyone. Alarms squalled at my head, and I did not understand them. My desire to talk to Ginny was so intense that I nearly quailed.

Sue *Rasmussen?*

What the fuck are you doing?

But of course I didn't walk away. In what you might call a moral sense, I didn't know how. I'd already put my feet on this path. And the idea of asking Hong to appraise the chops was simply too apt to reject without a better reason than blind fear.

"Again, thanks," I said vaguely. Then I made an effort to pull myself together. "It looks like she owes us all an explanation. I'm certainly going to ask her for one."

With that sop to T'ang Wen's tarnished face, I changed gears awkwardly. "Can I talk to *Sifu* Hong now?"

Since he didn't really have any choice, he bowed slightly and led me upstairs.

I was breathing hard, hyperventilating almost transcendentally. I felt like a man in a burning house trying to carry victims he couldn't identify above the reach of the flames.

Fortunately someone had flipped on all the lights, and illumination filled the meeting room outside the apartments. That steadied me. It seemed to expose my alarm to rational examination.

At Hong's door, T'ang composed himself for a discreet knock. If my mind hadn't been so congested with worry, I might've wondered whether Hong's "condescension" would extend to inviting me into his home. But it didn't. When he emerged, he closed the door firmly behind him before offering me an impersonal bow.

By now I understood that there were no accidents in Oriental manners. As he had yesterday, Hong meant to hear me out in public, at least symbolically. He wanted me—and T'ang—to know that he wouldn't tolerate any secrets between us.

Which must've reassured the hell out of T'ang. And it suited me fine, especially in my present condition. Despite what I'd said downstairs, I didn't have the slightest interest in keeping my proposal private.

With so many lights on, we could see each other clearly. T'ang stood a bit to the side, ready to intervene if I committed some uniquely *gwailo* gaucherie, while Hong and I faced each other. Trying to minimize the effect of my height, I made a point of keeping a little distance between us.

I answered Hong's bow with the best one I could muster. "*Sifu*," I began, "thanks for agreeing to see me on such short notice. I'm sure you must have a lot of demands on your time."

"Mr. Axbrewder." His flat features neither acknowledged nor denied demands on his time. "You represent Mr. Lacone and Watchdog Insurance. Their concerns should be discussed with T'ang Wen. However, I am willing to hear what you wish to say."

I felt the slap of reprimand, but it was a light one. By degrees I began to breathe a little easier.

"Ordinarily I wouldn't intrude like this," I said to appease him. "Mr. T'ang has been more than helpful." Another sop for T'ang—and an oblique apology for violating Hong's instructions. "As I told him downstairs, I have a request to make. But before I get to it, may I ask a question?"

Hong didn't say anything. His molded-clay features revealed nothing I could read. If I'd been talking to anyone else—even Hideo Komatori—I would've insisted on a response of some kind. Here I decided to interpret silence as consent.

"*Sifu*," I began as if there were lives in my hands, "have you had a chance to look closely at Mr. Nakahatchi's chops?"

T'ang made a hissing noise. His indignation was palpable. "Do you expect my master to belittle himself in that way?"

Presumably he meant "belittle himself" by inspecting the chops at the tournament, where anyone from *Essential Shotokan* might see him do it.

Hong flashed a warning glance at T'ang, but didn't give me any other answer.

"In that case"—every handhold in the face of the cliff seemed to crumble under my weight—"would you mind coming with me to Mr. Nakahatchi's *dojo* and telling me whether you think those chops are genuine?"

As soon as I said it, I knew what was coming. To forestall an eruption, I turned quickly toward T'ang Wen.

"Before you object, Mr. T'ang," I said while his eyes flamed, "I want to point out that I'm speaking for Mr. Lacone and Watchdog Insurance here. The idea is mine, but I have their enthusiastic support. They're eager for *Sifu* Hong's opinion."

Then I faced Hong. "I also speak for Mr. Nakahatchi. I have his support as well. Watchdog has already hired someone to appraise the chops—a local expert, Carliss Swilley. But Mr. Nakahatchi would be pleased to have your evaluation."

I felt anger pour off Hong despite his lack of expression. Every muscle in his body remained relaxed, impervious to threat. Nevertheless his gaze gripped mine like claws, and his iron hair seemed to bristle with outrage.

I kept talking to prevent a response I couldn't handle.

"For one thing, he knows you're better qualified than anyone else to appreciate the real importance of those chops. He's"—I wasn't sure how to phrase what Komatori had told me—"uncomfortable with the possibility that he has a genuine Chinese treasure in his possession, where it probably doesn't belong. And for another, he regrets the appearance of disrespect in his present situation. He'd welcome a chance to honor you in person."

That may've overstated what Komatori had told me. Under the circumstances, I didn't care.

Nothing in Hong's face shifted. For two heartbeats, three, his charged relaxation seemed to ooze danger, as viscid and fatal as nitroglycerin. Like a flash of prophecy, I seemed to see every movement of the *kata* he'd performed at the tournament, all compressed at once into his stillness, and available without warning or transition. He could've broken my neck before I saw him move, despite the distance between us.

How could a man like that be threatened by anything I asked of him? He was more truly capable of taking care of himself than I would've been if I were a solid gold seer, as reliable as sunrise.

Yet my fear for him didn't so much as flicker.

While the moment lasted, I hardly noticed that Hong had made a small gesture to control T'ang Wen. I was barely aware of it as Hong bowed to me smoothly, one hand closed into a fist, the other open to cover it, contradict it.

Then his voice snatched me out of myself.

"Mr. Axbrewder," he pronounced without a hint of tension, "I accept your suggestion. It is fitting.

"Some preparation is surely required. If you will name a suitable time, I will accompany you."

I should've felt that a crisis had been averted, but I didn't. Instead I had the gut-deep sensation that the catch on a guillotine had been released, and that the only thing I'd be able to do for the rest of my life was watch the blade fall.

20

Careful despite my intuitive shock, I spent a couple of minutes while T'ang Wen led me out of the *dojo* confirming the arrangements Deborah had made with Carliss Swilley. At the door, T'ang assured me that he and his master would be ready at 11:00.

Then I found myself out in the full force of Carner's sun.

I still had half an hour to recover my balance. Time enough, you would've thought. Unfortunately time wasn't what I needed.

I needed someone to give me the kind of hint I used to get from forlorn drunks and lost souls late at night back in Puerta del Sol—a suggestive twist of fact or inference which would resolve to clarify my instinctive groping. For years I'd relied on help like that, and on Ginny's straight-ahead tangible rationality, to anchor me against unfounded assumptions and flighty guesswork.

Here I was far out of my natural element, and I didn't know who to turn to.

Sunlight washed over me from all sides—up from the concrete, off the dimmed glass of the windows, out of the sky. For a moment or two I endured its harsh scrutiny. Then I got mad.

Slapping on my sunglasses, I strode back to the van, wrenched open the door, and jumped in. While the engine started and the AC whined to life, I swore at everyone I could think of—at Bernie's killer, at James M. "Turf" Hardshorn for getting himself killed, at Marshal's impenetrable superiority and Edgar Moy's disinterest, at the clotted arrogance of all martial artists, especially Hong and Nakahatchi and Sternway. Then I grabbed my cell phone and dialed the number directory assistance had given me for Sue Rasmussen.

Forty seconds later the receptionist at the Weathers, Slewell, Mallet, Rasmussen law firm informed me that Ms. Rasmussen was working at the IAMA offices this morning. I already had the number, but the receptionist offered it so cheerfully that I let him give it to me again.

That phone rang four or five times—just long enough to make me think that I was finally out of luck. Then a man's voice answered, "International Association of Martial Artists. May I help you?"

Despite my phone's limitations, I recognized Parker Neill.

"Parker," I said, striving to sound calm. "It's Brew."

"Brew," he replied pleasantly. "How are you?" Before I could answer, he added, "Rumor has it you've moved from tournament security to buildings. Is that progress, or should I offer condolences?"

Remembering our last conversation brought a sympathetic ache to the spot he'd poked on my chest. We hadn't exactly parted on good terms. But apparently he didn't hold it against me.

"It pays better," I told him. "I suppose that's an improvement." Then I added, "Looking back, I think I owe you an apology. Anson says I like kicking over anthills. Sometimes I guess I kick at things that should've been left alone."

"Forget it." I didn't hear any tension in his tone. "Tournaments make me irritable. They've changed since the days when I competed regularly. Or I have." He didn't elaborate.

Ned Gage had described him as a "true believer" who didn't know what to do with himself now that he had too much rank and responsibility to participate fully. But I'd picked up the impression that his unspoken disenchantment ran deeper, that the martial arts hadn't offered him anything with enough substance to replace the competitive intensity of his youth.

Which reminded me obliquely that Sternway was Parker's *sensei*. And Anson Sternway *definitely* hadn't found any useful substitute for competitive intensity. For him whatever ideals the martial arts espoused had degenerated into money grubbing and brawls.

In my opinion, Parker needed a new *sensei*. Not that anyone actually cared what I thought.

But this wasn't the right occasion for my anger, so I said, "It's forgotten. Thanks," and then asked quickly, before I talked myself out of it, "Could I call you sometime? Do you mind giving me your phone number? You've already been a big help. I'd like to ask you a few more questions when you aren't on duty over there."

I meant, when he wouldn't be overheard by Sternway's acolytes and sycophants.

"Sure, anytime." Without hesitation, he gave me his cellular number. Then he asked, "Were you looking for me, or is there something else I can help you with?"

"Thanks," I said again. "As a matter of fact, I'm trying to track down Sue Rasmussen. Her office told me she might be there."

"Sure. Let me put you on hold, and I'll get her."

The connection clicked onto the vacant sound of empty space. While I waited, my stifled fuming seemed to echo back from the void like the radio debris of some ancient astrophysical cataclysm. At least the IAMA didn't torment callers with Muzak. The homogenized dysfunction of popular love songs would've driven me mad.

A minute later, the handset clicked again, and Sternway's girlfriend said, "Mr. Axbrewder," with the kind of sweetness conspirators use to conceal hemlock. "This is an unexpected pleasure. What can I do for you?"

Not liking poison much, I wanted to charge right in, guns ablazin'. If even part of what I'd heard recently was accurate, she had a lot to answer for. But I'd been told that she was a no-holds-barred competitor as well as a hard-ass lawyer, despite her cheerleader's facade. And I already knew that she didn't much like me. The forthright approach probably wouldn't work.

I went on pretending I was calm.

"I'm glad you're willing to talk to me, Ms. Rasmussen. We didn't exactly hit it off at the tournament."

"Call me Sue, Mr. Axbrewder." Her tone didn't waver. No doubt she had a lot of fun that way during cross-examinations, confusing her opponent's witnesses with honey. "You're right, we didn't hit it off then. And we probably won't now. But Sternway *sensei* values the job you're doing for Mr. Lacone and Martial America, and he wants the IAMA to give you every cooperation. I'm sure we can be civil to each other, if we really try."

Well, *I* wasn't sure, but what the hell. I could go along with it, at least for a little while.

"That's good to hear, Sue." Deliberately I didn't remind her to call me Brew. "There are several things I think you can help me with, if you don't mind."

"I'll do what I can," she promised.

I waited a beat or two, mostly for effect, then said, "Anson may've told you that I'm interested in Bernie Appelwait. The Luxury security guard who was killed at your tournament. The cops are investigating, of course, and the detective in charge seems to be doing a pretty thorough job." Sweetness Axbrewder-style. "But I've been poking around anyway, asking the kinds of questions that might not occur to anyone else, just to see what turns up."

Apparently that caught her by surprise. She sounded perplexed as she replied, "I thought you identified Mr. Appelwait's killer last night. Sternway *sensei* told me that's why he attacked you."

"Well," I drawled with a hint of malice, "that's not quite accurate. I identified the man as a thief, not a killer. So far anything else is just supposition."

Then I got to the point. "But in fact I'm reasonably sure he *wasn't* Bernie's killer. So, as I say, I've been asking questions."

"I see." She considered the idea. "What sorts of questions?"

She disappointed me by recovering her honey—and by not pushing to find out why I thought Hardshorn wasn't the killer. But I didn't really care. I had plenty of ammunition.

Without a pause I brought my guns to bear.

"Did you know Bernie at all? I mean, outside The Luxury and your tournaments?"

"Know him?" Now I heard a little strain in her voice. "Bernie Appelwait?"

"Did the IAMA ever do any private business with him? Did you? Or *Anson Sternway Shorin-Ryu Bushido*? A bit of part-time security work, for example? Or maybe he arranged some quiet financing, helped you solve a cash-flow problem?"

"Mr. Axbrewder," she put in quickly, "are you suggesting that Sternway *sensei* is involved with loan sharks?"

I sensed a lawyer's instincts at work.

"I'm not suggesting anything," I told her firmly. "I'm just asking questions."

"Then the answer is no." She'd abandoned sweetness for asperity—the tone she probably used on opposing counsel. "In all the years I've known Sternway *sensei*, or been involved with the IAMA, we've never had any dealings of any kind with Mr. Appelwait outside his role as The Luxury's Chief of Security."

I refined my focus, continued maneuvering her into range. "Was he ever a student of yours? Can you think of any personal connection that might exist between him and anyone at the IAMA, or in Anson's school? Any connection at all?"

"No. Categorically not."

I made a pretense of pausing for thought. Then I inquired, "And you'd tell me the truth about this, Sue?"

Her reaction stung across the airwaves. "That's either an insult or a very stupid question." She bit off each word precisely. "What makes you think I might lie to you?"

"I'll answer that," I returned promptly, "if you'll answer another for me first." Before she could refuse, I asked, "What's the real reason Anson hasn't moved into Martial America?"

"What do you mean," she countered, " 'the real reason'? What reason have you heard?"

I snorted. "Money and politics. Martial America costs too much. And Anson doesn't want to get caught in the middle of potential conflicts between schools."

"And that doesn't make sense to you? It sounds perfectly reasonable to me."

"No," I retorted, "it doesn't make sense. Lacone has too much to gain by attracting Anson's business. He's eager to make a deal Anson can afford. And as for politics—"

She cut me off. "Stop right there, Mr. Axbrewder. You're already wrong. Mr. Lacone is eager to make a deal Sternway *sensei* could afford—*if* he didn't already have financial problems.

"In case you haven't heard, he's trying to divorce his wife. And she's contesting it. In fact, she's doing everything in her power to leave him destitute. She was extravagant before they separated. I swear to God, the man was a saint with her. But now she's determined to gut his assets. As a school, we survive where we are on a month-by-month basis. Under the circumstances, Sternway *sensei* certainly can't commit himself to the kind of long-term lease Mr. Lacone wants.

"I'm trying to be cooperative here," she finished, "but I think you have a hell of a nerve suggesting that I might not tell you the truth."

Gotcha, I thought. If Sternway heard what she just said, he'd probably demote her. Hell, he might even kick her out of his bed. The last thing a balls-to-the-wall fighter like him would want was to be exposed as a pussy-whipped weakling who couldn't defend himself against his own wife.

Sue Rasmussen—I was sure of this—had told me too much about money because she didn't want to talk about politics.

"That's all very interesting," I returned. "But you've only answered part of my question." At last I cocked one of my guns, let some of my anger show. "What about the conflicts in Martial America?"

She met me with exasperation. "What *about* them? They're traditional, Mr. Axbrewder—they go back longer than you can imagine. With the best will in the world, Sternway *sensei* can't resolve them. What little effectiveness he has as a mediator depends on his stature outside those conflicts."

Working to convey the impression that I took her response seriously, I paused again, relaxed into the silence. I wanted her to drop her guard. But I didn't drag it out. A moment later I remarked, "That's also very interesting. Unfortunately it's bullshit."

Then I opened fire.

"From what I've heard, both *Sifu* Hong and Nakahatchi *sensei* like Anson's idea of cooperation among *dojos*. They're in conflict with each other because *you've* been stirring up trouble."

I heard the hiss as she snatched a breath. The next instant she flashed back at me, "Mr. Axbrewder, I've had enough of this. I'm trying to answer your questions, I'm *trying* to get along with you here. I certainly don't deserve—"

I interrupted hard. "Correct me if I'm wrong, Sue. Didn't you prepare the leases for *Essential Shotokan* and *Traditional Wing Chun*?"

"Yes, but—" she began.

That admission was enough. "So you were in a position to know that Hong expected precedence. But you didn't mention his feelings until you'd already moved Nakahatchi into Martial America ahead of Hong. In fact, you created an insult that didn't exist."

"That's absurd! How was I supposed to know—?"

I kept right on interrupting her. "You just lectured me about conflicts between martial arts schools. How could you *not* know? Do you expect me to believe that Anson didn't *tell* you he'd offered Hong the chance to be first in Martial America?

"But you didn't stop there. As I hear it, you made a point of making Nakahatchi aware that Hong was offended. But you didn't explain Nakahatchi's circumstances to Hong. How am I supposed to interpret that? It sure looks like you didn't *want* Hong to understand that Nakahatchi wasn't trying to upstage him."

"*Mister* Axbrewder." Sue's vehemence caused a crackle of distortion in my phone's earpiece. "You're taking the entire situation out of context." Her disdain filled the connection. "I don't discuss one client's business with another. That's privileged information. I'm ethically bound not to tell either *Sifu* Hong or Nakahatchi *sensei* about each other's decisions.

"I only mentioned *Sifu* Hong's reaction when I realized he'd misinterpreted Nakahatchi *sensei*'s actions. I thought Nakahatchi *sensei* deserved a chance to correct *Sifu* Hong's misapprehensions. It's not *my* fault he didn't take advantage of the opportunity.

"And *that's* privileged information as well. I don't know who has been talking to you, but they should not have done it."

All right. So she was fast on her feet. Living up to her reputation. That didn't bother me. I could exchange volleys with her like this all day.

"Well—" I made a pretense of backing down. "Maybe you're right." Then I tried a more oblique attack. "But I have to say, I'm still confused by your role in all this. If you thought Nakahatchi deserved a chance to straighten things out, why didn't you think Hong deserved accurate information?"

"Because," she retorted with heavy impatience, "he's a Wing Chun stylist. I don't expect you to understand what that means, but believe me, it's relevant. He's too touchy to be reasonable."

I had her, and she didn't even know it. Grinning fiercely at my windshield, I let her bury herself.

"Soft stylists are like that generally," she pronounced. "They're flashy and dramatic because they don't want anyone to know that their techniques don't really work. Instead they cultivate secretiveness, trying to convince themselves that the rest of us aren't smart enough to recognize their real power. And they're *touchy*. You should hear the complaints at tournaments. The judges aren't fair, the refs won't give them points they deserve, everyone is prejudiced against them. Since they can't demonstrate any effectiveness, they've made the whole thing about ego.

"I didn't explain Nakahatchi *sensei*'s position to Hong," she concluded with mis-aimed sarcasm, "because I had no reason to think he'd listen."

"I see." I let my grin show in my voice. "It's starting to make sense now. There's just one more thing I don't get." Then I asked cheerfully, "Why did you tell Hong that I was hired to protect the chops from him? I mean, considering that he's so 'touchy' and all."

"Mr. Axbrewder"—my earpiece positively spat at me—"I've had enough of this." Righteous Sue Rasmussen in full cry. "From the beginning you approached our tournament with contempt, and all you've done since then is sneer.

"You forget that I know what you're like. When I heard Mr. Lacone made the mistake of hiring you, I knew you weren't qualified to deal with the situation in Martial America. You're too ignorant and 'superior' to appreciate the danger. So—" She took a deep breath. "I gave you some help. I made *Sifu* Hong aware that his school was being watched. *You* weren't likely to grasp what the ownership of those chops means, or how far almost anyone at *Traditional Wing Chun* would go to retrieve them. On your behalf, I made them nervous. I made them *cautious*. Otherwise they might have stolen those chops out from under your nose."

I wanted to applaud, but she didn't give me the chance.

"This conversation is over," she informed me. Then she slammed down the phone.

Well, gosh, I thought. Apparently she'd figured out why I suspected her of lying.

I'd finally won a round. For a minute or two I couldn't stop grinning.

Sternway's squeeze spent almost as much time and ingenuity undermining Martial America as he did promoting it. Bless his woman-ridden little heart, he had a saboteur in his midst.

Or—

With the suddenness of a cerebral hemorrhage, a window seemed to open in my head. Through it, I saw nameless intuitions tremble on the verge of clarity. Hong and Hardshorn and Bernie shimmered on the horizon like mirages, obscured or invented by heat, and accompanied by other figures with their faces hidden.

Maybe it wasn't her lover sweet Sue had sabotaged. Maybe it was me.

Before I could grasp all the implications, however, before I could catch even a glimpse of the danger I'd created for Hong, the window closed. I found myself in a muck sweat, despite the van's valiant AC. Even through my sunglasses, Carner's hard light had a mocking tinge.

God*damn* it, where was Ginny when I needed her?

Some part of me knew what Sue's performance meant, I was sure of that. But I'd lost the window. It wouldn't open again until it was good and ready. Or I was.

Maybe it was me.

Damn and *damn*. The sensation that people might get hurt because I couldn't understand my own instincts was almost more than I could stomach.

Unfortunately experience had taught me that I wouldn't get anywhere if I sat and stewed about it. Muttering curses, I forced myself out of my own head long enough to look around the parking lot for some indication that Deborah had arrived.

I didn't see any new cars. But it was getting close to 11:00, so I decided not to wait. Reluctantly I turned off the Plymouth and stepped out onto the griddle of the concrete.

Deliberately I tried not to hurry. I needed to relax somehow. Nevertheless anxieties I couldn't identify goaded me too hard. In spite of my best efforts, I burst into *Traditional Wing Chun* like a man with furies in his wake.

To my surprise, I found Hong and T'ang Wen ready in the hall.

They both wore formal kung fu silks. As usual, I couldn't read Hong's face, but his posture hardly hinted at violence. If he saw threats in meeting Nakahatchi, he may've been reluctant to prejudge them. At his side, T'ang appeared subdued, almost chastened. I suspected that he'd told his master about Nakahatchi's lease, and had been shaken when Hong took the information seriously.

Pulling off my sunglasses, I bowed to both of them. They responded without making a production out of it—measured courtesy, a tentative acknowledgment that waited for events to justify something more definitive.

"I'm a bit early, *Sifu.*" By using his title without his name, I hoped to suggest that he continued to rise in my estimation. My own form of measured acknowledgment. "I don't think Ms. Messenger and Mr. Swilley have arrived yet. Would you prefer to wait for them here, or shall we go on over to *Essential Shotokan*? I'm sure we'll be welcome either way."

Hong inclined his head. "We will go." He may've wanted to gauge Nakahatchi's reaction without Deborah and Swilley there to complicate matters.

"Good." With another bow, I swung the door open so that Hong and T'ang could precede me.

But as we reached the sidewalk, I saw Deborah and a man I didn't know emerge from a BMW so immaculate that it might've descended from the hand of God right there in the parking lot. She wore a pale blue business suit that seemed to turn her auburn hair the color of firelight and flames. When she spotted us, she waved cheerfully, then escorted her companion toward Nakahatchi's *dojo.*

Without transition my heart started thudding double-time. As surreptitiously as I could, I wiped my palms on my slacks, but it didn't help. Somehow I controlled my impulse to stare while she crossed the concrete. If I got caught up in the lissome sway of her gait, I'd forget that I still didn't know how to trust her.

We converged under the awning at *Essential Shotokan*'s symbolic door. Deborah gave me a smile that nearly dropped me to my knees, greeted Hong and T'ang with a subtle combination of familiarity and reserve, then introduced all three of us to her companion.

Carliss Swilley's appearance struck me as odd. From a distance, he'd looked both shorter and fatter than he actually was. In fact, he was a man of medium height and average weight, dressed in a rich, slightly shimmering blue suit that God could've handed down along with the BMW. Dark, horn-rimmed glasses gave his face a studious air. Well-behaved scraps of hair around his balding head suggested elegance. And yet somehow his aura, his presence, insisted that in reality he was short and pudgy, that the man who shook my hand was a facade for someone smaller and less fastidious.

Above his expert's smile, he had plain features a bit too broad for his height, and a substantial birthmark smack in the middle of his forehead. It increased the effect of his glasses, as if nature had marked him with authority. Or maybe it was the insignia of what lay behind his facade.

"A pleasure, Mr. Axbrewder," he informed me in a desiccated tone like the sound of dust settling. "I understand I have you to thank for this commission. Do you know Chinese antiques?"

"Not even a little bit. But I have a vague grasp on insurance." I flicked an involuntary grin at Deborah. "Enough to be sure we need a professional appraisal."

"I'm grateful nonetheless." He sounded as grateful as a tombstone. "A chance to study ivory and workmanship which may have come from early in the Qing dynasty, and which may indeed have been produced by Leung Len Kwai himself"—he rustled his hands—"well, suffice it to say that missing such an opportunity would be an occasion for regret."

I doubted that. He gave me the impression that he didn't take his "regret" out of the closet very often and hadn't quite finished brushing off the cobwebs.

"I hope you won't be disappointed," I put in bluntly. "The chops may not be authentic."

"I'll enjoy seeing them in any case," he assured me without enthusiasm. "Forged antiques often demonstrate as much skill and industry as their originals, and may be nearly as old. Indeed, any copies of Leung Len Kwai's work could well derive, as his originals do, from the eighteenth century. Historically—"

He was poised to deliver a disquisition, but Deborah interrupted him tactfully. "Shall we take this inside, Mr. Swilley? It's fascinating, of course, but I'm sure Nakahatchi *sensei* is waiting for us." Her smile paused on me briefly as she scanned our little group. "And I'm sure we'd like to escape this heat."

"Certainly," Swilley assented with no change of tone. Maybe dry-and-neglected was the only tone he had.

Deborah reached for the door, but T'ang Wen forestalled her, bowing each of us inside ahead of him.

The air of the *dojo* was a relief—cooled and dim, almost comforting. If I'd been that easily comforted, I might've relaxed a bit. But nearly audible mental voices insisted persistently that I'd entered the presence of threats I couldn't identify or defuse. That lives were on the line somehow.

Hideo Komatori awaited us at the foot of the stairs. He was formally dressed in a dark suit and understated tie which made him look like a pallbearer. Vaguely I wondered what that meant. If there were no accidents in Oriental manners, what message did Komatori mean to convey? For that matter, what did Hong and T'ang imply with their silks?

I wasn't qualified to guess. Certainly Hideo's smile seemed genuine. Ignoring Swilley, Deborah, and me, he bowed deeply to Hong—and almost as deeply to T'ang. "*Sifu* Hong," he said, "T'ang-*san*, I am honored to welcome you. We've desired this day for a long time, but didn't know how to bring it about. For that we're indebted to Brew-*san*."

Neither Hong or T'ang replied, but Hong gave Komatori a bow that looked adequately respectful. T'ang also bowed, although he couldn't match his master's reserve or grace.

Then Hideo turned his attention to the rest of us. He bowed to me as he had to T'ang, shook Deborah's hand, expressed gratitude for Carliss Swilley's presence—the perfect host. "My master is waiting." He gestured toward the stairs. "Will you join him?"

"That's why I'm here," Swilley announced. I detected a note of peevishness in his voice. Maybe he thought he deserved more "face" than he'd been given.

Confirming my impression, he started to talk as soon as Komatori approached the stairs. "As I was saying, the later decades of the eighteenth century were a time when such martial artifacts as Leung Len Kwai's Wing Chun chops would have been especially desirable. The martial arts in general, and Wing Chun in particular, played a significant political role during the first century of the Qing dynasty. They were considered subversive in the hands of the dynasty's opponents, and strenuous efforts were made to suppress them. For that reason, such artifacts as Leung Len Kwai's chops were uniquely valuable. They represented knowledge and traditions precious to the dynasty's opponents. Historically, the time was ripe for copies of all kinds. A skilled reproduction from that period would have considerable value of its own, regardless of its provenance."

He went on in that vein, throwing out references to "literati art," hanging scrolls, and bamboo carving—claiming authority with both hands—but I stopped listening. Without much effort, I maneuvered us so that Deborah and I brought up the rear of the group. Giving her hand a quick squeeze, I bent down to whisper in her ear, "I've got a bad feeling about this."

She looked at me quickly. "Why?"

"I can't explain it," I admitted. "Just a hunch."

She aimed a luminous smile into my heart. "Carliss has that effect on people," she breathed. "I had to ride with him all the way here. Until I saw you, I wanted to step in front of a truck."

My throat went dry as her breath kissed my check. I swallowed hard. "That's not it. It began before I met him."

Now she frowned. "Don't you trust Mr. Nakahatchi?"

I shrugged helplessly.

She gave me a squeeze of her own. "Let's see what happens."

I didn't have anything better to suggest. Hong could probably handle an entire roomful of thugs, if it came to that. And Nakahatchi had no discernible reason to turn this appraisal into a battlefield.

But that didn't reassure me. Whatever the danger was, it didn't come from Nakahatchi. Or from anyone at *Essential Shotokan.*

At the top of the stairs, we moved toward the meeting room. The door was open, and I noticed that Lacone hadn't yet installed any of the bolts I'd requested. The display was visible, but I couldn't see anyone inside until Komatori bowed us through the doorway. Then I spotted Nakahatchi.

Like his senior student, he baffled my expectations. Since Komatori was wearing a business suit, I'd assumed that Nakahatchi would do the same. Instead, however, he had on an elaborate Oriental outfit I could hardly describe. A brocade bathrobe—a *kimono*—with gold stitching and too many colors draped his torso, closed at the waist by a wide white sash fastened in a knot that must've taken him a week to tie. Below the bathrobe he wore voluminous black pantaloons like culottes on steroids. White socks and cotton sandals peeked out under his pant legs.

Apparently this ensemble was the Japanese equivalent of a morning suit, or maybe even a tux. By rights, he should've looked ridiculous, but he didn't. Instead he seemed to emanate grave dignity. His costume had a stately processional quality that made the rest of us look shallow, as if we'd joined a funeral cortege after way too many beers.

As an exercise in Oriental manners, it made my skin crawl. I felt sure that Hong wouldn't appreciate it.

Like Komatori downstairs, Nakahatchi began by concentrating exclusively on Hong and T'ang. With a bow as stylized as his garb, he said, "*Sifu* Hong, respected T'ang, please be welcome in my small home. Your presence does me great honor." The seams on either side of his mouth looked deeper than they had the last time I'd seen him, cut into his cheeks by care. "It fulfills one of my most cherished desires."

Hong bowed in return, but he didn't fool me. I could feel anger fume off his skin, so hot it boiled the air. As unobtrusively as I could, I shifted Deborah out of the way, moved closer to him.

"Nakahatchi, you shame me," he replied stiffly. "I was not invited to a formal occasion. I was asked to consider the authenticity of the chops. It is offensive—"

"Ah, forgive me," Nakahatchi put in. His air of unrelieved mourning robbed the interruption of rudeness. "That was not my intent. I have been very clumsy."

He took a small step forward, lowered his voice. "It is my wife, *Sifu* Hong. Mitsuku-*san* is entranced with pleasure at the thought of your visit. She instructs me to invite you to take tea with us when the matter of this appraisal is concluded. And nothing would satisfy her but that I must show my respect as such things are done in Japan, among the old families. I protested that surely you would wish to make your own preparations. But she would have none of it. '*Sifu* Hong,' she insisted, 'does quite enough by consenting to visit. No further effort is required of him.' At last it became clear to me that I must comply with her wishes.

"The fault is mine entirely if I have erred."

Again he bowed as if he were offering the back of his neck to a blade.

A small sigh of relief escaped me. Halfway through Nakahatchi's speech, I felt Hong's emotional temperature drop. Some arcane issue of "face" had been resolved. When Nakahatchi bowed, Hong did the same. Then he offered, "A good wife is a great treasure. They ask much of those who hold them, as all treasures do." He sounded almost genial. "Put my protest from your mind. I spoke in ignorance. T'ang Wen and I will take tea with you."

T'ang's face wore a congested expression, but he kept his mouth shut. Which was a good thing. If he'd started trouble now, I might've punched him.

Deborah gave me a tentative smile, like she didn't quite grasp what had just happened.

"You are very gracious," Nakahatchi murmured in response.

On cue, Komatori stepped forward. "*Sensei*, let me introduce Ms. Deborah Messenger, who represents Watchdog Insurance. Also Mr. Carliss Swilley, who is widely considered an authority on Chinese antiques. Mr. Axbrewder you've met. It was he who persuaded *Sifu* Hong to join us.

"Ms. Messenger, Mr. Swilley, Mr. Axbrewder, this is my master, Sihan Nakahatchi."

I took a few deep breaths while Nakahatchi shook hands all around. Swilley had surprised me by containing himself this long. He'd exhausted his patience, however. As he put his limp hand in Nakahatchi's, he said, "I *am* an authority, sir. I recognize Leung Len Kwai's work when I see it. And if your chops were carved by someone else, I should be able to date them quite accurately. That, as you know, is critical to determining their value. A more recent copy can't compare with an eighteenth-century reproduction, especially if the workmanship suggests an authorized reproduction.

"There are several crucial questions. First—"

Deborah rolled her eyes at me, then interposed herself smoothly between Swilley and Nakahatchi. "The chops are here, Mr. Swilley." Tucking her hand under his arm, she drew him toward the case. "Why don't you explain while we look at them? That will help the rest of us understand."

Apparently he didn't care who he talked to, as long as he got to talk. Still lecturing, he approached the display. Komatori opened it for him, then withdrew in my direction.

For a moment Hong held back. Maybe he didn't want to encroach on Swilley's expertise. Or maybe he just couldn't stand Swilley's manner. But Nakahatchi urged him to go ahead with his own examination. Followed by T'ang, they joined Deborah and Swilley at the case.

I stayed where I was. I wouldn't learn anything by watching other people peer at ivory carvings. And I didn't enjoy the unconscious insult of Swilley's pedantry, his implicit assumption that Hong and Nakahatchi knew nothing. He could expatiate on "the Qianlong emperor's eulogy" and "the application of *pidiao* techniques to ivory during the Qing dynasty" until his jaw broke, and it would still be rude.

Komatori approached me. The pale scar cutting across his eyebrow into his left cheek gave his smile an ironic cast. "You've done us a considerable service, Brew-*san*," he stated softly. "My master and *Sifu* Hong may finally be able to dispel some of their differences."

"Over tea?" I asked, just to keep him talking.

"Yes," he assented. "The occasion will be highly ceremonial. If you were present, you might find it too"—he considered adjectives briefly—"indirect to be useful. But it gives great face. I think Mitsuku-*san* is right. *Sifu* Hong will understand that any disagreement about the chops doesn't indicate disrespect."

"So why aren't you all dressed up?" I meant, like Nakahatchi.

He smiled more broadly. "Because I was born in this country, Brew-*san*. And my ancestors weren't aristocrats. My family has remained Japanese in many ways, but our traditions don't include formal aristocratic tea ceremonies. I don't own the right clothes. This"—he indicated his suit—"is the best I can do."

"Well, you've got *me* beat, at any rate," I muttered. "It's a good thing I'm not invited." I was sincere about that. An hour kneeling at a low table while I struggled not to use the wrong chopstick would've ruptured something. "I'm not that pretty on my good days."

Komatori didn't respond directly. Without any particular transition, he announced, "My master would like to speak with you later. Perhaps after lunch?"

That surprised me. "What about?"

Hideo didn't offer me any help. "He'll tell you."

For the second time my throat went dry, like I'd swallowed a lump of alum. New tension ran along my nerves. I had the sudden impression that something big had opened ahead of me, just out of sight. Something personal—

My instincts must've been working overtime. Or else I was so knotted up about Hong that I'd started flinching at shadows.

I forced moisture back into my mouth. "After lunch is good," I said, nearly croaking. I hadn't made any specific plans. "I'll be glad to talk to him."

Komatori bowed as if I'd granted a significant request.

Meanwhile Swilley continued hectoring his unfortunate audience. He'd produced a loupe which he used to scrutinize several of the chops from all sides, while he went on and on about secret artist's marks and scientific means of dating ivory. As far as I could tell, he hardly paused for breath. Maybe having a voice that dry enabled him to inhale through his ears.

At his side, Deborah listened and nodded, feigning attention.

Hong had examined a couple of the chops, primarily by rubbing them with his fingers. Then he withdrew as if he didn't want to get in Swilley's way. His face held no more expression than a clay pot. In contrast, T'ang watched Swilley like he expected the appraiser to grab a handful of chops and bolt.

From a respectful distance, Nakahatchi presided over the display. The sheer artificiality of his attire seemed to emphasize the sorrows ingrained in his features. He looked like a man with more bereavements than he could name.

The more I saw of him, the more difficulty I had imagining him as a martial artist. He looked like Death's Gatekeeper, immersed in the griefs of those who passed through his portal.

Abruptly Swilley put down the chop he'd been peering at, lowered his loupe, and turned around.

"Ms. Messenger. Mr. Nakahatchi." His voice held a tremor I hadn't heard before—excitement or alarm, I couldn't tell which. "There's no doubt. Other experts will agree with me. The workmanship is unmistakable. And the particular way that the ivory has aged is right."

He paused as if he needed to gather his courage. Then he announced, "The chops are genuine. They were carved by Leung Len Kwai."

Oh, shit. My heart kicked into a faster beat. Genuine? That sure as hell raised the stakes. For me, for Watchdog and Lacone. Definitely for Nakahatchi. And for Hong—

Somehow Swilley's pronouncement multiplied the danger I'd put Hong in. Suddenly the floor around him was littered with land mines, metaphorically speaking, and I didn't know where any of them were.

Deborah's eyes widened at the news. T'ang looked hard at his master, expecting some reaction, but Hong remained expressionless, silent. Nakahatchi bowed his head like a man in prayer.

Komatori glanced at me and shrugged discreetly. I guess he didn't know where the mines were either.

"I would be reluctant to assign a specific value," Swilley continued, "without consulting my sources." Now that he'd taken the plunge, his voice grew steadier. "And Mr. Hong may have relevant information which would clarify an important point."

Shifting to face Hong, he asked, "Do you know if this collection is complete, sir?"

After a moment Hong nodded ambiguously.

Did that mean, Yes, I know, or, Yes, it's complete? I wanted to ask, but Swilley didn't give me a chance.

"On that basis," he proclaimed like a desert wind, "I feel confident in suggesting that a complete set of this provenance cannot be worth less than one million dollars." He looked like he wanted to chortle. "Beyond question. Possibly more.

"Congratulations, sir," he finished, addressing Nakahatchi. "You are now a rich man."

Damnation. Killing Bernie probably seemed trivial to a man who aimed to get his hands on that much loot.

At the case, Deborah appeared to shake herself out of a daze. "Mr. Nakahatchi," she began earnestly, "I recognize that this may not be entirely good news. When Mr. Swilley is ready to name a precise figure"—she looked toward the appraiser—"by tomorrow if possible?"

"By three o'clock today," Swilley answered with a smug smile. "No later."

Nakahatchi raised his head. Whatever he'd felt a moment ago was hidden now. He might've been ecstatic, suicidal, or merely confused, and I wouldn't have known the difference.

Deborah nodded reluctantly. "When we get a figure," she continued to Nakahatchi, "we'll consult with Mr. Lacone and the IAMA. And our home offices, of course. We'll see what we can work out. I'll do everything possible to keep the insurance within your means. But that will take at least a couple of days.

"In the meantime"—she pulled in a deep breath—"I assure you that you're covered. Your policy, and the policy on Martial America, will protect you until we're ready to discuss new terms."

Nakahatchi should've been glad to hear that. A couple of days would give Lacone time to get serious about security. But Deborah's promise didn't seem to affect him. Apparently he'd raised stoicism to the level of an art form. Or else he just didn't care.

That I did not believe.

"You are most kind, Ms. Messenger," he said the same way he might've thanked her for mailing a letter. "We will await further discussion." Then he turned to Hong and bowed.

"*Sifu*, may I inquire if you are satisfied with your own inspection?"

"I am, *sensei*," Hong replied quietly. "No more need be said."

His answering bow looked just a touch deeper than the one he'd given Nakahatchi earlier.

The intensity on T'ang Wen's face resembled shock. But he effaced it quickly. Good disciple that he was, he didn't do or say anything to undermine his master, regardless of his own feelings.

Nevertheless he gave me the sudden impression that he knew where at least some of the mines were.

"Then," Nakahatchi continued with another bow, "I thank you for your time and attention in this matter, Mr. Swilley."

Swilley nodded back like he didn't think that an ordinary old bow did him justice.

Next Nakahatchi bowed to Deborah. "Ms. Messenger, when you are ready you will speak with Hideo-*san*."

"Of course, *sensei*." She used his title like she couldn't help it.

I knew how she felt. Despite his getup, and his diffidence, he commanded respect.

"*Sifu*," he went on, "will you now enter my humble dwelling? You will do my dear wife great honor if you and the esteemed T'ang Wen will take tea with us."

"It is we who are honored, *sensei*," Hong replied with an air of liturgical gravity. "We will join you with pleasure."

The fact that neither of them let Swilley's pronouncement affect their courtesies did nothing to ease my panic. I couldn't match them. Inside I reeled with the sensation that at least one of them had already stepped on a mine and blown himself to bits. I just didn't know how or why—or when the damage would show.

Then everyone bowed to everyone else. Again. Komatori joined his master at Nakahatchi's door. With an almost processional solemnity, as if everything they said and did carried spiritual weight, they ushered Hong and T'ang into Nakahatchi's apartment.

I found myself staring past Deborah and Swilley like I'd gone stupid.

"Brew." She reached for me with a smile. "I'm going to take Mr. Swilley back to his shop. Then I'll call Mr. Lacone, let him know what's going on."

I heard myself say thanks. Between her smile and my alarm, I hardly knew who I was anymore.

She came closer. "It looks to me like you've accomplished something pretty special. These schools can't go on distrusting each other now." Her eyes studied my face for hints of what was wrong. "Maybe you should take the afternoon off, get some rest." Holding herself so that Swilley couldn't see her face, she moistened her lips. "You've got a big night ahead of you."

I couldn't imagine smiling myself, but I tried. It felt like a skull's grimace.

Swilley looked ostentatiously at his watch. It was probably a Rolex, but I didn't care.

"Tell Mr. Lacone," I replied unsteadily, "he can't sit on his hands any longer. Those security measures I requested have to be installed *now*."

Deborah's smile shifted into a perplexed frown.

"Scare him a bit," I explained. "Even if it's not true. We need action here. And I don't think he takes me very seriously."

Her expression cleared. "Got it. If he won't listen to me, I'll sic Sammy on him."

Trying not to sound too fervent, I muttered, "Good."

She arched an eyebrow. "Same to you." Then she turned back to Swilley. "Shall we go?"

He didn't muffle his impatience. "Indeed."

Just for a second, before she escorted him out of the room, I could've sworn he glared at me.

I didn't care about that either. When they were gone, I leaned back against the wall, then slid down it to the floor.

Bernie was already dead. So was Hardshorn. How many more people would get hurt or killed before I figured out what was going on?

21

Unfortunately moping about it solved just about as many problems as sitting on the floor did. Also it made my butt hurt.

With a sigh, I labored to my feet and considered my options.

The only people I really wanted to talk to were Marshal, Detective Moy, and Ginny. But she was on duty with Mai Sternway. And the other two wouldn't appreciate being harassed for answers they didn't have. Marshal would probably call me if he learned anything—including whatever he heard from Moy.

So. What else could I do?

No question about it, the time had come to tackle Song Duk Soon.

I'd been putting that off, even though it was obviously necessary. He'd left the tournament hall in plenty of time to trap Bernie. And, as I remembered his location on the bleachers, he could've seen me watching the picks. If he were Hardshorn's spot—

I told myself I'd delayed confronting him so that I could learn more about the residual tensions in Martial America. However, the truth was that he scared me. I hadn't seen any sign that he shared Hong's and Nakahatchi's measured restraint.

And I still wanted to postpone encountering him. I didn't even want food. I was losing confidence by the hour, and I needed a shower. I wanted to blast hot water at my knotted doubts until they dissolved into soapsuds and steam. But I couldn't afford to wait any longer. Not if the chops were genuine.

Nevertheless I had to warm up for the challenge. On general principles, I let myself out of *Essential Shotokan*, coaxed the Plymouth back to life, and drove away in search of lunch.

An hour later I was back.

It wasn't 1:00 yet, which seemed a bit early for "after lunch." In other words, I'd run of out excuses. Bob Gravel and *Malaysian*

Fighting Arts didn't worry me—Song Duk Soon and his school did. After drumming my fingers fretfully on the van's steering wheel for a couple of minutes, I tightened my grip on myself and went to face Master Soon.

Under his awning, I found another wooden door engraved with Asian symbols and *kanji*. I couldn't tell the difference between this one and *Essential Shotokan*'s design, except that here everything had been gilt-edged. The intaglio effect made the door stand out like the portal of a trap.

Sternway shouldn't have admitted that he considered Tae Kwon Do a "toy martial art."

Inside, I took off my sunglasses and looked around. As expected, the basic floorplan matched the other schools—a main *dojo* to my right, a smaller one lined with specialized training equipment to my left. In the larger room, a youngish man wearing a crisp white *gi* and a black belt led twenty or more students, mostly middle-aged women in leotards and sweat shirts, through exercises that looked suspiciously like martial aerobics. The students bounced and flopped strenuously around the floor, yelling at regular intervals—punching and kicking their way to fitness. In contrast, their instructor seemed to coast through the movements.

The smaller room held four or five students of various ages, all male, all wearing white canvas pajamas and brown belts, with Master Soon's *Tae Kwon Do Academy* patches on their chests. They practiced drills in pairs. One partner launched an implausible attack of some kind—a two-handed punch, or an aerial kick—while the other attempted an equally implausible block. Snorting to myself, I turned away. Most of the street thugs I knew would've dismantled these "artists" in about four seconds.

While I waited for someone to notice me, I scanned the entry hallway. Maybe a dozen trophies, some of them four feet tall, stood on stands attached to the walls. Between them hung rank certificates in ornate frames, boasting of at least twenty black belts. And up out of reach near the ceiling hung a variety of weapons, all of them apparently old. Some I recognized—*katanas, tonfas, bos.* Others I'd never seen before. A couple looked so unwieldy that I couldn't imagine how they were used.

A cluttered bulletin board hung near the doorway to the main *dojo*. Mostly it held flyers for Tae Kwon Do tournaments all over the country. But after a moment I located a class schedule. Apparently Song Duk Soon ran a busy school. The women in leotards were studying "Fitness Tae Kwon Do." A whole series of kids' classes would take over the *dojo* from 2:00 until 5:30, after which the training divided into beginning, intermediate, advanced, and black belt sessions. Soon's *Academy* must've had at least two hundred students.

Since I didn't see a brown belt class listed for the afternoon, I assumed that the men in the smaller *dojo* were working out on their own. Demonstrating their diligence for anyone who bothered to notice.

A sheet of general information about the school hung near the class schedule. It informed me, among other things, that dues were $100 a month. $20,000 a month altogether. $240,000 a year.

Somehow I felt sure that *Traditional Wing Chun* and *Essential Shotokan* weren't doing anything like the same amount of business.

The straining women had stopped yelling. When I turned away from the bulletin board, I found their instructor in the doorway, staring at me with thick arms folded on a broad chest.

He was a white guy, aggressively so, with pale eyes, sandy hair, and enough freckles to make him look vaguely leprous. From a distance he'd seemed youngish, but up close he looked older. For a heartbeat or two, I couldn't figure out why. Then I realized that the skin of his cheeks was too worn for his years. He had the kind of cheeks you usually see on tired boxers, flesh beaten to the consistency of leather by too many fists over way too many years. His left cheekbone had been flattened with blows.

He also looked like you could smack him across the chops with a bundle of rebar and not faze him. He would've fit right in at Sternway's fight club.

"You're Axbrewder," he announced. His voice didn't suit his pugilistic features. It was incongruously high, a voice for whimpering in fright or whining complaints, not for intimidation. But that didn't stop him. "I remember you from the tournament. You humiliated one of ours.

"We don't like that around here."

Oh, joy.

Right on cue, the brown belts came out into the hallway and ranged themselves across from me, shoulder to shoulder, like a team of amateur enforcers. They all had belligerence in their eyes. At least a couple of them looked like they meant it.

Joy and wapture. Just what I needed, a testosterone check. And here I was supposed to be keeping the peace and all.

"Then I guess it's a good thing," I replied pleasantly, "that you're wrong. I didn't humiliate him. He humiliated himself. All I did was intervene before someone hurt him."

One of the brown belts opened his mouth, but another shut him up with an elbow in his ribs. Apparently students weren't supposed to express themselves in the presence of an instructor.

"Is that right?" the black belt sneered. "I guess you think you're pretty tough. Is *that* right, Axbrewder?" He made my name sound like an obscenity. "Do you?"

Sweat gathered against my ribs. Trying to be unobtrusive about it, I shifted so that I could keep an eye on the brown belts and their instructor at the same time.

"I'm sorry," I said in a neutral tone. "I didn't catch your name." Then I stuck out my hand optimistically.

My challenger didn't take it. Instead he grimaced like he was going to spit. "I'm one of Master Soon's senior black belts. That's all you need to know."

Two of the brown belts fumed at the ears. The rest just did their best to look fierce.

I smiled with all my teeth. "Oh, I don't think so. I'm sure I'll want to mention you by name when I tell Master Soon how I was welcomed.

"I'll have to talk to him, you know," I explained amiably. "Part of my job. I'm in charge of security for Martial America. Just in case"—I unsheathed a threat of my own—"anything happens to Nakahatchi *sensei*'s collection of Wing Chun chops."

"That's bullshit," freckles retorted. "Those chops are junk. We've got swords here worth more than any damn collection of printing blocks, and nobody ever hired security for us."

"I'm not so sure." Exercising my famous people-skills. "Did you ever *ask* for security?"

At the same time I slipped my right hand under my jacket, ostensibly to scratch my ribs. Let him think I took him that lightly. But I left my hand inside my jacket.

"Nobody hired security for us," the black belt snapped back, "because they've got it in for Tae Kwon Do. Especially for Master Soon. Hiring you for *Nakahatchi* is another way of sneering at us. We're the best, but nobody wants to admit it.

"We don't need you here. We don't need your fucking security. We take care of our own. So why don't you just get out of here before I show you how we do it?"

He was probably serious. An extravagant, almost rabid glare darkened his face. His fists tightened at his sides. Following his example, the brown belts clenched themselves, tensing to jump at me.

"Well," I drawled, "I still think you should tell me your name. It's the polite thing to do."

Hell, it was probably the *martial* thing to do. Hadn't I heard people talking about "respect" and "perfection of character"?

Deliberately freckles hawked and spat at my feet.

So much for respect.

The poor bozo couldn't spit worth a damn. His mouth was too dry. The little saliva he produced came out in an ineffectual spray. A bit of it got on my pants, but mostly it dribbled down his chin.

He was more frightened than he wanted to admit. That's what made him so belligerent. He'd been hit far too often for his own good, but he kept picking fights—and getting clobbered—so that he wouldn't have to recognize his own fear.

I didn't let that stop me, however. Some days scared fighters are more dangerous than nerveless thugs who know what they're doing. And if freckles was frightened, half his brown belts were downright petrified.

Before any of them could move, I swept out the .45 and lined it up on the startled face of the nearest brown belt. My left index finger I pointed like another gun at freckles' forehead.

Instantly he froze, and the blood rushed out of his face. Instead of glaring, he gaped like I'd stuck a knife into his crotch. For a second there, I thought he might piss himself.

Quietly—very quietly—I said, "Listen to me, junior. Before someone gets hurt. I don't *have* to think I'm tough. And I certainly don't need to prove it to you. I've been stomping on punks like you since high school."

Then I repeated, "I didn't catch your name."

He didn't answer. Maybe he couldn't. The poor clot didn't realize that I hadn't chambered a round.

"His name is Hamson, Mr. Axbrewder," a voice behind me said, full of compressed ease and violence. "Cloyd Hamson."

Past my right shoulder, I saw Song Duk Soon at the foot of the stairs.

"Perhaps you would do well," he went on, "to set your weapon aside and step into our *dojo*." He didn't move. "Allow Mr. Hamson to measure himself against you. We would all profit by observing how you 'stomp on punks.' It might be quite instructive."

I couldn't help noticing that he didn't reprimand Hamson. Or the brown belts.

"Master Soon." I wanted to wheel toward him, cover him with the .45, but instead I lowered it immediately, put it away under my left arm. "Do your students always treat visitors this way, or am I getting special treatment?"

He lifted an eyebrow. His brows were stark and black against his brown skin. They arched over his muddy eyes like lines of surprise, but the hard lines of his jaw and the inflexibility of his mouth contradicted them. "Are you a visitor, Mr. Axbrewder?"

Touché. "I guess not," I admitted. "I've been hired to take a look at security for Martial America. That practically makes me a resident."

Which to me meant that I deserved more courtesy, not less. But apparently he didn't see it that way.

"Then enter our *dojo*, Mr. Axbrewder," he retorted. "Demonstrate yourself to us. Or depart. I have no interest in the needs of those who cannot defend their own."

Damn, I was tempted. Life isn't much fun if you aren't willing to put your muscle where your mouth is. Besides, he pissed me off. I hadn't forgotten the way he'd humiliated one of his students at the tournament. I felt hot and ready, and all my frustration and alarm wanted to boil over at once.

But he'd left the tournament ahead of Bernie and Hardshorn. That made me think again.

In addition, getting into a brawl here didn't exactly fit my job description. I was supposed to ease tensions, reduce potential security problems, not alienate Soon and his entire school.

Swallowing my pride, as they say, I attempted a smile.

"Master Soon, I apologize. I got off on the wrong foot with Mr. Hamson. There's a serious misunderstanding here, and I'd like to correct it if I can."

By then my knees quivered with anger, and the frustration in my shoulders felt like overstretched cables. I hated backing down. *Loathed* it. Always had.

"Bullshit," Hamson muttered again. He sounded stronger with his *sensei* to back him up.

Somehow I ignored him.

"Truly?" Soon's eyebrows signaled disbelief again. "You were swift to exert yourself against a defeated brown belt, a mere youth. Yet now you decline to confront a black belt who challenges you. Are you not a coward?" His tone held no sarcasm. He didn't need any. "What have I misunderstood?"

"Everything, apparently," I snarled before I could catch myself. Then I bit down on my anger. "Whether or not I'm a coward"—my mouth twisted involuntarily—"is beside the point.

"The point," I pronounced more carefully, "is that Nakahatchi *sensei* owns a rather controversial treasure, and you need my protection."

My right palm ached for the necessary weight of the .45.

"*I?*" Soon scowled. This time I'd surprised him for real. "What foolishness is this? I need no man's protection."

I shook my head. "You're mistaken." Ire leaked into my voice despite my efforts to control it. "If anything happens to those chops, there will be only two primary suspects. *Sifu* Hong first. Then you." Soon tried to interrupt, but I overrode him. "*Him* because he resents seeing the chops in Japanese hands. *You* because you resent seeing them in *anyone's*."

And because he'd left the tournament.

"You think they diminish you," I finished. "You think they draw attention away from your school."

The small hairs on the back of my neck picked up hostility and discomfort from Soon's students. I felt exposed, vulnerable. The skin over my kidneys squirmed, but I kept my focus on Soon.

"They do so," he said between his teeth. "They do so." He'd lost his explosive relaxation. Tension knotted his shoulders. "We compete for students, Mr. Axbrewder. For students and respect. Perhaps you do not understand that. In any equal comparison Tae Kwon Do will stand above its competitors. But here the comparison is unequal. The attraction of antique *netsuke* grants *Essential Shotokan* an advantage it has not earned.

"That is the true source of Hong Fei-Tung's dissatisfaction," he stated flatly. "And it is the source of mine."

His students seemed to swarm like bees near my shoulder-blades. Behind the clenched surface of my professional facade, I wanted to pistol-whip them all. I was fucking *tired* of being treated like a personal insult. But I didn't do it. Instead I countered, "And it's why you need my protection.

"You probably consider yourself a man of honor. But if that display disappears, the cops won't even listen when you tell them you're too honorable to sully your hands by stealing. They know something you might not want them to know. They know you left the tournament just a few minutes before I found The Luxury's Chief of Security dead in the men's room."

Actually I hadn't told Moy anything about that. But I had no intention of saying so. I wanted Soon nervous.

"Incidentally," I asked as if I were merely curious, "why *did* you leave the tournament?"

For a long moment, he didn't answer. His gaze held mine, and in his eyes I could see my death, gathering like thunderheads. I'd practically accused him of murdering Bernie. If he couldn't control his rampant ego—or if he'd killed Bernie—I might never know what hit me.

But then, slowly, the darkness receded from his stare, pushed aside by calculation. By degrees the tension in his shoulders eased. Facing me squarely, he asked, "Am I suspected—?"

"You will be," I put in, "if anything happens to those chops.

"That's why you need me." The visceral shame of backing down serrated my voice. "I'm security here. If I do my job right, I'll be the best protection you can get."

Obviously he hadn't considered the situation in that light. When he spoke again, he'd made up his mind.

"You are Western, Mr. Axbrewder." It wasn't a compliment. "I am not. Perhaps your understanding of these matters has merit.

"What do you require of me?"

Maybe I should've let him change the subject. Bernie's death wasn't my responsibility. Martial America was. But I positively could not retreat another step. I'd already backed up more than I could bear.

"For starters," I told him harshly, "answer the question. Why did you leave the tournament when you did?"

That brought a new flicker of butchery into his glare, but he didn't waver. When he made a decision, he stuck to it.

"One of my students was expected to compete, but he had not arrived. I wished to call him, and went to the telephone."

If I hadn't been working for Lacone, I might've yelled, And you expect me *believe* that? Why didn't you send one of your flunkies? Unfortunately I couldn't go that far and justify it to myself afterward. Anger aside, I had no solid reason to accuse him of lying. And anyway I was mostly furious at myself for backing down.

Like an act of self-mortification, I nodded to accept his answer. Then I went back to the job Lacone paid me for.

"Thank you, Master Soon. What I need right now is pretty simple. If you'll answer a couple of questions, I'll get out of your way."

He gestured for me to go ahead.

Gritting my teeth, I asked, "How do you provide for your own security? I understand that you have some pretty valuable artifacts yourself. What do you do to protect them?"

As if in response, Soon looked past my shoulder at Hamson and the brown belts. "Return to your training," he instructed them. "Do not concern yourselves with Mr. Axbrewder."

That was as close as he came to reprimanding them. Apparently it was all the satisfaction I'd get.

I didn't turn to watch his students go. I could feel them disperse. And a moment later I heard the aerobics class start yelling again. Low voices came from the smaller *dojo*, but I couldn't make out what they said.

Grimly I slipped my hands into my pockets and dug my fingers into the tops of my thighs, clawing at my quads for restraint.

"Mr. Axbrewder," Soon announced, "you will not speak of what I tell you."

"Not unless I have to," I agreed. "But if the cops question me for some reason, I'll talk. For my protection as well as yours."

After an instant's uncertainty, he accepted that.

"I am my own security," he explained. "I sleep lightly." His tone suggested that every real martial artist did the same. "And I am attuned to my *dojo*. I would be aware of any intrusion.

"Further, my first student, Pack Hee Cho, makes his home here. He is talented and sensitive, and I have taught him well. Also"—Soon spread his hands slightly—"he is a large man. Even you would say so. In fighting his effectiveness is extreme."

"That's it?" I didn't even try not to sound skeptical.

"As an additional precaution," he went on more sharply, "and as part of their training, all my brown belts in turn sleep here. They place their pallets there." He tilted his head at the door behind me. "No one can enter without disturbing them."

A pretty good precaution, I had to admit. And it explained a few things to me—intuitively, anyway. Despite its obvious benefits, his approach to training said less about security than it did about solidarity, school loyalty. It ingrained an us-against-them attitude. After spending a few sleepless responsible nights on the floor, half expecting every cough and pit stop to bring down his master's disapproval, even a tough-minded brown belt might lose his ability to think for himself.

My mouth twisted as I considered the implications. "That should do it," I remarked, although I meant something different than Soon probably thought I did. If Hong and Nakahatchi taught us-against-them, Martial America would degenerate into a war zone.

All the front doors, as I'd already noticed, opened outward.

Which brought me to my other question. Before Soon lost patience with me, I said, "I need to ask you about keys. Just to cover an obvious point.

"Do you still use your original key? The one you got from Mr. Lacone?"

"Yes," he answered without interest.

"Your key works for the fire doors as well as this one?" The apartments upstairs didn't concern me.

"Yes."

"How many copies are there?"

He didn't hesitate. "Each of my black belts is given a key."

I raised my eyebrows. "So there are, what?"—I glanced around at the rank certificates—"twenty copies? More?"

"Yes," he said again.

"That's a lot, Master Soon." A bitter wind gusted in the background of my voice. "Can you trust that many people?"

Not to mention their girlfriends, spouses, buddies, co-workers. He pinned a lot on school loyalty.

He wasn't worried, however. Stiffly he informed me, "I do not grant a black belt to a student who has not earned my trust."

Oh, of course. Naturally. I faked a smile. "I'm sure you don't." Then, taking a precaution of my own, I said, "Thank you, Master Soon. That's all I need for now.

"We'll have the chops appraised in a few days. When we know whether or not they're genuine, we'll decide how much security they really need. I might want to consult with you again then."

Thinking while I talked, Come on, asshole. Tell me you know that's a lie. Tell me you know they're genuine.

Tell me you didn't leave the tournament to make a phone call.

But he disappointed me. Indicating the door, he said, "We will speak again at that time." *And not before*, his tone added.

Discretion and all that. The better part of fucking valor. I took my cue and left, snarling inwardly at the sensation that I had my tail tucked between my legs.

Outside the sun felt like a wash of fire against my heated face. I *abhorred* backing down. Maybe I was doing my job. Earning Lacone's money. But as far as I could tell, I'd accomplished exactly nothing.

I didn't know how much longer I could keep it up. I longed for the simplicity of Puerta del Sol's dark streets, the straightforward corruption of men who lurked in alleys and doorways to sell drugs or flesh or stolen property. Crimes like Bernie's murder and Soon's attitude were making me crazy.

Probably I should've driven away right then, given myself a chance to decompress a bit. I could always call *Essential Shotokan* from the van, let Nakahatchi know I'd talk to him later. No doubt that would've been sensible.

So of course I didn't do it.

Carliss Swilley had pronounced the chops genuine. *A complete set of this provenance cannot be worth less than one million dollars.* And Bernie was still dead.

Squinting against the light because I was too angry to put on my sunglasses, I rounded the building to Sihan Nakahatchi's *dojo*.

I had no idea what he wanted to talk to me about. Presumably it had something to do with guarding the display. In which case

I had a very simple suggestion for him—one that wouldn't impress Watchdog even a little bit, but that might do more to keep the chops safe than all the security measures I'd mentioned to Lacone.

As I pulled the door open and entered the building, I went blind for a few seconds while my eyes adjusted to the relative gloom. When I could see again, I caught a glimpse of a white *gi* through the doorway to the main *dojo*. Hideo Komatori shifted quickly in and out of view as he worked up and down the hardwood floor alone, practicing some *kata* or other.

And he did it without all the tension and threats, the strained breathing and flushed faces, that I'd seen at the tournament. Instead he moved like oil flowing down a cascade of worn stones, viscid and somehow out of reach, as if by the time you identified where he was he'd already slipped somewhere else. His reflection in the mirrors made him look like he filled the room. His breathing was deep and easy, inaudible. In fact, the only sounds came from the snap of his *gi* against his forearms and calves at the end of each technique. Even when he jumped, his feet returned to the boards as lightly as a falling breeze.

If I'd had the brains God gave lawn furniture, I might've taken it as a warning.

For some reason I felt sure that he was aware of me, but he didn't so much as glance in my direction until he'd come to the end of his pattern. Even then he didn't acknowledge me until he'd bowed to the room—a sign of respect for the *dojo*, apparently.

At last he turned and walked toward me, smiling. "Brew-*san*," he said when he'd bowed himself out of the *dojo*, and bowed again to me. "You've come to talk to my master."

I nodded. But I was still too angry for my own good. Procrastinating so that I wouldn't rush into a mistake, I asked, "Have any idea what it's about?"

He gestured me toward the stairs. Clearly he didn't want to keep Nakahatchi waiting any longer than necessary. As we headed upward, he said, "*Sensei* hasn't told me what he has in mind. Knowing him, however, I might hazard a guess."

"Guess away," I muttered. "If he doesn't want security advice, I'm in the dark here."

"Brew-*san*"—Komatori smiled again—"*I'm* eager to hear any

advice you can give me. As my master's senior student, I'm responsible for the chops. But Nakahatchi *sensei* won't discuss that with you."

I considered my options briefly while we left the head of the stairs and approached the meeting room. "So what's your guess?"

Hideo inclined his head, acquiescing to something I couldn't identify. "I expect my master wants to form a deeper impression of your character."

Oh, joy. And me without my references. Not to mention my characteristic good humor.

I ground my teeth. "How will he do that?"

Now Komatori shrugged. "I can't say."

"Can't, or won't?"

"Can't," he replied calmly. Instead of leading me into the meeting room, he halted at the foot of the stairway to the third floor. "His methods are his own. And they vary. He assesses different people in different ways."

I was in no mood to accept anything from anyone. Nevertheless his answer sounded perfectly reasonable.

Facing him squarely, I said, "OK. I'll cope.

"Here's my security advice." For what it was worth. "Understand that Alex Lacone won't want to spend the money for a really adequate alarm system. Oh, he wants to keep you and the chops here. He's pretty clear about that. But he's not exactly brimming with cash."

As it stood, Lacone's "dream" would only work if it grew big enough. He needed to put up more buildings, attract more schools. Otherwise he wouldn't be able to generate the traffic, publicity, and revenue that would suck in serious investors. But without those investors he might not be able to put up more buildings.

"I'll get everything I can out of him," I promised. "And you can bet that Watchdog will lean on him. But you'll have to take precautions of your own."

Komatori's face didn't show any particular reaction. He simply waited for me to go on.

I gave him the best I had.

"Don't trust this lock." I pointed at the meeting room door. "Move the display into your apartment at night. Every night. Or

Nakahatchi *sensei*'s. Then put extra deadbolts on your doors. And don't use the same key."

He nodded without hesitation. "I'll begin tonight. Tomorrow I'll have the deadbolts installed.

"Thank you, Brew-*san*." Then he added, "My master is upstairs. You'll be able to speak privately."

In other words, he wasn't coming with me.

The warning I'd missed earlier finally began to nag at the ends of my nerves. This was going to be such fun. I started up the stairs immediately so that I wouldn't have time to talk myself into a frothing rage.

Right away, however, I thought of another question. I stopped abruptly, turned to look down at Komatori. Trying to sound unconcerned, I asked, "By the way, how did your tea ceremony go?"

He laughed, a soft ripple of pleasure. "Quite well. I was"—he spread his hands—"surprised. I expected some discomfort. But Mitsuku-*san* is really an extraordinary hostess. And *Sifu* Hong was very gracious. Poor T'ang Wen and I found it hard to emulate such grand manners without embarrassing ourselves."

That was a relief. Apparently the danger I'd created for Hong didn't involve driving him into overt conflict with Nakahatchi. Something that I'd wanted to accomplish had actually gone right.

I'd expected Hong's pride to assert itself somehow—

When I thanked Hideo and started upward again, I had a bit less dread in my stride.

This was my first visit to any top floor in Martial America. Sternway had told me that Nakahatchi had a private *dojo* up here, as well as a library and a guest apartment. I hoped that I wouldn't have to blunder around knocking on doors. Fortunately, at the head of the stair I found myself in the library, with the *dojo* immediately beyond it through a wide entryway.

Ignoring the library—except to notice that the shelves along the walls held a number of books that looked old and weren't in English—I crossed to the *dojo*.

Like the rooms on the ground level, this one had a hardwood floor, the wood rubbed and cleaned until it seemed to glow with its own warmth. But this *dojo* didn't have any mirrors. Instead its long exterior wall held one long series of heavily tinted windows. Presumably the door in the neighboring wall gave access to Nakahatchi's guest quarters.

Below the precise center of the windows stood a small three-sided structure like a shrine of some kind. It was made of wood lacquered black, ornamentally carved in an austere way, with a line of incense holders nearly at floor level, a black stand supporting two slightly curved swords above that, and above them another stand which cradled a scroll. The swords differed in size, but looked identical in other ways. The larger one, I assumed, was a *katana*. I didn't know what to call its smaller twin.

On both sides of the shrine where you could look at them while you lit your incense or slit open your guts hung sheets of paper or parchment in plain black frames. The characters written on them looked like *kanji*.

Sihan Nakahatchi knelt there. He'd replaced his elaborate tea-ceremony garb with a white *gi* cinched by a black belt so worn that it'd frayed white. He didn't kneel the way Catholics in Puerta del Sol did, straight up from the knees. Instead he'd lowered himself onto his heels with his feet extended under him. A small curl of incense rose past his swords and his bowed head. The air held a faint tinge of sandalwood, so delicate that I almost missed it.

Since I didn't know what else to do, I stayed where I was, watching him from the entryway. But then I caught an ambiguous flash of intuition. Before I could question it, I bent down to take off my shoes. Leaving them in the library, I stepped onto the hardwood in my socks.

That may've been a signal of some kind. Or a clue. At once Nakahatchi lifted from his knees as lightly as smoke and turned toward me. Like he'd been watching to see how I entered the *dojo*.

He bowed in my direction, hands at his sides. When I'd bowed back, he beckoned me to join him in the middle of the room.

Up close he looked a bit less sorrowful than he had earlier, and his eyes were brighter, as if someone had rubbed a layer of tarnish off his gaze. I couldn't imagine that he felt better knowing his insurance rates were about to erupt like Krakatoa. Something else must've happened to ease his settled distress, reduce the rub of a worry that had galled him for a long time.

"Mr. Axbrewder." The lines at the corners of his mouth deepened—he almost smiled. "Your presence in my small *dojo* pleases me. I am much in your debt. Your invitation to *Sifu* Hong has lifted a burden from my spirit."

I was tempted to shuffle my feet and mumble, Aw, shucks. A side effect of being so pissed off, I suppose. The anger blowing through my head urged me to insult his thanks by mocking it.

Instead I muttered, "Just doing my job. We'll all be better off with a little less tension around here."

He didn't reply to that. "I have observed your actions with interest, Mr. Axbrewder," he went on as if I hadn't spoken. "Now I wish to teach you. You will spar with me, please."

I gaped at him—I couldn't help it. *Spar* with him? He wasn't serious. He may've been a great martial artist, but this was ridiculous. For one thing, he was hardly two thirds my size. If I sat on him, he'd never get up again. And for another, he had more than a decade on me. Occasionally his air of unrelieved mourning made me feel almost young.

And I'd just *backed down* from a fight at Soon's school, despite a hell of a lot more provocation.

"*Sensei*—" I groped for a response. "You flatter me." Or maybe he insulted me. I wasn't sure there was any difference. "They asked if I wanted to study with them. At *Sifu* Hong's school. Yesterday." I must've sounded like an idiot. "I turned them down. I've got a job to do. I don't have time to study a martial art."

Nakahatchi dismissed all that. It seemed to run off him like water. "*Sifu* Hong is a great master," he stated as if that answered my objections. "But Wing Chun is not for you. For you, Shotokan is best."

"Well, now," I replied, procrastinating shamelessly, "I'm not sure about that." I needed time to *think*. "What I've seen of Wing Chun looks pretty impressive. And—"

You're too *short*. You're too *old*.

I bit down on the inside of my cheek to make myself shut up.

"Much of Wing Chun is oblique," he said. Explaining something he thought I needed to understand. "It's purposes are likewise oblique. Shotokan is direct. For you, to be direct is necessary."

As if I needed the benefit of his wisdom on that point.

Exasperated now, and too angry to be polite about it, I countered, "Listen to me, Mr.—"

With no warning at all—no flick of his eyes, no catch in his breathing, no hint of intensification—he stepped toward me.

The room whirled, and I found myself on my hands and knees. The hardwood in front of my face had a long grain like flowing veins. It seemed full of remembered sunlight, too warm for ordinary wood. The lines between the boards looked deep enough to reach the center of the world, the center of reality. Shock paralyzed my solar plexus. That's how I knew he'd hit me. I certainly hadn't picked up any other clues. Until the room stopped moving I couldn't imagine how he'd swept me off my feet.

When I finally raised my head, I saw him standing several feet away—far enough for safety, too far to threaten me if I wanted to get up.

The paralysis in my chest eased. My lungs sucked small gusts of air. A distant roar in my ears sounded like advancing rage, a tornado gathering its forces on the horizon.

Unsteadily I pushed my legs under me and stood up.

Trembling, I went back to the place where I'd left my shoes, emptied my pants pockets into the pockets of my jacket, did the same with pens and notes from my shirt pocket, then pulled my jacket off and dropped it beside my shoes. I undid the straps of my shoulder holster, set the .45 on top of my jacket. Despite the way my knees shook, I crouched down to strip off my socks.

Ginny'd have my hide for this. If we were still partners.

If I still cared.

The roaring grew louder. It filled my head. Anything that might've objected to what I was doing couldn't make itself heard. I'd already had all the cowardice I could bear. While that wind tore through the room, nothing else mattered.

Deliberately I walked back into the center of the *dojo*. The center of the world. Toward Nakahatchi.

Evaluate *my* character? *Mine*? *I* wasn't the one who wanted to steal those chops. *I* hadn't killed Bernie.

Tremors mounted through me, hints of crisis.

He stood ready for me, waiting. This time he assumed what he seemed to consider a sparring stance, left foot forward, left hand open near the level of his chin, right fist relaxed on his hip. Somehow he conveyed the impression that he floated a fraction of an inch off the hardwood, impervious to such mundane concerns as gravity and mass.

Well, fine. Just stand there.

If he wanted direct, I'd show him *direct*.

Timing it in stride, riding the storm, I wheeled a punch at his head hard enough to stagger a lamp post.

Except that my bicep found the point of his elbow before my fist reached his head. A shredding pain like the path of a bullet ripped at my arm while Nakahatchi cross-stepped past me. His right hand touched my groin. I felt his fingers skim my crotch before they reached the underside of my thigh, but I couldn't do anything about it, it was happening too fast, lightning strikes of pain had burned their way through the gale inside my head, when he *pinched* the nerve center of my hamstring a cattle prod went off in my thigh, and all my muscles spasmed, flinging me backward across his hip. If he hadn't caught me at the last second, slowed my fall, I would've landed like a load of cinder blocks.

A warning. Komatori had warned me. Nakahatchi had just warned me twice. Evaluate my character. My damaged bicep wailed along the wind. The back of my thigh felt like the kiss of a high-tension line.

Rolling through the rest of the fall, I staggered upright. For some peculiar reason, my chest strained for air as if I'd just run the mile. Nakahatchi seemed to stand at a slight angle. Or, no, it was the floor tilting—

Hell, even Parker Neill had warned me. Sternway had practically jumped up and down on my head about it.

Barely audible through the howl in my ears, Nakahatchi announced, "It was written by Gichin Funakoshi *sensei*, 'If your hand goes forth, withhold your anger. If your anger goes forth, withhold your hand.' "

All right. If that's the way he wanted to play. I'd show him what "goes forth" really meant.

I went at him again, exactly the same as before. If you didn't count the weakness in one arm, or the involuntary hitch in my opposite leg. Or the fact that I couldn't tell the difference between rage and pain. This time, however, I didn't try to punch him. Instead I swung up a kick from the pit of my stomach, aiming to punt the little shit out of the stadium.

He slid aside effortlessly. I missed so hard that I would've smashed down onto my back if my pinched leg hadn't collapsed under me, pitching me forward.

Somehow I caught myself on my arms. The jolt rocked through me hard. If I'd stopped to notice, I might've realized that I'd dislocated a shoulder or two, or maybe a kneecap. But I didn't, and apparently I hadn't. The slam of the impact and the wind seemed to bounce me back onto my feet, and I could still stay there, so in some sense I must've been OK.

Nakahatchi had resumed his floating stance, one hand raised and ready. I could barely breathe, but he didn't show any sign of strain—or even exertion.

That was about to change. I'd already suffered enough beatings to last me forever. But I'd also delivered a fair number of them. There were still thugs in Puerta del Sol—enforcers, extortion muscle, bodyguards, and such—who couldn't look at me without flinching. And I hadn't let a little thing like a bullet through my guts stop me from putting Muy Estobal out of everyone's misery.

Evaluate my character, *fuck*.

Ignoring my sore bicep and hamstrung thigh, my bruised knees and shocked shoulders and stunned respiration, I attacked again.

More cautiously this time. More slowly. And straighter. I didn't try to swing a roundhouse, or bring up a kick. That sure as hell hadn't worked. Instead I concentrated on jabs. And careful footwork, so that he couldn't turn my momentum against me. Jab jab jab. A quick step in. Jab cross jab. Another step.

Also I kept my eyes on his, studying them for hints. He'd counterattack soon. When he did, I wanted to see it coming.

He didn't meet my stare. Instead he kept his gaze focused on the middle of my abdomen.

For the first few flurries, he seemed content to block and retreat, block and retreat. His blocks were so effortless, so nearly gentle, that I couldn't figure out why I hadn't hit him yet. No matter how hard I punched, he merely patted my fist or my forearm with one hand or the other and stepped back. None of my blows reached him.

Patty-cake, patty-cake, baker's man.

Jab jab. Jabjabjab. I could *not* get inside his defenses.

Nevertheless I didn't consider surrender. My inner tornado consumed me. That blast demanded release. Clearly I wouldn't get a real chance to hit him until he stopped retreating, so I used my attacks to steer him toward one of the walls.

If he couldn't back up, I'd connect sooner or later. Or come close enough to get my hands on him. Then I'd have him. Hell, all I had to do was *fall* on the sonofabitch—

That might've worked, but he didn't stand still for it. Just when I thought I'd trapped him, and my desire to finally land a punch had become fire in my veins, he turned one of his patty-cake blocks into a sweep and stepped aside.

Behind me.

Inspired by pain and gales, I wheeled in the opposite direction, all the way around, and lunged after him.

He must've sensed what I was about to do, felt it before I moved. By the time I dove at him, he'd already retreated two steps, three—

—out of reach.

Almost out of reach.

By stretching out headlong, and making no effort to keep my feet under me, I managed to grab the hem of his *gi* just above his sternum before the rest of me dropped to my knees.

Now, I thought through the roar, now he was mine. From here on it was just muscle, and he didn't stand a chance. If he believed that he could force me to let go by simply hitting me, he was about to learn an important lesson.

Only I was wrong. Again. He didn't hit me. While I scrambled to gain my feet, straining for leverage so that I could use my bulk, he calmly set the ball of his thumb into the hollow where my collarbones met. And pushed.

His thumb dug in. *Damn*, it dug in. He was going to strangle me. Crush my trachea. Already I couldn't breathe. Or see. Blackness stormed through my head, effacing everything else.

And it *hurt*. The nerve center in the supersternal notch has links throughout the torso. My brother taught me that, Rick Axbrewder, Richard, he'd learned it while he was with the Special Forces. The brother I'd shot to death in drunken negligence.

With my free hand, I hacked at Nakahatchi's arm. He stopped me somehow. Suffocating around the pressure of his thumb, I hardly registered other sensations. Had he taken hold of one of my fingers? Was he bending it backward? Did the agony of it pull me harder onto his thumb?

I clung to his *gi* anyway. Fuck him. In fact, fuck him with a crowbar. He couldn't make me let go. Not just by hurting me.

Not me. I knew things about pain that would make him howl at the moon if I happened to mention them.

He made me let go.

An autonomic desperation compelled me. Just when I'd decided to hang on until he killed me or lost his nerve, I snapped. Releasing my hold, I wrenched sideways to twist my throat off his thumb, then frantically heaved myself upward, up and forward, over his tearing grasp on my finger.

His finger lock helped me go. My legs pitched at the ceiling, and I plunged face first at the floor.

Broke my neck, crushed two or three vertebrae, severed my spinal cord. Or would have, if he hadn't caught me again. Anchoring me in the air until my legs finished their arc, he lowered my shoulders to the hardwood. Actually lowered them. Only my heels landed hard.

If I were lucky, I thought, stupid with shock, I'd shattered bones, and I'd never walk again. Then I wouldn't have to go on humiliating myself like this.

But I didn't stop. After a couple of seconds—or a couple of minutes—I rolled onto my side, then over to my chest. Pulled my knees under me.

Gasping for breath, I shifted my weight back onto my feet.

The pain made me gasp. My heels felt like they'd been hacked apart. Serrated agony sliced along all my nerves into my brain.

Nevertheless I could stand. My feet held me.

Nothing else held. The windows and the floor and Nakahatchi all existed in dimensions of their own, drifting on trajectories that made no sense in relation to each other. Air shuddered in and out of my lungs, but it didn't help. There wasn't enough oxygen in all the world to turn me back into the man I was.

Somehow I didn't fall over.

While the room went off in all directions like hurled water, something in my head found its center. A place where no wind blew. An imponderable stillness cupped the *dojo*, humbling me when I didn't know how to humble myself.

Soon I could hear again. First the declining racket of my heart, the edged urgency of my breathing. Then the ambiance of the room, the shrouded complaint of traffic outside, the small splash of sweat dripping from my face to the hardwood. The faint deified susurrus as Nakahatchi shifted his feet.

Well, hell. Maybe he didn't actually float after all.

My face felt strange. For a few moments I couldn't figure out why. Then I realized that I was grinning. I couldn't help it.

My list of hurts was too long to count, so I didn't bother. Instead I dragged my fists up in front of me, flexed my knees a bit, and took two or three fractured steps forward. When I was close enough to talk without raising my voice, I panted hoarsely, "You said you wanted to teach me. I'm ready to learn now."

I went on grinning.

For all I knew, grinning at your instructor was an insult. But he didn't look offended. And he didn't resume his fighting stance. With his hands at his sides, he bowed deeply. Then he announced, "We are done, Axbrewder-*san*. We will spar no more today."

"No, please." Straightening my legs, mainly because I didn't have the strength to keep them flexed, I opened my hands like an appeal. "I'm sorry it took me so long to get in the right frame of mind. I wasn't angry at you. I just needed a target. But I'm ready now."

I'd never been more sincere in my life. Whatever his secret was, I needed it. Badly.

"No." He shook his head gravely. "I honor your courage. And I will teach you. But first you must learn this. Pain is a means to an end, but it must never become the end. Today you believe you are ready because your pain has become greater than your anger, yet you are not defeated by it. That is important, Axbrewder-*san*. It is necessary. But you will not be ready indeed until your pain has become separate from your anger."

Again he bowed.

This time I did the same. I didn't think I had much choice. And he'd called me "Axbrewder-*san*." That counted for something.

Now he smiled. For a moment the old sorrow on his face lost its immediacy. "I will leave you," he said quietly. "You may remain or depart, as you wish. Return tomorrow at the same time."

With the kind of dignity you can only get from real mastery, he walked to the edge of the floor, bowed to the *dojo* and his shrine, then crossed the library and disappeared down the stairs.

Apparently he trusted me alone in his sanctum.

Separate from your anger.

I almost understood him.

22

Briefly I considered defacing his shrine. Not that I had the slightest desire to do so. In fact, I would've fought to protect it. But such lunacy helped distract me so that I could move. Become separate. Otherwise I might've remained stuck where I stood for hours, trapped between bruises and immanence.

Sure, deface the shrine. The world was full of spare excrement. I could probably find some if I put my mind to it.

Whee.

Then some of the tension in my chest released itself, and I began to breathe a bit more easily.

I let my shoulders slump, took a couple of tentative steps toward my shoes and jacket. At first everything in me seemed to hurt, and I felt damn near crippled. But as I breathed the pain receded to more realistic proportions.

Nakahatchi hadn't actually done me much damage. Apart from one throbbing bicep, one strung hamstring, a sore finger, and a lump of pain at the base of my throat which made swallowing difficult, I'd mostly hurt myself by falling a lot. And he'd softened that for me as much as he could. Hardshorn had hit me harder.

I finally concluded that Nakahatchi's lessons felt so dangerous because he'd disoriented me completely. I'd never been eluded and tossed around like that before. Everyone else who'd ever beaten me up—including Muy Estobal—had done it like Hardshorn, straight and brutal, in ways I understood.

Vaguely I noticed that my shirt looked like I'd used it to polish the floor. That disoriented me as well. I felt filthy—and transformed. Torqued into a new shape. No wonder I wasn't entirely sure which way was up.

I paused to rub my bicep for a moment, then shambled over to the edge of the hardwood. My heels weren't happy with me, but they didn't bitch too much when I pulled on my socks and stepped gingerly into my shoes. With that challenge behind me, I had an easier time slipping my arms into the straps of the shoulder holster and the sleeves of my jacket.

Now what? I had no idea. I'd recovered some small measure of mobility, but I still couldn't think effectively. The chops were genuine. Bernie was dead. Surely I was supposed to do something?

At last I got it. Take a shower. And a nap. Put on clean clothes. For my date with Deborah Messenger.

That seemed inadequate somehow. Insufficiently arduous. Us manly-type private investigators were born to suffer. That's why God put us on this earth. But what alternatives did I have? Figure out why Hong was in danger? Grasp the connection between Bernie's murder and Nakahatchi's antiques? Make everything right with Ginny? In my condition? Ha.

A shower and a nap sounded like Heaven. And I was getting *just a bit* tired of all this divinely inspired *angst*.

I decided to go back to the apartment.

Fortunately I didn't encounter anyone on my way out of the *dojo*. Unhindered, I stumbled out into the sun's glare like I'd just escaped a shipwreck.

The Plymouth seemed ridiculously far away, but under cover of sunglasses I managed to cross the blazing concrete, unlock the van, and climb in. God, I hoped I wasn't still here when summer came. Carner would be a furnace. Some people considered Puerta del Sol hot, but there the drier air and the elevation blunted the sunlight's cruelty. I didn't feel so belittled by it.

Still in a state resembling stupefaction, I coaxed the Plymouth to life, engaged the AC, and began to retrace the route I'd used to come here just a few hours ago, in a previous life.

Become separate from your anger.

I probably could've driven all the way to the apartment without actually thinking about anything. As it happened, however, my phone rang while I still had a couple of miles to go.

For a moment or two I couldn't figure out what that insistent electronic chirp meant. On automatic pilot, I fumbled around in my pockets until I found the phone. By the time I tugged it out, I'd remembered what it was for.

The possibilities gave me a little rush. I sounded almost awake as I announced, "Axbrewder."

"Brew, are you all right?" Deborah's voice answered. "You seem blurry. Or do we have a bad connection?"

Suddenly I was awake all the way. "No," I assured her quickly, without quite making sense. Then I pulled myself together. "I mean, no, we don't have a bad connection. I'm fine."

As fine as I needed to be, anyway.

"That's good"—her tone conveyed a grin—"because you have a date with me tonight, and I have no intention of letting you tell me you've got a headache."

I grinned back. "Don't worry. I could have the absolute apocalypse of all headaches, and I'd forget it existed the minute I laid eyes on you."

Deborah laughed. Even the cell phone's deficiencies couldn't disguise her warmth. "Ah, such gallantry. I do love the way you talk." Then she turned serious. "Especially since I'm afraid I'm about to give you a headache myself."

"Don't worry," I repeated. "What's one more?"

"In that case—" She may've nodded to herself. "I've been busy this afternoon. Mr. Swilley didn't keep us waiting for his appraisal. According to him, the chops are worth—"

She named a number that made me hold my breath and stare, despite the fact that I'd been braced for seven figures.

When I could inhale again, I murmured, "Christ on a crutch."

"My sentiments exactly," she returned dryly. "You see the problem. If the chops aren't adequately insured, Watchdog will walk away from Mr. Nakahatchi. We'll have to. And if Mr. Lacone won't accept a coverage exclusion, we may be forced to turn our backs on Martial America.

"Sammy would prefer to do that, by the way. He thinks we've reached the point where Mr. Lacone's business isn't worth the risk."

"But you disagree," I suggested.

"At the moment," she answered, "I don't agree or disagree. I'm exploring options. I've consulted with our home offices at length. I've spoken to Mr. Lacone. I've talked to Sue Rasmussen and Mr. Sternway." Presumably so that the IAMA could participate in a solution, if there was one. "Here's what I have so far.

"The good news is that nothing needs to be decided today. Mr. Nakahatchi is covered in the short term—the *very* short term. By Thursday we'll want him to pay the premium for a temporary rider which will cover him until our New York expert appraises the chops next week. However, that premium shouldn't be too burdensome. And Mr. Lacone and Mr. Sternway have agreed to share the cost with Mr. Nakahatchi. For obvious reasons, they both feel strongly that the chops should stay with Martial America."

I chewed my lip. A week wasn't much time for Nakahatchi to arrange heavy financing—or to consider other options. But it allowed plenty of time for someone to make an attempt on the chops.

Which put Watchdog in a precarious position. And Deborah herself, I assumed, since apparently no one else in the company was likely to fight for Nakahatchi or Martial America.

"Unfortunately," she continued with a sigh, "everything changes when our expert delivers his appraisal. Of course, there's always a chance he'll come in below Mr. Swilley." Her tone told me she didn't consider that likely. "But even that won't do poor Mr. Nakahatchi much good. Mr. Lacone and Mr. Sternway may want to keep the chops here, but they don't want it enough to make themselves financially uncomfortable. At the rates we'll have to charge—"

She paused briefly. When she spoke again, she sounded bitter. "Mr. Nakahatchi will be on his own."

"So what happens then?" Her bitterness held me.

"Then," Deborah pronounced acidly, "Sammy and Mr. Lacone will force him to accept coverage that excludes the chops. Unless he's willing to do without insurance, he'll have to keep them somewhere else. Or leave Martial America.

"But really," she admitted more quietly, "nothing will solve his problem. Whatever he does, wherever he goes, he'll want insurance. He'd be insane not to. And I've already squeezed our numbers as hard as they can be squeezed." She sighed again. "In the end, he'll be forced to sell the chops. He won't be able to afford to keep them."

The remnants of my brain considered the dilemma. I'd seen similar situations too often to dismiss her concerns. And someone always profited from them. Always.

"Makes you wonder, doesn't it?" I murmured into the phone.

"Wonder what?" Deborah asked quickly. She may've been looking for a little hope.

"Whether anyone we know could afford to buy Nakahatchi out."

I was thinking of Hong Fei-Tung and his platoon of cash-wise relatives. But she had different ideas.

"If you mean Carliss Swilley"—her bitterness returned—"the answer is no. As it happens, Watchdog writes his insurance, too. His resources are limited. If they weren't, he'd be better known—trust him for that—and our home offices wouldn't feel the need to insist on a New York expert."

I still hadn't shaken off the effects of Nakahatchi's instruction. For a moment or two I lapsed into a kind of daze, wondering about Deborah's role in all this. She sounded like she sincerely wanted to help him keep the chops. But why was she so eager to spend an evening with *me*? What did she gain—

—by distracting me?

I couldn't think it through.

I must've been silent longer than I realized. Abruptly I heard her say, "Brew? Damn this phone. Did we lose the connection? Are you there?"

"I'm still here." Looking around, I discovered that I was close to the apartment. "I'm just trying to think. But I must've strained something in the attempt."

She accepted my version of humor gracefully. "Nothing critical, I hope." Her tone lifted a couple of notches. "I am *counting* on tonight."

"Nope," I assured her, "nothing critical. Nothing that seeing you won't fix."

With a renewed smile in her voice, she reminded me of the time and place. Unnecessarily. While I parked in front of the apartment, she said goodbye and hung up.

For a minute or two afterward, I left the engine running and leaned back in my seat. My eagerness to see Deborah again despite my uncertainty about her conflicted with a smoldering indignation on Nakahatchi's behalf. As far as I could tell, he was an honest man troubled by the ethical ambiguity of owning a Chinese national treasure. He didn't deserve to have a decision imposed on him by his insurance rates.

I couldn't solve his problem. But I didn't like it either.

Ah, shit. Groaning complaints against the moral order of the universe—as personified by Watchdog Insurance and Alex Lacone—I finally turned off the Plymouth, left it parked, and went into the apartment. After all, I still needed a shower. Positively required one. And the idea of a nap hadn't lost its seductiveness.

Ginny wasn't there. As expected. I had the place to myself. Which suited me just fine.

Unfortunately when I glanced at the answering machine I saw its message indicator flashing red.

Damnation. I didn't want to play the message back. It probably wasn't for me anyway—and I positively did not want to hear a message for Ginny, something that was none of my business.

Sure of my ground, I made a firm decision to ignore the machine's stubborn indicator until I'd had my shower. A *firm* decision, by God. So firm that I stuck by it just long enough to cross the room and jam my thumb down on the playback button.

There was only one message. It was from Ginny.

It said, "Brew, call me when you get this. We need to talk."

She'd used her lives-at-stake voice. Don't ask questions, don't hesitate, just do it. If she'd told me to throw myself out the window in that tone, I'd have done it.

There was only one problem. I didn't know how to reach her.

Dropping my bulk into the armchair, I jerked the phone onto my lap and dialed Marshal's cell phone number.

As soon as the ringing stopped, I said, "Marshal, it's Brew. I got a message from Ginny. She wants to talk to me." By then I could hear myself hyperventilating. "But I don't know how to get in touch with her."

"Brew." He sounded distant, untouchable, like a man who couldn't be compelled by anything I said or did. If he noticed my breathless urgency, he didn't comment on it. "What's going on?"

"She didn't say." My voice twitched and spattered.

"Well," he drawled back, "your timing is good, anyway. I was just about to call her myself. You can give her a message for me."

Grinding my teeth so that I wouldn't lose control, I waited for him to go on.

"You have a pencil?" he asked. Maddeningly.

Somehow I said, "Go ahead." The effort nearly strangled me.

"Tell her my sources have finally tracked down the phone number she's been curious about. She'll know the one I mean." So did I, but I didn't interrupt. "I haven't heard yet who it belongs to, but we do have the number." Carefully he read it to me. And repeated it. Even though I was about to scream. Then he inquired, "Got that?"

"Yes," I choked out.

"Good." As if to himself, he mused, "Maybe our client will recognize it."

The receiver seemed to throb in my hand. I wanted to howl at him, She won't! I was sure of that, although I couldn't have told him how or why. Mai Sternway had no clue what was going on. But I kept my conviction to myself.

Instead I snapped, "Fine. I'll tell her. But I still don't have—"

He overrode me. "You would if you gave me half a chance. I was about to tell you." I heard teasing in his tone. "She's using a company cell phone." Then he took pity on me. "Here's the number."

The instant he'd recited all seven digits, I meant to slam down the handset and dial again.

I meant to. But I didn't.

We need to talk.

Despite Ginny's exigency, the pressure of her demand, something in Marshal's attitude held me like the spark at the end of an intuitive fuse, hissing and spitting down the length of its gunpowder string toward a explosion. I could almost see in advance what the detonation would do, almost measure its significance—

Ginny needed me.

I didn't even work for him. Nevertheless he treated me like I had the right to call on him any hour of the day or night.

And Ginny wanted to close the gulf between us. She'd demonstrated that last night. Even though a week ago she could hardly wait to disentangle herself from me.

"Marshal," I heard myself say, "can I ask you a question?"

I hadn't so much as known that I was going to speak until the words came out of my mouth.

"Ask away." He sounded too casual for the circumstances, too relaxed, as if he didn't know Ginny needed me. Or I needed her. Or we'd ever been partners.

"Why are you helping me? I mean, I'm grateful." That was the truth, but I didn't dwell on it. "If you weren't willing to give me a hand, I don't know how I'd cope. But I don't understand it."

He was still in a teasing mood. "Take a guess. I'm sure you have a theory or two."

Remembering Beatrix Amity, I almost snarled, Maybe it's because you like helping us handicapped folks. Maybe that's how you atone for your sins. Axbrewder at his most sympathetic. But the burning fuse in my head warned me to *think*. I'd already missed too many hints.

Slowly, carefully, I said, "Of course I do. I'm good at guesses. But these days most of them aren't worth shit. I'm floundering here, Marshal. I'll do better if you just tell me."

Abruptly the atmosphere of our connection shifted. Through the phone's impersonality, I had the impression that he'd leaned forward in some way, tuned his attention more sharply. With exaggerated precision, he replied, "OK, Brew. I'll tell you.

"You and Ginny have a gift for getting involved in real cases. I don't know how you do it, but everything you touch turns into something serious, something that matters. I envy that.

"Professional Investigations brings in a lot of money, but most of what we do is pretty boring. It doesn't make any particular difference, even to the poor souls who hire us.

"I want some excitement. I want real work."

Then his tone seemed to retreat, as if he'd already exposed too much of himself. More distantly he added, "Of course I'm helping you. And Ginny. I haven't had this much fun in years."

Which probably explained his irritation with me this morning. Inadvertently I'd made him feel insubstantial and uninformed.

"So I was wrong," I offered tentatively. "My theory"—my only real explanation—"was that you help me because you feel guilty. For fucking Ginny when she and I used to be partners."

Then I gaped at the wall in chagrin. *I* said *that*? How had he gotten so much honesty out of me? If I'd given the words any actual consideration, I would've bitten my tongue in half. Or said something unforgivably nasty.

In response, Marshal burst out laughing.

"Brew, Brew, Brew," he chortled. "Can you spell 'chemistry,' you overgrown moron? If Ginny and I were going to jump into bed, we would've done it years ago, and your whole life would've been different. I *like* her. I respect the pantyhose off her. But—" He laughed again. "Have you been acting like an insolent twit all this time because you thought—?" Finally he was done.

"There's no chemistry." He might've been wiping the mirth from his eyes. "I swear to God."

After a moment I muttered, "I told you that my guesses haven't been worth shit." What else could I say? "Later I'll explain how stupid I feel." Apparently telling myself the truth wasn't enough. I had to tell other people, too. "Right now I need to talk to Ginny."

"I understand." His grin reached me along the phone line. "When you're done working for Lacone, we'll talk about whether you want a job with Professional Investigations."

Then he hung up. Which spared me having to gape some more.

Until I tried to dial Ginny's number, I didn't notice how badly I was trembling.

No, not now. Not *now*. I absolutely could not afford to be this stupid, too fumble-brained to dial a fucking phone. There was too much at stake. Not with Ginny. Within me.

I put down the receiver, wrapped mental arms around my guts to contain my visceral frenzy, and tried again.

After an interminable stretch of dead air while the cellular connection went through and my bowels tied themselves in knots, the number rang.

Ginny answered so promptly that she must've been waiting with the phone in her hand. "Fistoulari."

"Ginny, it's Brew." Now that I had her, I could barely speak. "What's happened?"

She chuckled grimly. "Calm down, Brew." She knew me too well. "I wanted to talk to you before I pick up Mai. She's with her lawyers. She's supposed to call me when she's ready to come home, but I haven't heard from her yet."

In other words, I'd reached her in time.

Almost involuntarily I sagged back in the chair. "Don't mind me," I panted unsteadily. "I'm just having a small coronary. Nothing to worry about."

"I know how you feel." She wasn't amused. "But you might want to put it off for a few minutes. This can't wait."

"Right." I already knew that she hadn't used her lives-at-stake tone just to scare me. "Go ahead."

She hesitated, then said, "When you suggested searching her house, I thought you were crazy." Like Marshal, she spoke distinctly, but for different reasons. "I wanted to ignore you, but you're right too often for my peace of mind. Way too often. And the crazier you sound, the more likely you are to be right."

Recently I hadn't been right about anything—and I was getting crazier by the second. About Mai Sternway, however, I had no doubts at all.

"So—" Ginny's voice trailed off. When she went on, she sounded angry in the cold businesslike way that meant she was at her most dangerous. "You'll never guess what I found."

"Tell me," I murmured softly.

"It's like a duffel bag." Her tone had teeth in it. "The kind athletes carry gear in. With a shoulder strap. Black plastic, not cloth—do they make these things out of vinyl?"

Sweet Christ. I sat up as if she'd yanked me by the hair.

"It closes with a flap instead of a zipper."

There she stopped.

The inside of my head began to clang like a cathedral bell. At the same time I seemed to become translucent, the way flesh does in the glare of a thermonuclear blast. Piercing light shone through me. If I'd looked fast enough I would've seen everything.

"What's in it?" I asked, suddenly calm. A flood of illumination washed away my tremors.

"Well, for one thing," she replied harshly, "there are a dozen or so watches, wallets, bracelets, money clips. No more than that. Not a very successful haul."

"And—?"

"And nothing," she snapped. "A *flik*, for God's sake. With dried blood on it. Bits of skin. Maybe a few fibers of some kind. Hair or something, I don't know." Then her voice softened. She sounded sad, rueful over a crime that she couldn't have prevented. "It smells like a murder weapon, Brew."

That was it, right there in front of me. The connection. The link that bound everything together. If I could just grasp how that one link attached to all the others.

"No, it doesn't," I told her. "It smells like *the* murder weapon. The one that killed Bernie Appelwait. At The Luxury."

Ginny recoiled. I sensed it through the phone. "You didn't tell me he was killed with a flik."

Clanging and fuses, impossible translucence. A concussion like explosive decompression. I'd taken too many blows, landed none. My head should've been full of chaos, a *blitzkrieg* of possibilities

I couldn't process, but it wasn't. Instead I hung on the edge of unattained clarity, so tantalizingly close that I would've wept to reach it.

"I didn't know it was important," I answered thinly. "I couldn't have guessed—"

She'd found the weapon that killed Bernie? In *Mai Sternway's* house?

"Shit!" Ginny snarled hoarsely. "What's it doing *here*?"

I knew the answer. Or I didn't, but I almost did. My brain felt like a crash zone, the place where frames of reference collided to extinguish each other.

"One step at a time." I could hardly recognize myself. "Is there ID in any of the wallets?"

"Just a minute." I heard her shuffle through the contents of the bag. "Here's one. Woman's clutch purse, red, with a driver's license. Kerri Lee Fuller." She read the address. Then she demanded through her teeth, "What the *fuck* is this shit doing here? What does *Mai* have to do with *Bernie Appelwait*?"

"I don't know." Maybe I did. Almost. But it felt false somehow, misleading, like an intuitive leap in the wrong direction that lands, impossibly, on solid ground. "I've got a theory, but I don't like it. I'm not sure it makes sense."

"Spit it out, Brew." Without transition, her voice changed. She'd recovered her poise. "I know we're not partners anymore. But this is *my* business too, now. Mai Sternway is *my* client. We need to work together."

And she knew how to do that. She'd had years of practice.

A day or two ago—in a previous reality—I might've retorted, Fuck that. But not today. Not after Nakahatchi had jolted me out of myself, and Marshal had answered my questions. Not when Ginny had made it clear that she wanted to heal the breach between us.

"One step at a time," I repeated. For my sake this time, not hers. "Marshal asked me to give you a message. He's traced that phone number, the ID-blocked one." I recited it for her. "But he doesn't know who it belongs to yet."

"Got it," she muttered. Then she waited.

"You need to do two things," I went on carefully. "Get that bag to Marshal. Without letting Mai know you found it. Tell Marshal it's for Sergeant Edgar Moy. And try out that phone number on Mai. Look for *any* hint that she recognizes it."

Before Ginny could react, I went on, "I'm going to track down this Kerri Lee Fuller, ask her if she was at the tournament. Then I'll give that phone number to Moy. He'll identify it faster than Marshal can."

Ginny accepted that as if she routinely let me tell her what to do. "And your theory is?" she inquired when I was done.

"It doesn't feel right," I insisted. "I don't trust it." Then I took a deep breath and told her, "But I'd bet my left ventricle I know whose number that is. 'Turf' Hardshorn, James M. The goon who tried to kill me last night."

By rights, that should've confused the hell out of her. She knew how my mind worked, however. She couldn't leap blind the way I did—but she could catch up in a hurry.

"So your theory," she replied slowly, putting it together as she talked, "is that he's the thug Mai hired to frame her husband. You think the same bozo who ripped off the tournament also made those threatening phone calls, slashed her tires, did everything else." She paused. "That part makes sense. He sounds like the kind of bastard you'd want to hire if you were trying to frame your husband for stalking you.

"But the bag—" I could imagine the predator's concentration in her eyes, the sharp lines of her mouth, the unconscious flexing of her fingers and claw. She might as well have been standing in front of me. "What's it doing here?"

She answered her own question. "Maybe he stashed his haul at her house as a kind of insurance, to implicate her if she ratted him out." Again she paused. "Or they had some other idea, like planting it at Sternway's, only Hardshorn got killed before they could do it. He might've planned to leave the club as soon as he saw Sternway there, so he could get to Sternway's apartment while it was empty. But you ruined that by recognizing him. Or Sternway did by defending you."

Quietly she added, "Of course, none of that helps your theory that Hardshorn didn't kill Appelwait."

Listening to her, I felt my blast of clarity recede toward the horizons. The shock still resonated, but I wasn't translucent anymore. In another minute I'd be as blank as a stone.

And there was still too much I hadn't grasped.

I'd been *positive* that Hardshorn wasn't alone with Bernie in the men's room.

"That'll be Moy's interpretation," I admitted. "Unless I can come up with something better." Otherwise he'd close the case, and I'd be left like a fool with my brain hanging out.

Ginny didn't argue. "As a theory," she mused, "it sounds plausible enough. What's wrong with it? I already told you I don't think her husband is harassing her. The pieces don't fit.

"And I can tell you this. Mai hasn't had any more threats since last night."

Since Hardshorn was killed.

I couldn't contradict her. I had too many strands, all tangled, and no way to sort them out. Besides, they were pure instinct—about as tangible as that flicker you sometimes get at the corner of your vision, the one that feels like a fading glimpse into another dimension.

Mr. Sternway lets his wife treat him like dirt.

I made Sifu *Hong aware that his school was being watched.*

So the pieces didn't fit. What were the alternatives? Say Mai hadn't arranged to harass herself. And Anson wasn't responsible. Then who?

Sue Rasmussen? *The man was a saint with her.* To protect her boyfriend?

Don't say anything about the club.

What the fuck are you doing?

Sternway knew Hardshorn from the fight club. Why hadn't Anson spotted him at the tournament?

You will not be ready indeed until your pain has become separate from your anger.

Meanwhile the chops were worth an appalling amount of money to anyone with the expertise to recognize their value.

How about my fear? Was that supposed to be *separate* too?

I stifled a groan. "What's wrong with it," I said finally because I couldn't imagine where else to begin, "is that it doesn't explain why asking Hong to evaluate those chops scares me so much."

"Damn it, Brew, you've lost me again." Ginny wasn't angry now. She was just trying to shake me out of my confusion. "Is Hong in danger? *Did* he look at the chops? Did he say something strange about them?"

I shook my head uselessly. "Shit, Ginny. I've lost myself. A couple of minutes ago I was so close—"

I simply hadn't been quick enough. The back of my brain had offered me a chance, and I'd let it get away.

As far as I knew, Hong hadn't said anything at all about the chops.

"But," she stated flatly, "it was too much to take in all at once. Cut yourself some slack, Brew. You've been here before. You know how to cope. Just give yourself a little time. You'll get it back when you're ready for it."

Sure, I muttered to myself. What's a few hours among friends? Or a few deaths?

Nevertheless she was right. I *had* been here before, trying to see things that I already knew clearly enough to understand them. And my brain never worked worth shit when I tried to force it.

But I couldn't shake the conviction that Hong's death was already on my conscience, and it hadn't even happened yet.

"Probably," I sighed. "But it never *feels* like it's going to come back."

"Then stop thinking about it." Ginny was ready to get off the phone. "Go do something. Find Fuller. Talk to Moy. Warn Hong. Give yourself a chance. I need to figure out how I can get this bag to Marshal before Mai calls."

"Sure," I conceded wanly. The aftermath of missed opportunities left me desolate, as ruined as a wasteland. But before she could hang up I added, "Ginny," with the fervor of a prayer, "thanks."

She chuckled grimly. "Thanks yourself. I would never have thought of searching this house."

And I wouldn't have thought of asking Hong to evaluate the chops if she hadn't suggested it. If she hadn't wanted to close the rift we'd driven between us.

When she hung up, I didn't know whether to smile or weep.

23

A nap was out of the question now. I couldn't have slept with a quart of Seconal in my veins. But I needed a shower badly. In fact, I might not survive without one. I felt too grimy to function, so dirt-streaked and bespattered that it reminded me of my drinking days. Back then Ginny sometimes had to roust me out of the trash before she could put me to work.

A shower could wait, however. I had time. First things first.

The phone sat in my lap like one of those black boxes that would tell you why an airplane crashed if you could just figure out how to access it. Personally I loathed phones. I was spending way too much time talking to people I couldn't see.

Maybe Nakahatchi was right. Maybe you couldn't trust what people said over the phone because they weren't present to take responsibility for it.

Unfortunately I had to make calls anyway.

After a couple of minutes, I sank my teeth into myself—in a manner of speaking—and dialed again.

Finding Kerri Lee Fuller turned out to be easy. Directory assistance gave me her number. She answered on the third ring.

Yes, she was a *karate-ka*, although I'd never heard of her school. Yes, she'd competed in the tournament. Yes, she'd lost a red clutch purse there. It held her driver's license and all her credit cards. She was in trouble without it. Her relief was evident when I told her that it'd been recovered.

I gave her Moy's number, informed her that her purse was evidence and Moy would want to talk to her, and assured her that she'd get everything back in a few days. Then I hung up.

Calling Moy myself didn't work out so well.

After the phone rang three or four thousand times, I was connected to a voice messaging system. Press "1" to leave a message, press "2" to speak to another detective, that sort of thing. I didn't have the heart to repeat everything for Moy, so I left the important stuff to Marshal. Instead I just said that I'd come across a phone number and wanted Moy to identify it for me. When I'd given him that one as well as my cell phone number, I replaced the handset and put the phone back on the end table.

Then—finally—I went to take a shower.

I still intended to call Hong. But I put it off. I had no idea what to say to him.

Sifu Hong, your life is in danger.

Why?

You got a good look at the chops.

Yeah, right. Pull the other one, I need it stretched.

Sternway had assured me that Hong could turn me *into dog food with both hands tied.* And now I thought he was in danger because he'd seen the chops up close?

I had to have a shower.

Some days just peeling off dirty clothes was like molting. Removing encrusted sweat and inadequacy from contact with my skin made me feel like I'd become new. But not today. Today my befouled sensation ran a whole lot deeper.

Where was I when I needed myself most? How had my intuitive instincts, my unconscious impulse to make patterns out of hints, become so conflicted? The back of my head already had all the information I needed. And yet I couldn't see the truth.

You will not be ready indeed until your pain has become separate from your anger.

I didn't trust myself enough to see it.

What the fuck are you doing?

Sternway had referred to Tae Kwon Do as a "toy." And he was Parker Neill's *sensei.* Yet Parker had informed me flatly, *Any teacher who doesn't train his students to honor all the martial arts doesn't deserve to* have *students.*

Ginny had found Bernie's flik and Hardshorn's loot in Mai Sternway's house.

Almost desperately I climbed into the shower and turned the volume up to "brain jelly," hoping that enough pressure and heat would blast the confusion out of my skull.

Eventually the heat started to sink in. Hot spray worked at my muscles like fingers. Steam baked the grime from my pores. And the muffled roar and splash of the water deafened me to my own clamor. Then at last I could think again.

Still dripping from the shower, I went back to the phone and dialed the number for *Traditional Wing Chun*.

A voice I didn't know answered. Having recovered a degree of cerebral function, I asked for T'ang Wen instead of Hong Fei-Tung.

When he finally came to the phone, I told him straight out, "Mr. T'ang, I'm worried about *Sifu* Hong. I think he might be in danger."

" 'Danger,' Mr. Axbrewder? What manner of danger?" He sounded suspicious.

"Call it a hunch. I can't explain it. I wish I could." *God*, I wished I could. "But ever since he went to look at the chops, my instincts have been trying to warn me about something.

"When I invited him the situation looked harmless. It still ought to be. But I can't afford to ignore my instincts. They're right too often. And they picked up some kind of threat."

I couldn't say things like that to Hong. His stature as a martial artist—his "face"—precluded them.

T'ang was silent for a moment. Then he pronounced, "You distrust Nakahatchi *sensei*."

"No," I retorted at once. "That's not it." I was sure. "But it has something to do with the chops."

On impulse or inspiration, I asked, "Did *Sifu* Hong tell you if he considers them authentic?"

"If you wish to speak of such matters," T'ang informed me severely, "you must address them to my master. It is not my place to share his thoughts."

That might've been a hint. Or another warning. But I couldn't challenge T'ang Wen about it. "Face" again.

Cursing the exigencies of Oriental manners, I dropped the subject.

"All right. I respect that. But please tell *Sifu* Hong that I'm worried. Tell him"—I was in no mood for restraint—"I'm on my knees here, begging him to be particularly careful."

If something happened to him—

T'ang's tone softened. "I will tell him, Mr. Axbrewder." Apparently I'd gotten his attention. "And I will be careful for him. We will all do so."

Presumably he meant everyone at *Traditional Wing Chun*.

That was probably more reassurance than I had any right to expect, so I thanked him and got off the phone.

By then I'd stopped dripping. After checking the time to be sure that I wasn't late, I went into my bedroom and paralyzed myself wondering what I ought to wear.

My only suit was too rank to put on. And after today the jacket was worse. But I didn't have time to locate a one-hour cleaner, so I tossed the jacket and a sheet of fabric softener into the dryer and let it run while I tackled the Augean Labor of choosing a shirt and slacks.

Light blue with khaki? Khaki with dark blue? Civilization as we know it hung in the balance.

When I'd achieved a state of perfect silliness, I applied the Fuck-It Principle. Whatever happened between Deborah and me tonight didn't depend on my clothes. Or my assumptions. It rested squarely and solely on how clearly we saw each other. So fuck it.

On that basis, I got dressed, shaved, trimmed my fingernails, then strapped on my shoulder holster and clicked the .45 through its chambers. While the dryer finished groaning over my jacket, I unfolded my map of Carner on the kitchen table and figured out how to follow Deborah's directions to the restaurant.

When I retrieved my jacket it wasn't clean, but at least it didn't stink anymore. Shrugging my arms into it, I tucked my cell phone into one of the pockets and left the apartment.

As the sun retracted its fierceness toward evening, I saw a surprise in the distance. Dark clouds massive as thunder piled around the setting sun like storms ready to boil. If they kept coming, they'd block the light before long, shed premature night across the city. The air bore hints that I'd learned to identify in Puerta del Sol, suggestions of moisture and violence, a deluge of change. Back home clouds like that brought rain which flattened pedestrians, drowned headlights until you couldn't see to drive, ripped down tree limbs and TV antennae like rubble from the broken heavens. Grandfather storms, tireless and full of malice.

But maybe I was wrong. This was Carner, not Puerta del Sol. As far as I knew, they didn't have weather here. The city fathers didn't permit it.

Nevertheless the sight of those clouds tightened my nerves,

singing shrill harmonies across the neurons. Sensible people stayed home when they saw clouds like that, but I was aimed right into them.

As I wheeled the van away from the curb, I had the disturbed sensation that I was leaving the rest of my life behind—that I was about to cross a threshold, an event horizon, which only allowed passage in one direction, and which would definitively alter all my landscapes. Or maybe Nakahatchi had already pushed me past the boundary, and I simply hadn't recognized the change until now.

This was *terra incognita*. The kind of terrain that scared me spitless.

At the moment, it was the only kind that mattered.

Fortunately I'd allowed myself over an hour for what appeared on the map to be a forty-five minute drive. Before I was halfway to the restaurant, I hit preliminary spatters of rain. At first they smeared weeks or months of accumulated oils over the windshield, and I could hardly see. But that didn't last long. As the wipers rubbed the streaks away, the rain gathered force. Lashed from side to side by the wind, the soft drizzle thickened into a downpour. Within a couple of miles it'd become what Puerta del Sol called a "gully-washer," a rain so hard that it caused flash floods in arroyos which hadn't held streams for years. And then the rain turned torrential. It plunged out of the sky like cataracts from a shattered dam, releasing lakes of stored water as hard and fast as its weight and the wind could drive it.

Blackness and scourging rain shut off every vestige of evening. In fact, they nearly effaced Carner's unremitting electric illumination. I lost sight of each street lamp before I crept into reach of the next. The traffic signals appeared in front of me as suddenly as enchantments. Half the time I only knew that I hadn't lost the road because I was following taillights. Carner's systemic commitment to artificial daylight was all that enabled me to make out the occasional street sign.

The roar of the storm cut out every other sound. I drove in a bubble of reality, a space of isolation created by the pitiless hammering of rain and wind on metal.

The possibility that Deborah might decide not to come at all under these conditions didn't cross my mind until I finally located the restaurant—half an hour late.

By then most of the traffic had scurried for shelter. I found a parking space at the curb no more than ten yards from the entrance to Chez Amneris. Ten yards in this storm— There may've been covered parking somewhere nearby, but I'd never find it.

Naturally I didn't own anything as reasonable as a raincoat—or an umbrella. By the time I reached the restaurant's front door, I'd look like a puppy someone tried to put to sleep in a bucket.

For a couple of minutes, I sat where I was, hoping for a break in the deluge—and trying to convince myself that Deborah wouldn't let weather like this stop her. But the rain just came down harder.

Finally I swallowed what was left of my dignity. Leaving my cell phone on the passenger seat to keep it dry, I jumped out of the van, slammed the door, and ran like the damned for what Deborah had called her favorite restaurant.

Those ten yards felt like slogging along the bottom of a lake. By the time I burst into shelter, I wore enough water to irrigate a football field.

Slapping moisture out of my eyes while I fountained in all directions, I found myself almost nose-to-nose with the maitre d'. His disapproving mustache matched the hard glare in his eyes. He retreated quickly to protect his tux, flapped his hands to ward me away.

"Perhaps," he sniffed with immaculate hauteur, "*monsieur* is unaware of the invention of umbrellas."

"That's not all," I told him in a sputter of rain. "I also didn't know they'd invented rude waiters."

He didn't rise to the challenge. Instead he fixed his glare on my sodden shoes. "Of course *monsieur* has a reservation."

Like I needed one. The place was practically empty.

When I looked around, however, I spotted Deborah Messenger at a table near the back of the room. As soon as I saw her, she waved and smiled.

I grinned back. "I guess I do," I told mine host as I turned my back on him and strolled away, squishing.

Chez Amneris was done up in a pseudo-Egyptian motif, complete with potted palms, Moroccan tableware, and sand-strewn pyramids in fresco. But the management had replaced the traditional rush-strewn floor with a hearty maroon carpet that made the whole room look awash in drying blood.

As far as I could see, Deborah wasn't wet at all. Her hair flowed around her head like a nimbus, dry and full of life, and her face had the fresh moist gloss of makeup rather than rain. She wore a mauve silk blouse that would've shown every drop of water, but instead it seemed to float against her, teasing me with hints.

She must've brought an umbrella the size of a trampoline.

A welcoming glitter in her eyes matched her smile. What with one thing and another, she nearly ravished me off my feet.

I didn't try to sit down. I wasn't sure I could. When I'd grinned back at her for an hour or two, I muttered sheepishly, "I could use some paper towels."

She laughed and pointed. "The restrooms are that way."

Unsteadily I sloshed away.

By the time I returned—still wet, but no longer dripping—she'd ordered herself a glass of burgundy, and the maitre d' had taken advantage of my absence to set a menu at my place. As I sat down across from her, she laughed again.

"Apparently I forgot to tell you there's a parking garage next door." So much for the trampoline theory. "You poor man, you look like you've been through the rinse cycle once too often."

Since there was hauteur in the air, I tried to fake some. "I prefer to think of it," I sniffed like the maitre d', "as 'rode hard and put away wet.' "

Deborah bit her lip mock-solicitously. "Did you have a horrible time getting here?"

"Moderately horrible," I admitted. "But it's already worth it."

"You're too kind," she told me. "But don't stop. I like it." Then she turned serious. "This must have been a difficult day. How are you?"

I considered the question briefly. "Confused."

"Not about me, I hope."

"Actually, I am. I can't figure out what a woman like you wants with me." I smiled to take the edge off my clumsiness. "But on the Great Scale of Incomprehension, that's one of my lesser problems. The rest are bigger."

"Tell me," she urged.

So I told her. Even though I didn't know how to trust her. I needed to talk more than I'd realized.

Apparently I'd forgotten how much I used to talk to Ginny—and how much good it did me.

Once I got started, I lost track of the ordinary details of dinner. The fact that I felt like I was wearing wet towels stopped bothering me. I ordered and ate something without registering what it was, drank club soda without noticing the lovely, pernicious aroma of burgundy. Instead I just talked. About Puerta del Sol and Ginny. About Bernie and Mai Sternway. About Alyse and Marshal, Turf Hardshorn and *Sifu* Hong. Whenever I got stuck, Deborah asked an attentive question, and I went on.

Outside the storm grew stronger. Thunder crashed like granite through the downpour, and shots of lightning paled Chez Amneris's lamps in jagged streaks. But the effect was muffled, almost impersonal. It didn't get in my way.

I was still going when Deborah announced, "Brew, I want you to come back to my apartment." From the look in her eyes, you would've thought that I'd been seducing her for hours.

"Please," I answered ardently. Nevertheless I couldn't stop. While she summoned the check, I asked, "What do you remember about Saturday—when Bernie was killed? You were in the lobby, weren't you? Talking to Sternway and Lacone?"

"That's right." She didn't push the question away. "Alex had asked me to meet him, but he didn't really have anything to discuss. He just pretended he did. He doesn't take me seriously—as a professional, I mean. All he wants is a chance to stand close and proposition me." She shrugged. "But he's an important client, so I do my job and make nice. Most of the time his propositions are easy to ignore.

"Mr. Sternway joined us after a while. I suppose we'd been making small talk"—she consulted her memory—"for maybe five minutes when we realized something was wrong."

"How did you know?"

She claimed the check before I could reach it. "We saw hotel security running. They looked upset. And one of them blocked the men's room." She smiled wryly. "That was enough for me."

"Can you remember where you were standing?" I pursued. "Which direction were you facing? What could you see?"

"Brew." She put her hand on my arm. "I'll think about it. I'll tell you everything I can remember. But I'd like to go now.

Please?" Mischief and desire shone in her eyes. "The way you talk about your work—I don't know how much longer I can keep my hands to myself."

I nearly fell over getting out of my chair. Then, just in case I didn't already look foolish enough, I bowed to the floor. "Yours to command, my lady."

Laughing again, she stood to join me.

Through the windows the storm looked fierce enough to overturn cars. After each hot strike of lightning, the thunder fell like buildings under demolition. She offered to give me a ride, bring me back to the Plymouth tomorrow, but something nagging in the back of my head told me that I might want the van. So she led me out the restaurant's rear entrance and up an escalator to the parking garage, then drove me in her sleek robin's-egg blue Audi into the lashing torrents and around the block until we were right beside the Plymouth. From there I heaved myself out in one stride, hauled open the van, and dove in. Altogether I wasn't exposed to the storm for more than three seconds.

It soaked me to the skin. Drenched me completely. I couldn't have gotten any wetter if I'd strolled here from Chicago.

The Plymouth didn't want to start. I could barely see the lights from Chez Amneris. The rain fell like reified darkness, driving every scrap of illumination to its knees. Whenever a bolt of lightning hit, the buildings on both sides of the street seemed to jump into existence as if they were crowding closer. Then the sudden impact of thunder restored the dark, tightened its noose around me. I felt like a fugitive from justice, desperate for escape, as I cranked the starter again and again.

Invisible through the rain, Deborah waited for me. Only her headlights showed that she was still there.

Finally the engine coughed a few times and sputtered to life. I revved it hard, trying to burn the damp from the plugs. When I'd snapped on my headlights and flicked them two or three times, Deborah's Audi began to creep ahead of me.

Guided by her taillights, I followed her through the smothering storm.

I didn't know where her apartment was, so I concentrated on not losing her. Unless lightning cracked open the torrents at just the right moment, I couldn't make out street signs. And I had too many other problems to wrestle with.

Clinging to Deborah's taillights as if they might save me, I asked myself the same question I'd almost asked her. What did she want from me? I couldn't avoid it any longer. I was on my way to spend the night with her when some part of me believed that I should be standing guard over the chops and *Sifu* Hong.

Lightning gave me a clear white look at the Audi. Buildings that might've been banks crowded the road, leaning inward like they were being thrashed by the rain. Thunder pounded overhead, so close that it made the Plymouth shudder on its tires.

What did she gain—

—by distracting me?

By distracting me tonight?

From a loyal insurance company employee's point of view, Watchdog would lose major bucks if something happened to the chops. Therefore of course Deborah wanted me to do my best for Lacone and Nakahatchi.

But suppose she wasn't a loyal employee—

What if instead she was a greedy woman with tastes too expensive for her salary and a secret yen for—just picking a name at random—T'ang Wen? Think of the cash she could get her hands on if she helped him steal and fence the chops.

The idea made me want to puke Chez Amneris' cuisine all over the van. According to this theory, she'd arranged for Hardshorn and his team to make Posten and Watchdog nervous by working the tournament. Then, when she was sure that I'd jump through any number of hoops for her—including ditching my former partner—she'd urged Lacone to hire me. So that she could get me away from Martial America tonight.

Then it followed that Hardshorn had killed Bernie. They must've been alone in the men's room. Deborah was out in the lobby with Lacone and Sternway, and no one else had a motive to crush Bernie's larynx and take the flik.

But—

I didn't believe that Hardshorn killed Bernie. Hardshorn's willingness to kill *me* only made sense if he had more at stake than a bag of petty loot. But nothing except the presence of a recognizable partner explained Bernie's death.

And the bag later ended up hidden in Mai Sternway's house? How crazy was that?

No matter whose name I substituted for T'ang's in this theory,

I couldn't make the pieces fit. If Deborah had larceny in her heart when she invited me to her apartment, nothing added up, and I was utterly lost.

For a moment her taillights eluded me. The deluge swarming down my windshield drained my self-confidence as it ran, washing me by scraps and shreds into Carner's overfilled sewers. If I were *that* wrong, absofuckinglutely anyone could've killed Bernie.

Then the Audi braked for a turn. I'd almost overshot it in the blackness.

Maybe everything in my head was just so much lightning and thunder, a tension reaction, neurons making themselves insane under the strain of the storm. Or maybe Carner itself lay so far beyond any reality I understood that I couldn't think straight.

I needed an answer, and I needed it soon.

At the next slash of lightning, I heard myself yelp. How long had I been doing *that*? My throat felt tight and raw, as if I'd already howled half a dozen times without noticing it.

Incoherently I began to fear that I'd have to follow Deborah through this pummeling chaos for the rest of my life. God alone knew how *she* coped without a set of taillights to guide her.

When she swung left, I assumed that she'd turned to another street. But the roadway sloped suddenly downward, and then between one heartbeat and the next the rain stopped, cut off as cleanly as if we'd fallen over the edge of the world. We were in an underground parking garage. A swollen river accompanied us downward. As the pavement leveled out the rainwater spread into a surging lake that covered the Audi's wheels to the hubcaps.

Deborah sculled her car into a parking space. I found one nearby for the van. When I opened my door, she stood on the Audi's running board, facing me over the roof.

"Now *that*," she called through the muffled clamor, "was horrible." Enforced gaiety strained her voice. "I haven't seen a storm like that in my *life*."

"Stay there," I shouted back. My whole body ached with the absence of torrents. My head felt like it'd been packed with cabbage and buried to rot. "I'm already wet. I'll carry you."

She made a noise that might've been laughter or hysteria. "Don't be silly. I'm a big girl." She removed her shoes, then hopped off the running board, closed her door, and splashed toward me. "Although I have to say," she added as she got closer, "I'm tempted. It sounds just too gallant for words.

"Besides, the water is *cold*."

As soon as I stepped out of the van—in past my ankles—she gave me a febrile grin and sprang at me. I braced myself just in time to catch her without falling over backward.

One arm under her knees, the other around her back, I held her above the lake. She kissed me quickly, then flung one arm outward like a command. "That way, Sir Knight," she ordered imperiously. "To the elevator, and at once. I need a drink. And *you*"—she slapped my shoulder—"need to get out of those clothes."

She hadn't dropped her purse. I've never understood how women do that. Ginny had the same gift. She could fall down a logging flume, and when she splashed out the end she'd still have her purse. Hell, it probably wouldn't even be damp.

Awkwardly I reached back into the van to retrieve my phone. I had to release one arm to do it, but she compensated by clinging to my neck. Once I'd settled my arms under her again, I leaned against the door to close it and headed for the elevator, high-stepping to avoid concealed obstacles.

She was right—the water was cold, bitter as a serpent's tooth. Soon the clenched concentration of driving caught up with me, and I started to shiver.

"Brew!" Deborah protested at once. "Put me down. You're *freezing*. We should hurry."

I didn't obey. "Forget it." Chills shuddered through me. "Right now you're the only warmth I've got."

I wanted her in my arms. The cold wasn't the only thing that made me shiver—

Nevertheless I tried to take longer strides. She hugged herself against me, ignoring the possibility that she might ruin her blouse.

At the elevator, rainwater no longer drained into the shaft. It was already full. If the elevator's motor and wiring were in the bottom of the shaft, and they weren't insulated—

I didn't know how many stairs I could climb in my condition.

But when Deborah hit the call button, lights over the door showed the elevator descending from fifteen floors above us.

Fortunately the car came straight down. When the doors opened, water flooded in. But it leaked back out as we rose. By the time we reached her floor, my shoes were no longer submerged.

Carefully I set Deborah on her feet. Waves of shivering undermined my balance. Holding my arm, she supported me into the hallway.

The hall gave off an impression of muted gentility—framed prints in soft colors interspersed with ornamental lighting fixtures along the walls, a carpet with a comfortable pattern. Four or five doors down from the elevator, she produced her keys, undid the lock, and hustled me inside. Then she hurried away.

"Take off those clothes," she ordered over her shoulder. "I'm going to turn on the shower and start some water boiling."

Take off those clothes. Ha. Would've been a good idea if my hands weren't shaking so badly.

I stood in a short entryway like a mini-foyer, complete with a delicate side table and—I assumed—a coat closet. A light blue carpet several shades richer than the one outside led to a living room on the left and a kitchen on the right, with half-open walls between them above a sideboard for the living room, counters for the kitchen. The room she'd disappeared into beyond the kitchen must've been the bathroom. Presumably the doorway opposite it led to her bedroom.

A nice apartment for a woman living alone. Not quite wealthy, but definitely upper-middle-class. Maybe Watchdog paid well. Maybe she'd inherited money, or struck gold on the stock market, or won a modest lottery. Or maybe—

I still held my phone. I put it down on the side table. Fighting shivers, I managed to work my jacket off my shoulders and down my arms. The holster came next. That was harder. While I fumbled at the straps, I wondered distantly whether the .45 would still fire. Probably it would. I'd used enough gun oil to make the damn bullets waterproof.

Shirt buttons? How?

Deborah bustled out of the bathroom, leaving the door open. I heard water running, glimpsed a wisp of steam. She started for the kitchen, then veered toward me instead. "Let me," she instructed firmly as she tackled the buttons. With matter-of-fact efficiency, she undid them all, loosened my belt, bent down to tug off my shoes. She'd had practice, apparently.

Finally she worked my shirt off and dropped it on my jacket. The skin of my chest looked like I'd spent a week underwater. Pointing at the bathroom, she said, "Leave the rest of your clothes on the floor. I'll put everything in the dryer. I'm going to have a drink. Do you want coffee or tea?"

"Coffee," I mumbled. I sounded like I had frostbite in my mouth.

With a nod, she nudged me into motion.

I shut the bathroom door behind me, mainly to keep the steam in. That warmth restored enough sanity to get me undressed the rest of the way—and to make me test the temperature before I stepped into the shower.

I'd already had more water than I knew what to do with. But this was *hot*, and it stung my skin like needles of bliss.

While I soaked away my chills, I heard the door open and close as Deborah retrieved my clothes. When I finally emerged with a parboiled blush on my skin and a towel clamped around my waist, she had a steaming cup ready for me. The coffee smelled like nectar.

On an ordinary day Ginny's coffee was sludge. On a bad day it tasted like turpentine. I'd done most of the cooking so that we wouldn't have to get our stomachs pumped after every meal.

If Deborah wanted to seduce me out of my senses, render me too stupid to think, she had the right approach.

She appraised me frankly for a moment, then nodded approval. "That's a definite improvement." Her mouth twitched into a grin. "Lose the towel, and it'll be flawless."

Luxurious amber filled the glass in her hand. It smelled like Macallan's, an old revered single-malt Scotch, more costly than blood. Against the stifled backdrop of the storm, I heard a dryer rumble softly.

Sipping coffee to disguise my yearning, I tightened my grip on the towel.

"Don't rush me. Us Knights Errant are supposed to be shy. It's in the manual." Unsteadily I added, "You didn't finish answering my question."

She treated me to a perplexed frown, as beguiling as a

summer's day. "Did you ask me a question? The last thing I remember you saying was about warmth."

"Back at the restaurant," I explained. "I asked you where you and Lacone and Sternway were standing. In the lobby on Saturday. I want to know what you remember."

If she resisted, it would mean—

I didn't know what. Surely it would mean something or other.

"That's right." She seemed to give herself a shake. "You asked me which direction I was facing."

I nodded dumbly.

"And I said I'd tell you everything I could remember." She looked me up and down. "Now?" she countered almost wistfully. "Can't it wait?"

I swallowed hard. "Now. Later I won't remember my damn name, never mind Saturday."

And Bernie. And Hong.

She sighed. "All right."

Deliberately she shut her eyes. For a moment she frowned in concentration. Then she turned to face away from me, toward the wall of her bedroom. "I'm in the lobby," she murmured through thunder and rain. "The main entrance is there." She nodded at the wall. "I arrived before Alex did. He's usually late, I knew that. But I hoped I'd see you, so I came a few minutes early."

Fortunately she didn't look at me while she spoke. The lines of her back and neck were alluring enough. Her eyes might've made me lose myself completely.

"There aren't very many people in the lobby. You aren't one of them, and I don't recognize anybody else." Her tone sounded dreamy, distant with recollection. "I find a place to wait where I can watch the front doors and the hallway to the convention center, just in case. When Alex arrives, I turn more toward the doors.

"He starts his usual flirting. I smile and talk without playing his game. He stands close to me, on my right, so he can touch my arm and stare at my breasts."

I visualized the lobby with her, tried to see what she saw. The registration desk at 10 o'clock. The doors at noon. Alex leering at 3. The convention center hallway at 7:30 or 8.

The short corridor toward the restrooms at 8 or 8:30.

"Eventually Anson joins us. He comes from the convention center. He stands two or three feet away on that side, facing Alex." 9 o'clock. "Alex stops flirting. We make small talk.

"Occasionally I glance behind me. I see you leave the hallway. I smile at you, but you don't respond. You hesitate, looking around. Then you head for the men's room. You're almost running." She chuckled softly. "I wonder if you've eaten something that doesn't agree with you.

"How am I doing?"

"Don't stop," I warned her quickly. "Keep your eyes closed."

She continued to face her bedroom wall.

Keeping my voice low so that it wouldn't shake, I asked, "Did you see Sternway leave the convention center? Or did he just show up on your left?"

Had she simply assumed—?

Without hesitation, she answered, "I didn't see him at first. Alex glanced in that direction, and I turned my head. He was ten or fifteen feet away."

"So you didn't actually see him leave the convention center?"

"No," she admitted dubiously. "I guess not. But where—?"

"As far as you know, he could've come from the men's room?"

Abruptly she turned back to me. Distress filled her eyes, darkened them until they looked bottomless. Her hands held her glass as if she'd forgotten it.

"Brew—" she began, then bit her lip. "I don't want to say that."

"Why not?"

"Because," she protested, "it sounds like I think he could have killed Bernie Appelwait. And I don't.

"My God, Brew, he's the Director of the IAMA! He's had his own school in Carner for fifteen years. Every martial artist I talk to thinks he sits on the right hand of *God*."

I knew what she meant.

"I know I called him a coward around women." She might've been pleading with me. "But that doesn't make him a murderer. The world is full of men who are terrified of women, and they don't go around killing hotel security guards."

As she spoke, slow relief eased into my heart. One small muscle at a time, my distrust began to let me go. She didn't plead for him personally. My nerves were sure. Instead she pleaded for her reality. In her world killers were people she didn't know and couldn't understand, men and women driven by demons that her mind refused to acknowledge.

A different heat rose along my pulse.

Of course, I ached to believe that she was exactly and only what she seemed. I couldn't hide that detail from myself. It affected my own reality. As a general rule, however, crooks who needed to protect their accomplices didn't try to convince me that other potential suspects were innocent.

But I still had to be careful. Distrusting her was one thing. Distrusting myself was entirely another. Quietly I asked, "Did you say any of this to that cop, Detective Moy?"

Deborah frowned like a wince. "No. He didn't ask. I mean, his questions weren't that specific. And I didn't think of it. I was so shocked by what had happened—

"Is it important?" she demanded. "Do you *actually*—?"

I gave her a thin smile. "Relax. It's my job to be suspicious." Gripping my towel, I shrugged awkwardly. I hadn't pursued all this with her because I distrusted Anson Sternway. "I've known too many people with blood on their hands."

I was one of them.

"The fact is," I continued more easily, "I like Sternway as a suspect. He pisses me off every time I see him. But murder isn't just means and opportunity. It's also motive. And for the life of me I can't imagine why he'd want Bernie dead."

Even the bizarre fact that Ginny had found Hardshorn's bag in Mai Sternway's house didn't shed any light. Ginny believed Mai wanted to frame her husband so that she could extort a fat divorce settlement. If Sternway went into that men's room to protect Hardshorn, he was cooperating in his own financial castration.

"I'll tell Moy what you've said the next time I talk to him," I added. "He'll follow up on it if he thinks it matters. Until then—" I gestured hopefully with my coffee cup. "You've answered my question. I'm done."

All at once she raised her glass to her mouth and drained it. The Scotch brought tears to her eyes, made her breathe open-mouthed as if she'd swallowed a lump of fire.

The rain sounded like scrubbing outside her windows, a storm to scourge away every doubt I had.

Dropping her glass on the carpet, she wiped her eyes with the backs of her hands. When she could take a normal breath again, she lifted a tentative smile toward my face. "Well, if you're really *done*—"

I did my best to grin for her. "With questions, yes. Absolutely."

For the second time, she jumped at me. I caught her in both arms, forgetting all about the towel.

We kissed like we were trying to drink each other down. And after that I forgot about any number of things.

24

I didn't go to sleep. I was determined not to. Stretched out and deeply comfortable on Deborah's bed with my arms around her, I didn't want the night to end. I'd arrived at a place of peace that simultaneously soothed me and left me hungry for more. The ceaseless rain outside and the thunder bombarding the city like an exchange of Howitzer shells seemed to make staying where I was the most desirable thing in the world.

But I must've drifted off without knowing it. And my dreams must've disturbed me, gnawing like beasts at the marrow of my bones. Otherwise I wouldn't have gasped and fallen out of bed when the phone rang.

For a moment I couldn't get my bearings. Where was I exactly? And whose phone was that? It didn't sound right—at once too distant and too piercing to mean anything except disaster.

Deborah didn't stir. Her nerves weren't attuned to intimations of ruin—

Lightning drove back the dark. I sprawled on the carpet in an unfamiliar bedroom, craning my neck toward an open doorway.

The phone rang again. The sound didn't come from anywhere around me. The phone wasn't in the bedroom.

The living room? The kitchen?

When it rang for the third time, I recognized it.

My cell phone. Which I'd left in Deborah's small foyer.

How long would it ring before it switched to voice mail? I didn't know, so I jumped to my feet and ran, waving my arms blindly to fend off obstacles, collisions. Remnants of dreams confused my steps, hounding me like nightmares.

Somehow I located a light switch on the fourth ring. Snatching up the phone, I thumbed the button to accept the call and panted, "Yes. Hello?"

"Axbrewder?" a man's voice demanded. "It's about damn time."

I didn't recognize the voice, but it dug into me, gouging too deep for such a small sound.

"What—?" I stammered, floundering. "Who—?"

"You're in serious trouble, boy. You better get your ass on down here, and I mean right now."

The voice— "Moy?" I asked. "Detective Moy?"

"You were expecting maybe your parish priest?" he retorted. "Where the hell *are* you? You're supposed to be working."

Finally his tone worked its way through the scraps of my dreams. Edgar Moy, no question about it. I'd left my phone number on his voice mail. He didn't ordinarily sound this exasperated.

Back in the bedroom, a light snapped on.

"I was asleep," I explained uselessly. "Where are you? What's going on?"

"Martial America." He paused, then added harshly, "There's been a murder."

Abruptly the storm no longer raged outside. It crashed in my head, lashing through my skull like the wrath of the Almighty. Confined thunder knelled at my ears. But I could still hear him.

"The guy who runs *Traditional Wing Chun*. Hong Fei-Tung. Looks like somebody broke his neck in his sleep.

"Isn't security here supposed to be your job?" Moy finished sweetly.

Deborah emerged from the bedroom wearing a robe that would've been sheer in better light.

I dropped to the floor like I'd had my hamstrings severed. "I tried to warn him," I told the phone. But my voice was so small that Moy probably couldn't hear it.

"The way I see it, Axbrewder," he informed me with a touch of his familiar disinterest, "there's a whole shitload of stuff going on here that you haven't told me about."

Hong. *Hong*.

Christ!

I'd tried to warn him, but on some level I'd known that wasn't good enough. I should've protected him myself. But I hadn't trusted my instincts.

"Brew?" Deborah asked. "Brew? My God, what's going on?" She sounded stricken.

I trusted them now. Now that it was too late. I'd have Hong's blood on my hands for the rest of my life.

I swallowed at a knot of grief or fury. As clearly as I could, I announced to Moy, "I'm on my way. I'll get there as fast as I can." As fast as the storm allowed. Then I hung up.

Deborah dropped to her knees beside me. "My God, Brew." She put her hands on the sides of my face, forced me to look at her. "What's wrong? What's happened?"

The cannonade in my head needed to break out somehow, positively required an outlet, but I could hardly form words, nothing that I could ever say would carry enough force to release what I felt. I had to whisper. Otherwise I wouldn't have been able to speak at all. Not without screaming in her face.

"*Sifu* Hong has been murdered."

As soon as I said the words, I knew who did it. Lightning etched the truth out of the tumbled chaos in my head.

And I was responsible. Absolutely. Hong would still be alive if I hadn't talked him into appraising the chops.

It hurt so bad that I almost wailed aloud.

She retreated with a gasp. "Oh, Brew." Horror and tears filled her eyes. "*Sifu* Hong?" Her mouth trembled. "That's terrible."

She didn't ask, How did it happen? She asked, "What're you going to do?"

If I hadn't wasted so much energy doubting her, I might've been able to do something in time.

If I'd trusted myself—

Thunder goaded me to my feet. Every blast and flail of the storm brought more into my head, pieces of the picture like shattered bones and streaming veins. I almost had it *all*, I was close—I still didn't know why. Not exactly.

But I knew exactly what I was going to do about it.

Deborah rose beside me. She wanted an answer. Maybe she needed it. But I wasn't ready. I had to know—

As fast as I could with sheets of rain confusing my fingers, I dialed the number for *Essential Shotokan*.

What time was it? 2:00 in the morning? That felt about right. I didn't have my watch on.

The number rang until I thought it would break my heart. Then Hideo Komatori answered warily, "Yes?" I heard vestiges of sleep in his voice.

"Hideo, it's Brew." I couldn't muffle my fury. It must've sounded like an attack. "Check on the chops."

He recoiled. "Brew-*san*? What do you mean? The chops are safe. We moved the case into my apartment this evening, as you advised. I passed it as I came to the phone."

No! I wanted to scream, the chops aren't fucking *safe*! Somehow I stifled the storm. "Take another look," I insisted. "Please."

A pause. "Very well." The connection conveyed a dull thunk as he put down the handset.

Deborah tried to get my attention. "The *chops*, Brew? I thought you said Hong— Has something happened to them?"

I ignored her. With everything I had, I clung to the phone.

"Brew-*san*?" Komatori's tone had changed utterly. Now he sounded like he was fighting for his life. "They're gone."

Of course.

"The case is intact," he went on. "But it's been opened. All the chops are gone."

Of fucking *course.*

"Brew?" Deborah pleaded.

"Don't ask me any questions," I told Komatori. "I don't have time to explain.

"*Sifu* Hong has been murdered. Detective Moy is already there. I'm on my way, but I won't be able to stop him. It's only a matter of time, minutes, before he comes for Nakahatchi *sensei.*" Naturally. Who else would T'ang Wen accuse? "When Moy hears the chops are gone, he's going to arrest your master."

Because *of course* Moy would assume that Nakahatchi had found the chops gone, believed Hong stole them, and killed Hong to get even. The fact that the case was in Komatori's apartment wouldn't mean anything to Moy. Hideo had already demonstrated that he could sleep through the theft. He could've slept through a visit from his *sensei* as well.

"You *must* explain," Komatori put in. "Can this Detective Moy believe that my master killed *Sifu* Hong? That is insane."

"I don't have *time*!" I shouted back. "Just wake up Nakahatchi. When Moy gets there, tell him about the chops. Don't hide anything. And don't resist. *I* know your master didn't do it. I'll clear him as soon as I can. Right now I have to *go*!"

Before he could object, I hung up.

Deborah stared at me wide-eyed. As I lowered the phone, she

breathed, "The chops are gone." She looked smaller, diminished by the sheer scale of the disaster. "Oh, God."

"Listen to me," I demanded. As if I thought maybe she wouldn't. "I have to get to Martial America. I don't have time to talk, and I do not have time to explain.

"I need directions. And I need you to make some calls for me. I can't stay to make them myself, and once I'm outside I won't be able to hear myself think."

"I have to call Sammy," she offered in a small voice.

"Do that last," I ordered. Knowing Posten, he'd reach Martial America before I did. He'd teleport if he had to. If he weren't already there. "First call Marshal Viviter. Professional Investigations. Tell him what's happened. I have his cell phone number."

I recited it like I expected her to memorize it on the fly.

She nodded gravely. Either she didn't have any trouble remembering phone numbers, or she wasn't listening at all.

"Then call Ginny Fistoulari. My former partner." I repeated her cellular number. "Tell her not to answer the apartment phone tonight. *Not.* Tell her to let the machine get it."

Our answering machine was one of the old-fashioned tape models. Once it started to record, it would keep going until the caller hung up. Or until it ran out of tape.

Deborah nodded again. I had the sensation that I'd lost her, but I couldn't afford to stop.

"Then call Parker Neill." I gave her a third number to remember. "Tell him what's happened. Tell him I need him at Martial America. As fast as he can get there."

I needed him to keep me alive.

Once more she nodded.

I had to trust her. Shoving myself into motion, I headed for the dryer and my clothes. "Do all that," I told her, "*after* you give me directions."

"What are you going to do?" she called after me. "Brew, I need to know."

She deserved an answer.

"My *job*," I snapped as I hauled open the laundry closet. "My fucking job! Hong is dead because I didn't figure this out. The chops are gone because I didn't figure it out.

"It ends *tonight*."

She caught up with me, pulled the rest of my clothes out of the dryer while I shoved my legs into my pants. Without looking at me, she asked, "*Have* you figured it out?"

"Yes." I buttoned my shirt partway. I didn't even think about tucking the tails in. "Or else I dreamed it. But I can't explain it yet. I don't understand all of it."

I meant that I didn't have even one scrap of evidence to make it credible.

I definitely needed Parker to keep me alive.

Carrying my jacket, I hurried back to the foyer. My shoes were still damp, and I couldn't untie the laces. Deborah tackled them for me while I shoved my arms into the shoulder holster, spun the cylinder of the .45. While she helped me into my shoes, I pulled the jacket on.

I already had the door open when she started to give me directions.

Right out of the parking garage, right again, count three blocks, turn left, keep going to the freeway. Head east. She named an exit. If I didn't miss it, or turn in the wrong direction, I'd be on a road that led straight to Martial America.

I'd almost reached the elevator before I heard her say, "Keep yourself safe, Brew. I want you back."

God, I hoped she could remember phone numbers.

While the elevator sank interminably toward the parking level, I keyed my apartment phone number into one of the cell phone's speed-dial locations. Then I searched the phone's menus until I found the command to silence the keypad.

Rainwater leaked into the car as soon as it reached bottom. The water was colder than ever, and without socks I lacked even the illusion of protection. But the sodden chill only tightened my nerves, sharpened my concentration.

Through the deepening lake of the garage, I splashed my way to the Plymouth.

The van started with a roar because I'd already shoved down on the gas too hard. Wheeling backward out of my parking space, I pointed the van at the exit ramp and plowed like a battering ram up into the storm.

A battering ram way too small for the gate it aimed to shatter.

Right through the cudgeling torrents. *Right again* almost immediately.

From the bottom of my heart, I prayed that Deborah would do what I'd asked. That Parker and Ginny would come through for me.

Count three blocks wasn't easy. I gave it my best guess, then hauled the Plymouth left into the wrong lane of a street that appeared to be my only option.

I couldn't see buildings or street signs except at unpredictable intervals when lightning cracked open the night. Most of the time I could barely locate curbs.

Keep going to the freeway.

I wasn't worried that Moy would finish in Martial America and leave before I got there. He needed backup, his lab boys, an ambulance—and all of them faced the same obstacles I did. And Nakahatchi lived right there. He and Komatori both had too much self-possession to do anything stupid. His arrest might go down as one of the most leisurely collars in history. Hell, if I were Edgar Moy I might just keep Nakahatchi confined to his apartment until the storm let up.

The deluge had wiped out the world, smothered any sensation that I was actually going somewhere. The speedometer indicated more speed than sanity, but the impregnable rain contradicted it.

I'd started to believe that the freeway didn't exist, that the whole concept of freeways was mythological, when a ragged glare exposed massive concrete supports with a louring darkness above them. The after-flash on my retinas left the image of a sign that said *east*.

In that direction another ramp opened onto a wider surface than the ones I'd driven so far.

At intervals the windscreen fogged over. The Plymouth's vents blew cold into my face, but when I added even a touch of heat the condensation thickened. I had to accept the chill.

Pushing the speedometer higher—ludicrously, moronically higher—I resumed my prayers.

As I saw it, my biggest problem was to keep the cell phone dry. I meant, my biggest problem apart from extracting all the information and evidence I needed. And staying alive— If the phone shorted out, I might as well just shoot myself in the head and go home.

I tried to test it by calling a number at random, but I couldn't hear anything. The sledgehammering rain covered everything. I felt like the inside of a gong.

Since my life depended on my driving anyway, and I was already going at a berserk rate, I wedged off my shoes, picked them up, and set them upside down on the passenger seat to drain.

In the real world, however—the sane world—my *biggest* problem was finding the right exit off the freeway.

Somehow I did it. Pure luck. So far, the gods of storm and violence were on my side. Approximating caution, I gushed down off the freeway and headed for Martial America.

Hong Fei-Tung was dead.

Looks like somebody broke his neck in his sleep.

How fucking likely was *that*?

Rain lashed at me from all sides. Between splitting bursts of lightning, thunder boomed like denunciation.

As I finally shouldered the Plymouth into Martial America's parking lot, my headlights picked out way too many cars. CPD cruisers I expected, four or five of them, lights winking frenetically against the dark. An ambulance. A Crime Lab van. But where had all these other cars come from? I'd never seen the lot this full.

My stomach squirmed. Bile crowded against the anger and sorrow in my throat. I'd taken too long to get here. The disaster had already expanded into new dimensions, grown to proportions I hadn't anticipated. Someone had kicked over something a whole lot worse than an anthill.

Sweet Jesus, just let one of these cars belong to Parker.

Through the blurring downpour, I saw that *Essential Shotokan* had all its lights on—with the exception of the top floor. The same was true in Master Soon's *Tae Kwon Do Academy*. The bulk of the building hid *Traditional Wing Chun*.

But *Malaysian Fighting Arts* remained completely dark. Apparently Bob Gravel and his students had more sense.

Swearing to myself, I searched the parking lot until I found a space near the intersection of the two buildings. After that I didn't hesitate. I'd used about a decade's worth of spare time just getting here. Now I had to go or give up.

Retrieving my shoes, I tucked the cell phone into one of them and clamped them against my chest, heels up, soles out. That was the best I could do. With my free hand, I flung open the door and plunged barefoot into the torrents.

At least the lot didn't hold water. The rain rivered elsewhere as soon as it fell. On the other hand, the concrete felt cruel on my unprotected feet, bitter as ice. Already drenched, I jogged for the entrance to *Essential Shotokan*.

Maybe I should've headed for *Traditional Wing Chun*. The lab boys were probably still there. I might get a look at Hong's bedroom—and even his body before they carted it away. If they let me in. But Moy had had plenty of time to finish there.

Heaving the ornamental door open, I lunged into Nakahatchi's *dojo*.

The sudden cessation of the rain nearly knocked me off balance. I hadn't realized how hard I'd braced myself against it. The comparative warmth of the entryhall stung my skin to gooseflesh. I was soaked to the marrow of my bones.

"Hold it!" a CPD uniform barked. He guarded the foot of the stairs with his partner, a woman who would've looked slim without the bulletproof vest and all that cop gear. "No farther!"

I lurched to a halt, sluicing water in all directions.

"This is a crime scene," the man announced. "You shouldn't be here. I'd chase you out if it weren't raining so damn hard. What the hell do you think you're doing?"

Apparently Moy hadn't warned his underlings to expect me.

Now I didn't hurry. I didn't need to—I knew why the uniforms were here. When I'd scrubbed the rain out of my eyes, I bent down to place my shoes on the floor.

That gave the uniforms a glimpse of the .45 under my arm.

They both shouted, "Freeze!" Faster than her partner, the woman had her automatic out first. From my angle, it looked like a Glock.

I didn't freeze, but I lifted the .45 out of its holster with two fingers and tossed it to the carpet a few feet away. When I'd taken out the cell phone and set it down, I worked my numb feet back into my shoes.

"My name is Axbrewder," I told the uniforms. "I'm a security consultant for this building. Detective Moy called me here. He wants to talk to me." I tried to smile, but I couldn't do it. "If I promise to be a good boy, can I take off my jacket?"

Slowly they lowered their weapons. "He's upstairs," the man muttered.

I wanted to ask who was with him, but I'd find out soon enough.

Tugging my arms out of the sleeves, I removed my jacket, wrapped it around itself, and twisted it in my fists to wring it out. When it stopped dripping, I draped it on the floor beside the .45. Maybe it would dry enough to keep the phone functional.

"I want everything back," I informed the cops. "I'll need them. I'm on cleanup. When you guys leave, my job starts."

The woman nodded. "They'll be right here."

Her partner shifted aside to let me at the stairs.

Trying not to hold my breath, I went up to the second floor.

The door to the meeting room stood open. Through it I saw Edgar Moy, Komatori, Nakahatchi, and an Oriental woman dressed in a flowing *kimono.* I'd never met her, but she must've been Nakahatchi's wife, Mitsuku. Moy didn't have any backup with him. Apparently he realized that he didn't need any.

Their silence felt like the fatal quiet after a crash of thunder.

The detective occupied the center of the floor. For the first time, his trench coat didn't look out of place. Dark streaks showed that it'd lost some of its waterproofing over the years. His hands held a damp fedora with enough brim to keep most of the rain out of his eyes.

Komatori stood to his left, wearing his full *karate-ka* regalia, a crisp white canvas *gi* cinched with his black belt. Obliquely I wondered if Moy caught the symbolism. It meant that Hideo was willing to go to the wall for his master. Literally. If Nakahatchi told him to fight, he'd feed Moy and every other cop in reach to the guppies. He had that look in his eyes. If Nakahatchi allowed it, he'd take his master's place under arrest.

But Sihan Nakahatchi hadn't allowed it, that was obvious. He had on a dark blue business suit that would've looked dapper if he hadn't worn it with such sorrow. He didn't so much as glance at me when I entered the room. As far as I could tell, he never looked at Moy. Maybe he hadn't even shared a gaze with his wife. He'd withdrawn into himself to face a crisis worse than dying.

Mitsuku comported herself with as much dignity as he did, but she didn't suffer his bereavement or dishonor with the same stoicism. Her lower lip quivered at intervals. Strands of grey hair straggled at her neck. Time had crossed her face with so many vertical lines that it looked pleated. By slow poignant degrees, tears seeped from her eyes into the wrinkles. Small spots displayed her distress on the front of her *kimono*.

"Axbrewder," Moy said by way of greeting. "It's about time."

I thought I heard an uncharacteristic strain in his voice.

Hideo gave me a brief bow. "Brew-*san*, I must thank you." His gaze searched me for something. Help, probably. Or hope.

"But I don't have to," Moy put in before Hideo could explain. "It seems you called them before I got here, warned them I was coming. Later I'm going to tell you exactly what 'interfering with an officer of the law in the performance of his duty' means." In this case it meant that I'd given them a chance to ditch any incriminating evidence. "But right now—" He wasn't just feeling the strain, he was outright uncomfortable. "The four of us have been standing right here ever since I arrived."

His tension enabled me to relax a notch. Faking detachment, I drawled, "What seems to be the problem, Sergeant?"

Moy glared at me. "You mean, apart from grand theft and murder? I'll tell you what the *problem* is"—he bared his teeth under his thin mustache—"because I expect you to fix it."

"If I can," I offered.

He didn't stop. "After that I expect you to explain this whole goddamn mess to me."

I couldn't think of a sensible response, so I kept my mouth shut.

"The problem," he went on more quietly, "is that Sihan Nakahatchi here has been accused of killing Hong Fei-Tung next door, and he won't talk to me. He won't even tell me his damn name. He doesn't say a thing when I read him his rights. I can't find out if he wants a lawyer."

Moy was a cop. He wanted Nakahatchi to at least deny the accusation.

I thought I knew why Nakahatchi wouldn't talk. I'd learned a few things about Oriental manners and honor. But it wasn't my place to answer for him. Turning to Hideo, I asked, "Why haven't you—?"

Komatori shrugged. "What would be the point?"

"The point of what?" Moy demanded.

Nakahatchi studied oblivion. His wife's eyes clung to me like desperation.

I faced Hideo's shrouded distress squarely. "You have to say it. The Sergeant may understand, or he may not. But he can't understand if you don't say it."

Komatori considered for a moment. Anger seethed behind his self-containment. Then he relented with a sigh.

Turning to Moy, he said, "Sergeant, my master is Sihan Nakahatchi *sensei*. Therefore the accusation is absurd. To answer such a mortal insult is to tolerate it"—his voice rose—"and we won't tolerate it. We won't 'account for our movements.' We won't give you 'alibis.' He is Sihan Nakahatchi *sensei*. That's sufficient."

Nakahatchi himself wouldn't even say that much.

"No," Moy began, "it's not." But I interrupted him.

"Sergeant." Deliberately I let my outrage uncoil like the thong of a whip. "You don't need to talk to them anyway." He wasn't my enemy. Under the surface, we were on the same side. But I had to get his attention. "You need to talk to *me*.

"I'm security here." The fact that I'd done a lousy job was beside the point. "Grand theft and murder are my department, not theirs. If you want to understand *honor* the way they do, ask them nicely." Without realizing it I'd clenched my hands into fists like a death grip. "But if you want to understand what happened here"—I forced my fingers open—"ask me."

Unfortunately I couldn't offer him evidence.

"If I were you," I added before he had a chance to reply, "I wouldn't even arrest Nakahatchi *sensei*. You don't need to. He'll be here whenever you want him."

Some of the streaks on Mitsuku's face looked like gratitude. As far as I could tell, her husband hadn't heard me.

For a long moment, Moy stared at me like he was trying to guess how much of my mind I'd actually lost. Then, slowly, he shook his head. "You know I can't do that." A heartbeat later he announced, "But *you* are most definitely going to talk to me."

"Sure." I let a bit of my anger go. "But let's take it downstairs."

I meant, Let's spare Nakahatchi and his wife the indignity of listening to us. Moy accepted the suggestion for a different reason, however. He didn't want *Essential Shotokan*'s people to hear anything that might help them invent an alibi.

Hideo let me see the raw, bleak questions in his eyes. I wanted to reassure him, but I couldn't. Not without facts. The truth was that I didn't really have anything to tell Moy. I just wanted to get him alone. Maybe then he'd share what he had so far.

Despite the detective's impatience, I took the time to bow to Nakahatchi. He surprised me by bowing back.

Shaken by his response, I blurted out, "*Sensei*, I'll deal with this." Somehow. "I know I'm not ready to be your student. But I can do my job. This insult won't stand."

Nakahatchi said nothing. He'd already returned to his contemplation of distances and depths I couldn't see. But Mitsuku offered me a wan troubled smile and bowed deeply.

I replied awkwardly, then bowed to Komatori and turned away.

Together Moy and I trudged down the stairs. My shirt stuck to my arms and torso. The damp fabric rubbed at my armpits. My pants felt like a cold second skin. Soon I'd start shivering again.

Moy nodded to the uniforms, sent the woman upstairs to keep an eye on Nakahatchi, then led me into the smaller *dojo*, the one with all the training equipment. I left the .45, the phone, and my jacket where they were.

He confronted me in the middle of the floor. "Not exactly impartial about this, are you, Axbrewder?" He'd lost his usual disinterest. "You need to be careful here. You're looking more and more like an accessory."

"I can see that." I didn't waste time denying the obvious. "But for the record, I didn't call Komatori to warn him you were coming. That was an afterthought. When you told me Hong was dead, I wanted to know if the chops were safe."

My wet shoes clamped a chill around my feet. The leather stuck to my skin.

"Alex Lacone didn't hire me to bodyguard anyone," I explained. "Men like Hong are better qualified to take care of themselves than I am. My job is the chops. When you called, my first reaction was the same as yours. Why would anyone risk tackling a trained killer like Hong? Whoever did it must've had a powerful motive.

"I don't know anything about Hong's personal life. Maybe he's got enemies. From what I've heard, he imports his relatives into this country as fast as he can. Maybe one of them offended some Hong Kong triad, or a Chinese Tong." This was all chaff, but I threw it in Moy's eyes with both hands. "I wouldn't know.

"But here, in Martial America, those chops are the only motive I can imagine. I called Komatori because I had to know if they were safe."

Shivers started in my legs. My knees shook. I locked them to try to hold them steady, but it didn't work.

"Since they aren't—" I finished lamely.

"That's not what I heard." Moy sounded calmer. Maybe he thought my obfuscation meant that I was being cooperative.

I frowned. "What did you hear?"

Why had T'ang Wen accused Nakahatchi?

"When we got the call," Moy told me, "the only other person over there was Hong's head student, T'ang Wen. According to him, he heard something during the night. He was worried about his master—he says *you* warned him his master was in danger—so he went to the other apartment, knocked a few times. When his master didn't answer, he used a spare key to let himself in."

"Just a minute." I needed details. "The apartments had different keys?"

I didn't want the detective to ask me why I'd warned T'ang.

"According to T'ang," Moy answered.

"Does either one of them open the *dojo*?"

"T'ang's does. Hong was the only one with a separate key for his apartment."

I nodded. That complicated the killer's situation.

Lightning glared through the windows. God's kettledrums pounded hard enough to rattle the glass.

"Go on."

With one finger, Moy stroked both sides of his mustache thoughtfully. Considering the question of access? Wondering why I thought keys were important? Then he shrugged to himself.

"T'ang found Hong dead in his bed. It didn't take a forensics expert to know he had a broken neck. T'ang called us. He said he didn't touch or move anything."

Tremors climbed into my belly. In another minute my voice would shake.

"If the door was locked, how did the killer get in?"

Moy let disgust twist his mouth. "Bedroom window."

A *window*. Oh, shit. That possibility had never occurred to me. Carner lived on AC. I'd assumed that no one here ever left a window open on purpose.

"It was open," Moy explained. "T'ang says Hong always slept with it open. He liked the night air.

"We've already been up on the roof. Not that we can see shit in this storm. But one of the utility grates sure looks scratched. And we found fifty yards of rope tied to a grappling hook out in the Dumpster. Ordinary towing rope, the kind you can buy in about a hundred hardware stores."

"Spell it out for me." I didn't need the help, but I wanted to keep him talking. "What do you think happened?"

Moy rolled his eyes. "Nakahatchi heard a noise and went to check on the chops. When he saw they were gone, he figured Hong took them. He went out the fire exit to the utility shaft, climbed up to the roof, hooked the grapple onto a grate and shimmied down to Hong's window. When he'd killed Hong, he went back up the rope, took his rope and grapple out to the Dumpster, and let himself back into *Essential Shotokan*."

"Isn't that kind of stupid?" I asked dishonestly. "Leaving the rope and grapple where you're sure to find them?" I already knew why they'd been disposed of so obviously.

Torrents blinded the windows. The parking lot might as well have existed in a different dimension. Full of cars like I'd never seen it before—

"There's no IQ test for killers," the detective retorted. "Nakahatchi may be a moron. God knows he acts like one."

"Bullshit." I couldn't stifle the shivers in my chest. My voice shook like I was feverish. "I've spent too much time around him. I know better."

He hadn't had any difficulty finding my weaknesses.

"Maybe," Moy countered, "he didn't have time to ditch the rope anywhere else. Not in this storm. He couldn't risk being gone when Hong's body was discovered. Hell, maybe he was still in Hong's apartment when T'ang Wen knocked. He had to hurry."

I conceded the point. What choice did I have? Instead of arguing, I threw more chaff.

"That doesn't explain why you considered Nakahatchi a suspect in the first place." I sounded the way I felt, chilled to the bone. "Unless T'ang already knew the chops were gone when he talked to you—"

I didn't believe that for a second. Hong hadn't stolen the chops. And T'ang Wen would never have left his master open to that kind of suspicion.

"He didn't," Moy stated flatly. "He didn't mention the chops at all. In fact, he doesn't know they're gone." He stared at me hard. "Unless somebody called him after I came over here." Like me, for instance. But Moy didn't pursue the question. "I asked him if Hong had any enemies. He named Nakahatchi. But he was reluctant about it. He kept insisting that Nakahatchi behaved honorably toward his master as recently as yesterday."

"He must've given you some kind of reason," I countered.

Moy nodded. "He said the Japanese are hostile toward all things Chinese. Especially the martial arts. He claimed it's traditional, almost hereditary." The detective paused briefly, then added, "And he's sure Nakahatchi was jealous of Hong."

I let my jaw drop. "Jealous—?"

"Hong had more students. And Nakahatchi had to recognize Hong was a better martial artist. It's obvious to everybody."

I got the impression that Moy wasn't impressed.

"Says T'ang," I insisted.

"Says T'ang," he admitted.

"Well," I went on, "he's right about the traditional hostility." Tremors gave my tone a cutting edge. "But the part he didn't tell you is that it works both ways. The Japanese and the Chinese and the Koreans all distrust each other. Soft styles and hard styles sneer at each other. Traditional styles think modern styles are junk. Modern styles think traditional ones are ossified. Martial America is a hotbed of ingrained suspicion. Everyone here wants precedence.

"That Tae Kwon Do school next door is one of the worst." More chaff. "They don't think Nakahatchi *deserves* the chops. They give him too much 'face.'

"And speaking of 'face,' " I continued, hurrying so that Moy wouldn't notice my efforts to distract him, "who do you think inherits *Traditional Wing Chun* now? The head student, T'ang Wen. With his master out of the way, he stands to gain major 'face' if Hong was murdered by a Japanese *sensei*."

That was cruelly unfair to T'ang. He esteemed his master too highly to be selfish about it. But I ached to deflect Moy from Nakahatchi. That was crucial. I couldn't tell Moy the truth. If I did, he'd have only two choices, a cop's choices—believe me and get in my way, or doubt me and take me in as an accessory. Somehow I needed to make him question his assumptions about Nakahatchi without turning him in the right direction. Otherwise I'd never be able to extract the evidence I needed.

Moy held up his hands, urging me to slow down. "Are you trying to tell me T'ang Wen had a reason to kill his master? He took the chops to throw suspicion on Nakahatchi, then killed Hong so he could take over the school?"

I shook my head. I couldn't go that far. Not even to protect Nakahatchi—or myself. Shivering in gusts, I admitted, "I think T'ang is a decent guy. But maybe he's figured out that he could be the big winner here. If Nakahatchi goes down, the only rival T'ang has left in Martial America is Master Soon."

For a moment, Moy looked out into the storm as if he hoped all that rain and violence would help him think. Frantically I rubbed my hands up and down my arms, chafing my skin in an effort to generate some warmth. If I couldn't stop shivering, my brain might start to rattle in my skull. Then I wouldn't be able to put one coherent idea in front of another.

But I was too angry to let that happen. I'd pick a fight with the wall, batter my blood back into circulation, before I allowed myself to fall apart now.

When Moy faced me again, he changed directions. "Speaking of keys, Axbrewder," he asked in the bored tone I remembered, "how do you get around in the building?"

Shit! He was still interested in me as an accessory.

I met his gaze as innocently as I could. "I have a master."

"Where did you get it?"

"Lacone." Indirectly that was true.

"And it opens all the doors here?"

I didn't look away. "It opens all the locks that haven't been changed since these schools moved in. If T'ang's key works on the front door to the *dojo*, mine unlocks his apartment. But Hong had a new lock installed. My key won't open it."

Moy held my eyes for another moment. Then he smiled thinly. "Try to relax. At this rate you'll shiver yourself sick."

Relax? He had no idea. Roughly I slapped at my chest, trying to sting in a little warmth. "Are we done here?" I did not want him to ask me anything else. "I should get over to *Traditional Wing Chun*." The people who'd driven all those cars to Martial America had to be *some*where. "I know you've covered it, but if I don't at least take a look I won't be doing my job."

"Just a couple more things." His eyes told me that he still wondered about my involvement. "T'ang said—"

A loud whoosh as the front door burst open interrupted him. We both wheeled in that direction.

Driven by a rush of rain, a short figure wrapped in a raincoat splashed into the *dojo*. At first I couldn't see who he was. An umbrella concealed his head. Right away, however, he dropped the umbrella so that he could pull the door shut.

I'd never have thought that I'd be grateful to see Sammy Posten. Maybe he'd distract Moy for me.

"Hold it right there," the uniform guarding the stairs ordered. "You can't come in here. This is a crime scene—"

Posten ignored the warning. The instant he spotted Moy and me, he stomped toward us. But he wasn't interested in the detective. As soon as he got close enough, he hit me in the chest with both hands. Like he thought he could knock me backward.

"Goddamn it, Axbrewder!" he shouted up at me, "this is unforgivable!" His face reminded me of a perforated ulcer. "You call yourself a 'security consultant'? *Where were you*? Probably out fucking some whore, you incompetent sonofabitch!"

Moy put a hand on Posten's shoulder to intervene. "Take it easy. We're investigating every possibility. We'll find—"

The little man flung him off.

"Let me tell you something!" he practically screamed at me. "We won't pay for this! Not a penny. It's your fault, *your fault*, and I am personally going to take it out of your hide." His raincoat shed water like froth. "You're going to make restitution if you have to sell your soul for the money!"

"Sarge?" the uniform asked from the doorway. "You want help?"

Moy smiled again, without enthusiasm. "No, thanks. I think Axbrewder and I can handle it." Now he sounded bored. Normal. "If nothing else works, we'll sit on him."

The uniform chuckled harshly and returned to his post.

"Sergeant Moy." If I hadn't been so angry, I might've laughed in Posten's face. "This is Mr. Sammy Posten. He's a security advisor—a *senior* security advisor—for Watchdog Insurance. They hold coverage on the chops.

"Mr. Posten, this is Sergeant Edgar Moy, Homicide."

"I know, I know." Posten gave us his best imitation of a dismissive snarl. "Hong is dead. I don't care about that.

"Axbrewder, if you don't—"

Since he'd already hit me, I gave him a jolt of my own. It turned his face the color of apoplexy. "Tell you what, Mr. Posten." I let shivers carry my rage. "I'll make a deal with you. You go home. Let the Sergeant do his job. You can't accomplish anything right now anyway. And I'll take my chances with my soul." I grinned like the blade of an ax. "I've been in that position before."

Posten started to sputter a retort, but Moy stepped in front of him. Posten wasn't tall enough to fume at me past him. He was reduced to sputtering like a sodden chicken.

"Mr. Axbrewder is right, Mr. Posten," the detective said flatly. "You should go home. But there's one question you can answer for me first. How did you know there'd been a crime?"

"My associate called me," Posten huffed. "Deborah Messenger. She said she heard it from Axbrewder." He tried to aim his indignation at me past Moy's shoulder. "Ask him how he knew."

"He knew because I told him." Now Moy had a grip on Posten's elbow. It didn't look hard, but his fingers dug in enough to turn Posten toward the front door. "I assume he called Ms. Messenger because of Watchdog's involvement."

Sure. That's why I told her. Because of her—

—involvement—

"Just a minute," I demanded. Lightning echoed the glare of intuition in my head. Thunder spread its impact over the city.

Moy paused.

"Deborah called you," I said to Posten. "Who did *you* call?"

Who had he involved?

He was too sure of his righteousness to squirm. "People who need to know," he snapped. "Our offices. Mr. Lacone. Sue Rasmussen." He did his best to sneer. "Unlike you, I do my job."

Oh, joy. Now I knew why there were so many cars in the parking lot. I wasn't the only one who understood obfuscation.

I'd lost whatever advantage I might get from surprise.

Moy hadn't told the uniform he'd sent upstairs to keep Hideo Komatori there, and I thought I knew exactly what Komatori would do. Unless Nakahatchi stopped him—

In the entryway Moy released Posten. Mildly he instructed the uniform to make sure that Mr. Posten reached his car safely. Then he walked back in my direction.

He had to let me go. Before Komatori did something I'd regret. Unfortunately the look in his eyes told me he wasn't ready to do that. He didn't trust me yet.

"Posten raises an interesting point, Axbrewder," he commented with all the excitement he might've shown for a case of athlete's foot. "Where *were* you when I called?"

Did *I* have an alibi?

The deluge outside sounded like the end of the world. Tremors ran through me from head to foot. I bit down on them in an effort to control my voice.

"I was with a friend. A woman. I'll tell you her name if I have to. But she isn't part of this." I was sure now. "I think her privacy deserves some respect."

Moy studied me for a moment, obviously trying to decide how much leeway he could afford to give me. When he spoke, he didn't ask for Deborah's name. Instead he said, "Tell me something else first. Where did you get that phone number you left on my voice mail?"

Damn him, he had to let me *go*. I didn't have much time.

Practically dancing from foot to foot, I replied, "I can't answer that. Client confidentiality."

Literally, of course, Mal Sternway was none of my business. Nevertheless Marshal had given me more help than I had any right to expect. I owed him a little discretion.

"Axbrewder—" The sheer disinterest in Moy's tone warned me that I was losing ground.

I blundered ahead. "But you can ask Marshal Viviter. Professional Investigations. It's his client. What he tells you is up to him."

Moy took a look at his fingernails. They bored him, too. "I'll do that. But he isn't here." He meant, Viviter isn't the one in trouble. You are. "And all of a sudden you don't want to give me a straight answer." He frowned up at me. "I'll offer you one more chance.

"T'ang Wen says you warned him Hong was in danger. What the hell was that about?"

Christ! The one question I absolutely did not want to answer. If I did, Moy wouldn't have any choice. He'd have to get in my way.

"It was a hunch, Sergeant." I wanted to shout, Let me go! I'll explain everything when I've got some *evidence.* "That's all. A bad feeling in the pit of my stomach.

"I swear to God"—I forced all the conviction it would hold into my voice—"if I'd known what might happen, I would've spent the whole fucking night with him myself."

Moy peered at me like he would a particularly distasteful lab specimen. "As hunches go," he asked slowly, "how does this one compare with your theory that Hardshorn didn't kill Appelwait?"

I nearly cracked. The violence of the storm centered here, in me. Thunder broke against the windows like blows. I started yelling because I feared that if I didn't I might hit him.

"You don't get it, do you? I *know* Hardshorn didn't kill Bernie! I *knew* it last night. If I'd been even five percent that sure about Hong, *we wouldn't be standing here.* I'd have *shot* the bastard who did this before I let him get away."

Or he would've killed me, too.

He still might. If Moy ever released me.

The uniform reappeared in the entryway. He had his hand on his weapon. "Sarge?"

Moy made a placating gesture. For the uniform or for me, I couldn't tell which.

"All right, Axbrewder. Take it easy. You'll work yourself into a seizure. I believe you.

"I get hunches myself." I thought I saw calculation in his smile. Or malice. "I'll cut you loose. You can go."

Maybe he wanted me to leave so that I'd crucify myself.

I could scarcely breathe. Instead of thanking him, I headed for the entryway. When I'd retrieved the phone, the .45, and my jacket, I went back into the small *dojo.* That was my quickest route to the fire exit.

As I passed him, Moy cleared his throat.

"In case you're still interested. That phone number. It's Hardshorn's home number. He may not have had any friends, but he sure made a lot of calls."

That stopped me momentarily. Like Marshal and Deborah and quite a few other people—Ginny included—Moy was treating me better than I deserved. Better than I'd treated him.

"Thanks, Sergeant," I said with a hoarse shiver. "I'll remember you in my will."

Part of me itched to take him along. To keep me alive. And repay his trust. But if I did I'd never get the proof I needed.

From the back of the *dojo* I crossed the dressing room to the fire door and punched it open with the heel of my palm.

25

The fire door let me out onto the ground floor of the building's utility well. Wet and damn near frozen as I was, entering the well felt like walking face first into a space heater. The boiler, furnace, and AC units put out enough BTUs to liquefy Styrofoam.

I went straight to the equipment cage, spread out my arms, and pressed my shivering against the grate. I couldn't afford the time to hang there like a heat sink, soaking warmth while my clothes dried. Nevertheless I stayed motionless for twenty or thirty seconds—long enough to restore blood to at least some of my muscles.

Duct and conduit insulation gave the air a faint sulfurous tinge I hadn't noticed the other day. Floodlamps in the walls filled the well with a glaring shadowless artificial illumination. The whole place resembled the atrium of an inferno.

Fortunately it was quieter than I'd expected. Or feared. Despite the thrashing fury outside, only a muffled sibilance penetrated the well. The skylights overhead must've been just about bulletproof.

As soon as I could move without quivering, I shoved the .45 back into its damp holster, hid the cell phone in a jacket pocket, and tugged the jacket up my arms. I wasn't much concerned with concealing the .45, but I needed to keep my phone hidden and accessible without risking it in my sodden pants.

Wrestling out my keys, I hurried around the equipment cage to *Traditional Wing Chun*'s fire door. If I got in there before the lab boys, paramedics, and uniforms left, I might be able to prevent this disaster from getting any worse.

My key released the lock. I pulled open the door and went in.

The dressing room was dark. Likewise the small *dojo* beyond it. But enough light leaked in from the entryway to let me see where I put my feet. In any case, I didn't need light to hear that I was already too late. Again.

The confusion of angry voices sounded like thirty or forty people primed to tear each other's throats out. A hell of a crowd must've gathered in the main *dojo*. The consequences of Hong's death multiplied faster than I could imagine them.

Trying not to run, I crossed the dressing room and the *dojo* to the entryway.

Ahead of me the front door swung open, letting a slash of rain carry a man and a woman inside. They wore canvas *gis* with their belts—purple and brown respectively—cinched tight. Neither of them paid any attention to me. Tossing their umbrellas to the carpet, they hurried into the main *dojo*.

I followed on their heels.

Instead of thirty or more people, I saw only twenty or so. Maybe half of them wore street clothes. Three or four still had on raincoats. The rest had donned their martial uniforms—silk pajamas, canvas *gis*. I was tall enough to see over most of them.

They crowded around a clear space in the middle of the floor, shouting furiously at each other. The *gis* were mostly to my right, opposite the pajamas. I didn't know any of the pajamas, or the men and women in street clothes. Among the *gis*, however, I recognized one of Nakahatchi's students, Aronson, and the two kids who'd helped him and Komatori move the display case to Martial America.

Words like "murder" and "revenge," "unforgivable," and "stolen" raged back and forth, but I didn't try to sort them out.

In the center of the crowd stood Hideo Komatori and T'ang Wen. Hideo's wet *gi* dripped on the hardwood. Water cast a sheen along his scar. He must've taken the fire escape route out of *Essential Shotokan*, then run through the rain unprotected to *Traditional Wing Chun*. Unlike their supporters, he and T'ang didn't yell. It wasn't necessary. They faced each other with the deceptive menace of martial artists, self-contained and calm, ready to detonate. From where I stood, I couldn't see T'ang's face, but Komatori's eyes held a killing intensity that made my guts ache.

I couldn't locate Parker Neill.

His absence hit me like a club. I'd been hoping fervently that he'd arrived ahead of me. That Deborah had reached him, and he'd agreed to do what I asked.

Without him—

Oh, fuck.

Then some of the shouts penetrated my alarm. *Stolen*? Moy had told me that T'ang Wen didn't know the chops were gone. What in God's name was Hideo doing? Had he come over here to accuse Hong of *stealing*—?

Using my bulk, I plowed through the crowd into the clear space around Komatori and T'ang. My presence struck the *dojo* silent, at least for a moment. Suddenly all the hostility in the room refocused on me. When Komatori and T'ang noticed me, I stepped between them.

Quietly I demanded, "What the hell's the matter with you two?" If I kept my voice down, the crowd might stay quiet to hear me. "You don't think we already have enough trouble? Now you want your students to beat each other up?"

Hideo didn't hesitate. "Brew-*san*, this affront to my master is intolerable. You know that I can't—"

"No!" T'ang put in hotly. "*My* master has been *slain*! I did not insult that Japanese. I said to the police only what I know to be true, that I can think of no one else who might wish my master ill. Yet he comes here to accuse *my master* of the theft of the chops. It is indeed intolerable, and we will not suffer it!"

"He lies, Brew-*san*," Komatori retorted. "I haven't mentioned the chops. I haven't accused *Sifu* Hong in any way. I came because I won't endure the claim that my master has any desire for *Sifu* Hong's death. My master's esteem for *Sifu* Hong is boundless. His death is an affront to all martial artists. I *will not* allow it to be placed on my master's shoulders."

I believed him. Hell, I believed both of them.

But if Hideo hadn't said anything about the chops—

"He's right, Axbrewder," a hard voice put in. "It *is* an affront to all martial artists. But who else took the chops? Who else wanted them as badly as Hong did? And if you don't think Nakahatchi killed him, tell us who did. Who else had a reason?"

Turning sharply, I faced Anson Sternway. He stood with his back to the windows like he'd just materialized out of the storm.

Reflected lightning strobed behind him, emphasizing him against the dark glass.

He wore virtually the same clothes he'd had on last night, a grey sweatshirt and warmup pants over canvas deck shoes.

Between one heartbeat and the next, my pulse rate about tripled. Maybe he'd been there all along. Somehow I hadn't spotted him. Too busy praying that Parker would show up, probably.

"Mr. Sternway," I gritted through my teeth. "What the fuck are you doing? This'll be great for Martial America's reputation. Just great. I need help here. You're stirring these people up. We should be calming them down."

He shook his head. "No, Axbrewder. You don't understand." His lack of inflection was the viscid surface of a pool of acid. "This has to be resolved. If it isn't, it will tear Martial America apart. They're approaching it the traditional way, the only way it *can* be resolved. A challenge between schools. Both Komatori-*san* and Mr T'ang are prepared to fight for their masters' honor. Their students are ready to back them up. I suggest you get out of their way."

"Do you mean to tell me," I protested, "that you *buy* this bullshit? You think Hong stole the chops, and Nakahatchi killed him to get even? In case you haven't heard, Hong was killed in his bed. Do you actually believe that Nakahatchi could sneak up on a renowned fighter like Hong Fei-Tung, break his neck in his sleep?"

Never mind the obvious fact that Hong had no known access to *Essential Shotokan.*

Without faltering Sternway countered, "Do you know anything about Ninjitsu?"

I stared at him. He had everyone's attention now. Even Komatori and T'ang shifted in his direction.

"It's an assassin's art," he explained. "It teaches stealth and an imaginative use of weapons. Similar arts have developed in other countries. The Thuggee in India, for example. But no one has ever surpassed Ninjitsu.

"It's a Japanese art."

He shocked me. Nakahatchi? A Ninja? Surrounded by men and women so charged with adrenaline and fear that they could hardly hold themselves back, I could still feel a kind of horrified admiration.

The IAMA director was that confident.

Despite my shock, however, I had to admit that he might be right about one thing. Maybe a fight was the best way to resolve this.

Komatori sure as hell thought so. "Withdraw, Brew-*san*," he told me like the stroke of a blade. "Mr. Sternway indulges in fancies. I don't hear him. I leave the theft of the chops to you. And *Sifu* Hong's murder. You've earned that much respect from me. But the accusation against my master I leave to no one."

"Yes, withdraw," T'ang Wen sneered. "It may be that you have earned honor from this Japanese, but you have dishonored yourself to me. With your own mouth you promised that your presence would protect my master. Now I have seen how your promises are kept. You have no word to speak that I will hear."

Inwardly I cringed. He was right. I'd bought Hong's cooperation with promises I couldn't keep.

And I'd given his killer a reason to take him out.

But I was still *bigger* than Komatori and T'ang. I was bigger than most of their students. And I could yell louder.

"You want me out of your way?" I barked at both of them. "Fine. I'll 'withdraw.' " My voice rose. "On one condition. *No one else fights.* Your students stay out of it. They accept the outcome." In a brawl any number of them would get hurt. With so much martial expertise running loose, someone might be killed. "Otherwise I'll haul the cops in here, have them arrest the whole pack of you."

An empty threat. In this weather I couldn't summon anyone except Edgar Moy and his two uniforms. But that might be enough—

"No!" Aronson shouted immediately. Damn fool. Half the *karate-ka* with him were kids, but he was old enough to know better.

At once T'ang's students roared back. In an instant the whole room erupted with challenges. Pajamas and *gis* and street clothes started for each other.

Sternway watched me nervelessly.

Before I could react, however, Hideo wheeled on his people. His voice rang out with a command I didn't understand.

His students jerked to attention as if he'd cracked a whip in their faces. He had that much moral authority for them.

"You will do as Brew-*san* says." Each word struck with the force of a fist. "You'll watch and do nothing. Otherwise you'll dishonor Nakahatchi *sensei*—and you know I won't allow that."

I wanted to give him a round of applause, but I didn't have time. As soon as he finished, I turned on T'ang Wen.

I didn't speak. I didn't have to. Komatori's example was more eloquent than anything I could've said. I simply glared into T'ang's face until he gave a reluctant nod.

"This Japanese has given me face," he told his students bitterly. "You will not take it away. While those of *Essential Shotokan* remain only to witness, you will do the same. If you do not, I am dishonored regardless of the outcome."

I thought that some of his supporters would object. They had more at stake—Hong was dead, Nakahatchi wasn't. Nevertheless they agreed ungraciously, muttering to each other as they did so.

That was the best I could do. To no one in particular, I muttered, "Fine. Knock yourselves out." Feeling like a coward, I moved into the crowd toward Sternway.

He considered my approach scornfully. As soon as I reached him, I took hold of his left forearm and dug my fingers in hard, just to get his attention. When he winced involuntarily, I let go.

"Don't leave," I breathed in his ear. "I want to talk to you when this is over."

Without warning his right hand flicked under his left arm. His fingertips brushed my ribs, he hardly touched me—and yet a sudden spasm of pain clenched my chest. He must've caught a nerve. For a moment or two I couldn't move. If he'd decided to put his entire arm down my throat, I wouldn't have been able to stop him.

"I'll be right here," he replied like a warning.

I sneaked a quick gulp of air.

At least we understood each other. He knew what I wanted to talk to him about. And I knew I was as good as dead.

In the center of the *dojo* Hideo Komatori and T'ang Wen prepared themselves for battle.

They stood six or seven paces apart. Hideo bowed to T'ang with his palms on the sides of his thighs, then shifted into a fighting stance like the one Nakahatchi had used on me earlier. T'ang replied by dropping into a kind of crouch, his right leg doubled under him, his left extended ahead with only the ball of his foot on the floor. In that position he covered his right fist with his left hand and straightened his arms toward Komatori.

Neither of them moved.

Everyone else in the room seemed to have suspended breathing.

Then T'ang moved his lead foot, stroked the hardwood with his toes in a circle that brought his left foot under him. Flowing up from his crouch, he poured his weight onto his left leg, tucked his right foot behind the knee, cocked his left arm over his head with the fingers of that hand pinched together, and gestured toward Komatori with his right hand open, palm upward.

That hand beckoned for Komatori to attack.

Without warning Komatori surged forward.

At the same instant T'ang sprang at him, yelling fiercely.

In unison, as if they were both part of the same technique, they burst into a flurry of movement. Punches from all angles met blocks, blocks became punches and more blocks, Komatori and T'ang swayed in and out from the waist while their arms fired like bolts off a static generator. The spasm in my chest eased, yet I hardly breathed. I couldn't believe that they weren't pummeling each other bloody. But I didn't actually see a blow land.

Abruptly T'ang whirled into a spin so swift that he seemed to flicker. His leg flipped out, snapping his heel at Komatori's head.

Komatori ducked under the kick, swept one of his own at T'ang's supporting leg. T'ang hopped over the attack into another spin and kick that would've taken Komatori's head off if Komatori hadn't dropped to the floor and rolled away.

T'ang went after him. By the time Komatori regained his feet, T'ang had leaped high into the air. For an instant, a small shard of time, he seemed to hang there, poised to crash down on his opponent like a boulder from a trebuchet. Then he dropped, driving both heels at Komatori's chest.

He hit hard enough to pulverize cement, never mind ordinary human bone—or he would have if Komatori hadn't slipped aside. While T'ang was still in the air, Komatori fired a punch from his hip straight into T'ang's sternum. Komatori's hoarse shout covered the thud of impact.

T'ang didn't fall. I couldn't imagine how he managed that. A blow like Komatori's would've dropped me to my knees for life. But somehow T'ang got his feet under him, landed staggering backward. Two steps later, he recovered his balance.

His flat eyes burned silver with mayhem.

At the edge of my attention I thought I heard the front door open. I turned reflexively. Parker—?

No.

A second later half a dozen people in *gis*, no, ten, fifteen, charged into the *dojo*, streaming rainwater as they came. Their *gis* sported patches that said Master Soon's *Tae Kwon Do Academy*. They all wore black belts. Apparently Song Duk Soon had brought most of his senior students with him.

What the fuck—?

Before anyone could react, Soon's people rushed into the middle of the room, forcing the combatants apart.

Shock held the *dojo* for a moment. No one moved. Komatori stood at attention, his expression shrouded. Panting at the force of Komatori's blow, T'ang poised himself on the balls of his feet. The lines of his stance shed threats the way Soon's black belts shed water.

Sternway cocked an eyebrow at me. He might've been laughing.

Goddamn it, how many phone calls did Sue Rasmussen make?

Then Soon spread his arms, cleared a small space around him. The look on his face resembled triumph.

"Disgraceful!" he almost crowed. "Chops stolen. Masters murdered. Fighting in your *dojo*. This is the work of children! You disgrace yourselves and your schools. You disgrace the martial arts."

It was Rasmussen's doing. All of it. Unless Sternway himself had told T'ang Wen about the chops.

Any doubt I might've retained was gone, burned away in a flare of perfect outrage.

"I will not allow it!" Soon went on. Water dripped from his *gi* like eagerness. "You are fortunate that we were informed. For you yourselves I care nothing. I would leave you to pummel each other like babies. But I will not allow this insult to the martial arts. The newspapers will not make distinctions between us. They will say that all martial artists are wild dogs." He closed his fists. "It falls to *taekwondo-ka* to act responsibly."

The sonofabitch sounded like he'd gained the pinnacle of Heaven. Anointed by the Almighty to achieve his rightful superiority.

Which would've been fine with me. As long as he stopped the fight before T'ang or Komatori got hurt—as long as he sent everyone home—I didn't give a shit how much stature he assigned himself afterward.

But that wasn't really what he wanted. I could see it in his eyes. One of his black belts was Cloyd Hamson, looking even more belligerent—in other words, frightened—than he had yesterday. Another was a big Korean man, practically a giant, with a face like a hatchet and the closed remorseless aspect of an ax murderer. He was probably Pack Hee Cho, Soon's chief enforcer.

What Soon really wanted was a fight. He wanted to beat the crap out of every *karate-ka* and Wing Chun stylist in sight, force the whole damn building to admit that he was the best.

Stung by dread, I started forward. But I was too late. Always too late. Before I'd taken a step, T'ang Wen brought up a yell from the bottom of his heart and struck Soon's nearest black belt hard enough to double the man over.

Instantly the room went up like a high-octane gas fire. Howling their anger and fear, thirty-plus men and women with too much training and too little restraint hurled themselves at each other. By the time I'd finished one step and started another, the uneasy balance of the *dojo* had shattered into a brawl.

Kicks, punches, throws, yelling and cries, gasps, frantic respiration. Aronson went down with a gash over his eye that hadn't yet had time to start bleeding. From the floor he kicked his antagonist in the crotch, then clawed his way back to his feet. Komatori cracked heads with his elbows, jammed his palms into ribs. T'ang flashed from opponent to opponent, striking each of them so fast that he was two blows away before they reacted. The giant picked up pajamas and *gis* indiscriminately, threw them against each other. With every punch and kick he felled someone. A couple of them didn't get up. They lay still and let themselves be trampled.

In the middle of the confusion, Soon measured out spinning kicks that staggered everyone they hit.

Wrenching myself away, I grabbed onto Sternway, shouted, "Do something!"

He sneered in my face. "Such as?"

Fuck him. Covering my head with both arms and crouching to protect my torso, I crashed into the melee.

Somewhere nearby, a scream pierced the storm. I ignored it. Bodies collided with me, fists jolted my arms and ribs. Kicks landed on me, heavy as bags of sand. I ignored all that as well. Single-minded as a bulldozer, I drove my bulk through the battle.

Toward Pack Hee Cho.

I didn't consider him the most dangerous fighter in the room. Not even close. But he was doing the most immediate damage. And I needed to make an example out of *some*one. Otherwise none of these misguided lunatics would listen to me.

I got lucky—Cho had his back to me. If he'd seen me coming he would've knocked me in half. A blow to the small of my back staggered me, but I shrugged it off, forced my feet back under me. Then I snatched out the .45, reared up, and pounded it at the side of Cho's head.

At that moment I didn't particularly care whether I broke his skull or not.

Although breaking a skull like his was probably impossible. It could've been bone from ear to ear. For the first second or two after I hit him, I actually thought that he wouldn't fall.

Finally he did. Instead of toppling, he slumped almost gently to the floor.

At once fighters stumbled and stomped over him. Bodies slammed into me from one side, then the other. A kick came at my face so fast that I almost didn't duck in time.

Racking a round into the chamber, I pointed the .45 at the ceiling and pulled the trigger.

In that crowded space the shot sounded as lethal as a grenade.

And like a grenade, shrapnel scything wheat, it cleared a circle around me instantaneously. Reacting on instinct, *gis* and pajamas and street clothes jumped or blundered or fell away. In moments Cho's supine form and I had the middle of the room to ourselves.

Without hesitation I located Soon and aimed the .45 at his stomach.

Loud enough to abrade my throat, I shouted, "No one moves! *No one*! You do, and I shoot Master Soon in the gut! You move again, and I *start blazing*. I don't give a fuck *who* I hit!"

Fury congested Soon's face, but he stood still.

Komatori spread his arms to hold his people back. His stare searched me for an explanation I couldn't give him. Not without exposing the whole place to more violence.

T'ang Wen looked even angrier than Soon. A yearning for blood poured off him like flame off napalm. Yet he, too, didn't move. I'd clubbed Cho, not one of his students. I held the .45 on Soon, not him. Apparently that bought me a moment of his restraint.

He was the one I needed to convince.

Back against the windows, Sternway appeared to be having fun.

"This is a setup!" I roared hoarsely. "You're all being manipulated. This whole disaster was staged! To distract you from what really happened.

"Do you," I nearly screamed, "*like being puppets*?"

I didn't even glance at Komatori. Him I trusted. But I watched Soon, saw the passion in his eyes shift toward suspicion. And T'ang's stance eased slightly as a hint of uncertainty crossed his face, eroding the righteousness he stood on.

Taking my life in my hands, I uncocked the .45 and tucked it back into its holster. Then I faced T'ang Wen.

"We need to talk," I told him quietly. "Here. Now."

As soon as I put the .45 away, half the room moved. Anticipated blows flared along my nerves. But no one came toward me. Men and women on the floor got up if they could. Their fellow students went to help those who couldn't. A couple of pajamas remained unconscious. One of the kids who'd helped Komatori and Aronson with the display case had a crushed knee. Their friends supplied what assistance they could.

No one approached Pack Hee Cho. I still stood over him.

T'ang glared back at me. "My master treated you honorably when I would not have done so. Now I have seen how you repay such courtesy. I say again what I have already said. You have no word to speak that I will hear."

"You're right," I retorted, too angry myself to pretend otherwise. "You said that already. And I *did* fail your master. But I didn't kill him. I was miles away when it happened. And Nakahatchi *sensei* didn't kill him. He was asleep in bed with his wife. If the two of them weren't being so damn dignified and insulted about it, they would've told the cops that already."

When I saw that I'd shaken his confidence just a bit, I announced harshly, "Mr. T'ang, *you* have a word that *I* need to hear."

The doubt in his eyes didn't last long. He clenched his teeth, said nothing.

"I think I know why your master was killed." My tone spat like overheated cooking oil. "But I can't be sure until you answer a question for me."

Through the room's quiet I could hear rain thrash the windows, despite the hard breathing of the fighters and the choked moans of the injured.

"*Sifu* Hong looked at the chops yesterday." I ignored everything else, concentrated exclusively on T'ang. "But he didn't tell any of us what he thought of them. Maybe he told you."

I paused to gather my courage. Then I demanded, "What about it, Mr. T'ang? Are the chops genuine?"

He straightened his shoulders. "They are not."

He was willing to go that far, if no farther.

I felt rather than heard Komatori's surprise behind me. His students raised a low murmur of protest. Even Soon's black belts objected.

"How could he be sure?" I had to know. Too much depended on it. "A professional appraiser declared them genuine. He sounded convincing enough. What made your master think he's wrong?"

T'ang snorted his contempt. "My master did not 'think' your appraiser was wrong. He was certain of it."

"But how? What made him certain?"

T'ang shook his head. "No." His jaw knotted angrily. "This is not a matter for outsiders. It is private, secret to Wing Chun. Only the greatest masters know of it. I myself did not know until my master entrusted it to me yesterday." The admission cost him a visible effort. "I will not speak of it, not to you, not to these"—he gestured around him—"intruders. I will not betray my master's confidence."

Confidence. Secrets. I wanted to throttle him, squeeze the truth out of his narrow-minded throat.

"Oh, stop," I snarled. "Not even to catch your master's killer? Are you so *content* with his death that you're willing to let the man who broke his neck go free?" Not to mention Bernie's murderer. "If you insist on keeping your precious secret, I won't be responsible for what comes next. Maybe *Sifu* Hong's killer will kill you, too. He'll sure as hell try."

As long as Hong's secret died with T'ang, the bastard might still come out on top.

There T'ang hung fire. I could see his internal struggle as clearly as if he'd drawn me a schematic. Pride in his master and his style, an almost genetic instinct for secrets, ingrained combativeness, a sore ego, grief, and a kind of transcendental rage warred with the insult I'd thrown in his face. He wanted revenge on Hong's killer, he wanted to *crush* me for putting this kind of pressure on him, he wanted to make Soon eat his air of superiority and his interference. And maybe, just maybe, he wanted to prove that he could match Hideo Komatori's self-possession.

Through the veiled threats of the storm, I seemed to feel the *dojo* lean in on me, concentrating three schools worth of "face" and pain on my vulnerable shoulders. At my feet Cho groaned, shifted his shoulders. I stepped aside just in case he'd regained enough consciousness to grab at me.

By slow degrees, T'ang Wen sagged. He had to surrender *something*, that was obvious. I hadn't left him any choice. He couldn't preserve his master's secrets without refusing to help me identify his master's killer.

But he didn't let himself sound beaten. His tone was defiant when he finally said, "I spoke to you of Ng Mui, the Buddhist nun who escaped the destruction of the Northern Shaolin Temple, and who taught her secrets to Yim Wing Chun." At the tournament on Saturday. Before Bernie died. "That tale is a legend spread to protect Ming adherents from the Manchurian Qing dynasty. In truth, Wing Chun was developed in the south, with the aid of certain masters from the north. They sought to supply Ming supporters with an effective fighting style after the burning of the Southern Shaolin Temple.

"Perhaps Leung Len Kwai carved the chops," he finished roughly, "but he knew nothing of Wing Chun."

In other words, if Swilley hadn't certified the chops as historically valuable artifacts instead of mere antiques, Watchdog could've measured its risk in tens of thousands of dollars instead of millions. Artistically the chops may've been as beautiful as

Seraphim, but they lacked authority. Their value as a martial record of Wing Chun was nonexistent.

Now I had everything I needed.

Anson Sternway, bless his little heart, didn't look like he was having fun anymore.

26

Cupping my left hand over my right first, I bowed to T'ang Wen. "Thank you." I was too scared and angry to sound as fervent as I felt, but I gave it my best shot. "You humble me. *Sifu* Hong must truly have been a great master to teach a student like you.

"He was killed because he knew that the chops weren't genuine." I made sure everyone in the room could hear me. "If the bastard who did it had realized your master shared the secret with you, he would've killed you, too. But now we all know. There's no point in killing any more of us, unless he kills us all."

I'd accomplished that much, whatever happened. No one remained in the line of fire—except me.

Unfortunately I'd also raised the stakes. Greed drives some people hard—but survival drives them harder.

I had everything I needed, but I didn't stop. One more question cried out for an answer. "Help me understand something," I said to T'ang. "Knowing the truth, why didn't your master tell Nakahatchi *sensei* about the chops?"

T'ang's hostility had collapsed when he surrendered. He swallowed at the distress in his throat.

"How could my master speak? Nakahatchi *sensei* showed him respect." Presumably by welcoming his evaluation of the chops. By inviting him to tea. "And your appraiser proclaimed his superior knowledge. To contradict that *gwailo* would deny face to my master's host, into whose care the chops had been entrusted.

"My master could not foresee what followed." T'ang's tone hardened. "He would have shown his own respect in deeds if he had perceived the danger."

I believed him. Once Hong had accepted Nakahatchi's hospitality, he would've gone to war to square the debt.

Leaving the window, Sternway came toward me, a fixed expression on his face, his hands relaxed at his sides. I had to get moving.

"Care for your students," I told T'ang more quietly. "Protect your *dojo*. I'll resolve this tonight."

If I had the strength. Or the brains.

Before Sternway reached me, I turned to Song Duk Soon.

He was helping Cho stand. The big man looked dazed, vaguely bewildered. Maybe he still didn't know who'd hit him. But Soon met me with a glare hot enough to sizzle bacon.

"Master Soon," I said so softly that I almost whispered, "I need your help."

Maybe I did, maybe I didn't. Nevertheless I had to soothe his aggrieved pride somehow. Otherwise I wouldn't be able to turn my back on him. And I owed at least that much to Alex Lacone's dream for Martial America.

Soon's angry stare didn't waver. However, he raised the palm of his hand toward Sternway.

The IAMA director stopped obediently just out of earshot, calm as a man with all his questions answered.

In a low voice, I told Soon, "This isn't done." I indicated the *dojo*. "There's going to be more trouble. I need you, or one of your black belts, to keep watch on the empty school," the unoccupied fourth side of the building. "If anyone goes in, find out who it is. If anyone comes out, stop them. Then call the police."

He appraised me indignantly. After all, I'd threatened him once—and insulted him at least that often. But apparently he didn't like the idea that he'd been manipulated any more than T'ang and Komatori did. After a moment he nodded.

"Thank you," I murmured.

Despite the alarm that scraped the lining of my stomach, the visceral desire to break and run, I took the time to offer him a bow as well. Then I stepped past Cho toward Hideo.

At once Soon gathered his people to leave.

Sternway came to join me. But now I didn't care what he heard. At this point I only wanted to keep Komatori and his students out of harm's way. Like T'ang Wen and *his* students.

The IAMA director watched with an expression that might've indicated bemusement while I told Hideo essentially what I'd said to T'ang. I thanked him for his restraint earlier, urged him to call an ambulance for the kid with the ruined knee, promised I'd clear Nakahatchi's name by morning, and asked him to take his supporters back to *Essential Shotokan.* Now, however, Sternway's threatening presence marred my sincerity. Sending Komatori away left me alone, unarmed apart from the .45, my cell phone, and an anger so deep that I could've drowned in it.

Exertion had dried Komatori's face, but his *gi* remained damp. "If you have your key," I added, "you can go out the back here and let yourself into your *dojo* by the fire door." That way he and his students wouldn't have to carry the kid through the rain.

He'd regained his self-containment, but I saw shadows in his eyes, suggestions of turmoil, and his scar had darkened. "We'll go, Brew-*san*," he answered quietly. "But I don't understand what's happening. You've taken too much onto yourself."

Dishonestly I tried to reassure him. "It's not as much as you think." I wanted him safe. Innocent men were already dead. Not to mention Turf Hardshorn. My conscience couldn't bear any more victims. "As long as no one except *Sifu* Hong knew the truth, a man could get rich stealing the chops. But now—" I faltered, shrugged. "There's no money in it. We'll get them back. And prove your master's innocence."

Glancing at Sternway to avoid Hideo's scrutiny, I finished, "I'm not alone. Between us, Anson and I'll work everything out."

Sternway's thin smile reminded me of his eagerness in the fight club, where he'd killed Hardshorn.

I still had no evidence. None at all.

Finally Hideo nodded. He made a point of crossing the room so that he could bow to T'ang Wen. When T'ang responded, Komatori collected his students. Carefully they carried the moaning kid out if the *dojo.* A moment later I heard the fire door clash open. The sound was barely audible against the background of the storm.

"Now what, Axbrewder?" Sternway asked flatly. "You said you wanted to talk."

Instead of answering, I returned to T'ang.

He knelt beside one of his students now, checking the extent of the man's injuries. He looked up as Sternway and I approached.

"Mr. T'ang, Mr. Sternway and I have a lot to discuss." Fear

and the aftereffects of shouting left my voice rough. "We'll need privacy. But I don't want to intrude on you. We'll let ourselves out the back."

T'ang nodded a dismissal. I'd already taken more from him than he thought he could afford.

When I'd given Hideo enough time to get his people back where they belonged, Sternway and I followed him. At the fire door, I gestured Sternway ahead of me. He shrugged incuriously and complied. He'd seen me club Cho, but apparently he wasn't concerned that I might do the same to him.

While he had his back to me, I slipped my hand into my jacket pocket, touched the cell phone preset to bring up the number for my apartment, and pushed the dial button.

Praying that the answering machine wouldn't fail me, I stepped out into the heat of the utility well and let the fire door shut itself behind me.

Sternway went as far as the equipment cage. Light glared down from the floodlamps, casting accusative shadows across us from the catwalks overhead. His features appeared to slip in and out of existence as he shifted through the shadows. For some reason, the smell of brimstone seemed stronger. After the comparative quiet inside *Traditional Wing Chun*, the rain rattled in the air like distressed sheet metal. Whenever thunder struck nearby, it raised a muffled vibration like keening from the grills and catwalks.

Too late, I realized that the answering machine might not hear anything except rain and faint metallic woe.

Ah, shit.

At the cage, Sternway turned to face me. His arms hung expectantly at his sides. "Well?" he demanded. "Spit it out, Axbrewder."

I could hardly hear him myself.

I didn't have any choice. If the answering machine couldn't pick up our voices, I'd just have to survive. Somehow.

Staying at least three long strides away from him, I moved until the fire-escape corridor was at my back. Now he couldn't escape unless he got past me first. There I straightened my spine, let him see my teeth in a harsh grin.

"Tell me something, Anson." I raised my voice to carry

through the muffled downpour. "I think I have the rest of it figured out." The parts that mattered, anyway. "But how did you know you were going to need that rope and grapple?"

He laughed sharply, like the crack of a handgun. "What rope and grapple?"

"The ones the cops found in the Dumpster. You made it too easy. When you handed off the chops to Swilley, you could've given him the rope and grapple too. He could've ditched them anywhere."

That got his attention. He opened his mouth to laugh again, then changed his mind. His frown caught the shadows.

"Swilley? Carliss Swilley? I don't know what you're talking about. I've never met the man." He feigned a dawning surprise. "Do you mean to say you think I—?"

I cut him off. "Never mind. It doesn't matter. Let's just assume that you left the evidence where the cops couldn't miss it because you wanted to implicate Nakahatchi.

"The part that really pisses me off—and I mean *really*—is killing Bernie Appelwait. Hong sure as hell didn't deserve to die, but at least there was always a chance that he'd wake up in time to defend himself. Not Bernie." For a moment rage constricted my chest. I had to fight it down in order to breathe. "He couldn't have saved himself from you and Hardshorn with a fucking *cannon*, never mind a mere flik."

"Stop!" Sternway ordered. "Damn you, Axbrewder, *stop*." Now I could hear him better. All I had to do was keep him angry. "I don't know what you're talking about! I hardly knew Appelwait. Hardshorn was just a man I saw around the fight club. Until he tried to kill you—until I saved your *life*—I never had anything to do with him.

"You better have a good excuse for accusing me like this. If you don't, I'll sue you for harassment. Slander. I'll call that detective, what's his name, and have you arrested!"

Pure bluster. I ignored it.

"Here's the way I see it." I spat out every word so that he wouldn't miss it. "You tell me if I miss anything.

"You knew the chops were fake. That particular secret wasn't hard to ferret out. Not for a martial arts *god* like you. But Nakahatchi didn't. Watchdog didn't. If you stole them, you could make a fortune selling them. As long as your buyers believed they were genuine.

"That meant you had to get them appraised as genuine. But of course Watchdog's New York expert wouldn't do that, so you had to make sure he never saw them. Instead you approached Swilley, offered him a share of the take if he authenticated them for you.

"He's a greedy little weasel, and he jumped at it."

Sternway changed his approach. I guess he'd realized that righteous indignation wouldn't work. "Do you have children, Axbrewder?" he inquired sardonically. "You should. You're good at bedtime stories."

His sarcasm didn't touch me. I understood it too well.

I knew it was a sign of weakness—

Keeping my voice loud—goading him to do the same—I continued.

"Next you needed to make Watchdog nervous. They had to want a local appraisal before their expert could get here. And you already knew Hardshorn. You'd hired him to frame your wife so that she looked like she was trying to set you up for a fat divorce settlement. Now you had him bring a team to the tournament.

"You weren't particularly interested in petty cash"—I gave him another bloodthirsty grin—"although you always need money. You wanted to scare Watchdog, make them think ordinary security wasn't good enough to protect the chops.

"Naturally Hardshorn didn't intend to risk getting caught, so you arranged to meet him in the men's room, just in case he needed help.

"Unfortunately," I growled, "you didn't expect me to tag the picks." Sternway must've been Hardshorn's spot. "Bernie caught you by surprise. He was probably already in the men's room when you got there, flailing his flik at Hardshorn.

"And he *knew* you." Again I had to struggle for breath. The heat of the utility well and the sound of the rain seemed to clog my lungs. "That was his only crime. As soon as he saw you, you weren't looking at millions anymore. You were looking at prison."

Fury mounted in my raw throat. "So you took his flik—right

after he gave you that nice bruise on your left forearm, the one you keep hidden—and you *crushed his larynx*!"

For the second time Sternway opened his mouth to respond, then thought better of it. Apparently he'd run out of jibes.

Instinct told me that I'd set him up as well as I could. Now I had to blindside him somehow, hit him with something he didn't expect. Otherwise he might never give me what I needed.

"Afterward," I informed him, "you went out to the lobby, blended in with Lacone and Deborah Messenger. Later you got the bag from Hardshorn, put the flik inside, and hid it in Mai's house. You were still trying to incriminate her, make her look like she'd hired Hardshorn to frame you."

That shook him, I could see it. Obviously he believed that he could bluff his way out of anything I said about the chops and Swilley. But the fact that I knew what he'd done with Hardshorn's gear-bag undermined his confidence.

At last I'd found a vulnerable spot. Like the bruise on his forearm. I dug into it as hard as I could.

"The cops have the flik now. They can prove it's the murder weapon. Since you didn't bother to clean it," I explained trenchantly, "they'll find Bernie's blood on it. And the same fibers they found in his throat.

"Once they match those fibers to your IAMA blazer, they're going to *fry* your ass.

"Of course, they don't suspect you yet," I drawled. "You've been pretty clever so far. But a friend of mine is searching your place right now, looking for that blazer."

Which was pure bullshit. I hadn't thought that fast, or that far ahead, when I'd asked Deborah to call Marshal. But he might figure it out for himself. Or Ginny might.

"And even if he doesn't find it," I added, "you're still fried. You didn't clean the damn flik." That I knew for sure. "It has your fingerprints on it.

"Really, it's too bad you're so fucking determined to punish your wife. Otherwise you might've gotten away with it."

Now I couldn't read Sternway expression. He'd draped a shroud over his gaze. Instead of watching my face, he'd lowered his eyes to the center of my chest. Like Nakahatchi sparring—

I probably should've pulled out the .45 right then. But he still hadn't admitted anything. My connection to the answering machine—if it worked at all—had recorded nothing except my accusations.

I needed him to say *some*thing I could use.

"But of course," I went on, "you didn't realize any of that. You thought you were getting exactly what you wanted.

"Sammy Posten panics. Lacone hires me. I help convince Watchdog they need an appraisal right away. Hell, you probably hung around with Lacone on Sunday to make sure he hired me.

"Mission accomplished.

"The downside is, I want Lacone to improve his security. A lot. You know all about my suggestions because you and Lacone are such pals. And you know he isn't stupid enough to drag his feet once Swilley authenticates the chops. So you have to act fast—which means taking the chops *and* killing Hong."

If I hadn't invited Hong to take a close look—

"But first you want to get rid of me. Once Watchdog decided to bring in Swilley, you and Hardshorn would both be safer that way. That's why you convinced me to go out with you Monday night. A big dumb rent-a-cop at a fight club—what could be more natural? Brain-dead Axbrewder catches sight of Hardshorn, chases him out into the alley. Then he's dead. He can't tell anyone that you helped Hardshorn kill him. Chances are the cops won't even realize you were there. And they aren't likely to track Hardshorn down. He's safe unless you rat him out—which you won't do because he knows too much."

I sucked thick heat into my lungs.

"But you changed your mind."

What the fuck are you doing?

"At the last minute you killed Hardshorn instead. That's the only thing I really don't understand. You had me right where you wanted me, and you let me live.

"Why?"

Through the sheet metal obstruction of the rain, the echo of thunder in the catwalks, Sternway answered as if I'd invoked the truth from him with blood and sacrifice.

"Because you were no danger. Him I couldn't control."

Yes! *Got* you, you sonofabitch.

Scornfully he explained, "You're one of those big men with a gun and no real courage. If I thought you had the stones to get into the ring with Hardshorn, I would have let him break your neck. He had it all planned. But I knew you wouldn't.

"After that"—Sternway shrugged—"I couldn't risk letting him kill you. You'd already used your phone. I could assume you told someone you were with me. Then the police would wonder why I hadn't tried to help you. And if I only pretended to help, Turf would have gone berserk. He would think that I was setting him up. That I was going to testify against him."

I let triumph into my voice. "And since I'm a big man with a gun and no guts, you knew you could handle me.

"Still, it must've given you quite a jolt when I told Moy that Hardshorn hadn't killed Bernie."

Sternway didn't react. I forged on anyway.

"So you went ahead with your original plan. You'd already talked Lacone into letting you take me and the chops to Martial America. And of course you couldn't stand in for him without his master key—which you copied before you handed it over."

He nodded indistinctly.

"That gave you access to the chops." I was winning. "Now all you had to do was wait until Swilley did his part. As soon as Deborah Messenger called Sue Rasmussen to discuss the problem, you knew how fast you had to act.

"And you knew that I'd asked Hong to take a look at the chops. You had to kill him when you stole them. Before he told anyone the truth."

Shadows from the catwalk filled Sternway's eyes. I couldn't tell whether he regarded me with contempt or alarm.

I locked my arms across my chest to contain my anger.

"As for the rest— Your Sue is good at incendiary phone calls. Once you had the chops and Hong was dead, she started talking to people like T'ang and Soon, selling the idea that Hong stole the chops and Nakahatchi killed him for it. You wanted to stir up enough good ol' 'traditional hostility' to convince the cops that they didn't need to look any farther for motives."

Sternway had resumed his lethal relaxation. He stood like mockery, waiting for me to finish.

Through my teeth I pronounced, "Which brings me back to my original question. How did you know you were going to need a rope and grapple?"

He snorted. "That's easy. I'm surprised it isn't obvious."

For the first time, he shifted his position, took a step toward me. "T'ang told Sue Hong had changed his lock. He even told her Hong liked to sleep with his window open." Another step. "It's amazing what you can learn from people when they think you share an enemy like the Japanese. Or the Koreans."

And when Posten called Rasmussen, she let Sternway know. He returned to stoke the fires—all that talk about "Ninjitsu"—and keep an eye on me.

Uncrossing my arms, I pulled out the .45 and pointed it dead at his face.

"That's close enough, asshole."

He sneered. "You won't shoot me, Axbrewder. You said it yourself. No guts. And I'm unarmed. Even a coward like you can't kill people in cold blood."

He started into another step.

With my left hand, I chambered a round. Background noise dulled the sound.

"Maybe I'll shoot you, maybe I won't. Unlike you, I've still got a couple of scruples." Anger poured from me like venom. "But I've been known to let them slip on occasion.

"However," I admitted bitterly, "I'm a terrible shot. I could probably miss. Even at this range." Not bloody likely. "So I took precautions."

I lifted the cell phone out of my pocket, held it up so that Sternway could see it. The connection counter hadn't stopped. My link to the answering machine remained open.

"When we left the *dojo*, I called a tape recorder. It's been running the whole time. It'll have a lot of background noise—rain, thunder, that sort of thing. But the crime lab can clear it up. When they're done, you'll be perfectly audible."

Abruptly a storm of fury seized his features. All at once he looked rabid and unstoppable, like he could walk through machine-gun fire, tear me apart with his teeth. But that passed almost immediately. Without effort he relaxed his shoulders, let the tension out of his hands. A twist of his mouth dismissed my precautions. Ready as a stick of dynamite, he flashed a glare into my face.

"That won't save you, Axbrewder," he announced distinctly. "I don't care how many lies you tell about me. I don't care if you shoot me. You can't hide the truth. Eventually the police will hunt you down."

That sudden change in his stance scared me worse than a direct charge. If he'd come right at me, I could at least have tried to whack him on the head. If nothing else, I should've braced myself.

Instead I dropped the phone back into my pocket, steadied the .45 with both hands.

"Oh, give it up," I rasped back. "Maybe you're too tough to die." I sighted at his guts. "Maybe you're the fucking Ebola virus of martial artists. But too many people know what I know. The cops have a piece, Marshal Viviter has a piece, the friend who found that bag has a piece." I wasn't about to say Ginny's name. Just in case. "They'll put it all together sooner or later."

"Lies," he retorted. "You're lying. I have to wonder where you've hidden the chops. You haven't had time to take them far. If you're as careless about that as you've been about other things, they may still be in your car."

"That's enough!" What the hell was wrong with him? He couldn't wipe out what he'd already said by accusing me. "Get down! *Now*! On the floor. Face first. I don't want to kill you, but I do *not* mind leaving a hole you can put your fist through in your goddamn stomach!"

He stepped back like I'd scared him—like he suddenly believed that I'd blow him away when scarcely a minute ago he'd actively dared me to shoot him.

I didn't get any other warning. I'd already missed too many danger signs.

Out of nowhere a weight like the business end of an Abrams tank plowed into my kidneys. My head cracked back, my arms jumped at the ceiling. I held onto the .45 as hard as I could, but that didn't prevent me from sprawling heavily onto the cement.

My back felt like my spine had snapped.

Sternway kicked at my right wrist, wrenched the .45 out of my fingers.

"What kept you?" He didn't sound angry—or even irritated. He sounded smug, satisfied. "Another minute, and he would have killed me."

A voice answered, "We had to be careful." A man's voice. "If he heard us coming—"

Numbness washed everything away for a moment. Numbness

and rain. It was never going to stop raining. Then the man's voice came back.

"—didn't want him to kill you."

Whoever he was.

Sternway said, "He has a phone, Sue. Left jacket pocket."

Sue? Hell of a name for a man. I'd always thought so.

Hands rummaged in my pocket. The phone appeared on the cement in front of my face. I could almost focus on it. Then a foot wearing an athletic shoe came down, crushed it.

"Did he use it?" A woman's voice this time.

Or not? With my back broken, I couldn't be sure.

"He says he did," Sternway replied. "He says he called a tape recorder. It got the whole conversation."

"Oh, shit!" She sounded like she might be pretty when she was angry. "You didn't tell him anything?"

"Enough." Sternway still sounded pleased. "Enough to keep him from shooting me."

"Jesus Christ, Anson!" The woman wasn't pleased. Not at all. "What were you *thinking*?"

"What was there to tell?" A man's voice again. "I thought he wanted to—"

Sternway had two rescuers. Definitely. At least two.

"He did," Sternway retorted. "I can't explain right now. We don't have time. We have to get rid of him. Before somebody comes looking for him."

"What do you mean, get rid of him?" the man asked. "If Sue hadn't ruined his phone, you could call the police. I'll go out to *Essential Shotokan*, use their phone."

"Shut up!" the woman barked. "You don't understand. Anson's right. We have to get rid of him. Now. We'll explain everything *when we have time.*"

I didn't much like the idea that they'd broken my back. They could get rid of me all they wanted, but I did not want a broken back. And I couldn't feel anything. Not anywhere.

But when I told my right hand to move, it twitched.

My numbness vanished in a sudden jolt of pain, as incandescent and irrefusable as lightning. Bruised bones, torn muscles, there was no distinction.

It galvanized me like lightning. Without noticing how I did it,

I squirmed onto my back. My wrist and kidneys hurt like the fires of hell, but at least now I could see.

Outlined by floodlamps, a woman who looked exactly like a cheerleader I used to know in high school stood over me. Sue Rasmussen. She wore a warmup suit and athletic shoes. When I flopped over, she retreated a step, but she didn't take her eyes off Parker Neill.

He also wore a warmup suit. And athletic shoes. Uniform of the day. Neither of them was wet. They must've left their rain gear at the end of the fire escape corridor.

Parker—

Ah, Christ.

He was the tank that ran me over. Rasmussen had the rep of a killer martial artist, but she lacked the sheer mass to hit me so hard.

The cavalry had arrived, all right. For Sternway.

Parker didn't look at her. His attention focused on Sternway. Shadows and uncertainty confused his round face.

"Anson—" he tried to say. "*Sensei*—"

"Trust me," Sternway ordered. He'd lost his smugness. His patience. "This will all make sense, I promise.

"What do you think, Sue? If we shoot him—"

She shook her head violently. "That could attract attention."

I agreed with her. A shot might be heard in one of the *dojos*. Despite the storm.

Sternway nodded. "What I would like to do," he said in a speculative tone, gazing upward, "is drop him off the top catwalk. Make it look like an accident. We can dispose of the gun later. But I don't think we can wrestle him up there. He's too heavy." He glanced down at me. "And he's conscious. He'll resist."

"Then we break his back," Rasmussen announced harshly. "If we arrange him by the cage, he'll look like he fell, killed himself."

"Good." Sternway grinned at her. "Let's do it."

"You're serious," Neill said. "You're going to kill him."

"*Because we have to*," she spat at him. "Get it through your head. We don't have any *choice*!"

"Oh." He sounded shaken. "I see. OK."

"Finally!" Rasmussen didn't disguise her exasperation. "Help me pick him up."

Neill ducked his head, defeated. "OK," he said again.

He came over to my right. She took the left. Clearly they didn't expect their revered *sensei* to do any of the work.

Together they manhandled me to my feet. When they had me upright, they turned me to face Sternway.

He still stood in front of the cage, no more than six feet away. If I fell at him, I could butt him in the kneecap. The .45 rested in his hand like it weighed nothing, meant nothing.

If he fired from this range, the slug would tear out half my back.

I shut my eyes. I could feel my legs now. Jagged blades stabbed up and down my thighs and calves. The small of my back was a sodden mass of hurt. Parker may've injured one of my kidneys.

But pain was a good thing. In a manner of speaking. As long as I felt it, I knew I wasn't dead.

"How shall we do this?" Rasmussen asked Sternway.

"OK," Neill said for the third time. He nodded to himself. "I have an idea."

Rain pounded like retribution onto the roof of the building. I reopened my eyes.

He let go of me, and I nearly crumbled. Somehow I managed to lock my knees, keep myself upright. He put himself between me and Sternway. Between me and the .45.

"How about," he suggested, "we do this?"

His left fist lashed out. His knuckles struck Rasmussen on the bridge of her nose. I heard it shatter.

At the same time, his right forearm hacked at Sternway's hand. At the .45. His left fist rebounded from Sue's nose to punch at Sternway's head.

Sternway had trained her well. Parker caught her by surprise, yet his blow hardly cost her half a second. Then she flung herself after him.

The .45 arced away, skidded across the concrete.

Sternway blocked Neill's punch, countered hard.

I toppled myself like a stack of cinder blocks onto Rasmussen's back.

Parker wheeled aside, blocking furiously. Sternway went for him like a whirlwind.

With my bulk crashing down on her, Sue couldn't control her momentum, deflect herself, avoid— She didn't even have time to get her hands up. Head first, she slammed into the utility cage.

The heavy grate rang like falling rebar. I stumbled into it, hooked my fingers through the links to hold myself up. She bounced back a step or two, then folded quietly to the floor.

Blood stained her face. I didn't like the angle of her neck. It looked final.

Sternway drove Parker backward. They exchanged blows like barrages, kicks with the impact of mortar shells. I'd never seen fighters move so fast, not even at the fight club. Concentration flamed in Neill's eyes, rapt and consuming. But he was overweight, couldn't match Sternway's conditioning. And he lacked—

Clinging to the cage, I turned. Pain thundered in the air. I couldn't hear blows or breathing. I couldn't hear desperation.

—lacked Sternway's eagerness for combat, the keen joy that lifted him out of himself and made killing easy.

Frantically I searched the floor. As soon as I spotted the .45, I pitched forward onto my hands and knees, and began crawling toward it.

Hell, it wasn't more than twenty feet away. I could reach it easy. Fuck Sternway, I could *reach* it. Parker hadn't broken my back. And pain was my friend, my oldest companion. Every shift of my knees and scrape of my palms hurt like rage. Like courage. And if it hurt like this, it had to be worth doing. Simply had to be. All I needed, absolutely all, was for Parker to hang on.

Long enough.

Sternway had killed Bernie. He'd killed Hong. For money.

I wanted to shoot him straight in the head.

I thought I heard laughter. "You're slow, Parker." Taunts. "You're no fighter. You've always been slow." Taunts and blows, hammered flesh. "I can take you whenever I choose."

"Show me," Parker gasped.

Halfway to the .45. Two thirds of the way.

Hang on long enough.

More jeering. "I'll let you wear yourself out first. I want you to see it coming."

Fuck him.

Pain was a good thing. Oh, yes. As good as rage. I wedged my legs under me, lunged into a dive.

Landed hard.

Rolled.

Came up onto my knees with the .45 in both fists.

Their struggle had taken Neill and Sternway over by one of the catwalk ladders. They were too far away. And too close together. Parker fought with his back to the wall now, defending frantically while Sternway inundated him with blows.

I raised the .45 to fire a shot over their heads.

Except I couldn't. My fingers didn't work right. Sternway must've hurt a nerve in my wrist. I couldn't pull the trigger.

Awkwardly I shifted the .45 to my left. It felt like a club, inert and too heavy to lift. I'd never be able to aim this way.

I didn't need to aim.

The concussion nearly knocked me off balance. For an instant the storm and the fight fell silent, deafened by the blast. Then I heard the slug ricochet off concrete and spang into one of the catwalks.

Involuntarily Parker turned his head to look at me—

—and Sternway hit him in the solar plexus with a two-knuckled punch that dropped him like a sack of discarded clothes.

Sonofa*bitch*!

I staggered to my feet, stood wavering with the .45 stretched out in front of me. "That's enough," I panted. "Don't move." When had my voice become so weak? "Don't even think about moving." I started toward him, lock-kneed and rigid, one step at a time. "You've already done too much harm. You won't do any more."

Had anyone heard the shot? Even that demanding sound might not penetrate the walls and the storm.

But if it did—

More cannon fodder for the IAMA director.

Shadows hid his expression. He glanced at Sue Rasmussen's huddled body, then looked back at me.

"Do it, Axbrewder." He sounded like butchery. "Shoot me. If you don't, I'll tear your heart out through your ass."

Parker didn't move.

"Fuck you." Some chances I had to take.

I fired on the move, lurching through the recoil. I didn't expect to hit him. All I wanted was to make him remain still until I got closer.

Entirely by chance, my shot spalled a cinder block three feet from his head before it angled away, whining like a drill in granite.

I saw outrage seize his face again, the recognition that he was trapped. I was willing to shoot him after all. And I must have a few rounds left. If he let me get close enough, he was finished. He couldn't fight a bullet.

And no one else would get hurt.

Snarling, he turned and jumped for the ladder.

I tried to hurry after him, but he was faster. By the time I'd covered enough distance to aim the .45 adequately, he'd already scrambled up to the second floor catwalk. There metal bars and railings protected him. He was out of my reach before he started up the next ladder to the top floor.

Damn him. Damn him inside out and backward. I *wanted* him, but I'd never get him now. He still had his key, he could let himself into all four sides of the building. I'd have to try to intercept him before he gained an exit.

If he doubled back while I hunted him, I'd never stop him.

And if he didn't, if he entered one of the schools and headed for the front door, he'd find innocent people in his way. Hideo's students. Hong's. Soon's. I couldn't tell myself that they'd all gone home by now. And Komatori and T'ang lived here. So did Soon.

And if Sternway chose the unoccupied side, he'd encounter one of Soon's black belts. Or Soon himself.

More innocent people. More death.

It was too much. I couldn't let it pass.

Coughing to clear my throat, I shouted, "Anson!"

The rattle of his feet on the ladder stopped. I didn't hear him clang along the catwalk.

"*Anson*!" I had to cough some more. Fortunately I didn't hack up blood. My kidneys hadn't been damaged as badly as I'd feared.

He didn't answer—but he didn't move either. Maybe he didn't like his chances inside any of the *dojos*. If nothing else, *some*one would see him running away—

"You beat Parker!" Parker still hadn't moved. From my angle, he hardly seemed to breathe. "I saw that. But you can't take *me*!"

Sternway didn't answer.

Desperately I tossed the .45 so that it skittered across the floor into the white scowl of the floodlamps. Where he could see it.

"I didn't avoid fighting Hardshorn because I'm a coward! I did it because I wanted him alive. I wanted him to tell me who killed Bernie. If he hadn't ambushed me, you'd already be in jail!"

Abruptly Sternway leaned out over the railing, sneered down at me. "You're lying, Axbrewder. You couldn't take him with his head tied between his legs. You'll need a platoon to take me."

I beckoned. "Come back down here. I'll show you."

He snorted a laugh. "You come up. I'll let you show me."

What, climb all the way up there? With misfiring nerves in my wrist, and bruises riding my kidneys? Just so he could kill me?

What choice did I have? If just one more innocent *karate-ka* paid the price for my mistakes, I wouldn't need Sternway to tear out my heart. I'd already mastered that surgical procedure for myself.

"Fine," I coughed up at him. "Just don't rush me. I'm conserving my strength."

He grinned, a flash of eagerness. After a moment he moved away from the top of the ladder to the corner of the catwalk, where he could watch my progress without threatening me. A show of good faith. He meant to slaughter me in a fair fight.

Somewhere during the past few hours, he must've lost his mind. Otherwise he would've paid more attention to his own survival.

I was counting on that.

First I knelt beside Parker, checked his pulse with my good hand. When I found it strong and steady in his neck, my heart gave a little leap of relief. He was still unconscious, but he wasn't dying. I could risk leaving him while I challenged Sternway.

I tugged off my jacket, dropped it over Parker to keep him warm. Then I raised my arms to the ladder and began to struggle upward.

Which would've been impossible if Sternway had stomped on my wrist instead of kicking it. But my right hand began working better as I climbed. On the down side, Parker's blows had left my legs as weak as a drunk's. Nakahatchi had thrown me around the room hardly fourteen hours ago. Just last night Hardshorn had pummeled me nearly unconscious.

Nevertheless this was the work I'd been born to do—the work

of pain and endurance, the unforgiving task of standing in harm's way. *Today you believe you are ready because your pain has become greater than your anger, yet you are not defeated by it. That is important.*

It is necessary.

If I didn't understand anything else, I understood *that.*

Instead of thinking about my hurts while I climbed, I concentrated on the clarity of unmarred rage—anger as cold and ready as black ice, and as fatal. Sternway had killed two innocent people. Plus Turf Hardshorn. He'd used my efforts to ease the tensions in Martial America as an excuse to break Hong's neck and get Nakahatchi arrested. It didn't matter *how* much I hurt. Or that I was scared almost witless.

Only stopping him mattered.

"What's the problem?" Sternway crowed over me. "At this rate you'll take all night."

I remembered Nakahatchi's face, and Mitsuku's, and went on climbing.

Gradually I found more strength. My muscles worked out some of the congestion in my back. The fingers of my right hand tightened on the rungs. I began to make better progress.

I wanted to rest when I reached the second floor, but I kept going. I was no match for Anson Sternway, I understood that. Nevertheless I had one advantage he couldn't match.

I knew I'd lost my mind.

I knew why.

"Come *on*, Axbrewder." He still watched me from the corner of the catwalk. "I hate waiting."

What's the matter? Getting nervous?

I didn't try to hurry.

Finally I reached the top. By then my lower back felt like a bucket of lead clamped to my hips. I hauled it after me up onto the catwalk.

Paused to gasp for air.

This close to the skylights, the downpour sounded louder. Lightning leered across the darkness. But I could still hear the ragged labor of my heart. It drummed like panic in my temples, pounding out an autonomic message of terror.

Sternway was going to kill me.

Fuck that.

He backed around the corner. With the fingers of one hand, he beckoned me forward. When I didn't obey, he cocked his fists on his hips.

"I hate to say this, Axbrewder, but you look pathetic. Don't you ever exercise? I train harder than you do in my sleep."

I thought I knew why he backed up, why he wanted me to follow. To get me away from the ladder. So that I couldn't escape—

The bastard didn't understand me at all. He had no clue.

Panting from the pit of my stomach, I started after him.

He retreated until he reached the middle of the catwalk, a step or two past the nearest fire door. I quickened my pace.

But he ignored the door. Apparently the exit didn't interest him.

I slowed down. Still outside his kicking range, I wobbled to a halt.

His eagerness had reached manic proportions. Light flashed off the whites of his eyes. He bounced gently on the balls of his feet, warming up to spurn gravity. His hands flexed like springs at the ends of his arms. Like fliks.

"Speaking of carelessness," I panted, "what makes you think you'll accomplish anything if you *do* beat me?" The effort hurt my throat. "Have you forgotten that tape? Once they hear it, the cops will come after you. You won't stand a chance. Not against the kind of manhunt they'll organize."

He shrugged. His shoulders conveyed a hint of fever, urgency. "I'll find the tape after I finish you. The police have no reason to suspect me. And Marshal Viviter has no evidence."

He smiled like the blade of a table saw. "The tape is in your apartment."

I shook my head speciously. "That's not a mistake Sue would've let you make. You'll have to do better."

He exploded at me as if I'd lit a fuse by saying her name.

I tried to counter him as Nakahatchi had countered me, gently, without alarm. My right hand still felt stiff, so I held it up, covered my stomach with that elbow. My left hand I used open, striving to slip every high punch aside with my palm.

Some of them I missed. Those ones landed like hammers. Whenever my elbow blocked his foot or his fist, the blow wailed along my nerves. With enough breath I might've wailed myself.

Nevertheless this was my work, *my work*, and I didn't back down from it. He forced me to retreat slowly, a few inches at a time, but the wall and the railing hampered him. He couldn't swing kicks around at my head. For every blow that reached me, I stopped two.

All I needed was a grip on him, one second with my fist closed in his sweatshirt. Then I could kick him, swing the toe of my shoe into his guts with every ounce of my bulk and fury behind it.

When I got the chance.

If I got it.

I didn't. He struck too hard, too fast. Too often.

But the second, no, the third time his fist rocked my head, something changed. Instead of knocking me out, the impact seemed to translate me into a state that resembled Nakahatchi's impregnable tranquility. Without transition I found myself in a place that held no anger and no fear.

Pain no longer distracted or drove me, and I relaxed.

I could move faster now. My left skidded his attacks away earlier. My elbow adjusted to deflect him more effectively. Fewer strikes made contact. Every breath came a bit more easily.

If only Nakahatchi had given me one more lesson—

Sternway felt the change. I saw it on his face. A new glee for combat flared in his eyes, ignited by eagerness. He stopped kicking, speeded up his punches. Put less force into each blow.

I thought nothing, felt nothing. The explosive discharge of his fists consumed all of my attention, my whole world. Reality. The instant I allowed anything else to exist, anything at all, he'd break every bone in my face. And he wouldn't stop there, oh, no, he'd go on breaking and breaking me until—

Shit!

—until I woke up enough to realize that I was wrong. He had no intention of breaking me. Not with his fists.

Too late. Always too late.

Suddenly he surged forward, ducking under my defense faster than I could react. In one fluid motion, he braced himself, hooked one arm under my right leg, clenched his other hand in the back of my shirt.

And heaved.

Walls and skylights and floodlamps reeled around me. The catwalk jumped away.

In spite of my size, he tipped me over the railing.

Flailing instinctively, I managed to hook my right elbow over the top rail somehow, catch the lower bar with my left hand. My entire weight snapped along the length of my body like the strike of a scourge.

I screamed. I couldn't help it. My left hand hadn't caught enough of my weight. Most of it dropped onto my right elbow. Dislocated the joint, shattered it, both, neither, I had no idea. After the first instant, the first tearing howl of pain, I couldn't even feel it. Just hanging there took everything I had.

Now I knew why he'd wanted me to climb up here. He still intended to make my death look like an accident—killed by a fall from the top floor. If I struck the cage on the way down, the damage to my body would disguise everything he'd done to me.

He'd positioned me near the fire door, in the middle of the catwalk, so that I'd hit the cage.

Leave Rasmussen where she was. Kill Parker. Make it look like I did it. Once I fell, he could tell Moy anything he wanted.

He stood at the railing, lit by floodlamps and triumph—stark as an angel. All he lacked was a flaming sword. His arms relaxed as he grinned down at me. "What a shame. Just when I thought the fight might become interesting, you decided to commit suicide."

If I hadn't been in so much pain, I would've wept at my own blindness.

Casually he lifted his foot, nudged at my right hand.

Now I was gone, erased. Nothing at all remained except white staring agony and the long plunge to darkness.

Behind him, the fire door crashed open, slammed back against the wall. Metal rang in protest as Ginny sprang out onto the catwalk.

He whirled toward her.

She had her .357 in her hand. Her right hand. He was on her left. And he was too fast, she couldn't swing the .357 toward him and shoot quickly enough.

She didn't try. Without hesitation she slashed her claw across his face.

Yelling, he fell back a step. Instant blood filled his eyes.

And still he was too fast. As she brought the .357 to bear, he lashed up a straight kick that caught her under the chin.

It whacked her head back. Whiplash compressed her brain against her skull so hard that it rebounded, hurt itself again.

The gun dropped from her hand, clanged against the bars of the catwalk, slipped through and fell. I saw it go like the pinching out of a candle flame, the extinguishing of my life.

He crouched over her, splashed blood into her face. "Bitch!" A howl of madness. "*Whore*! Get up! *Get up*! I'm not *finished* with you!

"You *cut* me!"

His fists grabbed her shoulders. He jerked her up and down, whipping her head back and forth. He was going to break her neck. If he hadn't already—

I couldn't do anything about it. I was about to fall myself. My elbow wouldn't hold.

No.

Separate from your anger. Wasn't that what Nakahatchi had said? *You will not be ready indeed until your pain has become separate from your anger.*

Not greater than your anger. Or less. Separate.

The flawless black ice of fury and the detached impersonal calm of concentration. Not combined, but simultaneous.

Together they canceled the cruel gravity of my helplessness.

I had to reach Ginny.

I knew how.

I could do it.

Took damn near forever. Nevertheless Sternway didn't notice me. He'd gone berserk. He dropped Ginny so that he could wipe the blood out of his eyes, but it streamed down his face anyway, his hands couldn't keep up with it, she must've gashed the hell out of him. Once he let her go, she sprawled like death on the catwalk. He stood over her, still yowling insults that made no sense.

I swung my legs hard, hooked my right heel up onto the catwalk to take some of the weight off my elbow. I couldn't balance there, but in the small instant of support before my foot slipped I swung my left arm upward, snagged a grip on the top rail. Then I could pull without crucifying my elbow.

As soon as I got my right foot back onto the catwalk, I lunged up and over the railing.

Landed like bricks on my right arm.

Didn't care.

He must've heard me, felt the vibration of the catwalk, something. He turned before I got my feet all the way under me.

Blood veiled his face. It throbbed out of him along a ragged tear that crossed his forehead from one temple down into the opposite cheek. The intense white of the floodlamps turned it black and slick. His eyes made gaps of madness in the dark stream. Madness or mortality.

Roaring my name, he launched another kick like the one that felled Ginny.

I made him miss by lurching aside and forward. Which enabled me to plant my right foot. Then I straightened up under his kick.

His leg came down on my left shoulder. I couldn't do much with my right arm, so I swung my left around his leg and up under his left armpit, shifted my hips forward—

—strained to rise.

I may've screamed again, but I didn't hear it.

He did it for me as he went over the railing.

I never saw him hit. I never saw him again at all. I lasted long enough to kneel beside Ginny, fumble for her pulse, see that she was still breathing. I think I tried to call for help. But of course the fire door had shut itself.

Then I disappeared into a darkness like the storm outside and the blood on Anson Sternway's face.

27

The hospital let her go late the next afternoon. Concussion, severe whiplash. X-rays ruled out a broken jaw. She needed rest and ibuprofen, regular physical therapy, frequent check-ups, but the doctors said she'd be all right.

Parker Neill spent a few hours in the emergency room, being poked and peered at for signs of internal seepage. But once the shock to his solar plexus eased, he recovered well enough. He called one of his friends to give him a ride, and went home.

Me they kept for a day and a half. "For observation," just in case my kidneys started bleeding. They bandaged a few contusions, trapped my hand and arm in a cast to protect my dislocated elbow. No problems. Nothing to worry about. It was their considered medical opinion, however, that I needed a different hobby. Getting beaten half to death wasn't good for me.

I would've laughed if I hadn't been so full of morphine. Getting beaten half to death was what I did best.

That, and getting through it.

Maybe eventually I'd even understand Sihan Nakahatchi. The IVs made his lessons look easy.

During the day I had a succession of phone calls and visitors. Fortunately most of them came in the afternoon, when the nurses had eased back on my morphine. I hurt more then, but occasionally I could think.

Most of the calls were from Marshal and Sergeant Moy. With their help, and Ginny's, I pieced together what had happened behind my back.

When Deborah reached her, Ginny had decided not to wait until she heard whatever the answering machine might record. Instead she'd called Marshal, told him the little she knew. Then she headed out into the storm for Martial America.

Once she arrived, however, she wasn't sure what to do next. I wouldn't welcome interference, I'd made that clear. And she had no idea what might be going on inside. She only knew that Hong was dead and the chops had disappeared. But she figured that I couldn't be in too much trouble with all those people around, so she waited in the Olds until the parking lot began to empty.

Even then she hesitated. Every time she tried my phone, she got a busy signal. But eventually, when most of the other cars had left, she saw two people run for the building. Under the circumstances, she didn't get a look at them, and wouldn't have recognized them anyway, but they didn't go into one of the schools. Instead they entered through the fire exit.

That was enough for her. She went after them.

Of course, she couldn't get in. No key. So she followed the edge of the building to *Essential Shotokan*. Inside she found herself talking to Hideo Komatori.

By then the cops had taken Nakahatchi away, and Komatori wasn't feeling cooperative. Fortunately he adjusted his attitude when he learned that she worked with me. He confirmed that I'd been there recently. Unfortunately he had no idea where I was now.

After some hesitation, however, he offered to call *Traditional Wing Chun*, ask if I were still there. T'ang Wen informed him that Sternway and I'd gone into the utility well.

Now Ginny well and truly didn't know what to do. She had no reason to consider Sternway dangerous. He'd saved my life at the fight club. And I hadn't reacted well the last time she'd arrived unexpectedly. If Marshal hadn't called to tell her what he'd heard on the answering machine, she might not have done anything at all.

But she still couldn't be sure that I was in trouble. I might have Sternway under control. After all, I had the .45. On the other hand, the two people who'd entered through the fire exit worried her. Maybe I'd called them to help me, maybe I hadn't. Finally she decided to go up to the top floor and ease open the fire door. From there she might see or hear something that clarified the situation. If I were OK, she could withdraw without intruding.

Hideo wanted to go with her. Convincing him to stay behind cost her a minute or two. But she didn't want to endanger him if I needed her, or to waste his time if I didn't. Finally she climbed the stairs to Nakahatchi's private *dojo* alone.

She was outside the fire door when I screamed.

As for Marshal, he hadn't wanted to be left out. When Ginny told him she was going to Martial America, he braved the storm and jimmied his way into our apartment so that he could listen to any messages I left on the machine. He heard most of my confrontation with Sternway—at least the parts that weren't covered by background noise.

As soon as Sternway started to incriminate himself, Marshal called Ginny. Then he called Moy, caught the detective a mile or so from Martial America. Still dragging Nakahatchi along, Moy turned back.

By the time the detective reached Martial America, Hideo had already found Ginny and me. When she hadn't returned after a few minutes, he'd gone upstairs and opened the fire door. Then he'd called 911, given us some rudimentary first aid. As Moy arrived he and Mitsuku were improvising a makeshift stretcher out of two *bos* and a blanket so that they could carry us downstairs.

At that point, Moy released Nakahatchi—"pending further investigation." At least Nakahatchi didn't have to spend the night in jail. That was a relief.

Before dawn Moy took a search warrant to Carliss Swilley's place of business. His uniforms found the chops hidden in a storeroom under a pile of "genuine" ratty-looking Oriental rugs. Swilley himself crumbled without much persuasion. Apparently he hated driving in the rain so much that he'd assumed everyone else did too, so he believed that he didn't need to hurry. Instead he preferred to wait until the storm let up before stashing the chops in an anonymous storage locker, as he and Sternway had agreed.

Within a few more hours, the cops had searched Sternway's apartment. They found his IAMA blazer. Its left forearm showed subtle signs that it might've been struck with an object like a flik. Moy would know more when the lab boys compared the fibers.

By midafternoon a forensics team in the IAMA offices had appropriated the organization's financial records. The cops weren't ready to make a statement yet, but a quick analysis of the books and Sternway's personal accounts suggested that he'd been skimming for years. Nevertheless he was practically broke.

Naturally this infuriated Mai Sternway. As his widow, she'd inherit everything he had left—which was mostly karate gear and unpaid bills. Poor woman. She'd have to get a job.

For his part, Parker Neill hadn't heard anything that tied Sternway to Hong or the chops. But he told Moy in no uncertain terms that Sternway and Sue Rasmussen meant to kill me. Which effectively protected me from any kind of "wrongful death" charge.

When Marshal told me his side of the story, he sounded almost envious, like he wished that he could've traded places with me. I spared him the benefit of my usual poor grace. I was just grateful that he'd taken me seriously enough to get involved.

Moy was more businesslike, but that didn't stop him from chewing me out. Where did I get off, he wondered, facing Sternway alone when I could've had half a dozen uniforms with me if I'd just bothered to tell him what I suspected? Didn't I trust the police? Well-meaning loose cannons like me did more harm in Carner than almost any number of plain criminals. And so on. He enjoyed his Stern Officer of the Law shtick so much that he nearly ruined it by laughing.

I thanked him anyway. Mainly for letting Nakahatchi go.

Alex Lacone also called—by proxy. I actually spoke to his personal assistant, the enduring Cassandra Hightower. In a quavering voice, she advised me that Mr. Lacone was pleased with my work. He considered my assignment completed. Naturally he would pay me in full. In addition, he and Watchdog had put together an attractive bonus which would more than cover my medical expenses.

Later Deborah Messenger revealed that most of the bonus money came from Watchdog. In lieu of a "recovery fee."

She saw me several times. The first time—she said it was the second, but I didn't remember one earlier—I had too many drugs in my system to concentrate. But that afternoon we talked for quite a while. I gave her a bowdlerized version of events, with all the parts where I screamed and felt sorry for myself edited out. Even that upset her more than I expected. Her eyes spilled tears until I thought she might break down. Then she got mad.

"You arrogant, inconsiderate—" Her voice rose. "All you *men*! You charge off into the night without explanation. You leave me alone to panic, you risk your life *stupidly* against a man you've *seen* kill. Everybody who *glances* at TV knows you need backup. A so-called *professional* ought to know that better than anybody.

"Did you ever stop to think I might not *like* it if you got yourself murdered?"

I grinned at her, I couldn't help it. She looked so delectable that I wanted to pull her clothes off on the spot. And her anger touched me—

She warmed me in ways I hadn't felt for years. Lots of them.

Still fuming, she started to sputter, "If you *ever*—"

There she stopped herself. For a moment she looked away. When she faced me again, her tears were gone.

"I'm sorry. I get emotional sometimes. This is what you do. It's right for you. I'll get used to it."

Then she asked anxiously, "Every case isn't like this? Is it?"

"No," I admitted, "every case isn't like this."

Just the important ones.

We held hands until she had to go back to work.

Nakahatchi *sensei* surprised me with a visit. His wife and Hideo accompanied him. None of them said much. They were too dignified. But they brought gifts—which they presented formally, like promises of friendship.

Nakahatchi gave me a scroll which unrolled to reveal a beautifully indecipherable hand-painted inscription. It was, he informed me, a quotation from Gichin Funakoshi. "The ultimate aim of the art of *karate* lies not in victory or defeat, but in the perfection of the character of its participants." We would resume my lessons when I was fully recovered.

Mitsuku proffered a self-contained ornamental fountain the size of a mailbox. Add water, plug in the pump, and listen to the soothing trickle of water over polished black stones. Unexpectedly modern of her, I thought. Maybe it would help me relax.

And Komatori presented me with a white canvas *gi*, including what he called an "honorary" black belt. I wasn't supposed to actually wear it. Nevertheless I'd earned it, he said, by defeating such a renowned fighter.

They left me feeling better than I had in years.

T'ang Wen also put in an appearance. And gave me a present, a pair of polished fire-hardened rattan sticks, maybe twenty inches long, which he called "Kali sticks." They weren't traditional Wing Chun weapons, apparently, but he'd studied them in another *dojo* on his master's urging. If I granted him the honor of letting him teach me, he'd show me how to use them.

I hardly knew what to say except, "Sure," and, "Thanks." Hong Fei-Tung was dead because I hadn't trusted my instincts. Instead of reproaching me, however, T'ang covered my bewildered guilt by giving me "face"—by telling me more about the origins of Wing Chun and the chops.

According to Hong, the *Joi Si*, the 'first leader,' of Wing Chun wasn't either Ng Mui or her disciple, Yim Wing Chun. Rather, he was a Ming military officer who studied in the Southern Shaolin Temple. He called himself Da Jung, although that wasn't his name. After the Manchurian Qings burned the Temple, his style was developed and preserved by Yat Chum Dai Si, twenty-second in a continuous lineage of Shaolin grandmasters, and by his disciple Cheung Ng, who spread Wing Chun under the guise of performances by the Red Boat Opera Company.

The true chops were carved under the direction of Cheung Ng as part of his efforts to expand Wing Chun against the Qings. Those by Leung Len Kwai may've had great value as examples of his art, and as antiques. But to Wing Chun they were fakes.

Later Watchdog's New York expert said they weren't even that. In some obscure way, he determined that the ivory was too recent for Leung Len Kwai's work. The chops were forgeries of fakes.

Sammy Posten about had a seizure. Deborah Messenger just threw up her hands and laughed at him.

For some reason, being entrusted with a piece of Wing Chun lore which T'ang hadn't known himself until a day ago helped me accept his gift. In his oblique courteous fashion, he seemed to be offering me forgiveness.

Parker Neill stopped by as well, unhappiness dragging at the flesh of his face, but once he'd asked me how I felt he couldn't think of anything to say. Trapped misery closed his throat.

I couldn't bear to lie still and watch him ache. "You saved my life," I informed him hoarsely. "Maybe you don't realize that. When you jumped in, I couldn't have defended myself against an autistic Girl Scout. You gave me time to pick up my gun."

He didn't look at me. "He taught me everything I know," he murmured, "but it wasn't enough. If you hadn't stopped him—"

"Bullshit." I might've been gentle with him, I suppose, but I didn't think that would work. "He didn't teach you everything you know. You're the one who told me, *Any teacher who doesn't train his students to honor all the martial arts doesn't deserve to* have *students.* You sure as hell didn't learn that from Anson Sternway," the man who'd tried to undermine every school in Martial America. "And *you* have scruples—"

"He was my *sensei.*" Parker kept his head down. "Do you know what that means? It means 'revered teacher.' I—" He spread his hands helplessly. "I did that. I revered him. He was God, and my father, and Gichin Funakoshi, all rolled into one."

"Fine," I snorted. "Do you know how your 'revered teacher' spent his spare time? He went to a fight club. And he didn't go there to earn any fucking *reverence.* Instead he got into the ring and made pulp out of anyone stupid enough to face him. And he picked up some easy money betting on himself.

"That's how he stayed sharp."

At last Parker met my gaze. "Is that true?" He sounded shocked.

"I went with him Monday night. I saw it."

Something in his face lifted. After a moment he said slowly, "I've been wondering what to do about his school. I couldn't imagine taking over for him. But maybe—"

"Maybe," I put in, "you're the best man for the job." Then I added, "You're probably the best man to take over the IAMA as well. You already know everyone. They all respect you. And you had the courage to oppose your own *sensei* when he went crazy. Right now you've got enough 'face' to start your own hall of fame. If anyone can keep the IAMA going, you can."

The challenge suited him. As he considered it, his eyes lost their tarnish. For the first time, I got a chance to see what he looked like when he wasn't dying of boredom. As he left, I thought he might burst into song.

Aside from the usual parade of nurses, aides, and technicians, plus the occasional doctor, Ginny was my only other visitor. She came to my room twice, once in the afternoon after the doctors let her go, and again late the next morning. The first time, we concentrated on practical matters—who did what to whom, in which order. Other than that, we left each other alone. I didn't even try to tell her how I felt about being rescued. The subject was too complicated for morphine.

Her second visit was different. Behind her bruises, she had something heavy in her eyes. She looked like a woman who'd spent the night in surgery having the features of her life rearranged.

I owed her more than I could ever hope to repay, so I went first.

"I have a problem," I admitted as she sat down in a chair against the far wall. "I can't find the words to tell you how much your help means to me.

"Just in the past few days, you found the real connection between Sternway and Hardshorn for me, you put me on the right track about the chops," by suggesting that Hong evaluate them, "and you saved my life for the umpteenth time.

"I owe you a desperate apology."

She studied me sharply. "For what?"

"Well"—I faltered momentarily—"for being such an asshole in general." Then I rallied. "But specifically for the way I reacted when you came to The Luxury." Meeting her gaze was tough, but I did it. "When you decided to end our partnership, I felt so betrayed and angry that I couldn't think. First I lost you as a lover. Then I lost you as a partner. It never occurred to me that I hadn't lost you as a friend."

Ginny shook her head. "Don't be so hard on yourself. God knows I gave you plenty of reason to think that way."

Then she stood up and came to the side of the bed so that I could see her swollen face more clearly. The contusion along her jaw made her look like a victim of domestic violence.

"The truth is—"

To my amazement, she faltered as well. But she didn't back down.

"The truth is," she began again, "*I* thought we stopped being friends months ago. After I lost my hand. I felt so damn dependent, and I *loathed*— I decided we weren't friends because I didn't deserve to have any. But I couldn't admit I felt that way. Even to myself. I couldn't face it.

"Even after I started to function again, I still couldn't face it, so I took it out on you. I decided you were a drunk by nature, even if you never had another drink. Your weakness was permanent. You weren't worth trusting."

She paused to gather her courage, then said, "But it wasn't

permanent. Ever since Estobal put you in the hospital, you've been trying to prove yourself to me, earn back my respect. Only you couldn't. I wasn't paying attention."

I swallowed roughly. "What changed?" I wanted to know what she'd seen in me. But she didn't answer that.

Instead she told me, "Marshal." The edge in her voice sounded like anger or regret. Or both. "Ever since you two met, we've been arguing about you.

"Knowing you, you probably think he's too successful to be honest. But let me tell you, he's pretty damn perceptive. And you impressed him. I mean, except for your manners. He is impressed. He's been telling me for days that I was wrong about you." Her eyes flared. "He called me a coward. He said I was blaming you for things I didn't have the courage to face in myself."

She glared through me hard enough to crack the wall behind the bed. "He isn't easy to argue with. And when I made myself look, I started to see what he was talking about."

That explained the shift in her attitude when I got home from the fight club Monday night.

"Hearing from your girlfriend clinched it." Once she'd finished demolishing the wall, her gaze softened. "You needed help, but you couldn't ask for it, no matter how much trouble you were in, because I'd made you think I'd sneer at you if you did. When your girlfriend called, she told me almost nothing. I assumed you hadn't explained anything to her because you didn't want her to pass it on."

"Actually," I put in uncomfortably, "I didn't explain it because I didn't have time. And I hadn't figured it all out. I was just reacting on instinct."

Ginny dismissed my objection. "That's not the point. The point is, I *believed* you couldn't ask me for help because I've been so unfair to you."

She studied me briefly, then asked, "If you hadn't been in such a hurry, would you have called me to back you up?"

I shook my head. She was telling me the truth. She deserved the truth in return.

"Brew—" Her throat closed. She had to look away for a moment before she could speak again. "I want us to be friends.

This"—she indicated her jaw—"is a small price to pay if it means I can ask you for a second chance."

Not as a lover. I understood that.

Or as a partner. Not yet.

But as a friend—?

Yes. In fact, *hell*, yes. No question about it.

"Ginny." I reached out with my good hand, took hold of hers. "I'm sorry I've made you think you have to ask. I've been in pain, and I've taken it out on everyone in sight." Marshal included. "I couldn't bear the thought that I'd lost you completely," couldn't bear that much grief, "so I turned everything into anger.

"You talk about not deserving any friends. I never believed I deserved you. But ever since I stopped drinking, I have been *trying*—"

I couldn't go on.

Fortunately I didn't have to. "I know," she murmured. "Like you haven't already proven yourself a hundred times over. You made one drunken mistake, and you've punished yourself for it ever since. Satan Himself couldn't whip you any harder."

That was true, too.

And maybe I'd done it enough. *Pain is a means to an end*, Nakahatchi *sensei* had told me, *but it must never become the end.* Maybe that's what he meant. Enough was enough. God knows I'd already spent a lifetime of hurt on Richard's death.

When the hospital finally let me go, I went back to Bernie's apartment. I wanted to look Alyse Appelwait in the eye while I said goodbye. And thank you.